THE OLD BRIDGE

A Joe Johnson Thriller

ANDREW TURPIN

The Write Direction Publishing

COPYRIGHT

WELCOME AND THE NEXT BOOK

Thank you for buying **The Old Bridge** — I hope you enjoy it!

This is the second in the series of thrillers I am writing that features Joe Johnson, a US-based independent war crimes investigator. He previously worked for the CIA and for the Office of Special Investigations—a section of the Department of Justice responsible for tracking down Nazi war criminals hiding in the States.

The other books in the series about his various war crimes investigations are all for sale on Amazon. In order, they are:

Prequel: *The Afghan*
1. *The Last Nazi*
2. *The Old Bridge*
3. *Bandit Country*
4. *Stalin's Final Sting*
5. *The Nazi's Son*

If you enjoy this book, I would like to keep in touch. This is not always easy, as I usually only publish a couple of books a year and there are many authors and books out there. So the best way is for you to be on my Readers Group email list. I can then send you updates on the next book, plus occasional special offers.

If you would like to join my Readers Group and receive the email updates, I will send you, **FREE** of charge, the ebook version of another Joe Johnson thriller, *The Afghan*, which is a prequel to the series and normally sells at $2.99/£2.99 (paperback $11.99/£9.99).

The Afghan is set in 1988 when Johnson was still a CIA officer. Most of the action takes place in Afghanistan and Washington, DC.

To sign up for the Readers Group and get your free copy of ***The Afghan***, go to the following web page:

https://bookhip.com/LFMAWM

If you only like reading paperbacks you can still sign up for the email list at that link. A paperback of ***The Afghan*** is for sale on Amazon.

Andrew Turpin, St. Albans, UK.

"After so much bloodshed and loss, after so many outrageous acts of inhuman brutality, it will take an extraordinary effort of will for the people of Bosnia to pull themselves from their past and start building a future of peace. But with our leadership and the commitment of our allies, the people of Bosnia can have the chance to decide their future in peace. They have a chance to remind the world that just a few short years ago the mosques and churches of Sarajevo were a shining symbol of multi-ethnic tolerance, that Bosnia once found unity in its diversity."

— President Bill Clinton, excerpt from a speech on Bosnia, November 27, 1995.

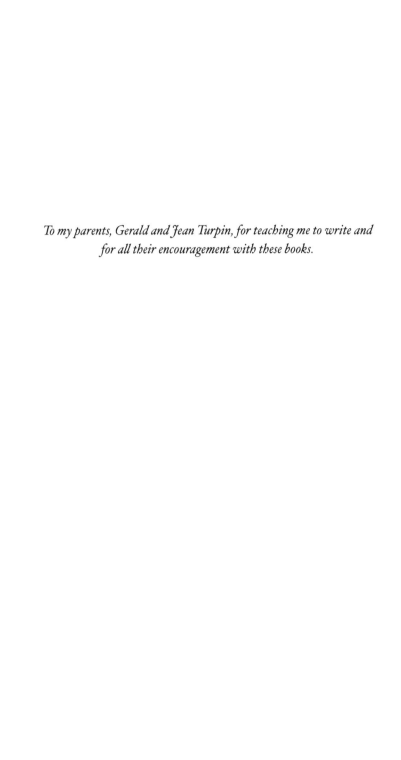

To my parents, Gerald and Jean Turpin, for teaching me to write and for all their encouragement with these books.

PROLOGUE

Tuesday, November 9, 1993
Mostar, Bosnia and Herzegovina

Adrian Turner pressed the red record button on his camera and ducked down behind a pile of rubble. Seconds later, another shell whined overhead and crashed into the parapet right in the center of the ancient stone bridge. It exploded with a deafening bang.

A large cloud of gray smoke and dust rose against the azure sky. A clatter of automatic gunfire sounded in the background.

Turner stood and assessed the situation. "You've got about ninety seconds before the next one," he muttered to his partner, the British TV news reporter Martin Baron, who crouched next to him.

Baron's face was as ashen as the layer of dust that now covered his hair and the shoulders of his blue flak jacket. He scrambled to his feet and walked a few yards to stand in front of the camera, which sat on a tripod among piles of smashed old stone, brick, and wood. It was all that remained of an old cottage on the riverbank.

"Behind me you can see the wreckage of one of the most famous stone bridges in the world, the Stari Most, or 'Old Bridge,' in Mostar," he said into the lens. "It was built in 1566 on the orders of the Ottoman Empire's greatest ruler, Suleiman the Magnificent. But today, this once beautiful old bridge is coming under heavy fire. A tank situated on Stotina Hill, further down the Neretva River and manned by gunners from the mainly Catholic Croatian army, the HVO, has been attacking all morning in an attempt to destroy it. The Croats want to smother morale among the 25,000 remaining Bosnian Muslims who live just across the other side of the river in eastern Mostar."

As he spoke, Baron half turned and indicated with his hand toward the crumbling structure, which was covered with a makeshift tangle of scaffolding, corrugated iron sheets, planks, and old rubber car tires in a vain attempt to protect it from the shelling.

To his left and his right, all the buildings along the riverbank, which together had formed the medieval heart of one of Eastern Europe's most beautiful old cities, lay in ruins.

"The Bosnian Muslims rely on this bridge for access to drinking water here on the western side of the river and also use it to get supplies to the front line in this increasingly bloody civil war. They have to run across the bridge to try and avoid the Croatian snipers who are up in the hills surrounding this city," Baron continued.

Next to the wreckage of an archway that led onto the bridge stood four people: an older man, a woman in her late teens, and two men in their twenties, holding a stretcher on which a wounded man lay, a bloodstained bandage wrapped around his head.

Baron glanced over his shoulder and pointed at them.

"You can see just over there four people who are waiting to try and carry a wounded man back from the front line across the bridge to the only hospital functioning on the eastern side. So far, this bridge has remained just about usable, but if this shelling continues for much longer, it may not be."

Baron was interrupted by the telltale whine of another incoming shell. Turner and Baron simultaneously threw themselves facedown to the floor, their fingers in their ears, eyes shut.

This time, the shell exploded much nearer, right next to the former archway, causing the ground beneath the two newsmen to shake as pieces of stone and other debris landed on them.

When the noise died down a little, Turner lifted his head. His camera was still intact on the tripod. But beyond it, next to the ruined arch, he saw that the four people carrying the stretcher, and the man on it, were no more. Only a mess of blood, body parts, and the misshapen stretcher remained.

To Turner's left, another man yelled loudly into a walkie-talkie. On the far side of the bridge he could see a woman in a bright blue dress screaming nonstop. Other people were wailing.

Turner glanced at his camera. They'd caught everything.

"We got it all on film. Do another minute, can you?" Turner asked Baron.

Baron stared at him, then brushed pieces of stone and dust from his hair. "You're mad. Five people have just died. We should get out of here now."

But he got to his feet, picked up his handheld microphone, and staggered around in front of the camera one more time. He coughed and then began to speak.

"We've just seen firsthand the devastating effect of this war on all who live here. An injured man on a stretcher and four others who were trying to save his life have just been blown apart by a tank shell. That one landed unexpectedly near to us. The others have been hitting the center of the bridge. Yet another senseless loss of life in a senseless war. As the tank seems to have suddenly begun to target the area here on the western side of the bridge, rather than the center, we're going to move to a safer location."

Turner stepped over and turned off his camera, then picked up the tripod. He and Baron strode to a new position about a hundred yards from the bridge, where Turner set up his equipment again. He focused on the smoking bridge structure, zoomed in a little, and then pressed the record button.

As he did so, the woman who had been screaming on the other side of the bridge suddenly sprinted across it, her blue dress blowing in the wind, hair trailing in her wake, ignoring the shouts of those behind her who yelled at her to stop.

She knelt in the dust and the blood next to the mangled bodies of the stretcher bearers. There she prostrated herself beside the torso of the older man, placing her head on his red-stained chest. Then she did likewise with the woman lying next to him.

Baron watched her for a moment, then shook his head, stood in front of the camera, and resumed his report.

"It is clear there's now a concerted effort by the Croatians to destroy this old bridge," he said. "It was once described in the 1930s by British author Rebecca West as one of the most beautiful bridges in the world. She wrote about its architecture, the slender arch that stretched between its two round towers, about how its parapet was bent in a shallow angle in the center. Well, all of that might soon become no more than a memory for those who still live here, some of them clinging to life, many others dying by the day, in a city that is slowly being destroyed. This is Martin Baron reporting from Mostar."

As he stopped speaking, there was another whine behind him, and an incoming shell smashed into the center of the bridge, exploded loudly, and sent another cloud of debris up into the blue sky.

Several large chunks of masonry fell off the bridge and down into the river eighty feet below. Then a few more dropped.

Suddenly, as if in slow motion, and with an almighty crash, the entire thirty-yard-long bridge collapsed into the river.

Hundreds of tons of carefully handcrafted medieval stonework plunged, causing an immense geyser of displaced water to shoot skyward, reaching almost up to the point where the bridge had been until a few moments earlier.

Turner stepped over to his camera and peered through the viewfinder to check what he was recording. He'd gotten it all.

In the center of the frame the Croatian army soldiers, still firing their weapons, came into view as they drew near to the bodies of the five people who had died a few minutes before.

The woman kneeling next to the bodies now had her head in the gutter, her hands on the torso of the older man, and she wept uncontrollably.

Turner ended the recording. "We'd better get this film off to London, quick as we can," he said to Baron.

"Yes, we should."

Away to his right, Turner saw a small group of Croatian army soldiers dancing and triumphantly firing their automatic rifles into the air.

PART ONE

CHAPTER ONE

Wednesday, July 4, 2012
Dubrovnik, Croatia

Joe Johnson emerged from the hotel's windowless conference room and blinked in the sun that reflected off the Adriatic Sea, just a short distance away.

One of his fellow conference attendees, a tall blond German academic who was an authority on the Holocaust, had already changed into her bikini and was laying a towel on a sun lounger next to the pool.

Johnson gazed for a few seconds at the woman's Amazonian figure through the floor-to-ceiling plate glass that separated the bar from the pool. Then he walked to the bar and threw his speaker's notes and slide deck printout onto the shiny black granite surface. "Thank God that's over," he muttered to himself.

"Death in Yugoslavia" ran the title in large letters on the front of his pack of PowerPoint slides. The subheading beneath it read, "1991–1995: Atrocities of War That Shocked the World." Then came a further heading, which referenced the heart of his speech: "An international approach to tracing war criminals."

Johnson's presentation to the 330 delegates at the Balkans War Crimes Conference had gone as planned. The deck of about fifty slides was graphic, including a few photographs of emaciated Muslim and Croatian prisoners in Serbian-run concentration camps at Omarska and Keraterm, but it made all the points he wanted to get across to his audience.

The conference venue was one of Dubrovnik's largest hotels, the Valamar Lacroma, on the Lapad peninsula, ten minutes' drive from the historic Old Town. It made for an idyllic setting.

Johnson had just reached into his jacket pocket and taken out his sunglasses when someone nudged his elbow. "Relieved that's over, Joe? Can I get you a beer?"

Johnson turned to see Professor Philip De Vere, a stooping Oxford historian whom he vaguely knew and who had also delivered a paper to the conference.

"Thanks, I need one," Johnson said.

And he did. The nervous buildup to a conference speech was always the same: a restless night, the 2 a.m. whiskey, then the black coffee that overstimulated his nervous system. Then, when it was over, the wave of relief was often accompanied by a craving for alcohol.

De Vere ordered two local Ožujsko beers before turning back to Johnson. "An interesting talk you gave there," De Vere said. "But you were rather generous toward Bill Clinton and his policies on Bosnia in the early '90s. I suppose you are American, after all." He chuckled.

Johnson put on his sunglasses and placed his documents into his leather briefcase. "I think Clinton got most things right. Dayton was a good agreement, despite Clinton only doing it because he wanted it finished before the '96 election.

Can't stand the guy personally, but someone needed to stand up for the Bosnian Muslims, and he did it."

"Depends whether you take a long-term view or not, and how closely you look at how he went about it," De Vere said. He paused and peered sideways at Johnson. "Do you do a lot of research work? You're not a full-time academic, are you?"

Johnson eyed him. *Always the snob*. He explained that he worked as a visiting lecturer at American University in Washington, DC, within its College of Law, speaking periodically if its War Crimes Research Office required he do so. Otherwise, he ran his own business doing private investigations but was increasingly trying to focus on jobs with a war crimes element. That was his passion.

"Interesting work," De Vere replied with a smirk.

Johnson had had enough of being talked down to. He picked up his beer and said, "You're going to have to excuse me, I need a smoke." He walked out the door of the interior bar to the far side of the patio, where a path wound its way past a couple of palm trees.

He continued for a few yards along the path, out of sight of De Vere, then pulled a pack of Marlboros and a lighter out of his pocket. He ripped off the cellophane wrapper and lit one.

Staring out to sea, where the dark azure of the Adriatic met the paler sky as the sun began its descent behind the Elaphiti Islands beyond, Johnson found it hard to imagine this as the backdrop to a raging battle that had erupted only two decades earlier. Croatian forces had somehow defended Dubrovnik, whose Old Town was a UNESCO World Heritage Site, against an ultimately fruitless bombardment of shells, mortars, antitank missiles, and bombs from the Yugoslav People's Army, the JNA, as well as the Yugoslav air force.

He had developed a strong interest in the region during

the course of two separate stints in 1999 in the Croatian capital, Zagreb, and in the Bosnia and Herzegovina capital, Sarajevo, when he had gathered evidence on war criminals hiding in the US. That was during his time at the Office of Special Investigations, based in Washington, DC. A prolific linguist, he had picked up a decent knowledge of Serbo-Croat there, to add to his Russian, German, Spanish, and Pashto.

Johnson finished his cigarette, drained his beer, and set off back to the outdoor bar, where a busy crowd of conference attendees now gathered. There were a couple hundred there now, he calculated, and the number grew as those who had gone back to their hotel rooms to change into more comfortable clothing returned to the bar.

Johnson couldn't be bothered to change, although he felt too warm in his crumpled dark blue linen jacket and chinos. He removed the jacket and threw it over one shoulder. Sweat stains were starting to spread from his armpits across his pale blue cotton shirt. It was still at least eighty-five degrees Fahrenheit, he guessed.

A waiter offered him a glass of prosecco, which he accepted, and he joined the edge of a group, including De Vere, that was debating the value of pursuing war criminals in their eighties and nineties who were no longer a danger to those around them.

Johnson listened for a moment, then shook his head and snorted to himself.

What kind of justice would it be to let them off just because they were old?

He turned away from the group, then jumped slightly upon finding himself face-to-face with a thin, dark-haired man.

"Mr. Johnson?" the man asked in heavily accented English.

"Yes, hello." Johnson felt slightly nonplussed at the stranger's silent approach and proximity.

"Have you got a minute to speak to me?"

Johnson ran the back of his hand across his chin. "Sure."

"I was listening to your talk today, which was interesting —especially the part about how you go about tracking down war criminals who just disappeared without a trace. I live in Bosnia, in Mostar, and I think the authorities should have made more of an effort to make sure they covered all the allegations."

Johnson squinted a little as he weighed the man's point. "I thought they did a good job here, personally."

"You think so?"

"Yes, in my view," Johnson said. He folded his arms. "Well, the international tribunal's nearly finished processing the 161 people they indicted. And I think the local court in Bosnia's been effective since it took over war crimes prosecutions after 2005."

The man shifted from one foot to the other. "Yes, that's what you said in your talk. But the truth is, there were people who did things that never came to the authorities' notice, crimes that they didn't pursue, so they were never indicted in the first place."

Johnson glanced to his right. A couple of people from De Vere's group were staring at them, as were those from another small group from Sarajevo University, whom he'd briefly spoken to earlier. He turned back to the man.

"What are you trying to say? And sorry, who are you?"

"I'm Petar Simic." He held out his hand and Johnson shook it. "This is your expertise, isn't it? Hunting war criminals. I had a quick check, so I've seen your record. Nazis, right?" he said. "There are things I'd like to discuss that you might be interested in, as an investigator. I'm sure you're busy here right now, but maybe we could meet somewhere else at another time?"

Johnson paused and sighed inwardly. It was typical of the

kind of approach he had often received over the years at the OSI, the US government's Nazi-hunting organization, before he had become self-employed.

The man was obviously going to tip him off about someone who'd supposedly done something evil and gotten away with it. Virtually always, such leads came to nothing.

"When and where were you thinking of?" Johnson asked.

"Tomorrow morning, down in the Stari Grad, the Old Town." He smiled. "You should see the Old Town if you haven't done so already. It's a beautiful historic place."

Johnson thought about it. He *had* been planning to visit the Old Town the next day anyway, given that he had nothing scheduled. And it might be interesting to chat with a local rather than the usual cluster of international academics.

"Okay, we can have a quick chat for half an hour," Johnson said. "Say ten o'clock? Where do you want to meet?"

"Café right on the harbor, near the boats—Poklisar is its name. Good coffee, okay? Tomorrow at ten, then?"

Johnson took a step back. "Okay. I hope you're not wasting my time." He gave the man a questioning look.

Petar shook his head. "No, I won't be wasting it. But you might need plenty of it." Then he turned and walked away.

* * *

An hour and a half after Petar had left, Johnson drained his fourth Ožujsko of the evening and reached into his jacket pocket for his cigarettes.

He lit one, leaned on the bar, and took a deep drag just as the sun finally disappeared over the horizon.

"Of all the gin joints in all the towns in all the world . . ."

Johnson jumped upon hearing the low-pitched, gravelly voice, but he knew immediately whom he'd find standing there when he turned around. It was a voice he had known well for more than two-and-a-half decades, ever since his days with the CIA in the sweat and dust of Pakistan and Afghanistan in the late 1980s.

He pivoted to face a familiar tall, bespectacled figure.

"Vic! What the hell are you doing here?"

"Business, I'm afraid, Doc. Sorry, I would have called first, but I knew you were here, so I opted for surprise. I got sent here at short notice—only flew in from DC this morning."

One of Johnson's oldest friends from his CIA days, Vic Walter had long ago nicknamed Johnson as "Doc" because of his Ph.D. in history from Freie Universität Berlin.

"You knew I'd be here?" Johnson said. "Of course, you would. How stupid of me. So, what's going on? Would you like a beer?"

Vic nodded, and Johnson signaled to the barman for two more beers.

Vic scratched his graying temple. "I was given a job a couple of days ago and thought of you straightaway. So I called your home, and your sister said you'd gone to Dubrovnik for a conference. Bit of a coincidence, as that was where I was heading. Is Amy watching your kids?"

"Yes, Amy always steps in for me if I'm away on business. But now I'm intrigued," Johnson said. "You thought of me? Why? And what are you doing here, anyway?"

The barman put two bottles on the bar in front of Johnson.

"Well, I thought of you because I need someone to subcontract out to." Vic grinned. "It's actually an old Yugoslav issue, a Balkan job. That's why I'm here. I might need your help with something a little delicate. And I needed to be in Dubrovnik for a meeting at the port. The counterparty refused to fly to DC, so I had no choice but to travel. But it worked out in the end, with you being here anyway."

"So, what's the story?" Johnson asked.

Vic perched his angular frame on one of the black-leather-covered barstools and sipped his beer. "Well, I've been asked, on the quiet, to do what you might call a tidying up job. And I thought it was a job that's right up your street."

"I'm sorry?"

Vic grinned. "Okay, you remember who was in the hot seat at the White House during the Bosnian civil war twenty years ago?"

Johnson didn't need reminding. "Hillary's dear husband, Bill."

"Correct, it was Clinton. And you might also remember that Bill had a tough time because his policies toward Bosnia went against the grain. They were different than those of other Western European leaders."

Again, Johnson knew about that—he'd just talked about it earlier with De Vere. Clinton had taken some flak because he supported the Muslims during that war, whereas the French, British, and Germans were all far more cautious.

"The story is," Vic said, "that there was a sheaf of documents relating to Bill's policies toward Bosnia that the Bosnian government in Sarajevo had. Bill's people requested the documents be destroyed. This was when the Bosnian president was Alija Izetbegović."

"Okay," Johnson said, wondering where this was going.

Vic sipped his beer. "Izetbegović's office had promised to destroy the documents," he said, "but later admitted they'd gone missing and the foreign ministry couldn't find them. Or so the office said. And they hadn't been seen since, so people forgot about them." He leaned forward. "But I was called up a couple of weeks ago and asked if I could try and track them down."

Johnson lit another cigarette. "So why were you asked to track them down? And who's doing the asking and how high up?"

Vic averted his gaze from Johnson and looked out over the Adriatic. Then he said, "I'm not sure why. And the request came indirectly, so I'm not sure of who made it, either."

Johnson avoided the temptation to roll his eyes. It was typical CIA doublespeak.

"Okay," Vic said, "the truth is, the request came out of the director's office. I can tell you that much—on the quiet."

All right, so it was critical, Johnson thought.

"Right, so spit it out. What do you want?"

Vic leaned back. "Well, I've had clearance to use someone who's not CIA, at least not currently, who's independent but trustworthy, who can try and find these docs. It would be harder for us internally to cover it for a whole load of reasons that I won't bore you with."

He gave Johnson a look, head lowered, from beneath his eyebrows. "You know what I mean?"

Johnson snorted. He knew exactly what Vic meant. There was no point in even replying. The bottom line was, as often was the case in the Agency, they needed someone who was deniable.

Vic read his expression and shrugged. "I could employ you as an anonymous contractor. It won't be an easy job—a needle in a haystack. But we've got to give it a go so we can at least say we gave it our best shot."

He raised his eyebrows. "What d'you think?"

Johnson shook his head. He did need to find another major job or project to work on, although he wasn't going to admit that to Vic. Time was moving on, and he definitely didn't want to go back to hometown searches for lost people. He wanted it to be something really worthwhile.

However, working with the Agency again?

"Nothing personal, because you're an old buddy and I know I owe you a favor," Johnson said, "but I'm not keen on anything CIA-related. I mean, the organization's screwed me, fired me, and even last year, when I was trying to track down that old Nazi, that asshole Watson did his best to block me. How he stays in his job at his age is a mystery. Is he still focused on Syria?"

He was referring to Robert Watson, who had been Johnson's boss in the CIA as chief of station in Islamabad in the late 1980s.

"Yeah, Syria's his baby right now," Vic said. "He should concentrate on the big picture in his job, but he can't resist getting into the detail of operations. He's effectively been heading up Syria since he switched from Special Activities, running the Pakistan drone strikes."

Vic walked to the other end of the bar and picked up a small tub of complimentary olives, then returned and put them next to his beer. "You're right," he said. "I think they'll need to retire him soon. He's sixty-five now. But you don't need to worry. He's not involved in this particular project."

Johnson gave a wry smile and sipped his beer. Vic was working hard on him this time.

"The other thing is," Johnson said. "I can't stand the Clintons. I don't like this sort of dynastic thing going on where you've got father and son Bush or husband and wife Clinton trying to follow each other into the White House. It's not healthy."

He paused, then said, "Sorry, buddy, but you're going to have to find someone else to do the dirty work on this job."

"I'd make it worth your while," Vic said. "There's plenty of budget, and if you're here now anyway for this war crimes conference, it seems like a perfect opportunity. A few days extra in the sun. Kill two birds and all that."

Johnson ran a hand through the graying semicircle of short-cropped hair that bordered his extensive bald patch. "The answer's no. I've got a few possible work options at the moment. I just need to check them all out properly. I'm going to grab a few days here, then on to Istanbul on Monday morning for a meeting, then home Monday night. If the Clintons need someone to drag them out of the shit, I'm not the man."

Johnson took a deep drag on his cigarette and exhaled smoothly. "Also, we're meant to be having a long family weekend break in Castine, north of Portland, at the end of next week. I promised the kids. Amy and her husband are coming along as well. They would all kill me if I don't make it. We haven't had a break for ages."

"Mmm, a tricky one," Vic said. He drained his beer bottle.

There seemed no obvious reason why Vic couldn't have the job done internally. It seemed fairly routine. Unless there was something Vic wasn't telling him, which was quite likely and would be rather typical.

"You know, this is the second time I've been propositioned tonight, so to speak," Johnson said.

"Oh, yeah, who was the first?" asked Vic.

"Strange guy, a local, wants to meet me down at the Old Town tomorrow morning. Got something he wants to discuss, wouldn't say what, but he'd done his homework. He knew I was a war crimes investigator and ex-Nazi hunter. It'll probably be the usual bullshit, though."

Vic raised his eyebrows. "Good luck with that then, Doc. I'm going to have to get moving. I need to make sure I get the late flight back to DC tonight, otherwise I'll be in trouble."

He paused. "If you change your mind about these documents, let me know."

Johnson shook his head. "No thanks, not this time, buddy. Appreciate the thought, but it's not for me."

CHAPTER TWO

Thursday, July 5, 2012
Dubrovnik

"I never intended to tell anybody about this, not initially, but times change, thoughts change," Petar Simic said.

Just as he had promised, Petar had arrived at Poklisar at ten o'clock. The colorful café was right on the harbor and built next to the imposing stone wall that encircled the Old Town. It was busy at this time in the morning, full of tourists who were either waiting for boats to the various islands surrounding Dubrovnik or stopping off for refreshments after returning.

"Actually, I'm not comfortable sitting here talking," Petar said. "There are too many people, and you never know who's around. Instead of ordering coffee now, why don't we walk around the city walls for a while, then we can chat as we go? You can do your tourist bit at the same time, then."

Johnson, who had been looking forward to a jolt of

caffeine, sighed and nodded reluctantly. He put on his sunglasses and stood.

Petar got up and apologized to the hovering waiter, then led the way through an archway. He turned right and took Johnson up a steep stone staircase that led to the pathway around the top of the walls, a formidable barrier to potential invaders that dated back to the fourteenth century. At the top he handed over some money to a man in a kiosk and took two tickets.

"I'll pay—consider it me doing my bit for American-Bosnian relations," Petar said.

Johnson nodded and followed him onto the walls. Standing sixty feet above the narrow paved streets, Johnson looked down at the Old Town spread out below them. With its red tile roofs, stone bell towers, and tiny cramped houses, it truly looked like a medieval city dragged into the modern age.

To their left was the harbor, with its ferryboats and milling crowds of camera-wielding tourists. Ahead of them, beyond the city, was the Adriatic. A white haze rose from the horizon and blurred the lines between sea and sky. Johnson turned around. Behind them was a steep hill; a cable car slowly rose to the top.

Already the heat was stifling, and it was only just after ten o'clock.

Johnson took his phone out, quickly turned on his voice recorder, and put his phone back into his pocket. Recording conversations was an old habit.

"Okay, then, tell me what's on your mind," Johnson said. He thought Petar was probably in his mid-forties, with his dark hair that was going a little gray. Not much younger than Johnson himself.

"First, you need to think back to 1992," Petar said. "I'm a Bosnian-Croat. I grew up in eastern Mostar, which is about

150 kilometers north from here, over the border," Petar said. "My brother, Filip, me, and a couple of other guys I knew, Franjo Vuković and Marco Lukić, were in the HVO, the Croatian Defence Council, the army. Initially we fought with the Muslims, the Bosniaks, in the Bosnia and Herzegovina army to get rid of the Serbs. But then it all went wrong, and we started fighting each other instead toward the end of '92."

Petar took a long drink from a bottle of water he was carrying and explained that things had really started to go downhill with the start of a miniwar within a war, with fighting between the Catholic Croats and the Bosnian Muslims—the Bosniaks.

"It was vicious," he said, "with Mostar right in the thick of it."

Johnson listened intently. "So what went on between the two sides then? I did some work in Bosnia and in Croatia in 1999, so I've heard a few stories, that it wasn't just straightforward fighting. But tell me in your own words."

Petar gave a sardonic laugh. "Not straightforward. That's one way of putting it. It was bad on both sides. Any prisoners were treated like pigs. Many died or they were tortured. Franjo, Marco, and Filip were in a unit that spent some of the time looking after Muslims locked up in a concentration camp at the Heliodrom, just south of Mostar."

"Don't misunderstand me," Petar said. "All the soldiers on both sides were doing this kind of stuff. I did things I wasn't proud of. But the Heliodrom—that was something else."

He explained how at the Heliodrom, which consisted of a three-story prison building and a sports hall, Muslims had been continually beaten up, given little food and water, and were frequently tortured. Many were eventually killed.

"Here, read this," Petar said. He reached into his back pocket and took out a folded sheet of paper and handed it to Johnson.

It was a printout from an amended indictment issued in 2008 against various HVO officers at a war crimes trial conducted at the International Criminal Tribunal for the former Yugoslavia in The Hague. Johnson flicked through the six pages Petar had given him, many of them annotated with scribbles, underlines, circles, and other marks in red pen.

He stopped when he saw one particular reference. "Approximately 1,800 Bosnian Muslim civilians were detained by the Herceg-Bosna/HVO forces at the Heliodrom," it read.

And then, a little further down, came the damning detail. "The use of Bosnian Muslim detainees held at the Heliodrom in forced labor or as human shields resulted in at least fifty-six Muslim detainees being killed and at least 178 being wounded."

Another paragraph, heavily underlined, read, "Many Bosnian Muslims held by the HVO were forced to engage in physical labor, such as building military fortifications, digging trenches, carrying ammunition, and retrieving bodies, often in combat and dangerous conditions, which resulted in many Bosnian Muslim detainees being killed or severely wounded."

The indictment described how Muslims were forced to dress like HVO soldiers, ordered to carry wooden rifles, and made to walk toward Bosnian army positions in order to draw fire and enable the HVO to identify enemy gun positions.

Johnson shook his head as he read a paragraph that described conditions at the Heliodrom. "Conditions were inhumane, with severe overcrowding, inadequate medical and sanitary facilities, insufficient food and water, inadequate ventilation, and in the summer, suffocating heat. Detainees often slept on concrete floors with no bedding or blankets. On some occasions, HVO guards withheld all food and water from the detainees in retaliation for HVO military setbacks."

It said that HVO soldiers often beat detainees until they were unconscious, causing severe injuries, fired bullets at them indiscriminately, set attack dogs on them, and subjected them to sexual assaults.

The indictment referred to numerous acts of torture, inhumane treatment, and killing of Muslims between April 1993 and March 1994.

"Is there more of this?" Johnson said as he handed the sheets back to Petar.

"Yes. That's just a few extracts. The indictment's eighty pages long. And of course, that's just the crimes and offenses they could identify, which were a tiny fraction of the whole," he said.

Johnson knew very well that there had been many serious war crimes committed during the civil war on all sides, but the ones listed here were extreme.

Petar put the sheaf back into his pocket. "Franjo, Marco, and Filip were responsible for quite a lot of those deaths, no doubt about it," he said. "But it was only Filip who they caught and tried at the International Criminal Tribunal in The Hague and then sent to prison. The other two, Franjo and Marco, got away with it, as did very many others."

"They must have murdered dozens," Petar continued. "When I first knew Franjo and Marco, they were quite happy to live alongside Muslims. Franjo was even married to one. But they changed massively—really seemed to hate them in the end."

Johnson stopped walking. The two of them were now on a high section of wall overlooking Lokrum Island, a mile or two out to sea, with the harbor to their left. He leaned back against a stone parapet and folded his arms.

On a clear day, according to Johnson's guidebook, it was possible to see Italy across the Adriatic from Dubrovnik, but there was far too much haze for that today.

Johnson scratched the small nick at the top of his right

ear. "So do you know what happened to these guys, Franjo and Marco? Where they are now?"

"Franjo vanished not too long after that—gone," Petar flicked his wrist away from him to emphasize the point. "He was a bit of an enigma. Some said he was killed when his truck ran over a land mine. Other people said he vanished somewhere and got a new identity. But nobody seems to know the truth."

Franjo and Filip had both trained as journalists together, Petar explained. That was how they knew each other. After studying at university in Zagreb, they had trained together for a while as copy editors and producers at Radio Televizija Zagreb, the Croatian state-owned broadcaster, working across both radio and television stations.

But then the war had started, and both men had joined the armed forces, as everyone did.

"Franjo could well be dead for all I know," Petar said. "But Marco's still definitely around—nasty guy, made loads of money, I'm not sure how. There were whispers about illegal arms sales or something but obviously no proof. It was Marco who ratted on my brother to the authorities, the investigators. That's why Filip ended up in jail while Marco and Franjo went free. The authorities never believed Filip when he said that the man who turned him in was part of it, too. And Marco paid off the ones that looked into it. But I know it can be proven."

Petar stopped talking as a group of tourists went slowly past with a guide. They all took photographs from both sides of the wall, looking down into the Old Town on one side and out over the Adriatic on the other.

"So, this guy Franjo has disappeared," Johnson said. "Has anybody checked out his files, I mean his VOB military records?"

Johnson knew from his previous work in Croatia in 1999

that if Franjo had been in the HVO, then he would have a *vojno-evidencioni obrazac*, a master military service record, which would be held by the local office of the Ministry of Defence where he lived. It would include details of his conscripted military service, postings, the units he had served in, and other information, and would have been maintained, even during the chaos of war. It crossed Johnson's mind that there might be references in there to where he was now, as the VOB was an important record for state pension purposes.

But even as he spoke, Johnson suspected what the answer would be. The VOB files were not easily accessible without a good reason.

"No," Petar said, as if reading Johnson's mind. "You'd need someone on the inside to get them for you."

Johnson nodded. There would be ways around that if necessary, especially in countries like Bosnia and Croatia, where the wheels of bureaucracy could be oiled by dripping bank notes into the machinery.

The last time, he had done exactly that and had found ferrets to dig out what he needed: two good intelligence service sources he had carefully cultivated. One had been in Croatia, at the Security and Intelligence Service of the Ministry of Defence, and the other in Bosnia, at the civilian intelligence service, the Agency for Investigation and Documentation. Both men were still in their jobs, although the names of their agencies had changed. Maybe he could call on them for help again.

"But why have you taken so long to do anything about this?" Johnson asked. "Haven't you talked to anyone before?"

Petar shifted from one foot to the other. "I was never going to tell anyone," he said, "partly because I didn't want people targeting me or my brother when he finally comes out of jail. These are dangerous people. You start talking, and before you know it . . . " He shrugged. "But I've changed my mind over the years. It's been eating away at me, seeing my brother holed up in prison while these other guys go free. I approached a senior policeman I know, privately, but he said that without proof, it would be difficult to pin anything on Marco. Likewise with Franjo, although he had disappeared anyway."

"Okay," Johnson said. "Do you have any old photographs of Franjo? At least that would help for ID purposes."

Petar shook his head. "No, nothing. But there is one thing that makes his disappearance even more peculiar. Franjo was, to my mind, quite easily identifiable, not because of his looks generally but because of his eye. He had a slightly odd iris. You know the circular pupil in the middle of a normal eye is black, then there's a colored surrounding bit, the iris? Well, Franjo's right eye had a very narrow black line that ran from the pupil down across the iris. It made his eye almost look like a keyhole."

Johnson nodded. "A coloboma, you mean?" He knew exactly what Petar meant because an old school friend had something similar. It was a very distinctive identifying feature, but when he was older, his friend used to wear a colored contact lens to cover it up.

"Exactly," Petar said. "A coloboma. That's what it's called. He also used to have a thick beard. He was a skinny guy but strong. Well muscled."

The more Petar talked, the more Johnson felt intrigued. But he was now also starting to fade a little. After the alcohol he'd drunk the previous night and waking up early, plus the absence of caffeine, his mind was now slightly fuzzy.

"Shall we go for that coffee now and continue talking at the café?" Johnson asked.

"Yes, I've said most of the sensitive information now. Let's go." Petar smiled for the first time that morning, his forehead less furrowed. He retraced their steps around the wall and down the steep stone staircase to ground level, then back to the café.

They sat down at a white wooden outdoor table beneath a canvas awning. Petar signaled to a waiter and ordered two cappuccinos.

Johnson watched him carefully. If all that Petar had said was true, then it sounded potentially interesting, but he would definitely need to have the story verified before he could start to think about pursuing it further.

Then Petar's phone beeped loudly. He took it out of his pocket and read a message, completely focused on what was on the screen. He put the phone down on the table in front of him. His shoulders hunched, and he unconsciously stroked his chin, staring straight past Johnson, deep in thought.

"Everything all right?" Johnson asked.

Petar jumped a little. "Yes, yes. Just thinking."

As the waiter arrived with their coffees, Johnson took the opportunity to take out his own phone to make sure the recorder was working properly and to check his emails. There was a note from his fourteen-year-old son, Peter, asking if he was enjoying the sunshine and saying it was raining hard in Portland; he said he was looking forward to the family getaway in Castine.

Johnson smiled and tapped out a short reply.

Petar seemed to partly recover his poise, then excused himself to go to the bathroom. Johnson watched as he walked into the café, then cut left between the tables and disappeared through an open doorway at the back.

Johnson took another sip from his coffee, then put it down. Just then, a high-pitched shriek came from inside the café. Johnson saw a woman in a red dress emerge from the bathrooms. Clearly agitated, she yelled something in Croatian that Johnson didn't understand, and a white-shirted waiter ran across to her. They both disappeared back through the door.

Something was wrong. He slowly stood, a shard of anxiety digging into his stomach, then walked into the café and made his way to the door leading to the bathrooms, just as the woman in red came running out past him, babbling something unintelligible.

Johnson found himself in a long, dark corridor. At the far end, right outside the entrance to the men's bathroom, the waiter was crouched over someone lying on the white stone floor.

The person on the floor was Petar.

Johnson felt the skin on the back of his neck prickle involuntarily. "*What the hell . . .* " he said out loud, before remembering to switch to Croatian. "What's happened?"

The waiter turned his head sharply and stood. He waved his hands in a gesture of helplessness. "He is shot in the head," the waiter said.

Johnson bent down. Petar was facedown, his legs splayed and right arm trapped under his body. There was a dark red pool of blood spreading across the floor. Now he could see where a bullet had entered the back of his head.

"Go and call an ambulance, quickly," Johnson ordered. He said the words almost instinctively, but he knew it was pointless.

"The lady is calling," the waiter said.

"No, she was panicking. You do it—now, quickly," Johnson said firmly, again in Croatian.

The waiter nodded and ran back toward the exit.

Johnson took a deep breath, then slowly turned over Petar's body. There, to the right of his forehead, below the hairline, was a ragged exit wound, where the blood was coming from. Johnson gagged a little and swallowed hard to quell it.

Then he noticed there was a phone in Petar's right hand, under his body. Johnson picked it up and stood. He knew immediately what he was going to do. He gently put Petar's body back as it had been, then slipped into the bathroom, where he removed the battery and the SIM card from the phone and pocketed everything. Opening the door a fraction, he made sure no one was in the hallway and then exited the bathroom. Then he walked back along the corridor and out into the main café area.

He looked left. The waiter whom he had told to phone for an ambulance was standing, a receiver clamped to his right ear, speaking quickly and gesticulating, facing away from Johnson.

The woman in red was standing near the waiter, now wailing loudly, waving her arms and telling other customers at a nearby table what had happened. A couple of them jumped to their feet. Some of the people queuing on the quayside for the ferries, attracted by the woman's shrieks, were drifting over.

It was obvious to Johnson how the scene was going to play out. Within minutes the café would be swarming with police and ambulance crews. Yet nothing could be done to help Petar.

Johnson walked toward the waiter. As much as he disliked the idea of getting involved with the authorities, he knew he was going to have to give a statement of some kind.

But he just might omit a few details.

CHAPTER THREE

Thursday, July 5, 2012
Dubrovnik

An hour later, Johnson left the café. He had been questioned by two police officers and had told them that he'd met Petar for the first time at a conference the previous day. He said they had decided to meet for coffee that morning to discuss history and work and had taken a short walk around the walls before heading for the café.

He omitted details about pocketing Petar's phone and that they had discussed searching for war criminals. That would have opened a can of worms. The last thing Johnson wanted was for police to start inadvertently alerting the men Petar had mentioned, Marco Lukić and Franjo Vuković, assuming they were still alive.

So, after his statement and ensuring that several patrons in the café had verified that he hadn't left his table while Petar was in the bathroom, he was allowed to leave. The police took his contact information in case they had more questions.

Once Johnson had escaped the confines of Dubrovnik Old Town and its claustrophobic maze of narrow streets, he looked around for somewhere private where he could check Petar's phone.

He saw a tourist office and walked inside, then made his way to a bathroom in the corner. There he locked himself in a stall, took out the phone, replaced the battery but not the SIM card, and scrolled up the list of text messages on the device, all of which were in Croatian.

Johnson knew enough of the language to get a good sense of most of the messages. After checking the translations of a couple of words on his smartphone, he quickly pieced together the contents of the final message listed.

I've been watching you with the American. You're making a mistake. He's not what he seems. Be careful.

Johnson frowned. The number from which the message had been sent was visible, but there was no name attached to it. It worried Johnson that the person who had sent it had apparently been watching him and Petar—and therefore, logically, he had to assume it was probably the same person who had shot Petar.

But why is he warning Petar about me?

Johnson had taken no countersurveillance measures as there had seemed to be no need. But now he quickly cycled through his memory of the moments before Petar's death. There had been so many people in the café, and Johnson had been taking in many of the faces and their clothing as he waited for Petar to return from the bathroom. It was an old CIA street habit that had stuck with him.

Who had come from the bathrooms? There was the

woman in the red dress, the waiter, two middle-aged women and then—there had been a man. Johnson concentrated. The man had been wearing sunglasses and a navy baseball cap over his dark hair.

After the murder, he had seen all the people again, apart from the man in the baseball cap, who must have left. He had to be the most likely suspect.

Johnson glanced down at the phone in his hand. It was an old, basic Nokia model, not a smartphone, so there were no emails on the device. Johnson put the phone back in his pocket, then went outside again. This time, he carefully checked around him for any sign of the man who he now believed had shot Petar. There was nobody in view.

The departures board at the bus stop at Pile, outside the main gate to Dubrovnik's walled Old Town, showed that the next number six bus to the Babin Kuk peninsula, where his hotel was located, was due in two minutes.

An ambulance screamed past, its blue and red lights flashing, siren blaring, heading in the direction of the Old Town harbor.

Johnson leaned against the bus stop post and turned his attention back to Petar's previous text messages.

There were a few suggestive messages from a woman called Olga, clearly not Petar's wife, who signed off with "xxxx Olga" on all her messages. There were a whole series of exchanges with some friends that appeared to be about a soccer team, Hajduk Split, and a few to and from another number. These last messages said something about it being his mother's birthday, had she still been alive, and about trying to arrange a visit. The sender was presumably Petar's father.

Then, going back six weeks, there was another threatening message from the same number as that morning's missive, saying that the sender had heard that Petar had talked to someone about "our wartime activities" and that he should keep his mouth shut—otherwise there would be "serious consequences."

That was it—no signs of other contact from the same number. No incoming or outgoing calls listed on the calls register.

Johnson removed the phone battery again. He didn't want it to be traced while it was in his possession.

A number six drew into the bus stop. He joined the short queue, paid the driver, and made his way to the back of the bus. The air conditioning was a welcome relief from the rising heat outside.

He tried to think through the best course of action. He was away from the scene of the killing, not being followed, and was on the way back to his hotel. But now what?

Was this thing worth his attention? Petar had said there was no proof, and the detail was vague. The issue lay in evaluating the importance of what Petar had said and the significance of what might be, in reality, just a few straightforward wartime killings.

But someone clearly thought it was important—the person pulling the trigger on Petar at the café.

Johnson also had to bear in mind the other work options he had. The discussions he had lined up in Istanbul, relating to arms deals for Syrian rebels, seemed quite promising.

Johnson knew that the prosecuting authorities, originally the International Criminal Tribunal in The Hague, and then, since 2005, the local courts in Bosnia, Serbia, Croatia, and other countries of the former Yugoslavia, had taken their responsibility to prosecute war crimes very seriously. So if he could come up with evidence, the prosecutors would use it. But the question was, should he simply tip off local police and let them handle it.

Johnson was due to head to Istanbul on Monday. Perhaps

he could look into it until then and make a decision based on what he could find out.

Clearly, his best bet now would be to get in touch with Petar's brother, Filip. But he was in jail, Petar had said, without indicating which jail or when he might be released.

Then there was the father, for whom there was a phone number stored but no address. That might be a good starting point, but Johnson doubted whether a cold call to an old man who might not speak very good English would work well. Johnson could try speaking Croatian, but it wouldn't be an easy conversation, especially if the man had been informed about his son's death, which Johnson estimated would happen quite quickly.

Johnson felt somewhat at a dead end.

Then he thought of Jayne Robinson. Jayne was a long-standing friend, and for a brief period in the late 1980s, when they were both stationed in Pakistan—she for the British Secret Intelligence Service, MI6, and he for the CIA—they had been more than just friends.

Jayne had also helped Johnson with his most recent job, at the end of the previous year, tracking down a Nazi war criminal, and she was priceless as a partner on that type of investigation.

He knew, too, that Jayne had also done a four-year posting in the Balkans in the early 2000s, where she helped collect information to prosecute war criminals across the former Yugoslavia and fed back intelligence on political and economic issues to London.

That had come to an end when her cover, along with that of several of her colleagues, had been blown by a leak to local media in 2004.

But she might be able to put some context around everything Petar had said and help him out. Given her longer experience in the region, she would probably have a better idea than him about how to navigate her way through the labyrinth of government bodies and sources of information in these parts. It was certainly worth a try.

Johnson got off the bus when it stopped outside the Valamar Lacroma hotel. Instead of going to his room, he turned left down a road, past two other large tourist hotels, the Neptun and Royal Palm, and onto a pathway running along the rocky coastline. After a few hundred yards he came to the Cave Bar. Tucked underneath the cliff, the bar was built into a cave that extended deep into the cliff face and had an outdoor seating area right next to the water.

He sat down well away from the few other customers and ordered a beer, still feeling spooked by the shooting.

Johnson waited until the beer arrived, then checked carefully around him for possible eavesdroppers, pulled out his phone, and placed an encrypted call to Jayne, as was his habit with her.

She answered almost immediately. "Joe! Hello, good to hear from you. Where are you? What are you up to?"

Johnson pictured Jayne, her shortish dark hair and slim figure. She sounded excited to hear from him.

"I'm in Dubrovnik—work, not holiday," Johnson said. "I flew over earlier in the week to speak at a war crimes conference."

"Sounds good. Beautiful spot there. I miss it sometimes. How's it going?"

"It *was* going all right—but I've just come from drinking coffee with a guy who was shot dead outside the men's room of the café we were at, in the Old Town."

There was a pause as Jayne digested what he had said.

"What was that all about, then?" It was a typically low-key response from her.

Johnson explained the background to the morning's events and the information Petar had given him; he also told her about the visit from Vic and what he had asked him to find.

"So," Jayne said, "you've had Vic asking you to go look for some lost Bosnian government documents, which obviously must be highly critical if the Americans need them after twenty years. And then this guy Petar comes and tells you about a couple of war criminals who have evaded prosecution for two decades. Then he's shot dead, after receiving warning messages. Sounds like something of an odd coincidence to me."

"Yes, that just about sums it up," Johnson said.

"It might be worth investigating, then," Jayne said. "You could take the money from your friend Vic, do that job, and then, while he's paying your expenses, have a look at this other situation at the same time."

"Maybe, but it's difficult to know the significance of Petar's story," Johnson said. "Yes, he was murdered, but whether it's worth chasing from a war crimes perspective— and whether there's any evidence that could be used in a court to prosecute them—that's the hard question. Maybe I should just leave his murder to local police and drop the rest of it. What do you think?"

"If evidence does emerge of something that war crimes investigators weren't aware of before, then yes, it's worth pursuing. I know the Bosnian prosecutors are still pressing new charges all the time, having people extradited from various countries, including the US," Jayne said. "Another problem is, if you just hand it to local police, you can't be certain how seriously they'll pursue it or how capable they are. The bottom line is, how strongly do you feel about it?"

"I don't know, honestly," Johnson said. "But I was thinking of going to Split over the next two days to visit anyway, while I'm in Croatia, so I thought I could try and track down Petar's father, if I have time. I don't want to put you through a lot of trouble, but I was wondering if your technical guys at GCHQ might be able to track down the address registered against the father's cell phone number? Otherwise I can get Vic to try the NSA."

The Government Communications Headquarters was the British signals intelligence agency, responsible for a huge range of activities, including monitoring internet, telephone and email traffic for the Secret Intelligence Service (SIS) and other government functions, as required. Johnson knew that, as a member of the SIS, Jayne would have any number of contacts within the agency whom she could call on for a favor.

"I'll have a go," Jayne said. "Email me the details and I'll see what I can do. My friend Alice at GCHQ should be able to help."

Johnson also asked her to request from GCHQ a trace on the cell phone number from which the warning text message to Petar had been received.

She agreed, then paused. "You seem keen on this, Joe."

"No, really, I haven't decided that yet," Johnson said. "I've got other jobs I'm looking at. And anyway, I need to get home. I'm meant to be flying to Istanbul on Monday morning for a meeting, then home Monday night from there. What about you, what are you up to?"

Jayne paused. "Actually, I'm leaving Six. I've had enough. I've done twenty-six years. They're just taking costs out all the time, flogging us senseless, and with these London Olympics kicking off at the end of this month and all the security stuff flying around, it's just gone nuts. I've paid off the mortgage on my little apartment, so I handed my notice in some time back. You might remember I was getting close to quitting last year?"

Johnson remembered very well. But now he was surprised that she had actually taken such a bold step—and that he was learning of it only now. He thought they were closer than that.

It must be nice, in some ways, to be single, child-free, and footloose like Jayne, he thought. "So what are you planning to do when you leave?"

"I was thinking maybe something like you do," Jayne said. "Some private investigation work for corporates, governments, or intelligence agencies, maybe looking for wanted people who have removed themselves from the radar. There's plenty of work like that once you start looking around internationally. Actually . . . how about if I come and give you a hand now? It's a vipers' nest down there, Joe. You might need a little assistance and some extra local experience. And I'll get to explore the job that way, figure out if I like the reality as much as the idea."

Johnson laughed. "Really? You would? If I were going to do this job, then absolutely, but I don't think I will end up on it." But something in the back of his mind made him ask, "When could you do that, anyway?"

"Next week. Tuesday probably. I finish here on Monday afternoon."

For a second Johnson really considered it, but then reality hit him. "The kids would kill me, I'm afraid. We're meant to be going on a short break in northern Maine for a few days next weekend with my sister and her husband. I can't possibly miss that. So I'll be heading home Monday as planned."

"Okay, but if anything comes up, you know where to find me."

CHAPTER FOUR

Thursday, July 5, 2012
  London

The British Foreign Secretary Ian Owen wagged his finger at the *Wolff Live* studio audience to emphasize his point and raised his voice a couple of tones.

"What I would like to see, what most people in the Western world would like to see," he said, "is for democracy to thrive in the Islamic countries of the world. We've seen over the past decades, centuries, millennia even, a democratic culture evolve across much of the globe that is based very much on Christian principles. By that I mean Westernized countries have put in place the real building blocks of democracy, chiefly the independence of the judiciary, the rule of law, a free media and rights of individuals, and strong and diverse political parties. I'd like to see that kind of democracy spread to Islamic countries as well."

He took a sip of water, then leaned forward in his black armchair once again.

The interviewer, Boris Wolff, nodded. "That's fine, foreign secretary, but these systems have evolved over centuries. You're now saying to countries that have gone down the dictatorship route—just change overnight?"

"No, that's not what I'm saying," Owen said. "It's not an overnight process. But people bring about change from within. Strong, peaceful pressure for change can make a real difference."

"Okay," Boris said, running a hand through his clipped dark hair, "but in some ways you're seeing the tide go the other way, away from inclusion and diversity. Look at the United States, where we've seen Patrick Spencer, the Republican speaker of the House, trumpeting his anti-Muslim rhetoric, calling for bans on Muslims and getting huge support from various corners of the population."

"Yes, that's true," Owen said. "There are groups even in Western countries who are fighting to defeat us and our values. Spencer and his like are a threat to our vision of democracy because they want to exclude people who don't, say, have the right ethnic background or family group."

Boris leaned forward. "Foreign secretary, thank you for taking the time to be with us this afternoon. Strong views as always and much food for thought."

Owen nodded in acknowledgement, adjusted his tie, and sat back with a self-satisfied smile, clearly believing the interview had gone according to plan.

As the credits rolled and the show closed, Owen got to his feet and shook hands with Boris before his public relations staff swiftly ushered him out of the SRTV studios.

As the audience exited the building, in London's Paddington Basin, Boris wandered over to the program's editor, David Rowlands, who stood at the side of the set.

"I thought that mainly went very well," David said, looking up at Boris. "You did a good job. You pushed him just about hard enough on his points about internal change and Spencer and so on, without being too aggressive."

"Yes, hopefully I got the balance about right," Boris said, fingering the side of his face, which he had carefully shaved that morning, prior to the interview.

David smiled. "You've come a long way in the past few years. Amazing how you've grown into this role."

Boris nodded his thanks. David was right. It had been a long, sometimes hard journey from a junior copy editor, working shifts through dark winter nights on the BBC World Service, to a top TV political interviewer.

"Actually, on the subject of Spencer, I recently put in a pitch to interview him in New York," Boris said. "I thought it would make a good follow-up to the Owen interview. You know, he's got such a different viewpoint than Owen does, and he's coming from the other side of the Atlantic. It would make a great contrast and give a different perspective on the same issues. Also, Spencer's going to come across as a real thug, a mindless idiot, really, on some things. He's bound to say something strong—probably anti-Muslim or something—that will make a big headline and get us some great publicity. Management will love it."

"Great idea," David said. "The commercial boys will sell a ton of airtime on the back of that. We'll make a killing. You never mentioned that before."

"No, I wanted to see if it would get any traction with Spencer's publicity people first. But his main guy came back this morning and said they like the idea and could do it at quite short notice. Spencer's very publicity-keen at the moment, and we basically just need to find a studio that could handle it and fix it up. If the timing is right, we could do it as a live show, rather than a pre-record."

"When are you looking at?" David asked.

"I asked if Friday the twenty-seventh was doable."

David smiled. "Okay. Let's hope they bite, then. Nice one, Boris. We're on a roll at the moment, but we need to keep it up. The bosses upstairs are breathing down our necks, given that the ratings are slipping."

* * *

Thursday, July 5, 2012
  London

Later that afternoon, Boris steered his Porsche out of the SRTV studios parking lot, through London's Hyde Park, past the Royal Albert Hall and Imperial College, then onto Ennismore Mews, a quiet cobbled road tucked away just off Knightsbridge.

He felt a quiet sense of satisfaction as he drove; the Owen interview had been a job well done.

Boris pulled up outside his broad-fronted two-story house, a white-painted property with sky-blue doors and window frames, and glanced up at the bell tower of the Russian Orthodox church standing at the northern end of the street like a sentry on duty.

He pressed a remote control button attached to his car key, and his double garage door began to rise. When it was fully open, he drove in, closed it behind him, and let himself into the house through an interior door.

"Hayley, are you in?" he called up the polished mahogany staircase.

"Of course," Hayley said. Her long blond hair swung a little as she appeared at the top of the stairs. She wore a thin silk robe that fell slightly open, betraying the fact that she had nothing on underneath it. "Of course," she said. "Champagne's on ice down there. How did the interview go?"

"It was good," Boris said. "I gave Owen a good grilling. He started going on about the need for democracy in Islamic states, so I probed him quite strongly on that."

"Excellent," Hayley said. "When we've had a little champagne, I don't mind if you'd like to probe me too." She smiled and walked down the stairs, letting her garment slip a little further to reveal her long legs.

Boris laughed. "That'll definitely be a lot more enjoyable than probing Owen, and certainly a lot more enjoyable than probing the next person I'm lining up—Patrick Spencer."

"Ooh, Spencer. That's in the States then, not here?"

"Yes, it'll probably be in New York, and hopefully very soon."

"I can't stand him, but just make sure you wangle me onto that trip. Perhaps we can do a little shopping at the same time?" Hayley asked.

"Yes, sure. We can probably stay with Edvin and do a little partying as well." Edvin Matić was an old HVO army friend from Mostar, who had moved to New York in the mid-1990s. The two men kept in fairly close touch.

Hayley reached the bottom of the stairs, then walked over to Boris, her robe now fully open. She wrapped her arms around his neck and pressed her body into his, then began to kiss him. After a few minutes, she broke it off. "Hmm, I think you're definitely ready for the interview now."

"I am, but I just need to make a Skype call first. I fixed it for half past, and I'm already late, so I'd better get on," Boris said. "I'll do it in the office, then come down and join you for the champagne, okay?"

Hayley put on an exaggerated pout and theatrically closed her robe at the front again, then tied the belt to hold it in place. "I'll be waiting," she said.

Boris kissed her, then climbed the stairs, two steps at a time, walked around a set of weights in a recess on the landing that he occasionally used for a workout, and removed a key from his jacket pocket that he used to open his sound-proof first-floor office. He closed the door behind him and locked it again.

Hayley knew she wasn't to disturb him when he was making work-related calls, but nevertheless, he didn't want to take any chances. There was no way he would be able to explain to her the rationale for what happened in the other parts of his compartmentalized life, and when their relationship came to an end, as it undoubtedly would sooner rather than later, he didn't want any loose ends left behind.

Boris brought his desk computer out of sleep mode, entered a password, and clicked onto Skype, which he knew would automatically encrypt the call he was about to make.

He scrolled down his list of contacts until he came to a certain name, then pressed the call button.

After a couple of rings, the video screen opened, and gradually, the flickering picture stabilized. Boris could see a man with short dark hair wearing a pair of sunglasses. The sound came on, and Boris could hear background noise.

"Marco, sorry, I'm a little late," Boris said in Croatian. "We've just had Ian Owen on our Sunday program—not that that's an excuse. How are things?"

Marco Lukić shook his head. "So the British foreign secretary comes before your old friend, does he? How things change."

"Very funny."

"Anyway, I'm okay. It's been a busy few days," Marco said. "Are you still coming here for the meeting with our Turkish friend?"

"Yes," Boris said. "They're still buying heavily. The Syrians seem to be taking everything we can channel through, so I'm hoping to tie up another big order with Mustafa. I'll be there on Saturday to see him in Split. I was thinking, as I've got a several days off after that, we could go to Mostar and chill out for a bit, have a few beers?"

"Yes, good idea. We can spend some of Mustafa's money, assuming you complete the deal. Is he still paying on time?"

"Yes," Boris said, "They pay all right. Straight into Zürich, no problem. So you'll get your cut as usual."

"Good," Marco said. "And if you feel like increasing my cut, that'd be even better, as I'm doing most of the work these days."

"Yes," Boris said, "but if you remember, it was me who secured all the hardware in the first place, twenty years ago. Remember that. Back then it was me taking all the risks, not you."

"Hmm, well it's different now," Marco said. "I'm starting to feel as though I'm being ripped off."

Boris stared into his webcam. He knew that Marco had an image of him doing a three-days-per-week TV job that paid a fortune but demanded little. If only he knew the reality: the long hours working at home, preparing questions, researching and reading until he knew his subjects well enough to ensure they received a thorough examination, no matter the topic of discussion.

Marco shrugged. "Anyway, there's something else I need to tell you. Two days ago I did something. Remember Petar Simic?"

Boris nodded.

"Well, I heard a few weeks back he'd been talking to people about our wartime activities, and I gave him a warning about it. Then I was in Dubrovnik on Wednesday and Thursday and had a tip-off from someone I know at Sarajevo University who was at a conference at one of the big hotels down there. The guy said Petar was trying to get close to a war crimes investigator, an American guy with a big reputation. I checked him out—Joe Johnson's his name. He finds people and brings them to trial. A Nazi specialist. I can think of only one reason why Petar would want to talk to a big-league war crimes investigator." He paused.

"Go on," Boris said.

"So, anyway, I tailed Petar Thursday morning, and sure enough, he spent an hour or more deep in conversation with this guy Johnson down in the Stari Grad, up on the city walls. Very secretive. I didn't like it. So I did what I should have done years ago."

"What?"

"What do you think?"

Boris remained silent for a bit. Then he said, "What, right there in the Stari Grad?"

"Yes. Outside the men's room in a café."

Boris took a piece of chewing gum from a pack on his desk and put it into his mouth. In a *café*? His friend was losing his mind. "That's extremely risky. Why there?"

"I was up on the walls and saw Petar and Johnson at a table in a café in the harbor," Marco said. "I sent him a message, warned him against talking to Johnson. He was drinking a lot of water, and I figured he would use the men's room at some stage. So I sat nearby, then followed him when he went."

Boris sat speechless. It wasn't the sort of thing he would have expected from an experienced campaigner like Marco—especially not in such a high-risk area as Dubrovnik Old Town, which was normally swarming with tourists and uniformed police.

"But you didn't touch the American?" Boris asked. "Did he see you?"

"I left the American. Didn't get an opportunity anyway. And no, he wouldn't have seen me, I'm fairly sure of that. He was at an outside table."

"Well, surely he's going to link it to you," Boris said.

"Petar must have mentioned you in the conversation. Isn't the American now going to follow up?"

"How?" Marco asked. "He wouldn't know who did Petar in."

"Hmm. That's what you think. There's Filip. He might put him on your trail."

"Nah, he's still in prison, over with you in the UK, as far as I know."

Boris shook his head. "You said you sent Petar a message. Did you grab his phone, then, after you shot him?"

There was silence. Boris could see on his screen that Marco was frowning. The answer was clearly a no.

Boris ran his forefinger down his nose, which angled a little to the right from a car crash he was in during his eighteen months in Munich in 1995. "Not smart," he said. "Anyway, we can discuss it further in Mostar."

Marco shrugged. "Sure. I think it'll be okay. Like I said, should have done it a long time ago. If the American proves a problem, we can think again."

CHAPTER FIVE

Friday, July 6, 2012
Astoria, Queens, New York City

The barman increased the volume on the television in the corner of the restaurant Ćevabdžinica Sarajevo as Patrick Spencer began his much-anticipated speech, which was being broadcast live on CBA's special afternoon political news program.

Aisha Delić sat up in her chair and pushed her sunglasses onto the top of her head. "Great, this idiot Republican," she said to her friend Adela. "I tell you, he makes me ashamed to be a New Yorker . . . and an American."

She picked up her glass of iced tea from the wooden table. The amount of airtime her employer, the broadcaster CBA, was currently giving to Spencer, the recently elected speaker of the House of Representatives, sometimes made her feel embarrassed to admit she worked for them. She, like many of her friends, struggled to believe so many people were buying into his rhetoric—even other Republicans in his party had difficulty accepting its extremism.

The afternoon crowd of late lunchers and coffee drinkers in the Bosnian restaurant, on the corner of 38th Street and 34th Avenue in Astoria, fell quiet as Spencer leaned toward a bank of microphones on the stand in front of him.

"We've got a problem in this country, a problem with immigrants. Yes, we all know about illegal immigrants, and we'll deal with those. We need a wall to keep them out, because the current system just doesn't work. But I'm also talking about Muslim immigrants—some of whom are even legal."

Aisha shook her head. "Here we go," she said, flipping her long dark hair over her shoulder.

Spencer squared his shoulders and ran a hand through his coiffured mop of iron-gray hair, then continued. "Muslims gather in neighborhoods, and they influence each other. Some become radicalized—and dangerous. They become anti-American, anti the country they've chosen to live in. And that's a big problem for all of us. That's what I want to see sorted out. For the next few years this issue is going to be at the top of my list. My goal is to draft new legislation to address this endangerment to the American people. President Obama chooses to downplay this concern, as does Secretary Clinton, and I think that's very wrong. Just take a look at what's going on in the Middle East—Islamic fundamentalists chopping people's heads off, torturing people. Until we can understand what Muslims are trying to do, I think we shouldn't allow any more into the United States."

As Spencer talked, the silence in the restaurant was broken by a hum of chatter, which became increasingly angry and vocal. One man shouted, "Republican scum, turn that TV off." Another yelled, "Shoot the racist bastard."

Spencer's televised speech, to a community group in

Brooklyn, continued for another ten minutes as he moved away from immigration and on to health care and other issues before concluding. By then, few in the restaurant were still listening.

What a joke, Aisha thought. She cupped her chin in her right hand, her olive-tanned forearm propped on the table. "America was *built* on immigration," she said. "When I moved here in '95, I was welcomed. Now you've got people like that just stoking up hatred. He thinks he's going to solve an issue, but it's going to have the opposite effect."

She looked at Adela. "How do you feel? I know you've always tried to fit in—even changed your name. Then we get this shit."

Aisha was referring to when her friend switched her name from Ademović to Adamson many years earlier.

Adela sipped her drink. "It makes me angry. The imams I listen to, mostly reasonably moderate guys, hear people like him, Spencer, and a few are becoming more interventionist, more anti-American. Can't blame them."

"It's getting worse at work," Aisha said. "I keep getting blocked from promotions. It's discrimination. I've been there nine years, and I'm still no closer to being a broadcast lighting designer. If you've worked at CBA as long as I have, you should at least get annual inflation-linked pay rises. I've performed well, but I've had three small rises in nine years. And I'm still just a lighting board operator. What's the point?"

Adela nodded her head in sympathy.

Aisha finished her drink and pushed her hair back over her shoulders. "I'm telling you, if Spencer ever decides to run for the White House in the future, like some people think he might, I'm going back to Mostar, seriously."

"You wouldn't, surely, not after everything that happened?" Adela asked.

Would I? It was a question Aisha often asked herself and never really answered. Maybe it wouldn't be Mostar, where there were too many bad memories and nothing to go back for. But somewhere. Would she want to stay in the States if the country started implementing a discriminatory political agenda? She doubted it.

"It won't come to that. We won't let it," Adela said.

"What can we do?" Aisha asked, a skeptical look on her face. "It's not exactly a war zone here, is it, where you just move on and do what's necessary, like we used to back home."

"Well, there's a meeting going on at my mosque next Tuesday about some of this stuff. There'll be an interesting speaker who's a bit more radical and a chance to chat more. We shouldn't stand by doing nothing while this man spreads his hatred. Do you feel like coming along? There's one most Tuesdays and Thursdays."

Aisha hesitated. As much as she hated Patrick Spencer, she didn't feel like getting involved with anything that had the label of "radical" attached to it. She knew only too well what "radical" could do to a person.

"No, thanks, that's not really my scene."

"Okay," Adela said. "But you'll see that it's going to be all of our scene soon enough."

CHAPTER SIX

Saturday, July 7, 2012
Split, Croatia

Johnson hauled himself up a steep set of stone steps that led from the promenade around the harbor toward Marjan, the imposing pine-covered hill at the western end of Split.

He checked his map against the address he had received earlier that morning from Jayne; her contact at GCHQ had quickly traced an address for the cell phone number and found the name of the owner, Antun Simic, Petar's father. Johnson walked on.

At the top of the steps, he stopped and took out his phone, then pretended to dial a number and held a two-minute imaginary conversation with someone about an equally imaginary restaurant. While he was speaking, he turned around and looked down the stone steps, then along the road on which he now was standing. There was no obvious sign of a tail. He pocketed the phone.

Johnson was more than a little concerned after the incident in Dubrovnik, about one hundred miles south of Split. If someone had tracked Petar and warned him about speaking to Johnson, then it seemed logical to assume he too might be targeted.

Johnson turned left onto Marasovića Street, a road with old stone houses on the left and the green expanse of Marjan on the right. Partway up the hill, Johnson stopped. Another imaginary call, another check.

By now he was sweating in the morning heat, the sun glaring down from a cloudless sky. Behind and below him he could now see Split's harbor.

This is going to be a waste of time, I can feel it, he thought. *And a tough conversation.*

As he resumed walking, another encrypted text message arrived from Jayne. Her friend Alice at GCHQ now had a name for the owner of the cell phone from which the warning text had been sent: it was Marco Lukić, the man whom Petar had said ratted on his brother Filip, causing him to be imprisoned.

Interesting.

Johnson continued until, halfway up the hill, on the left, he came to a house with a red-tiled roof set back from the road, down a driveway, behind a dense hedge of conifers. The house was built of white stone and had green shutters and a wide balcony running across the length of the first floor.

Johnson walked cautiously down the driveway to the front door, paused, checked the address details again, and then pressed a brass doorbell next to the front door. A loud set of melodic chimes came from within the house, but nobody came to the door.

He rang again. Still no response. Johnson walked carefully along the house toward the side that overlooked the harbor.

Now Johnson could detect the unmistakable musky smell of cannabis in the air. He reached the corner of the house and poked his head around. There, on an expansive stone patio, shaded by three tall pine trees, sat an old man in a deck chair. He puffed away at a large joint.

"Hello, are you Mr. Simic?" Johnson ventured, in Croatian.

The old man jerked, startled. "Who are you?" he asked, also in Croatian.

"My name's Joe Johnson. I'm an American here on some business. Sorry, I did ring the doorbell, but there was no answer. I was hoping to speak to Antun Simic."

The man put his smoldering joint on an ashtray next to the deck chair, got to his feet, and walked to Johnson. He appeared to be in his seventies, with a full mop of white hair, slightly hunched shoulders, a wrinkled face, and deep-set dark eyes.

"What do you want?" he asked, now speaking in English. "I'm Antun."

Johnson's first thought was that the old man didn't seem to be in mourning. His second was that he was glad he didn't have to worry about the old man's English. It was crystal clear, if heavily accented.

Johnson held out his hand and shook the old man's. "Hello," he said. "Good to meet you, and I'm sorry about your son."

Antun nodded sharply. "Thank you. You knew Petar?"

"Yes. That's actually why I'm here. I wanted to talk to you —but particularly to Filip, about his death."

"What do you know about Petar's death?" Antun asked.

"Well, I was actually with Petar when it happened."

Antun stood momentarily speechless. "Are you the man the police mentioned? The one he was having coffee with?"

"Yes," Johnson said.

"So have you come here to tell me about it?"

"Yes. And I was hoping you might be able to help me find

a way to talk to Filip. I know he's in prison, but there were a few things that Petar spoke to me about, and he wanted me to discuss them with Filip."

Antun peered at Johnson suspiciously. "Are these things you told the police?"

"Not entirely. That's what I'd like to explain to you."

The old man hesitated. "Come this way." He led the way over to a bench just outside the door that led into the house from his veranda.

"Sorry, I get all kinds of odd people coming here. Do you have any identification? Passport, driver's license, or something." Antun was clearly not going to take any risks.

"Sure," Johnson said. He pulled his passport and a business card from his pocket and gave them to Antun, who scrutinized them closely, then handed them back.

"Do you want coffee? I was making some."

"Thanks," Johnson said. "An espresso would be good."

Antun disappeared into the house, and Johnson sat down on the bench outside. He took out his phone and switched on the voice recorder, then placed the device in the breast pocket of his shirt.

A few minutes later, Antun reappeared, carrying two cups of espresso. He gave one to Johnson, sat down, and studied him for a moment.

"So tell me—tell me what my son told you."

"Mr. Simic, you should know that I'm a war crimes investigator. That's why Petar approached me at a conference in Dubrovnik on Wednesday, where I was speaking. He told me he wanted to talk to me about some crimes that were never accounted for, back in the war. Then when we met on Thursday morning, he told me about Filip, about how his so-called friends betrayed him while they went free. He told me what those friends did during the war, how they escaped justice, and that he wanted me to track them down and ensure they paid for their crimes."

Antun stared at Johnson. "Did he name these 'friends'?"

"Yes. Franjo Vuković and Marco Lukić."

Antun let out a huff. "Petar was trying to get you to investigate Marco?"

"Yes."

"Then Marco killed him, most likely. You need to tell the police."

"Mr. Simic, I can't. Not until I speak with Filip and not until I have the evidence I need. Trust me, if Marco is responsible for the things Petar told me about, he'll pay for his crimes. But we can't spook him into disappearing now."

Antun narrowed his eyes a little. "Petar hated the fact that those two were free when Filip wasn't. But I thought he'd let it go. Clearly not." He paused, then added, "Okay, we don't let Marco disappear. Understand? We will have our justice for Petar, or we will have our revenge."

"I understand."

Johnson decided not to mention that he had read the text that Marco had sent Petar. That would lead to awkward questions about when and why he had picked up Petar's phone.

Antun continued to study Johnson, but he seemed to let his guard down a notch, apparently satisfied with what he was hearing. "You need to speak to Filip?"

"Yes. But I don't know where he's in prison," Johnson said.

"Filip's been in Wakefield prison, in the UK," he said. "He was sentenced to sixteen years in 1996. The tribunal in The Hague sent him there, along with a few others. I've traveled there many times to visit him."

"Right," Johnson said. "Sixteen years, so he's due out this year, then?"

"Yes, correct."

"When is he out?"

"Tomorrow."

Johnson blinked. "*Tomorrow?* You mean he's being released tomorrow?"

"Correct. He'll be back here tomorrow night, I hope, if he can get his flight arranged." Antun sighed. "Then I'll have to tell him about Petar. And then he'll want revenge, because he'll know who did it, just as I know who did it. And I'll have to try and calm him down, but I won't really want to. But I can't see him go straight back to jail, so I'll have to."

Johnson paused. "There is another way. I understand he's going to be angry, but there are different types of revenge. Look, I'm a war crimes investigator. I worked as a Nazi hunter in the United States for a long time, and I have my own private business now. Let me speak to Filip when he arrives. I don't know if there's anything that can be done, but there's no harm in talking."

The old man considered the suggestion. "Yes, come back here later next week, then."

"I can't. I'm due to leave for Istanbul on Monday morning, and then I head back home to the US on Monday night. So it will have to be tomorrow night or not at all."

The old man sipped his coffee, picked up the joint that was smoldering in the tray, knocked off a long trail of ash, and took a deep drag.

They sat in silence for a minute or two as Johnson waited for an answer.

"Okay, tomorrow night, then," Antun said.

Just as he spoke, a loud chime sounded from within the house.

"Who the hell can that be?" Antun said, turning around. "I'm just going to have a look at the security video screen." He got up and disappeared into the house.

A few seconds later there was a loud exclamation from inside the house.

"My God!" Antun shouted in Croatian.

Johnson wasn't sure what to do. Was the old man all right?

Then Antun's words floated through to the patio. "I wasn't expecting you until tomorrow or Monday."

Is Filip here now?

After a few moments he walked through to the hallway, where he saw Antun embracing a younger man. Johnson didn't need to be told that this was indeed Filip Simic. He was almost a clone of his father.

"They brought forward my release by three days," Filip said in Croatian. "They said it was something to do with new arrivals and—" He stopped when he saw Johnson. "Who the hell's this?" He broke away from hugging Antun.

Probably the last thing Filip wanted after sixteen years in prison was some stranger in his father's house on his return, Johnson thought.

"It's okay, Filip, it's okay. He's an American guy," Antun said in Croatian. Then he switched to English and introduced Johnson to his son. "He's an investigator. He speaks some Croatian, but let's use English. I was chatting with him. He was with Petar when . . ." Antun's voice trailed away.

"When what?" Filip asked.

"Come, let's go and sit through there." Antun motioned Filip and Johnson to the kitchen table and sat down. Filip scowled at Johnson and remained standing.

"Come on, tell me. What's happened to Petar?" Filip demanded.

It didn't look as though his years in prison had been kind to Filip, Johnson thought. Although his features were very much like his father and his brother's, his hair was grayer than Petar's had been; his face was red, his cheeks lined and punctuated with small broken blood vessels, which Johnson thought to be a sign of high blood pressure. His nose angled a few degrees to the right, and a front tooth was missing, leaving a black gap.

"It's . . . he's been shot. It happened on Thursday, in Dubrovnik, in the Stari Grad," Antun said.

"What? Is he—"

"He's gone, Filip."

"No! No, no . . . "

His shoulders shook, and then he sobbed.

It appeared to be a dry sob, but it gathered momentum. He sat down, put his head between his knees, and held his forehead with both hands, his whole body trembling. His father stood and put a hand on his shoulder. Johnson could only watch in silence.

Eventually, the sobbing subsided. Filip finally raised his head and glared at Johnson.

"What happened?" Filip asked. "Who did this?"

It was Antun who spoke first. "When it happened, he was in a café, telling Mr. Johnson here, who is a war crimes investigator, about Franjo and Marco, what happened in the '90s, and how you ended up in prison and they didn't."

Johnson resisted the temptation to jump in and give his firsthand version of the conversation he had with Petar as he watched shock, then understanding, cross Filip's face.

"Those bastards," Filip's eyes snapped to Johnson.

"You listen to me. It was Marco that did this," Antun said, rapping both palms down on the table in front of him. It was a statement that did not invite contradiction.

"Petar spoke to me about Marco," Johnson said. "I was interested, from a professional point of view, because that's my job: tracing war criminals, among others. And I was planning to get some more information from Petar, to try and decide whether the whole thing was worth investigating, when he was killed."

"Of course it's worth investigating," Filip said.

Johnson leaned forward and placed his elbows on the table, then cupped his chin in his hands. "I have to confess, I didn't give the police everything when I gave my statement. As I explained to your father, I didn't tell them that Petar asked me to look into Marco because I didn't want to spook him and have him disappear."

"You damn well should have told the police," Filip said, his voice rising. "They are useless, but maybe you've got something vital that could help them. Did you not see anything, anyone suspicious?"

Johnson pressed his lips together. "Actually, yes, I did. Petar received a text message, then not long afterward went to the men's room, inside the café. A minute later, I saw a man walk quickly from the restrooms and leave the café. But I didn't get a good look at his face. And I didn't remember it at the time, honestly. It was only later when I was thinking through what had happened that it came to me."

There was a short silence and Johnson sensed both men's mood.

"You're right," Johnson said. "I need to tell the police this. Listen, I'll do that when I return to Dubrovnik. Even if it makes Marco run."

That seemed to satisfy Filip and Antun, who sat back in their chairs.

"I'd better go and let you and your father grieve in peace," Johnson said. "You probably have a lot to talk about, especially given what's just happened. I could come back tomorrow."

"No, I can handle it," Filip said. "I'm used to it, living here. Actually, you can stay. You might be of use to me. There's probably quite a bit more to it than what Petar told you."

He scanned Johnson up and down. "There are things I

could tell you. But I'm going to have to check you out first before giving you the whole lot, okay?"

Johnson had to consciously stop his eyebrows from rising. The guy had some nerve, given he'd just finished a long stretch in prison.

"Okay," Johnson said. "I've got nothing to hide." He told Filip that his story was on his website, that he was an investigator who specialized in tracking down people who had gone off the radar—cases about which the police weren't necessarily interested. He said he had a special interest in war crimes because of his background as a Nazi hunter for the US government, in its Office of Special Investigations, prior to starting his own business in 2006. He just needed someone to pay for his time.

"And before the Nazi hunting job?" Filip asked.

Johnson decided to be vague. "Before that I worked for the US government. I did a stint in Pakistan and Afghanistan."

Filip pressed the palms of his hands together, visibly thinking. "I've just done sixteen years in Wakefield prison."

Johnson nodded.

"Now, I did something wrong," Filip said. "It led to the deaths of quite a few Bosnians. I've regretted what happened, and I've paid a price for that. I'm not going to discuss it any further, so don't ask," Filip said. "But these other guys, Franjo and Marco, committed worse crimes, killed a lot more—I think at least forty based on what they said at the time—and they've got off completely free. You can accuse me of being bitter, but I don't care. They should be in jail. Franjo, especially. They tortured Bosnians at a concentration camp, the Heliodrom, near Mostar, every day for months while they were working there. They did indescribable things. Starved them and broke fingers, arms, legs, left them without water, made them drink urine."

"Yes, your brother told me about the Heliodrom," Johnson said.

Antun tapped the table with his fingers. "There might be one lead worth chasing. Wasn't Franjo married at that time, to a Muslim girl? But it didn't last long. I believe they broke up when the war started."

"That's a good point," Filip said. "He was married to a girl called . . . oh, what was her name. Aisha, that's it. Aisha Delić. And she had a gorgeous friend who was a Croat called Ana Dukić, whom I was completely obsessed with when I was about nineteen. I chased after her for months, and eventually we, um, got together. Then we fell out in a major way. It was very bitter. We haven't spoken since."

He smiled. "See, in those days before the war, we all used to mix together much more, drink together more, sleep together much more. Church or mosque, it didn't really matter. And when we fought, it was over women, not religion. It was a different country then."

Filip pointed at Johnson. "You should try and find Aisha."

"So where is Aisha now?" Johnson asked.

"As far as I know she went to America," Filip said. "That was the last I heard of her, but that was before I went into Wakefield, in another lifetime."

"And her father, Erol, was high up in the government, I remember," Antun said. "He had some sort of secret job. He worked for Izetbegović in Sarajevo."

Johnson raised his eyebrows. Izetbegović, the former Bosnian Muslim president, who had been close to Bill Clinton. This was getting increasingly interesting.

Johnson sat upright. "So this guy Franjo was married to the daughter of one of Izetbegović's henchmen. It sounds like a tangled web."

"Yes, it was," Filip said. "Look, you're a war crimes investigator. Well, maybe you've arrived at exactly the right time. I'd actually really like you to find these two murderers, Franjo and Marco, especially given what's happened to Petar."

Johnson nodded. "You could definitely help me. Would you be free to do that? What are your plans now?"

Filip averted his eyes. "I've been thinking about it the past few years while I've been in prison. I was a journalist before the war—that's how I knew Franjo. We trained together. Then, like everybody, we joined the army, and everything fell away. It's been a long time, but I could go back to doing that. Maybe as a freelancer. My English is good, and there's a lot to write about in this part of the world. But I also have a few things I worked on before prison, business ventures around here. I've still got a lot of contacts. Don't worry, I'd be able to pay you."

Filip's phone pinged as a text message arrived. He took the phone from his pocket and stabbed at the screen. "Dammit, these phones are hard to get used to. First thing I bought when I got out. Didn't see too many of them in prison, apart from the odd one someone smuggled in," Filip said.

"Do you need some help?" Johnson offered.

"No, no, it's okay. I'll sort it out. Just a message from a business contact." Filip pocketed his phone. "Maybe we could work together? I could help you, you help me. You might need some local knowledge around here, yes?"

Johnson struggled to keep his face neutral. That didn't sound like a good idea.

"Maybe," Johnson said. "We can discuss it."

Filip leaned toward Johnson and looked him in the eye. "Okay. And now, just tell me what you need for us to nail these bastards."

CHAPTER SEVEN

Saturday, July 7, 2012
Split

The man calling himself Stefan strode over the smooth concrete quayside, the blue-green waters of Split's marina to his left offsetting the array of bleached white yachts.

He glanced at his watch. *Right on time*, he thought, as he continued toward a clutch of large yachts at the far end of the concrete pier.

Stefan, with neatly clipped receding dark hair and stubble covering his fleshy face, stopped in front of the third boat, a long, sleek Sunseeker.

Standing on the deck was a swarthy man with a rather straggly black beard, flecked with gray, who wore dark glasses. He raised his hand in greeting but didn't smile. "Hello, Stefan. Come on board."

Stefan stepped heavily onto the gangplank, which creaked under his weight. He walked past two Jet Skis that were mounted on a hydraulic pulley system at the back of the boat and shook hands with his host, Mustafa Asan.

"This makes a change from the Hilton," Stefan said in slightly accented but fluent English.

"Yes, we're having a break from Ankara for a few weeks," Mustafa said. He led the way into a teak-lined cabin, carefully closed the door, then extracted a bottle of champagne from a silver wine bucket, and poured it slowly into two flutes. He handed one to his guest.

"There you go, Stefan. *Serefe*, as we say in Turkey, 'your honor.' Cheers."

"*Serefe*, indeed, thank you," Stefan said, carefully lowering his frame onto an ornate wooden chair. He gently clinked glasses with Mustafa, who sat opposite. "I'm assuming we can talk securely here. Did you have the boat checked?"

"Yes, of course."

"Now, how are things looking at your end?" Stefan asked.

"Good," Mustafa said. "The Syrian rebels are taking all the hardware we can give them."

Stefan knew that the forces opposed to Syrian President Bashar al-Assad were determined to put up a real fight. Their appetite for both weapons and ammunition was seemingly insatiable.

He nodded. "We can keep supplying what your people need. What's on the list?"

Mustafa reeled off the items. "More Kalashnikovs, more M16s, and ammunition for both of those. Antitank grenades, Milan antitank missiles, detonators, rocket launchers, and surface-to-air missiles—including Stingers, if they are available."

"No Stingers. They're almost impossible to get," Stefan said. "But everything else is not a problem."

Mustafa inclined his head, as if expecting that would be the response.

"We could get it all together by next Friday night," Stefan said. "If you get a plane into that little airfield at Sinj again, we can load it very quickly."

Mustafa nodded. "Yes, that's fine." The Turk's Antonov An-72 aircraft was well suited to the short grass airstrip at Sinj, not far from the border with Bosnia. It allowed for an easy nighttime mission, with a quick exit straight to Saudi Arabia. From there, the aircraft would carry out a drop in the target zone.

Stefan lit his cigarette. "I'll have my guys on the ground again. And the Americans will ensure there's no interference —provided I keep a certain person in their ranks happy."

Mustafa shrugged. "I hope keeping that certain person happy doesn't require too big a cut."

"He does well enough but nothing to worry about," Stefan said.

Mustafa drained the remains of his champagne and stood up. "I need to get back to work. Real work."

Stefan also stood, said his farewells, and strolled back the way he had come an hour earlier, around the marina. After finding a space on a wooden bench, he took both of his cell phones from his pocket. He turned off the "Stefan" pay-as-you-go phone, then switched the other phone back on. He needed to make a quick call before heading to Split's airport.

He called a number in the United States.

CHAPTER EIGHT

Sunday, July 8, 2012
Wolf Trap, Virginia

The pathway ran from the back of the expansive gray brick house at the end of Wynhurst Lane to a small summerhouse about ninety yards away, at the end of the garden. Beyond it was thick woodland and Difficult Run River, which curled through the trees.

Robert Watson, chief of the Near East Division in the CIA's National Clandestine Service, limped past the summerhouse and removed a cheap burner cell phone from his pocket.

He walked slowly through a gate to the woods and continued along a narrow grassy footpath. Halfway along it, he glanced behind him, then carried on. The early morning sunshine glinted through the trees.

Once he was near the narrow river, among thick pines, the veteran intelligence officer sat on a small wooden bench, smoothed his mop of white hair, and looked carefully around him. There was no sign of anyone nearby. He was far from certain that his house was free of bugs, and this was as good a place as any to make a confidential call.

He called a number. It rang several times before someone answered.

"Hello."

"It's Robert," Watson said in a gravelly voice.

"Ah, Robert. What's happening?" replied Alan Edwards, the CIA's chief of station in Zagreb.

The call cut off before Watson could answer. He looked at the reception indicator. Barely one bar.

Damn phone company, he thought.

That was the problem with the phones he used for such calls. His encrypted CIA work device had no such issues; his employer had made sure of that. He redialed, and the call went through again but still sounded distant.

"Sorry, cell phone reception around here is awful. Got cut off. Anyway, I was about to say, I had a call from our man RUNNER, who's been over your way. He's been talking to the Turks again. We've got another shipment due out of Sinj next Friday night. Can you take care of it?"

Watson had long ago given his agent the code name RUNNER for purposes of communication with the very few people who were familiar with this particular operation, and it had nothing to do with the man's athletic prowess.

"Friday? Yes, that should be okay. Presumably we're talking late?"

"Yes, probably one o'clock in the morning. You just need to close off the roads, keep people away, and keep a lookout."

"Okay, we'll probably do what we did last time—a burst water main. That did the trick. Nobody expects Croatian workmen to move quickly at night. We'll block the road with vans and put the signs up, so that should give us a good hour or so." There was a slight pause. "Just to be clear, you think we're still safe, dealing with RUNNER? It's been a long time now."

"I'll deal with him as long as it pays. As for safe—it's as safe as it can be after twenty years. I limit information flows on a need-to-know basis. Might sound odd for someone in my job, but I don't actually know much about him, and I don't want to. I've only met him a handful of times. We keep him off the intelligence radar plus the odd favor, like this Sinj thing, and as long as I get my cut—which I do—it'll stay that way. You get your cut, I pay EDISON a cut, I pocket the rest, job done. Everyone's happy. It works."

"But about RUNNER," Edwards said. "What's his job?"

"Don't know, really. Like I said, I don't need to know," Watson said. "I think some arms wheeling and dealing."

"And who's EDISON?"

Watson frowned. Why was Edwards suddenly asking questions?

Lying and deception went with the territory in Watson's role, as it always had done and he expected always would do. It was something he was quite comfortable with, and he assumed that Edwards took a fair proportion of what he was told with a grain of salt. But so far he'd hardly told Edwards a single truth. In fact he knew precisely what RUNNER did, apart from arms dealing, and what his alias was. And likewise, he certainly wasn't going to give EDISON's identity to Edwards.

After a few seconds, Edwards broke the silence. "I shouldn't have asked. Forget I did."

"All I'll tell you," Watson said, "is EDISON helped me out a lot when we set this whole thing up in '93, so I owe him for that. He's doing all right for himself now, and when he gets to where he wants to be, he'll probably do me a big favor in due course—maybe a nice fat consultancy fee in my retirement in return for whispering useful information in his ear every so often. So I keep him happy. Just as I keep you happy, I hope?"

"Yeah, it's good, for a few hours work. Where are you now?" Edwards asked.

"I'm at home in Wolf Trap," Watson said. He had lived there for five years. The house was way too big for just him, but given it was only twelve miles from Langley, it worked out fine.

"How's things there?" Watson asked.

"Hot, stinking hot. Temperature's been up to ninety these past few days. Looking forward to my August break back home, frankly."

"I'm sure. Okay, I need to go. Talk to you later."

Watson hung up and scanned his surroundings carefully again.

Then he rang another cell phone number, one that he used very sparingly.

"EDISON, it's SILVER here," Watson began when the call was answered.

The person he was calling replied curtly, "Yes?"

"Just to let you know, another shipment's going out. Not huge but decent enough."

"How much?" EDISON asked.

"Total probably one to two million US. Like I said, not huge, but it'll keep us ticking," Watson said.

"Okay, thanks. Just remember, the stakes are getting higher for me. Got to be damn careful now."

Watson gripped the handset. "Yes, I know, don't worry. It'll be fine. Talk soon."

He hung up. Then he picked up a stone and tossed it into Difficult Run River.

Bullshit. The stakes are getting higher. Aren't they for all of us, he thought.

CHAPTER NINE

Sunday, July 8, 2012
  Split

Johnson climbed a steep iron staircase that wound upward in a spiral inside the bell tower of St. Domnius Cathedral. He had decided that a walk around the city and a spot of sight-seeing might help to clear his mind.

As he hauled himself up to the top, Johnson clung to the handrail. Eventually, he found himself on a stone platform whose carved stone arched windows offered views in all directions across the city of Split.

The early afternoon sun was baking the city yet again. Looking west from his vantage point, high above the surrounding buildings, he could see Marjan, the green hill where the previous afternoon he had been at Antun's house.

Johnson read the leaflet he had picked up at the entrance. The cathedral, situated within the medieval heart of Split, dated back to the seventh century, it said, and formed part of the oldest building in the city, the mausoleum of the Roman Emperor Diocletian.

He peered through one of the unglazed open windows. There was his hotel, the Luxe, just a short distance out of the walled Diocletian's Palace area.

It seemed to him that the broad sweep of history in these parts, particularly the more recent bloody schisms that had savagely broken up the old Yugoslavia, had left deep wounds that were still festering. And not a great deal had improved since he had worked in the region.

The war from 1991 to 1995 had ripped the country apart, destroying friendships, families, and relationships. Sure, he thought, some—maybe most—of the perpetrators of murder, violence, and torture had been caught, indicted, and sentenced. But not all of them.

He remembered reading the headlines when the likes of Slobodan Milošević, president of Serbia, Ratko Mladić, head of the Bosnian Serb army, and Radovan Karadžić, president of the Srpska Republic, had been tried in court.

Further down the tree there were police commanders, generals, and ordinary soldiers like Filip who had been brought to justice, representing all facets of the ethnic divides whose fault lines ran through the entire Balkan region.

But how many others are still out there, guilty but unpunished? And where are they now? America? Britain? Australia? Canada?

That was what interested him—what had always interested him.

Johnson moved to the other side of the bell tower and gazed out over the harbor. Hundreds of passengers were disembarking from a cruise ship to go on sightseeing tours and shopping expeditions in and around the Old Town—doubtless a large number of them were fellow Americans.

But behind the tourism facade, old battles were clearly still being fought, though not with tanks and rocket launchers. Johnson himself was already a witness to the fact that blood was still being spilt. And there was the threat of more to come.

Johnson sat on the stone parapet and stared out across the Adriatic.

A young couple who had been kissing in the corner finished taking photographs of each other. It reminded Johnson of him and his late wife, Kathy, in the early days, before they were married and before the children came along. He offered to take a picture of the couple together, which they gratefully accepted. They posed, arms wrapped around each other, in front of the window, which faced out to sea; then they eagerly examined the results of Johnson's handiwork on the camera screen. They seemed happy and thanked Johnson profusely before starting the descent down the staircase to ground level.

Johnson was left by himself. He had his own camera in his bag, a high-quality Olympus OM-D E-M5, which he had bought only a couple of months earlier as a lighter alternative to his Canon 5D SLR. Normally, he would have taken the opportunity to frame a few photographs of the city from such a vantage point. But now he had other things on his mind.

He took out a pack of cigarettes and lit one, smoking it slowly as he watched the tourists sitting at café tables far below him. Waiters clad in smart white shirts and black waistcoats scurried between them and delivered drinks and food.

As he smoked, Johnson clicked onto the recording of the conversation he'd had with Petar prior to the shooting and pressed play.

"... *Franjo, Marco, and Filip were responsible for quite a lot of those deaths, no doubt about it ... They must have murdered dozens. When I first knew Franjo and Marco, they were quite happy to live alongside Muslims. Franjo was even married to one. But they changed massively—really seemed to hate them in the end . . . "*

He rewound certain parts of the conversation and listened again.

His mind was made up.

When he had finished the cigarette, he took out his phone and made an encrypted call to Vic, who was now back home in Washington, DC. He answered on the third ring, and Johnson spoke before Vic could open his mouth.

"Vic, it's Joe."

After a pause, a gravelly voice came on at the other end of the line. "Doc, I'm sure you remembered it's only seven o'clock in the morning here. Where are you?"

"I'm in Split. Sorry, yes, I did know it was early. I'm just checking in with you."

"Right."

"There have been a few developments at this end. Listen to this. You remember I mentioned that guy who approached me just before you met me in Dubrovnik?" Johnson asked.

"Vaguely."

"Well, I'm sitting drinking coffee with him the next day in the Old Town, and he's telling me an interesting tale about an acquaintance of his, Franjo Vuković, who's apparently got away with various war crimes that he believes need investigating. Then he gets a text, disappears to the restrooms, and gets his head blown off."

"*What?*"

"Yes. Right in the café. Bullet through the head. Then I met the dead guy's brother here in Split. He just got back from serving a sixteen-year sentence for war crimes and already wants to avenge his brother."

There was a slight chuckle, which Vic swiftly stifled. "So what are you trying to tell me—the job's interesting enough to accept?"

"Well, listen to this . . . "

Johnson went on to tell Vic in greater detail what had happened in Dubrovnik and then the previous day in Split.

"But this is where things get intriguing," Johnson said. "I then learn that Franjo's father-in-law was high up in Izetbegović's government. The same Izetbegović who was close to Clinton."

"Interesting."

"Yes. I'm thinking it might be a starting point in terms of what you want me to do here—the documents you need," Johnson said. "I'll need to check it out further. At the very least, it might be a line into the government at that time."

"Okay, sounds worth looking at," Vic said. "And I should tell you that there's a large success bonus in it for whoever finds those documents. I'm expecting to get the name of another person who used to work in Izetbegović's office at that time, which would give you two leads."

"Right," Johnson said, "and as for your orders for this job, have you learned any more about who originally issued them to the director and why?"

"No," Vic said. "And I never said anybody issued them to the director, just that they came from his office."

Johnson decided that Vic's no probably meant yes.

"So just how high up the political ladder are we talking? Nosebleed level, or just plain old vertigo?" he asked.

"High. No more questions."

There was a long silence. A group of four, two men and two women, all in their twenties, emerged at the top of the stairs in the bell tower and immediately took out their cameras.

Johnson clearly heard Vic rustling something and then a slight slurp. He could almost picture him as he unfolded his newspaper and sipped his coffee.

"You do realize that the kids are going to kill me, don't

you?" Johnson asked. "We were meant to be going to Castine for a few days' break this coming weekend. I was on a suspended sentence six months ago after I was away for a good while on the last job. This time I'll definitely be behind bars."

"So you're going to do the job?"

Johnson pursed his lips. "Will I regret it?"

"Probably. The Balkans is a bitch's brew."

After a few more minutes of banter with Vic, Johnson ended the call and sighed. Now to tell his children. He descended the staircase to the bottom of the tower, went into a small white stone courtyard, and dialed again.

After he had explained that he'd be gone a little while for work, his fifteen-year-old daughter, Carrie, said, "Dad, come on, you promised you'd fly home Monday evening after your Istanbul meeting. I was really looking forward to that trip to Castine. And Peter was too. He told me."

"I know. I'm really sorry, but I've got to earn some money to keep you two going with iPhones and computers and so on. You're not cheap to run, you kids," Johnson said. He gritted his teeth as he said it.

"But you can get work in the States, can't you, Dad?" Carrie asked.

In theory, he could, Johnson conceded, and the plan had been to head back after his visit to Istanbul. But now he was canceling that trip as well, he explained, hoping his daughter would understand.

"I'm really sorry, Carrie. I hate disappointing both of you. But we'll fix up another weekend soon. Castine won't disappear, you know." He paused. "The thing is, you're old enough to know what my passion is, what I need to do, and that's bringing these war criminals to justice. Quite apart from the money, I just have to do it. You'll be the same in a few years, when you find something you really need to do."

He walked in small circles around the courtyard, his phone clamped to his left ear. There was silence at the other end of the line, broken eventually by the sound of the family's chocolate-brown Labrador, Cocoa, barking in the background. Johnson could hear Peter trying to quiet him.

"Okay, Dad," Carrie said. "As long as you don't start smoking again."

Johnson laughed. "I'm trying, I'm trying. I hardly ever do these days. Definitely not at home. Only when I'm away, the occasional one."

He was keenly aware he needed to set a good example for his kids, especially given that he had been a single dad since his wife, Kathy, had died of cancer in October 2005, at the age of only forty-six. But sometimes temptation still got the better of him, especially when he was feeling stressed.

Johnson said, "I've brought my running shoes here with me. I might go for a run tomorrow morning. Are you going to athletics club this week?"

"Guess so. Will Aunty Amy take me, then, if you're not going to be back? I guess we'll be staying with her?"

Johnson breathed a sigh of relief. He could tell from her tone that Carrie had accepted the situation. They would be fine with Amy, who didn't have any children of her own. She and her husband, Don Wilde, loved looking after his two.

"Yes, I've texted her," Johnson said. "She knows what's going on, so she'll stay with you guys until I'm back. Don't worry."

He chatted with Carrie for a few more minutes, then spoke for a shorter time to Peter, who was always much more monosyllabic than his fifteen-year-old sister. He too was disappointed but was less vocal about it.

After he had finished the call, Johnson sat down on a stone ledge in the shade.

It was difficult, trying to resolve what he called the

trilemma of balancing his responsibilities as a single dad with his passion for his work and the need to earn enough money to keep the family afloat.

He thought back to one of his mother's favorite sayings when he was a kid: "*Come on, Joe boy, don't give up.*"

The words had drifted in the back of his mind for years and kept him going, even more so since his mother had died in 2001. Helena, a Polish-Jewish concentration camp survivor, had been an inspiration at many critical moments over the years, when he needed some fire in his belly to push forward, especially when it came to matters of justice.

He started to write a text message.

Jayne, confirming I'm going to do this Balkans job. Feel free to join anytime you wish. Currently in Split. May head to Mostar soon.

He pressed send, then stood and started walking toward his hotel, which was a few hundred yards away.

Johnson had reached the lobby when a reply from Jayne beeped on his phone.

Will see you Tuesday late afternoon. Really looking forward to teaming up again xox.

PART TWO

CHAPTER TEN

Sunday, July 8, 2012
  Mostar

"If you're an architect, yes, I agree, you'd say this bridge is beautiful. But symbolically, it makes me want to vomit," Boris said. He stood on the central apex of Mostar's Old Bridge and stared down at the waters of the Neretva River that meandered beneath him.

As was their habit whenever he and Marco got together for one of their occasional reunions in their former hometown of Mostar, they lingered on the bridge for a few minutes. Boris had driven there from Split that morning to join his old friend.

He grasped the iron safety railings that ran the length of the white stone structure and glanced down the sloping cobbled approach from the Muslim side of the river to the east. Its medieval center consisted of stone houses and shops, all tiny windows, crooked doors, and misshapen roofs.

Then he glanced at the western, traditionally Bosnian

Croat side, where the banks of the river were lined with an array of cafés and restaurants, their outdoor terraces full of tourists who sipped afternoon lattes and took photographs.

They might have rebuilt the bridge and joined up east and west again physically, but in terms of relations between the two sides, this had changed little. He faced Marco. "It would've been more truthful, more honest, to have left these stones lying in the river."

Boris spat over the parapet into the river far below. "Come on," he said. "Let's have a beer somewhere away from these noisy tourists."

They walked back to Marco's black Lexus 4x4, which he had parked nearby. Boris opened the trunk and put his sweater inside, noticing that Marco had a guitar case in there.

"Are you playing again?" Boris asked, as he eased himself into the passenger seat.

"A little. But the instrument in that particular case plays a different type of tune, if you see what I mean."

"What is it then?" Boris said.

Marco put on his sunglasses before answering. "It's a Zastava M76 guitar. Plus several rounds of ammunition."

Boris nodded. "I see. Very unobtrusive. Where do you keep that? Not at home, I assume?"

"No. At the unit in Split, along with the other guns and ammo."

"Of course."

Boris remembered that Marco owned an industrial unit in a run-down area of Split, near the main railway station, that he used as a storage and transit base for some of the weaponry they moved in and out of the country.

Then Marco said, "What about a beer on Marshal Tito Street?"

Boris raised his eyebrows. "Yes, sure. Near the old school?"

"Yes. I go every time I come here," Marco said. "It kind of helps."

"I've not been there for a long time," Boris said.

"Well, it might help you too," Marco said.

He started the car and nosed it out of the Old Town along Onešćukova Street and then swung northward onto Bulevar, the divided highway running parallel to the river that had formed part of the front line during the war.

"How did it go with Mustafa yesterday, then?" Marco asked.

"To be honest," Boris said, "It was a rubber-stamping exercise. He's a keen buyer. So we need to get the order together for next Friday night at Sinj, and he's got an Antonov An-72 that he'll fly in there to pick it all up."

Marco nodded. "You're doing a good job of keeping him happy." He paused. "Do you ever think about moving back here? It's lower risk than it used to be, and if you weren't so tied up with that TV job, you'd be able to do more on these arms deals, where the real money is. And I need to tell you as a friend, London media life is making you fat."

Boris smiled, despite the insult. Marco was right about that. He'd been as skinny as a broom handle when he lived in Mostar.

"I sometimes wonder about moving back," Boris said. "But my job is a bit like a drug. You get a taste of it, a big interview that makes a headline because the person says something he or she shouldn't, and there's massive follow-up. Anyway, it's what I do; I'm a journalist. I'm not doing it for the money. I've found something I'm good at. I don't know why—maybe it's the foreign thing, the accent, that makes me look and sound a bit naïve—but people say things to me on camera that they don't say to other interviewers. That's the trick."

Marco shook his head. "What would the English call you? A Jekyll and Hyde, I think."

Another smile crossed Boris's face. "Maybe. I like the double life, though. Thing is, when you don't have any family, you feel like you've got to make your mark, do something that people can recognize you for. I don't have kids, no wife. I mean, all right, I have a girlfriend in London, but it's not the same."

After a short distance Marco crossed a bridge to the eastern side, into a built-up area, past hotels, banks, shops, and the famous Karagöz Bey Mosque with its towering minaret.

"These days this town feels like a place I kind of know but don't really know," Boris said. A bit like a metaphor for himself, he thought.

"Do you still think of yourself as a Bosnian Croat?" Marco asked.

Boris half laughed. He wasn't even sure how to answer. In many ways he still felt very much Bosnian Croat, almost passionately so. But geography, language, and the significant physical changes that time had wrought on him over the years sometimes meant he viewed his former self in the third person, as if he were on the outside looking in.

They turned onto Marshal Tito Street, the busy arterial road that ran almost the full length of Mostar, parallel to the Neretva River on the eastern side of the city.

When he came to a long derelict stone building on the corner of Alice Rizikala Street, Marco slowed the car to a crawl and stared at it, as did Boris.

They could see now that the stone facade remained, but the interior had been largely removed, including the roof. It appeared to be undergoing preparations for renovation. Builders' fences encircled the property.

Marco parked opposite the two-story stone building. He

switched off the engine, and they both sat and stared at the structure in silence for several minutes.

They didn't need to speak. Speaking wouldn't change what had happened.

During the war, word had gotten back to Boris and his army colleagues that Croats were being chained to the walls, being beaten with truncheons, kicked into unconsciousness, and that women were being raped. Among the Croats there, Boris's brother, Šimun, and Marco's father, Niko, had both died horrible deaths at the hands of their Muslim captors in the basement of the building they were looking at now. The image of Šimun's mutilated body, dumped outside the family's front door by somebody, was seared forever into the back of Boris's mind.

He got out the car, as did Marco, and the two men set off on foot to their usual bar around the corner.

A group of schoolchildren walked past in single file, laughing and joking with each other, their teacher bringing up the rear. Up on the facade, a carved stone date stamp, 1909, marked the year the old Fourth Primary School building opened.

"That day I saw Šimun's body was when I knew my marriage was over—especially when I heard who gave the orders for it," Boris said. "I hated them all after that."

Some of the guards had been caught and sentenced, but not many. And those that were jailed only got three, four, or five years. What a joke that had been.

"I'm told they're going to rebuild this place as the new municipal court building, starting next year," Marco said. "I hope a better version of justice is handed out when it starts its new life."

Marco's phone beeped. He took it out of his pocket and stopped walking as he checked the incoming message.

"You coming?" Boris asked.

"Wait, I just got a message from a friend of mine in Split. A guy called Bruno Pavić—you won't know him. Says that he was out on his motorbike, dropped into the Hemingway bar in town for a drink, and saw someone we both know in there. Guess who?"

"No idea."

"Filip Simic."

"*What?* He's in prison," Boris said.

"I guess he's out. Shit, those brothers—you get rid of one and another one pops up. It's like a Hollywood alien movie."

Marco typed a message and pressed send. "I've asked him to keep an eye on Filip and stick close to him. He's good at tailing and following. Had plenty of practice."

Boris looked over the river toward the mountains. "He needs to make sure he does. Those two brothers are the only ones who really know enough to cause problems."

He paused, then went on, "I know why you did what you did to Petar. But I'm just worried that it might have stirred some shit up unnecessarily. You might now need to double up —with the other brother."

Marco grimaced. "You might be right."

CHAPTER ELEVEN

Tuesday, July 10, 2012
  Split

Johnson lit his second cigarette of the afternoon and put his feet up on the balcony rail outside his hotel room, which looked out toward Split's harbor.

He picked up his phone and checked his emails. There was a new encrypted note from Vic. The two of them had each other's public and private keys for all the various email addresses they used, so they could encrypt and read each other's secure messages.

Doc, the guy you need to speak to is Haris Hasanović, who I under-stand kept the minutes of many informal meetings involving US offi-cials in Sarajevo within Izetbegović's office. He's now presumably retired. Last known location Dubrovnik, but we don't know where exactly. Your job to find out. It's a starting point. Also, COS in Croatia is Alan Edwards. He's based in Zagreb but sometimes goes to

Split. I'll send you a text message with his details when I get them. He will help you.
Vic

Johnson noted that Vic had sent the email from his CIA address and shook his head. Vic should know to be more careful.

He decided that Hasanović and whatever secrets he might own could wait a little while. His first job was to get to Mostar and to find Aisha's family, and from there maybe Franjo, with luck. If Aisha's father had been an insider in the Izetbegović government, that seemed like the most promising line of inquiry.

And as for approaching Edwards for assistance, well, he just didn't have time to waste working out how far to trust the guy. In fact, he was surprised Vic had suggested it. After all, it was Vic who had once given him a framed quote from one of the CIA's best-known Cold War counterintelligence chiefs, James Jesus Angleton, that he felt summed up the world of espionage. It read, "Deception is a state of mind and the mind of the state." Johnson had it hanging in his home office.

He looked at his watch. Jayne's flight from London was due into Split in two hours. In the meantime, Johnson had a meeting with Filip in a café in the Old Town area.

Johnson finished his cigarette, picked up his wallet and phone, and headed out the door.

He took a left out of the Hotel Luxe toward the harbor, then cut through the impossibly narrow stone streets of the Diocletian's Palace, the vertiginous walls of the buildings on each side almost blocking out the light. Mindful of the situation, he then spent half an hour on a surveillance detection route, involving several sharp turns down narrow alleys and cuts through boutiques and cafés.

Finally, sure he wasn't being followed, he slipped into Figa, a small coffee and food bar tucked away on the corner of two alleyways within the Old Town. Soft cushions were piled on outdoor seats where a few tourists sat and wrote postcards or clicked through photographs on their cameras.

Once in the dimly lit interior, adhering to the instructions in a text message received from Filip, he sat at a wooden table at the back of the restaurant, ordered an orange juice and waited. Five minutes later, Filip appeared in the doorway. Johnson could only hope that he had also taken suitable surveillance detection measures, but he doubted it.

Filip ordered an espresso and sat down.

"Think we should be okay in here," Filip said. "I didn't want to sit outside, given what happened to Petar. You never know."

"You're right to be worried," Johnson said. "You were safer in jail. Are you getting adjusted to civilian life again?"

"Slowly. It's a little weird, being able to make my own decisions about where I go, what I do again. Just about got the hang of my phone, though." He attempted a smile. "And are you getting used to the culture around here? It's still a bit combustible at times."

"Combustible's one word for it," Johnson said. "This whole region feels a bit like a ticking time bomb waiting to go off."

Filip nodded. "Anyway, enough of that shit. You want a cigarette?"

Johnson nodded. "Yes, might help."

Filip took out a pack of cigarettes and a lighter, then offered one to Johnson and took one himself. He clicked his lighter and lit first his own cigarette, then Johnson's. Both men took deep drags.

"I've got one or two small bits of information that might help you," Filip said. "Are you going to Mostar?"

"Yes, I was thinking of going tomorrow or the day after," Johnson said. "I've got a colleague coming in from London who's meeting me here tonight. We'll be working together."

"Okay," Filip said. "I, or we, need to find Franjo, if he's still alive. I think your starting point should be Aisha's family—what's left of it. I've no idea where she is, but I remembered there was a family in Mostar who her family was very close to—Terzić, that was their name. They all lived on Drage Palavstre Street, just off Marshal Tito Street, which is the main road in eastern Mostar. I knew them a bit too. Speak to the old man Terzić. I think his first name is Omar. He was friendly with Aisha's father."

"Good. That sounds like a starting point," Johnson said. Maybe Filip would be useful to him.

"No problem. Another thing. Have you got a gun?"

Johnson was taken aback by the sudden question. "I came here by plane, not in an Arab dhow or something. So no."

Filip ignored the attempted joke. "But you know how to handle one?"

Johnson furrowed his brow. "You could say that."

Filip blew a long stream of smoke in the direction of the bar and then knocked the ash from his cigarette into the ashtray. He glanced out the window. "I'll see what I can get. Those two guys Franjo and Marco . . . you'll need to be careful. The Balkans is a black place."

* * *

Tuesday, July 10, 2012
   Split Airport

Jayne gave Johnson a lengthy hug and a quick hello kiss on the lips, then swung her suitcase into the trunk of the gray

Opel Astra sedan. She stood back and studied the car, which Johnson had rented from an independent outlet not far from his hotel an hour earlier.

"I'm glad to see you've gone for the anonymous option. What's Go-Cro?" she asked, glancing at the large sticker in the car's rear window.

Trust her to home in on the small details, Johnson thought. "Small local rental company," he replied. He had learned the hard way that BMWs and Audis were not the best choice, and he tried to avoid big international rental firms so that it was harder for anyone trying to track him down.

While she was looking the car over, he eyed her up and down. Shortish dark hair, tight khaki-green cotton trousers that clung around her slim waist, and a low-cut cream T-shirt.

She was in good shape, he thought, maybe even a little slimmer than seven months earlier when he'd last seen her. She looked gym-toned and wiry.

Jayne saw him staring and smiled. "I've been cycling quite a lot. I just need to get rid of the British milk-bottle look," she said. "This sunshine should help. Not too bad given I'll be fifty-one tomorrow, though, hey?"

He had somehow forgotten her birthday was imminent. There were too many distractions.

She opened the car door and gave Johnson a once-over. "You're looking good yourself. But have you packed in the smoking yet?" she asked.

"I've as good as given up. I smoke a bit when I'm away working, but never at home," Johnson said.

Johnson enjoyed watching her as she did a 360-degree check around the parking lot before climbing into the passenger seat. He eased himself in behind the steering wheel.

"So, what's the plan?" Jayne asked.

He started the engine and carefully edged the Astra out of the airport and back toward the city center.

"I thought we'd stay here tonight since it's now getting into evening, then head to Mostar first thing in the morning," Johnson said. "I've a list of people we need to see there."

"Good. Although in my experience of the Balkans, plans are a complete waste of time. I learned to expect the unexpected, and that worked best for me." She smiled.

On the way Johnson briefed Jayne on his discussion with Filip and his contacts in Mostar and gave her the background on Marco and Franjo.

"So this Filip Simic, what's his story?" Jayne asked.

"He's just finished sixteen years in prison for all the shit he carried out during the war, while these other guys, who appear to have done even worse things, have been free as birds. Then there's the fact that it seems Marco murdered Filip's little brother. Filip now wants revenge—although I think I've convinced him that justice is the best form of that. He also said he wants to set himself up as a freelance journalist, which is apparently what he did before the war."

"If he's done sixteen years in prison for war crimes, are you sure you're happy working with him?" Jayne asked.

Johnson shrugged. "I'm not happy about it, no. But he's the one with the information we need. I'm trying to be pragmatic about it. My view is that he's harmless now and might be of use in other ways. For example, he's getting me the gun I need. The risk is going to come from Franjo and Marco."

"Can we trust Filip, though?"

"Don't know. Probably not. We need to remember, though, that his brother's been murdered. We have to do anything we can to help."

He pulled into the hotel's parking lot around the corner from the main entrance, and they made their way into the lobby.

Sitting in a chair there was Filip, a sturdy black plastic bag with something bulky inside on his lap. "Delivery for you," Filip said. He handed the bag to Johnson.

"This is presumably what I think it is?" Johnson asked.

"Correct."

Johnson discreetly opened the bag and looked inside. An old towel, which Johnson unfolded a little, covered a slightly battle-scarred Beretta. He closed the bag again.

"Thanks," Johnson said. "That'll do the job. This is my friend and colleague Jayne. She's just arrived from London and is going to help me."

Filip shook hands with Jayne. He looked surprised when she greeted him in Serbo-Croat, which Johnson knew she had picked up while working in the Balkans, to add to her fluent French, Spanish, Russian, and German, if he remembered correctly. "Pleased to meet you," Filip said, regarding her with some respect. "I hope we can all work well together."

After a brief pause, Johnson broke in. "We're off to Mostar in the morning."

"Of course," Filip said, glancing again at Jayne. "Yes, I was just thinking, I really should come along too. You will probably need an interpreter and some local knowledge up there."

Jayne shook her head. "I really don't think that's necessary. I mean, I can speak the language reasonably fluently."

"No, I've decided. I feel a duty toward my brother and to help you. I will come, especially if you're taking my gun," Filip said. "What time are you leaving in the morning?"

"I don't know, probably early. But really you don't need to—"

Filip cut Johnson short. "That's fine, I'll be here at seven, and then I'll just wait and have a coffee if you're going to be later. In fact, I was going to suggest that I could drive you there in my car. I've just bought a Subaru Impreza. It's a useful car if you're in a tight spot. It's quick."

Johnson shook his head. "I doubt it. Those Imprezas are loud, obvious cars. What color is it?"

"Blue."

"Look Filip, thanks for the offer, but no. I'm going to stick with the anonymous Astra I've rented. Nobody will notice that. Okay?"

"Okay, fair enough. I'll see you in the morning, then."

Filip turned and walked out of the hotel.

Johnson grimaced at Jayne.

"I'd really rather not take him," Jayne said.

"He might have his uses," Johnson said. "He knows the region. We'll just have to manage him carefully."

He tucked Filip's plastic bag under his left arm, picked up Jayne's suitcase with his right hand, and made his way to the check-in desk.

CHAPTER TWELVE

Wednesday, July 11, 2012
Mostar

Despite the sharp mountainous road leading from the Bosnian border toward Mostar, a series of motorcyclists overtook Johnson's car and raced ahead around hairpin corners.

But Johnson was certain that he saw one rider, clad in black leather, hanging a few hundred yards behind, even when there were opportunities to pass.

Finally, around two and three-quarter hours after leaving Split, they began the descent from Dobrič into the Neretva River valley and Mostar.

As they did so, the motorcyclist whom Johnson had noticed accelerated noisily and passed him on a straight section of road.

Johnson parked outside the hotel he had booked, Muslibegovic House, and looked up to the hills surrounding Mostar on both sides. He tried to imagine mortar shells and sniper fire raining in on the Muslim side of town from Hum

Hill, destroying lives, families, homes and businesses day after day, month after month.

Muslibegovic House was unmistakably Turkish in origin, all curved arches, ornate wooden window frames, deep pile rugs, and carved ceilings.

"We'll drop the bags, then we should walk down to the Old Bridge. We can get lunch there. I want to get a feel for this place," Johnson said after they collected room keys. He and Jayne made their way to the first floor, where their rooms adjoined each other, while Filip went to his second-floor room.

When he was out of sight, Johnson said, "I wasn't going to say anything in the car, but I'm certain one of those motorcyclists was tailing us. All of them came past us apart from that one. Then he passed us just as we came into Mostar. An anonymous-looking guy, black leather gear, black bike, black helmet. No markings on the bike, which was unusual."

"I saw him," Jayne said. "Yamaha two-seater touring bike with Croatian plates. After he overtook us, he disappeared quickly. Might be nothing, but . . ."

"He wasn't a tourist, that's for sure," Johnson said.

After Johnson completed a security check outside the hotel, involving a pretend phone call as cover while surveying the road, the three of them headed down the sloping street toward the river and the bazaar. The pedestrianized Kujundžiluk Street that ran up to the Old Bridge was lined with restored stone shops and houses, plus craft and tourist stalls.

As they approached the bridge, Jayne carried out another surveillance check, which again proved negative. A gale now blew straight down the valley, and they had to work hard against the wind as they walked onto the bridge.

"What was this place like during the war?" Johnson asked Filip.

"Hell. That's all I can say. We, the Croats, were behind the other side of the front line a little distance across there," Filip said. He pointed to beyond the far riverbank on the west side. "We just fired rockets and bullets at each other for two years. Crazy."

They moved into the center of the bridge and stood side by side, hands on the metal railings above the parapet, looking south.

"So the day the Croats destroyed this bridge, back in what, November '93, where was the tank that did the damage?" Johnson asked.

Filip pointed south, straight down the river. "You can just about see that hump, on the west side, about a kilometer and a half down there. There's a few houses on the top of it? That's Stotina Hill. The tank was there, hidden in an old house, firing through a window."

"So what did you think about that?" Johnson asked.

Filip shrugged. "I'm Croat. This bridge is symbolically Muslim and Ottoman. But it wasn't necessary to destroy it. This bridge is such a part of this city's history and heritage. The HVO leaders made a strategic argument that it would stop the guys on the east side getting to the front line, but that was bullshit."

Just as he finished his sentence, there was a faint crack and a high-pitched whining sound next to them, which Johnson heard above the wind.

After that, things seemed to unfold in slow motion.

To Johnson's right, Filip jerked backward and sideways, grabbing his right forearm and lifting it up. A large gash just below his elbow was dripping blood.

At the same time, Johnson felt dust and debris peppering his exposed skin, emanating from a large chip in the stonework of the parapet in front of them, the clean white of the damaged area contrasting with the dirtier surroundings.

He knew instantly what had happened.

"Get down," Johnson snapped, his voice rising sharply. He pushed Filip down to the cobbled surface of the bridge and simultaneously dropped to the floor. "It's a gunman, sonofabitch."

Jayne also dropped to the ground and all three flattened themselves, Filip now groaning in pain.

As they did so, another high-pitched whine sounded as another bullet ricocheted off the bridge parapet right above Johnson's head. More fragments of stone landed on top of him.

An overweight middle-aged woman, standing nearby with her husband, saw them, then spotted Filip's bleeding arm and screamed twice loudly.

She ran toward the western side of the bridge, her body waddling as she struggled to make headway. Her husband hesitated for a fraction of a second, then ran after her.

Johnson pulled himself tight up behind the three-foot-high parapet. "Crawl that way," Johnson said, indicating to his left, back toward the eastern side of the bridge.

Jayne hugged the bottom of the parapet, leading the way, and the bleeding Filip followed her. They crawled on knees and elbows back in the direction they had walked just minutes earlier.

Johnson, bringing up the rear, could hear Filip groaning and whining every time his wounded arm came in contact with the hard surface, which had raised stone ridges running across it every couple of feet to prevent pedestrians from slipping.

The trio crawled along the sloping bridge for about fifteen yards before they came to a tall, battered stone house on their right, which gave them some cover from the shots.

A small group of Japanese tourists, who had been about to cross the bridge, shouted and screamed in confusion. Other pedestrians, possibly locals, inched backward toward the shops. Two younger women sobbed, visibly terrified by the chaos.

"We need to get out of here, quick," Johnson said.

Jayne nodded. She leaned over and examined Filip's arm. "How is it?" she asked.

Filip shook his head and clutched his elbow. "Not good. It's a deep cut. It's got to be that bastard Marco—again," he said.

"We need to get him to a hospital," Jayne said to Johnson. "He'll need stitches. I think it was a piece of stone that hit him, not the bullet."

Johnson stood, his back flat against the wall of the house, and pointed with his thumb toward the west side of the river, just south of the bridge, where there was a piece of derelict land with a dilapidated old stone building covered in ivy and surrounded by trees. "The shots came from that direction," he said. "So let's keep going the opposite way."

He led them back the way they had come, walking close to the wall of the stone houses, until they reached the crowd of shoppers among the stalls, most of whom had not realized what had occurred just a few yards away.

He went to a stall that sold head scarves, pointed to a large yellow cotton one, and gave the old woman sitting behind the cash desk a ten euro note. She handed it to Filip, a worried expression on her face.

Johnson wound it tightly around Filip's forearm, still oozing blood. "Better than nothing, until we can get to the hospital," Johnson said.

Jayne stared over the bridge. As she did so, carried on the wind from the other side of the river came the faint but unmistakable sound of a large motorcycle engine starting up and revving loudly.

CHAPTER THIRTEEN

Wednesday, July 11, 2012
Manhattan

"I just got the lighting plot from Tim. We've a lot of moving lights and other specials to rig because he wants plenty of color for this show," Aisha said.

She turned the diagram on her laptop screen toward the others. "I just want to get the equipment list finalized so we can get the gear out of the storeroom and start rigging the extra lamps and other stuff."

She glanced around the dimmer room next to the studio, buried deep in the bowels of the CBA television studio complex, set back just off 34th Street, near Penn Station.

The four TV lighting electricians sitting around the table groaned, virtually in unison. "You're joking? We've got all that to rig?" one of them said. "We're not going to have much time to put all that in."

"Yeah, it's got to be done. At least we'll be doing our part, but it's a bit like trying to polish a chunk of cow shit," Aisha said. "I mean, from what I've seen, this *Alumni Brain Quiz* show looks a bit of a flop. Who wants to see a quiz between university alumni teams? Unless they get someone famous on, a few celebs, it's a nonstarter."

Everyone laughed. "You nailed it there, Aisha," said Olly West, who had joined CBA on the same day as she had, nine years earlier.

"What I'd like to do is use the kit we have to the maximum for this show," Aisha said. "I want to impress Tim. If we try and utilize some of the moving lights, we might be able to create a bit of atmosphere. That's what this thing is lacking, based on the pilots I've seen so far. I can program some fancy cues to happen every time a contestant gets a question wrong, for instance. That would really make the person the center of everybody's attention, you know what I mean?"

Tim Burroughs, the lighting director, had criticized Aisha during the last show on which they had worked together, and she was keen to rectify that this time.

"Okay, guys, I think we've got it covered for now. Let's get a move on. If there's any kit missing, let me know," said Steve Abrahams, the charge hand for the *Alumni Brain Quiz* show. "Otherwise, go get some lunch."

The group headed for the door. Aisha wandered into the newsroom farther down the corridor, where the monitors all showed the extended lunchtime CBA news and current affairs program.

She stood and watched for a while.

For the third time in the previous ten days, the lead item on the news was Patrick Spencer's comments on immigration, race, and religion, a theme he had returned to in all of his speeches. The speaker of the House's focus remained on Muslim immigrants in particular.

"Not again," Aisha said to the news producer, Alice

Munro, who stood by the door, also watching the segment. "This guy is cranking up the volume. He needs to be taken down a few notches."

"Yes, I know," Alice said. "It's an embarrassment. There's talk that he might be coming in here to do an interview at some point soon, with a British TV interviewer. I'll be making sure I'm off duty that day."

"Me too," said Aisha. "I can't stand the guy. Is he really coming here?"

"Apparently so."

Aisha listened as the TV anchor continued his report.

"Spencer's latest comments regarding the immigration of people from countries where Islam is the dominant religion and the steps he would like taken to stop it are already provoking a fierce reaction right across America," the presenter said. "Two Muslim Americans were killed in separate attacks, one by youths wielding hammers, the other by a man with a handgun. Four others were seriously injured after a man opened fire with a shotgun outside a mosque in the suburb of Bevo Mill in St. Louis, Missouri, which has a large population of Bosnian immigrants, many of whom are Muslims.

"Spencer's speeches, together with these incidents, have resulted in protest marches in St. Louis. Protesters have issued a statement that argues that Patrick Spencer is deliberately trying to stoke tension to provoke unrest and to bring about a self-fulfilling prophecy of violence and alienation that will force the federal government into action."

As the report continued, Aisha turned toward Alice. "I lived in St. Louis for several years after I moved to the States from Bosnia. That was where I did my broadcast engineering training. There was *never* any trouble down there."

She walked away shaking her head, then a thought struck her. She took her phone out of her pocket and called an old friend, Nikola, in St. Louis, with whom she had worked at the Fox KTVI TV station a decade and a half earlier.

It was answered after a couple of rings. "Nikola? Hi, it's Aisha. I just thought I'd give you a call. I was worried after hearing about all the trouble down there."

"Aisha, I can't tell you how *awful* things are here right now. Have you heard about Ammar and Karim?"

It was the tone of Nikola's voice that did it.

A shock wave went through Aisha, as if she had been hit hard in the stomach. She leaned against the wall in the corridor where she was standing. After a few deep breaths, she managed to say, "No, what is it?"

There was a pause, then Nikola told her. "They were at that mosque. Ammar was shot and badly wounded, hit in the bowel. He needs emergency surgery tonight. And Karim was also hit. He's got a punctured lung and is also in the hospital in intensive care. It's so terrible, and I can't . . ."

Aisha heard her burst into tears and did likewise; the two of them wept, almost a thousand miles apart, unable to help each other.

Both Ammar and Karim had been close friends. The four of them had hung out, chatted, cooked food, and attended mosque together. They had all spent a long time living in poverty after arriving from Bosnia in the 1990s, and it had bonded them.

"Bastards. I don't believe it," Aisha said. "I just had a thought that came out of nowhere. I kind of knew there was something happening. I had to give you a call. They never did anything to anybody, those guys. Tell them I'm praying for them. They *have* to pull through."

"Something's got to be done about all this stuff going on. Spencer is stirring up shit with his speeches on TV. It's really bad," Nikola said.

"I know," Aisha said. "Someone needs to act, you're right."

She thumped the wall against which she was leaning. "I haven't felt so angry since . . ." Her voice trailed away.

Since the war.

Five minutes later, after she had finished her call, Aisha texted her friend Adela.

Hey, about those Tuesday meetings at your mosque. I'd like to come after all. Can you send the specifics?

CHAPTER FOURTEEN

Wednesday, July 11, 2012
  Mostar

Boris and Marco walked swiftly through the sliding doors of the Hotel Mepas, a modernistic building that included shopping and cinema complexes.

"What an almighty screwup that was. How the hell did you miss?" Boris said without looking at his friend as they strode across the sand-colored marble floor.

A porter nodded at them. "Can I carry that for you, sir?" he asked politely, pointing at the battered guitar case Marco was carrying, which was plastered with music and travel stickers. "You play in a band, sir?"

"No, you can't. And yes, I'm in a band," Marco said, glancing at him.

"Which one is that, sir?"

"Guns N' Roses, an American band," Marco said without looking back as he continued toward the elevators.

Boris didn't laugh. As the elevator doors closed behind

them, he pressed the button for the second floor, leaned against the wall, and folded his arms.

Marco remained silent and stared at the floor until the elevator stopped and the door opened.

"An odd one. Must have been the wind," he said as the two of them exited the elevator. "And he ducked below the parapet just as I fired the second shot. The other guy pushed him down."

"You're losing your touch, my friend," Boris said.

As soon as they got into the twin room they were sharing, Boris walked straight to the minibar, poured himself a large whiskey and ice, and went out onto the balcony. He lit a cigarette.

"I've spoken to Bruno," Marco said. "He's got a friend who lives in Mostar, works as a driver or something. He knows everyone, at least on the eastern side of town. He's going to put some feelers out to see if he can discover where Filip and the American are staying and keep track of them."

"How is it Bruno doesn't know that? Why didn't he follow them to their hotel?" Boris asked.

Marco shrugged. "He said he had a feeling they realized they were being followed, so he didn't want to push his luck. By the way, Bruno's bike shifts. Nearly threw us both off when I accelerated out of the parking lot. I forgot to ask him which room he's in. Do you know?"

"I've no idea which room he's in," Boris said. "I'm more interested in those three on the bridge. They're not here to take photos of the architecture, are they? What the hell are they doing? Filip needs to be taken out. But I'm not sure what to do about that American investigator. And who's that woman with them now?"

Marco raised his hands to indicate he had no idea.

Boris took another deep drag from his cigarette, then eventually exhaled. He tapped the table with his fingers. "I'm just thinking, if that guy's American and an ex-Nazi hunter, odds are that our friend over in Washington will be able to find out something about him and what he's up to."

"Definitely worth a try."

Boris picked up his phone and dialed a number for a burner phone belonging to his contact in Washington, DC. After a few rings, it was answered.

"SILVER, it's RUNNER. I'm in Mostar with SUNMAN. I just need to speak to you urgently about something," Boris said.

"Make it quick then. Go on," said SILVER, otherwise known as Robert Watson.

"We've got an issue here. You remember I told you only the Simic brothers really know the truth?"

"Yep."

"We found out that one of them was talking with an American war crimes investigator. SUNMAN has taken care of that brother, permanently. Now the other brother's just come out of prison, and we've just seen him also talking to the same investigator, so we're going to take care of that brother, too. They're both here in Mostar. But it's the American we have questions about."

"An American?"

"Yes, the investigator's American. Can you find out about him?"

"A name might help."

"The guy's called Johnson, Joe Johnson," Boris said.

There was dead silence for a few seconds. *"Joe Johnson? Are you damn sure?"* Watson said.

"Yes, I'm damn sure," Boris said. "What about him?"

"I know that guy. I fired him from the CIA, way back. I also had a tangle with him at the end of last year. What the hell's he doing in Mostar?"

"That's what I want to know," Boris said. He caught

Marco's eye and shook his head. "He was here for a war crimes conference in Dubrovnik, and the Simic brother who SUNMAN shot approached him. I presume it has something to do with that."

"And you think—"

"If he's a war crimes investigator and the brothers know about me, then you can reach a logical conclusion. So what do you know about Johnson?" Boris said.

"Well, he's a freelancer," Watson said. "I'd say someone's called him in—maybe these brothers, as you suggest—and asked him to poke his finger into the pie to check it out. It's probably just a fishing trip. This sounds damn typical of him."

"Okay. In that case, do you have any suggestions for how we find out what he's trying to do?"

Watson hesitated. "There is one route you could go down. He's got a real weakness. I know that. It's one reason why I fired the bastard."

"What's that then?"

"Women."

Boris listened while Watson explained what he had in mind.

As soon as Boris had finished the call, Marco stepped onto the balcony. "Here, have a look at this. I meant to show you before," Marco said.

He took a front-page clipping from *Slobodna Dalmacija*, one of the biggest Croatian daily newspapers, from his pocket and handed it to Boris. A large front-page headline read, "Four Hikers Die in Land-mine Blast."

The story described how the hikers, wandering through the Moseć area, a rural part of Croatia sixty kilometers north of Split, appeared to have either ignored or not seen the warning signs. They had been blown up when one of the group stepped on a land mine.

The report was accompanied by two photographs: in one,

a blood-spattered corpse was being carried away on a
stretcher by ambulance crews; in the other another a
policeman was standing next to a sign warning of the danger
from mines. The article continued:

*The four hikers were heading along a narrow footpath in the hills
east of the village of Moseć when one of the party triggered the land
mine. A farmer heard the blast from two kilometers away and realized what had happened. He drove to the scene in his tractor and
discovered the remains of the four bodies.*

*Police said they have identified the bodies from documents found in
the hikers' clothing.*

*The death toll from land mines in Croatia now stands at more than
500. The Croatian government estimates that about 46,000 land
mines are still buried in the country, all emplaced during the war of
independence from 1991 onward.*

*The ongoing issue of deaths from mines so long after the war finished
is causing international outrage.* Slobodna Dalmacija *understands
that the BBC World Service is planning a one-hour radio documentary about the issue, to be broadcast next month.*

Boris finished reading the story. *The BBC World Service*. It
momentarily took him back to when he worked as a copy
editor and a producer for the iconic broadcasting unit in
London during the 1990s, mainly on the now-closed Croatian service. It was where he had learned most of his skills
and—as his English approached native fluency, helped by
intensive voice training—had started to make a name for
himself. From the World Service, he had moved to the
BBC's Brussels bureau, where he handled a series of increasingly complex, high-profile European stories and interviews
across radio and TV. He did enough to be headhunted by
CNN's Brussels bureau and gradually evolved into a hard-
punching political interviewer, doing a stint with CNBC

before David Rowlands had headhunted him for his current job at SRTV.

"Shit," Boris said, glancing again at the newspaper and turning to face Marco. "Did you read this bit about the BBC? We don't want them crawling all over it. That's the fourth mine that's gone off around the barn. Do we know if it was one of ours that was triggered or one from the war?"

"I don't know," Marco said. "I suspect it was one of ours. The municipal people apparently were saying last year that they'd cleared all the wartime ones from that footpath."

Boris pursed his lips. "Yes, but they don't know we're putting them down. They just think they've missed a few from the war. The problem is, if it keeps happening, it's going to leave gaping holes in our barn defenses. That's the last thing we want, especially if Filip and Johnson are sniffing around. How far away from the barn was this one?"

Marco unfolded a detailed map and pointed to a spot. "There's the barn, and this is where the mine went off, just here, about two hundred meters away."

"Too near. Okay, I want to beef up the number of mines around it. I don't want anyone getting near it. Can you order another batch and put them in place? We'll reinforce the ring we have with another smaller ring inside it, and we'll also make sure the footpath where these hikers got blown up gets a few more, okay? We want to make sure no one gets within range of it."

"Yeah, makes sense. I'll get onto it." Marco said. "The only thing is, this is a hikers' footpath—"

"So?"

"Well—"

"Don't start going soft, Marco. Just get on with it, okay?" Boris snapped.

"Sure, I'll sort it."

CHAPTER FIFTEEN

Wednesday, July 11, 2012
 Mostar

The wooden black front door squeaked open a few inches, and an old man peered out, his ragged beard and white hair tinged yellow with nicotine, his lids drooping so far that Johnson could barely see his eyes.

Johnson was intrigued. So this was Omar Terzić.

He looked up. The house appeared almost as unkempt as its owner, with dark red paint peeling away from the window frames and white rotting shutters.

The old man eyed Johnson and Filip, who wore a large white bandage over his elbow and upper forearm after the hospital patched him up a couple of hours earlier.

Despite a phone call from Filip, Omar took a few moments to realize who was standing on his doorstep. He raised his hands and apologized, then pulled the door fully open and launched into a rapid exchange with Filip in Bosnian, gesticulating occasionally at Johnson, who understood enough to know that his presence was being explained.

Omar switched to English, which he spoke surprisingly well, albeit with a strong accent, and shook hands with Filip and Johnson. His sunken black eyes flicked between the two men.

Behind Omar appeared a thick-set younger man with short cropped dark hair and muscled forearms. He leaned against the doorframe, folded his arms, and watched.

Johnson immediately smelled the younger man's pungent aftershave and momentarily cringed.

Omar explained that he had lived in the three-story house on Drage Palavstre Street since 1961. He indicated to a house three doors farther up the street, where he said Aisha and her family had lived until the events of 1993.

Johnson glanced in the direction he was pointing. Aisha's former home, also three stories, was far better maintained than Omar's. It was neatly painted in a pale terra-cotta, with a white door and an ornate first-floor balcony on which a small table and two chairs were arranged to look down over the street.

Johnson faced Omar. He felt relieved that Jayne had decided to stay at the Muslibegovic. Three visitors would have been too many for this old man.

Omar led the way down a dark passageway with a black-and-white checkered tile floor, like a giant chessboard, and through to the rear of the house into a large kitchen.

The cupboard units were chipped and grimy and missing a couple of the opaque glass panes. The wooden countertop was laced with knife cuts, stains, and cracks. Only the microwave and the fridge, a large American-style affair, looked remotely modern.

Omar indicated that Johnson and Filip should take a seat at the battered square oak table, then began to make coffee.

The younger man with the dark hair sat on another chair in the corner, near the door, the smell of his aftershave now all-pervading. Johnson instantly disliked him.

"This is my helper, Tomislav. He's a Croat," Omar said. "He drives, cooks, cleans, gardens, that sort of thing."

Omar poured coffee into three large cups and pushed one across the table to Johnson, one to Filip. Meanwhile, Omar switched back to Bosnian and held a rapid-fire conversation with Filip. Although Johnson picked up most of the conversation, he asked Filip to translate, to be certain.

"I've told him we want to talk about the war, specifically how we're trying to track down Franjo Vuković, and that we want to know what happened to Aisha and her father, Erol," Filip said. "He hasn't got a clue about Franjo. Says he just vanished off the face of the earth. He thinks Aisha went to the States, like I told you, to St. Louis, along with a lot of other Bosnians. But that was many years ago, and other than that, he doesn't know."

Johnson sipped his coffee and asked Omar, in Bosnian, if he knew what work Erol had done for Izetbegović.

The old man visibly jumped at the question.

Old habits die hard, Johnson thought.

The old Communist era and its secret police regime had bred a culture of secrecy and evasiveness that was doubtless difficult to cast off. But eventually, Omar relaxed a little and spoke at some length, frequently gesticulating with his wrinkled hands.

"Erol was someone who rarely talked about his job, unless he'd had a few glasses of wine," Omar said. "He had a senior job as a kind of fixer, a problem solver, in Izetbegović's office in Sarajevo. He used to travel there early on Monday mornings and come back on Friday night, on the late train. Some weekends Erol didn't come back at all, especially once the war started. Even when he did, he used to bring work with him and spend the whole time holed up in his study, going through piles of papers, files, and documents, and drawing up plans. The place looked like some kind of vault. He always looked tired."

Now Johnson felt even more intrigued. It sounded as though Erol Delić was more than just a fixer for his boss.

"How close was he to the wartime decision-making processes? Was he part of that? Did he discuss things, hear things, meet key people?" Johnson asked.

"Erol was right in the middle of it, though he was very low-profile publicly. But he was definitely a right-hand man to Izetbegović internally," Omar said. "He once mentioned to me that he met all kinds of obscure and shady people who came into the president's office: men from the Middle East, Afghanistan, Saudi Arabia, all coming to discuss how they might assist Izetbegović in his war effort, in his agenda to turn Bosnia and Herzegovina into a state that was more based on Islam."

"Who were these shady people?" Johnson asked.

"I don't know names."

Johnson leaned forward and cupped his chin in the palms of his hands, elbows propped on the table. "Well, there must be a way of tracking Aisha down," he said to Filip. "What about her old friends? I would guess she must keep in touch with at least some of them. You mentioned that girl Ana, whom you had a fling with once. What about her family?"

Omar sat back and said something in Bosnian about Ana to Filip, which Johnson didn't quite understand. Omar lifted his forefinger in the air and wagged it several times in Filip's direction. Finally, the old man smiled for the first time.

"He says I behaved quite dishonorably toward that girl, and he's just told me off for it," Filip said to Johnson. "Maybe a bit late. More than twenty years too late. Anyway, he said she went to the UK to study architecture at university years ago, and her relatives were either killed or left town. But listen to this—he's seen her in town periodically over recent months, and he saw her walking down in Kujundžiluk, the market street down near the Old Bridge, only two days ago. He couldn't catch up with her to speak to her, but he says he is 90 percent certain it was her."

"Let's find her, if she's here," Johnson said, his voice rising slightly. "How can we do it? Can you call around the hotels? Will she be with friends?"

Filip shrugged. "We can try. Not sure what kind of welcome I'd get from her after so long. Not a good one, I'd imagine, given the way we broke up."

He glanced at Johnson. "If we do find out where Ana is, I can speak to the hotel reception people and leave a message, but it might be better if you actually go and do the talking. As much as I'd like to see her again, I'll stay out of it."

* * *

Wednesday, July 11, 2012
  Mostar

Immediately after Johnson and Filip had left the house on Drage Palavstre Street, Tomislav Novak went to the back garden and sat on a bench at the far end, next to a wooden shed, where he lit a cigarette.

After a few moments, he took out his phone and made a call.

"Hi, Bruno, it's Tomi here. About your little request. You won't believe this, but I didn't need to make much effort to find Filip and the American guy Johnson . . . actually no effort at all." He laughed.

"Why's that?" his friend Bruno asked.

"Because they came to old Omar's house an hour ago. Simic knows him from a long time back, when he lived in Mostar."

Bruno was somewhat taken aback. "What were they trying to find out from Omar?"

"Information about where Franjo is. They obviously don't have any idea. They were also asking where Aisha was, and again they know nothing."

Tomislav took a deep drag of his cigarette and listened to his friend Bruno, whom he could hear consulting with two other men in the background.

Then Bruno came back on the line and rattled off a series of instructions.

"Yes, sure, my friend," Tomislav said. "They are all staying at the Muslibegovic hotel, you know the one, on Osmana Dikića Street. Don't worry, I'll sort it out. I know exactly the right person for that job."

* * *

Wednesday, July 11, 2012
  Mostar

Eight phone calls, and Filip had drawn a blank every time. None of the hotels he had rung in eastern Mostar had an Ana Dukić staying with them.

He was sitting on a sofa, tapping his fingers on his thigh, clearly frustrated. "I'll give this one a try," he said, underlining another number in a directory.

He glanced at Johnson, who was sitting at the other end of the sofa in the reception area of Muslibegovic House.

Johnson leaned back and stared at the ceiling, slowly shaking his head. *A needle in a haystack, just as Vic said.*

But Filip's next call—to the Hotel Pellegrino on the banks of the Neretva and less than a half mile from where Johnson, Jayne, and Filip were staying—drew a result.

Yes, the receptionist said, she could take a message for Ana Dukić, to expect a visit from Joe Johnson around seven o'clock, but she couldn't put the call through to her room now, as she'd asked not to be disturbed. But if the gentleman would like to come along at seven and have a drink in the bar while he was waiting, he would be welcome.

Johnson turned to Jayne. "It's your birthday. Shall we go for dinner, or shall I go see this woman Ana? Your call."

Jayne hesitated. "You go. We haven't got time to waste. We can have a few birthday drinks later."

Thus, later in the evening, Johnson walked around to the Pellegrino. He approached the front desk, asked the receptionist to let Ana Dukić know that he was here to see her, and settled into a comfortable armchair.

Johnson glanced around, using the pretense of checking emails on his phone as a cover. The Pellegrino was a smart boutique hotel, with patterned marble floors, leather chairs, wrought-iron interior canopies, and attentive but unobtrusive staff. Whatever Ana was doing here, she was clearly not lacking funds.

Ten minutes later, Johnson saw a tall, willowy woman walk into the reception area. She pulled back her shoulder-length blond hair and surveyed the lobby, glanced twice at Johnson, and then finally approached hesitantly.

"Excuse me, are you Joe Johnson?" she asked in a distinctly English accent.

"Yes. You're Ana Dukić?"

The woman nodded and unconsciously straightened her black skirt. "I had a message from reception saying that you were looking for me?"

Johnson stood and shook hands. "Yes, good to meet you,

and thanks for taking the trouble to speak to me. I apologize for the intrusion. I'm a private war crimes investigator, and if you don't mind, there are a couple of things I'd just like to discuss. Nothing to worry about—I'm just hoping you might be able to help."

"That sounds intriguing," Ana said. "I don't exactly get many war crimes investigators trying to track me down. How can I help you?"

"The reason I'm here is that someone who knows one of your old friends, Aisha Delić, pointed me in your direction," Johnson said. He decided not to mention Filip's name.

"Aisha? I haven't seen her in a long time. Why are you asking?"

"To cut a long story short, I'm beginning a potential inquiry into Aisha's former husband, Franjo. I guess you knew him, during the war?"

Ana took a sharp intake of breath and folded her arms. "Yes, I knew him. An inquiry? Well, that's probably long overdue, I'd say."

Johnson looked around. "Perhaps we should sit somewhere quieter. Then I can explain."

She nodded and indicated toward a quiet table against the wall at the back of the cocktail bar, suggesting they sit and talk over a drink.

Johnson positioned himself against the wall so he had a view across the bar, and Ana sat opposite. She quickly scanned the cocktail list and ordered a mojito from the hovering waiter. Johnson settled for a gin and tonic.

"Okay, tell me more," Ana said.

Johnson scratched his right ear. "I started looking into this only recently, after a tip-off. You may know that most of the major offenders from the war in these parts have been prosecuted, but some obviously got away."

Ana half laughed. "You've just worked that out, have you? And what's the story with Franjo?"

"Well, he seems to have vanished a long time ago. So I was trying to find Aisha in the hope that she would know where he is."

She shook her head. "Don't waste your time. Aisha won't know."

"But she might know something that can help—even if she's not aware of it. That's what I'd like to check out. Where is Aisha? Are you in contact with her?"

"Not much. There's the occasional email. I haven't seen her for twenty years. She's in the US. She went to St. Louis and is living in New York now. That's the tragedy of Bosnia, of Yugoslavia, of the war—all the good people have gone."

"Hmm, it does seem to be a well-trodden path. Why do they leave?"

Ana's view was that most had been either driven out by rival ethnic groups, as Aisha had been, or left because they couldn't stand living in a pressure cooker environment where they were defined by their religion or their ethnicity, like herself. That was what she and Aisha had in common—they were typical of Bosnian exiles from the 1990s, she said. Others left simply for economic reasons; the country had been wrecked by war and there were no jobs.

Johnson studied Ana's face. Filip was right; though she was in her late forties her face was unlined, and she *was* still beautiful.

"Do you have an address for Aisha, or do you know where she works? Or could you give me an email address?"

She hesitated. "I'm not sure. I'll think about it."

Johnson suppressed a sigh. "Okay, it really would be extremely helpful if you could give me something so I can contact her. It's only because I'm interested in justice for Franjo."

"I know that. Like I said, I'll think about it."

Johnson decided to change tack. "So where did you end up, when you fled?"

"London. I'm still there. I went to study architecture and worked as an architect for a while. I write books on the subject now, often from a historical angle, which is my other passion. That's why I've visited here a few times recently. I'm doing a history of some of the famous bridges across the old Yugoslavia, obviously including the Stari Most here, and also the Mehmed Paša Sokolović Bridge over the Drina River in Višegrad, which you might have heard of. There was a novel about it; *The Bridge on the Drina*. They're hundreds of years old, with big histories—very interesting."

Her words struck a chord with Johnson, who told her about his love of history and international relations and very briefly mentioned his career and family background and decision to become a freelancer after his wife had died.

"I'd like to focus more on war crimes, if I can find the right jobs, which isn't easy," Johnson said. "For a long time, my passion for justice has kept me going—it's why I love the war crimes work. It's messy and gory but rewarding when you find someone who's guilty as hell and has been on the run for decades."

Ana smiled, and her voice softened a little. "Actually, some of the research I've been doing on the destruction of the Stari Most might be very relevant to what you're looking for —particularly in regard to Franjo Vuković. It's surprising what you can find out by talking to people around here."

Johnson raised his eyebrows and glanced around. The cocktail bar was filling with hotel guests and tourists having predinner drinks. "Yes, please tell me whatever you think is relevant. I'd be interested to hear about anything that might help the case."

Ana leaned in closer to the table, and he noticed her

perfume for the first time, which he was certain was Opium, the same Yves Saint Laurent brand that Kathy had sometimes used. The smell alone triggered memories and emotions.

Come on, focus on the job in hand, Johnson told himself.

"You know the Old Bridge was destroyed by a tank that was firing from further down the river, in November '93?" Ana said.

Johnson nodded. "Yes, it made international headlines."

"Well, I've been doing some research into how that happened, because it was quite a mystery," Ana said. "The international criminal tribunal in The Hague, the ICTY, got quite worked up about the bridge. It was a cultural treasure."

"Yes, I understand they haven't pinned down who really gave the orders to destroy it; they're blaming the Croat army commander, which is fair enough at the top level, but at the local level they don't know."

Ana nodded. "You've done a little research yourself, then. Good, just listen to this. I'm a Croat, but when I lived here, a lot of my best friends were Muslims, and I saw things that upset me."

Johnson nodded.

"There were three men in the tank," Ana said. "All of them were doing exactly what they were told by a commander. Except until now, nobody has known who that commander was, or they haven't wanted to say. The problem is that the soldiers in the tank are all dead now, as far as I can make out. But I've talked to a number of witnesses both in the army, the HVO, and in that area around Stotina Hill, where the tank was firing from, and there's no doubt who the commander was. It was Franjo Vuković."

Johnson sipped his gin and tonic and leaned forward. "Go on."

"He was controlling the whole thing, standing next to the tank with a walkie-talkie, masterminding it like a circus ring leader. I've heard that from two people who saw it firsthand. You catch him, and you can pin the destruction of the bridge on him, as well as whatever killings, murders, and whatever else he's undoubtedly done."

Johnson drained his glass and put it down on the table. His adrenaline was kicking in. "Would you like another drink?" he asked.

She nodded. "Sure, why not."

He signaled to a waiter and ordered two more drinks before turning back to Ana.

He suddenly realized he was feeling quite light-headed. The barman had poured generous measures.

"But that tank didn't only destroy the bridge that day, it killed a number of people, too," he said.

"Yes, exactly," Ana said. "It was devastating. That's why I want to tell the story about it, in my book." She leaned forward and cupped her chin in her hands. "But enough about my sad country. I love it, but it depresses me sometimes. So tell me. How did you end up involved in this type of work as a freelancer?"

Johnson took a deep breath. "You don't need to know all that. It was a very long time ago."

"I'd like to," she said, raising an eyebrow.

Normally Johnson was circumspect when discussing his background, particularly the CIA elements. But now, he felt an urge to tell Ana a little more.

So he gave her the short, sanitized version about how he had joined the CIA and why he had left.

In March 1988, he and Vic had been on a covert mission in Afghanistan out of their Islamabad station in Pakistan, dodging the occupying Russian forces for a meeting with a highly placed Afghan mujahideen commander, in the city of Jalalabad, roughly thirty miles over the border.

The meeting broke up early after a warning about a raid

by the KGB. Johnson and Vic escaped, but got into a gun battle with a KGB sniper. Johnson pushed Vic into the safety of a doorway, but caught a round at the top of his right ear, leaving him with a U-shaped nick, a scar for life.

"You were lucky, then, and you saved your friend's life, too," Ana said.

"Kind of lucky."

Johnson opted not to tell Ana that he had shot the KGB sniper, causing a huge diplomatic upset. Pakistan's Inter-Services Intelligence agency found out and demanded to know why the CIA was recruiting its own agents in Afghanistan and running operations in the country, rather than sticking to protocol and working through them, as had been agreed.

"It was a difficult time, made worse because I didn't get along with my boss," Johnson told Ana.

Ana inclined her head in a certain way. "It all sounds quite sensitive. I won't ask any more questions."

"That's probably wise," Johnson said. "There's obviously more to it, but I can't go into detail about it, although much of it's been declassified since."

The reality was that the incident had been the latest in a series of clashes between Johnson and Watson, who removed Johnson from the Afghanistan program and told him he had worked "asshole-fashion."

But both Johnson and Vic had been convinced they had run that Jalalabad operation perfectly. They were utterly certain they weren't under surveillance when they went into the meeting.

Vic and Johnson logically concluded that there was a mole inside the Islamabad CIA station who had leaked details of the meeting to the KGB. But Johnson never did find out who it was.

He and Vic suspected that Watson might even have been

the mole, although there was no actual proof, and Johnson had rarely discussed it since. Even though Johnson was no longer with the CIA, it wouldn't be wise to accuse a sitting desk chief in the CIA of treason.

Ana sipped her drink and leaned back.

"But you didn't leave after that Jalalabad incident?" she asked.

"Not immediately. I left later that year."

Johnson again left unspoken the details about his brief affair with Jayne—which Watson subsequently found out about. The upshot was that Johnson was recalled from Islamabad back to Langley in early September 1988. He packed his bags two days later, just after his thirtieth birthday.

"So was leaving the CIA a good or bad thing?"

"Not sure," Johnson said. "But in the end, I enjoyed my next job, hunting Nazis, much more. Less deception, fewer egos to battle with, more passion, and more satisfaction. And from there, I started my own investigations business when I relocated, which is why I'm now working on this job."

"Good experience for this project, then," Ana said.

"Yes, definitely." Johnson mentioned that his colleague Jayne was with him in Mostar and was helping him out, but he said nothing of their history.

Half an hour later, after finishing the second round of drinks, Johnson said goodbye to Ana, who said she was tired. But she did give him her phone number and email and also promised to send Aisha's details too.

By that stage Johnson felt thoroughly invigorated. It was partly due to the alcohol, and partly due to the information she had given him about Aisha, Franjo, the tank, and the bridge. Things were gradually starting to unfold, he felt.

CHAPTER SIXTEEN

Wednesday, July 11, 2012
  Mostar

After leaving the Hotel Pellegrino bar, Johnson stood outside and checked up and down the road. It was deserted. The floodlit outline of the Stari Most was reflected almost perfectly in the slow-moving waters of the Neretva below.

It was dark now but still warm, and the twinkling lights of the cafés, bars, and hotels lining both banks of the river seemed to beckon him.

He sent a text to Jayne and Filip to say he had finished with Ana and to ask whether they wanted to meet him for a few glasses to celebrate Jayne's birthday.

A reply came back immediately from Jayne. *Thanks, but changed my mind. Feeling really tired. Can we do it tomorrow instead?*

There was no reply from Filip.

So Johnson sat on a bench outside the hotel and called his children, suddenly wishing they were there with him to see this historic part of Europe, so different from Maine. He spent the first twenty minutes catching up on Peter's chances of being selected for the district basketball team at the weekend trials, and then he had a discussion with Carrie about a party she wanted to attend that Friday that Amy was unsure about. In the end, he agreed she could go, to squeals of delight.

After he had hung up, Johnson decided he would have a couple of drinks. In this mood, he didn't feel like going back to Muslibegovic House just yet.

Johnson checked carefully behind him a few times as he walked southward along Braće Fejića Street, but there was no sign of anyone following. He then continued onto Kujundžiluk, near to the Old Bridge again. Now all the tourists were out in droves, shopping, eating, and drinking.

He stopped outside a place that was sunk deep into the cliff face, the Ali Baba. Long Turkish sofas, drapes, and soft chairs were hidden under a rock overhang and surrounded by walls, with a semicircular bar in the center.

Johnson battled his way to the bar and bought a beer, then went up a short flight of stone stairs to the dimly lit rear, where he sat on a stool and surveyed the clientele.

The evening was getting into full swing. Drunken couples kissed in dark corners, men argued, tourists took blurry photographs, and two old men played chess and chain-smoked. It was an ideal spot for an hour of people-watching.

Johnson drank his beer quickly and ordered another, by now feeling as mellow as he had ever been since arriving in Dubrovnik almost a week earlier, despite the events on the Old Bridge that day.

People were dancing in the center area, and Carly Rae Jepsen's song "Call Me Maybe" blasted out from the speakers around the inside of the cave. A group in their twenties standing near the bar sang along, loudly and utterly out of tune, and then joined in the dancing.

A woman in a black dress sat on the stool right next to Johnson and sipped her drink, moving her bare shoulders slightly in time to the music. She caught his eye, then smiled. Her curly dark hair fell over her face, and she brushed it back with a hand.

"Great music here," she said in accented English. "You British, American?"

"Yes, American," Johnson replied. "How can you tell?"

"I can always tell."

"And where are you from?"

"I'm a Mostar girl, a Bosnian Croat," she said, "although I've spent more time away than here. I worked in the UK for a while, in Edinburgh and London, then France, and then came back. Mostar used to be a tough place, but I love it now. Are you a tourist or here for work?"

"A bit of both," Johnson said. "Mainly work. What's your name?"

"Katarina, although you can call me Kate, as everyone did in London." Johnson nodded and introduced himself.

They chatted about London for a few minutes, then Katarina finished her drink. "You like another beer or a spirit?" she asked Johnson.

"I was planning to go, actually," Johnson said.

"Oh, don't, we just started chatting. Go on, have a drink," she insisted.

I really should stop drinking and go back to the hotel, Johnson thought.

But instead, Johnson found himself looking at Katarina and saying, "Oh, all right, I'll just stay for one drink . . . yes, rum and coke, please."

Johnson watched Katarina with renewed attention while

she was in line at the bar. She was slim and tanned, good-looking, and probably in her mid-thirties, he guessed.

She came back and handed Johnson his drink.

Johnson took out his pack of cigarettes and offered one to Katarina, who accepted. He took one out himself, and lit first hers, then his own.

They smoked without speaking for a few minutes. The intake of nicotine made him feel a little sharper.

"So," he finally said. "Do you like the new Mostar?"

"Yes, I do. This place is much happier than it used to be," Katarina said. "During the war and for a few years afterward, it was miserable. The thugs were in charge. A lot of the war criminals were caught, but there's still many just walking around. Most people could name one or two who escaped justice, on both sides of the river, Croat and Muslim."

"Yes, so I hear," Johnson said as he sipped his rum. "That's part of my job actually, to track down war criminals. It's why I'm here."

"Really? Are you investigating anything particular?"

"Oh, you know, large-scale killings, brutalities, and the like. The ones responsible have disappeared. Nobody knows where they are, so it's my job to find a way."

"Who's on your list? It's a small city. I might know them."

Johnson instinctively reined himself in. He looked around. The music was getting louder, and the bar was becoming jam-packed. It was probably time to go. "I can't give names. It's sensitive," he said.

"Okay, that's fine," Katarina said, resting a hand on Johnson's thigh. "Listen, there is a quieter bar we could go to, just up the road. It would be easier to talk."

"Well, I think I'm going to head back now, actually," Johnson said. He finished his rum and glanced down at Katarina's hand. She removed it.

"Okay, whatever. We could just have one drink at the

other bar, then you can go," she said. Her hand brushed against his thigh again, but she didn't leave it in place this time.

Johnson's instincts told him to walk out of the bar right then. She was obviously just trying her luck.

"No, I really have to go. Sorry."

"Okay, well, I'm heading to the other bar anyway. I'll walk out with you."

Johnson felt he couldn't exactly say no to that. They walked out of the bar, and Johnson turned toward his hotel.

Katarina fell in step with him. "I'm going that way," she said. She tapped a message to someone on her phone as she walked. "Are you sure you don't want another drink?"

Maybe she was just a woman on a night out, looking for some company. But still.

"I'm sure, but it's been nice talking—"

A man wearing a black ski mask suddenly appeared from behind a van, blocking the way, and said something in Bosnian.

Johnson looked at Katarina. She was backing away from them.

"*What?*" Johnson said. He suddenly felt a surge of adrenaline kick through him. *Here we go,* he thought.

By then, the man, thick-set and muscular, had drawn level with him. The ski mask covered his face apart from his eyes and nose.

Johnson braced himself, his back to a tall brick wall.

The man, now silent, stepped toward Johnson and launched a punch hard and low, aimed just below Johnson's rib cage, with little windup or telegraphing.

Johnson saw it coming and managed to raise his left forearm sufficiently to deflect it a little, but it still connected with some force. He felt an immediate sharp, stabbing pain around his kidneys.

It had been a very long time since he had last been involved in a street fight. But like most CIA recruits, he had trained in martial arts and close-quarter combat. Those skills had occasionally come in handy over the years.

Instinctively he saw the man was slightly off-balance following his punch, so he made a short-armed jab with his right hand, aiming for the man's nose, but connected with his cheekbone.

The thug raised his hands, grabbed Johnson by both shoulders, and shoved him backward into the wall. Johnson's head crunched against the brickwork. The man pinned him there, one hand on each shoulder, his arms at full stretch, and then head-butted Johnson hard at the base of his forehead, between his eyes, jamming his head back against the wall again.

"You are trying to poke your nose into our business here in Mostar," the man said, now speaking in English as he continued to pin Johnson to the wall. "This is a warning to you. You need to leave now. Get out of town, get out of this country, and leave us all alone. It is nothing to do with you. Otherwise you'll be in the river."

Pain seared through the back and front of Johnson's head. The pungent scent of the man's aftershave filled Johnson's nostrils. It was unmistakably the same aftershave he had smelled earlier that day at Omar's house. This was his helper, Tomislav.

Johnson managed to get both hands up through the gap between Tomislav's two forearms. With his left hand, he slammed down as hard as he could against the man's right elbow joint, causing it to bend and rocking Tomislav back on his heels slightly.

Then Johnson used his right hand to strike as hard as he could with the flat of his palm straight into Tomislav's nose.

The man gave a deep-throated grunt of pain as his head went back.

At the same time, Johnson jerked to his right. Now Tomislav was completely unbalanced. Johnson used his right hand to shove the man's head around in a tight semicircle, straight into the brickwork.

The tables were turned. Johnson had Tomislav, his knees buckled, back against the wall.

Johnson fully expected Katarina to launch herself at him. But he could see out of the corner of his eye she was walking quickly up the road, away from them.

He switched his right-hand grip from Tomislav's face to his neck and managed to bash his head backward against the wall again, then pushed hard to keep him there.

He shoved the thug one more time against the wall. Tomislav's knees buckled further.

Johnson let go. "Don't try that again, buddy," he said. Then he ran toward his hotel.

By the time he got back to Muslibegovic House, he felt slightly dizzy. His head throbbed with a sharp, insistent pain at the back, where it had crunched into the brick wall, and he could feel a large lump at the front where he had been head-butted. He was now feeling drained as the adrenaline receded.

Johnson reached his room and managed, after two attempts, to get his key into the lock of the door.

A voice came from behind him. "What the hell's happened? The back of your head's a real mess. There's a ton of blood."

It was Jayne, standing in the doorway of her room.

Johnson turned around and groaned. "Don't say anything, Jayne. I screwed up."

"Oh, you've been hit. Your forehead," Jayne said. "What

bastard did that?" She walked across and put one hand on each of his shoulders.

Johnson shook his head. "It was a setup, and stupidly, I didn't read it early enough. A guy who works for Omar, name of Tomislav. Don't worry, I'm okay. I just need some sleep." He checked his watch. It was half past eleven.

"Joe, you've got blood trickling down the back of your head. It's all over your shirt. I'm going to clean you up first. Come on."

She led him into his room, then into the bathroom. "What happened?"

"I met a woman in a bar and had a quick chat. But I got a bad vibe and decided to head back here. Then she walks out with me. I was heading toward the hotel when, the next thing I know, this guy Tomislav appears from nowhere and lands a couple of punches, telling me he's giving me a warning. I got him eventually—slammed him against a wall. He'll be worse off than me."

"So Franjo sent his heavies in," Jayne said.

"Yes. It's got to be Franjo and Marco. Tomislav probably knows them or something. I couldn't see his face, but I recognized his aftershave. It stank."

Johnson winced and held the back of his head. "I hadn't even drunk all that much."

Jayne took some tissues from a box in the bathroom, dampened them under the tap, and began dabbing the back of Johnson's head. "At least it's stopped bleeding. Have you got any painkillers?" she asked.

"Yes, there's a pack in my bag."

"Okay. Hope you feel better in the morning." She folded her arms. "I guess the lesson is don't go out drinking late by yourself when you've got people on your tail. We were shot at today, Joe! What were you thinking?"

"You're right. I should have come straight back here after I'd finished speaking with Ana. I just felt like a beer."

After Jayne had gone back to her room, Johnson drank a glass of water, swallowed a couple of painkillers, and sat in bed.

He checked the emails on his phone. There were two from Ana.

Hi Joe, it was good to meet you. I would like to see something happen from this investigation you are doing. I hope what I said was useful, though I realize it wasn't much. I have an address for Aisha in New York. It is 34-12C 38th Street, in Queens. One thing you should ask her about that I forgot to mention when I saw you. I remember her one day being very upset. She said her father was in trouble because of some documents and that it was Franjo's fault. She never told me more, but it stuck in my mind. Thanks, Ana.

The second note from Ana included only an email address for Aisha that she had forgotten to include with the first.

Johnson forwarded the first one to Jayne with a note on the top. *Looks like a trip to NYC imminently*. Then he put his phone down and lay back on his pillow. Within seconds, he had fallen asleep.

CHAPTER SEVENTEEN

Thursday, July 12, 2012
 Mostar

Johnson woke to find the back of his head stuck to his pillow and the lump at the front still there. But the worst of his headache had receded.

He gingerly sipped from a bottle of water that Jayne had placed on his bedside table and checked his phone. It was nine o'clock in the morning, and the sunlight streamed into his room.

Then he remembered the email from Ana the previous evening and sat up straight. Immediately he felt a sharp pain below his ribs, where Tomislav had hit him, and winced heavily.

"Got to get to New York," he muttered to himself. He pulled himself slowly out of bed and padded into the bathroom. After using the toilet, he splashed some cold water over his face and examined his reflection.

"My God," he said when he saw the large purple patch at

the base of his forehead, between his eyes where Tomislav's head-butt had made contact. The color was starting to descend toward his eye sockets. He touched the bruise cautiously and cringed.

There was another large purple bruise below his ribs.

He put a bathrobe on, then walked carefully into the corridor and knocked on Jayne's door.

Upon opening it, she immediately suppressed a giggle. "Sorry, Joe, can't help it."

"They're going to pay for this, you do realize," Johnson said.

"Going to be a big bill, then. Plastic surgery doesn't come cheap."

"Ha! Just make me a coffee, will you? We need to discuss what we do next."

Jayne opened the door fully and let him in. "Yep, I read your email from Ana. I think you're right. You need to be on the next flight to New York. Hopefully the bruising will go down while you're en route, otherwise Aisha will get a shock. I can stay here and start thinking about how we try and track down this guy Haris Hasanović, the elusive keeper of all things Izetbegović."

Johnson walked in and sat in an armchair near the window while Jayne made coffee.

He took his phone out to search for a flight. "Let's see, I can get away this afternoon, Croatia Airlines into Nice, then direct to JFK from there. That'll do the job." He finished the booking just as she handed him a steaming mug.

"There, drink that. Should improve your mood," Jayne said.

He took the mug. "Thanks. I was thinking that if I'm going to New York, I could pop up to Portland and see the kids and my sister, but I can't go looking like this."

Johnson reclined in his chair. "Anyway, it completely

underlines the fact that Franjo or Marco are desperately trying to block an investigation."

Jayne sat on the bed and folded her arms. "We should make sure word gets back to Franjo and Marco that you're gone, out of the country, as per the threat from that Tomislav guy."

"Yes, good point. Maybe Filip can think how we could do that. Perhaps a message via Omar and his thug helper."

Jayne eyed him. "Yeah, good idea. Speaking of Filip, he seemed quite down earlier. He'd had an update from police who are apparently making little headway in tracking down Marco for questioning about the Petar murder."

Johnson sat up. "They are slow. You'll just need to keep him focused on our inquiry. I don't want him going off by himself trying to find Marco."

* * *

Thursday, July 12, 2012
   Wolf Trap, Virginia

Robert Watson picked up the plastic water bottle from his desk and hurled it across his private office at the back of his six-bedroom house.

Then he stood up and kicked his wicker wastepaper basket, which tumbled and flipped across the floor, cannoned into the door, and spilled its contents of old chocolate bar wrappers, paper tissues, and plastic soft-drink bottles onto his office carpet.

"Shit, what the hell is that guy playing at," he said out loud. He sat back down and blinked as the early morning sunshine caught his eye through the window.

Watson once again studied the secure email received from his friend Mike at the National Security Agency.

Robert, I've done a check as requested on Joe Johnson. I can confirm email traffic and phone calls to and from him in both Croatia and Bosnia and Herzegovina over the past week. I can't read the emails, they're all encrypted. However, further cross-checks show one email to Johnson that I have been able to read—because it came from Langley, from Vic Walter's account. See attached copy. I've done a remote trawl of VW's hard drive, but there's nothing else on there that seems relevant to this or to Johnson.
Thanks,
Mike

Watson clicked onto the copy of the email to Johnson from Vic, dated July 10.

Doc, the guy you need to speak to is Haris Hasanović, who I understand kept the minutes of many informal meetings involving US officials in Sarajevo within Izetbegović's office. He's now presumably retired. Last known location Dubrovnik, but we don't know where exactly. Your job to find out. It's a starting point. Also, COS in Croatia is Alan Edwards. He's based in Zagreb but sometimes goes to Split. I'll send you a text message with his details when I get them. He will help you.
Vic

Watson picked up his phone and made an encrypted call to RUNNER's number. It rang four times and then was answered.

"Hello?"

"RUNNER, it's SILVER. Listen, our problem is bigger than I thought. It's not just Johnson doing this on his own initiative."

There was a pause. "What do you mean, it's not just Johnson?"

"It's bigger than him. He's under instructions."

"From who?"

"Some other part of the CIA," Watson said. "I won't go into exactly which departments, but someone else here has asked Johnson to investigate something related to Haris Hasanović, who, as I'm sure you may be aware, used to keep the meeting minutes inside Izetbegović's office—including those of meetings with US officials." He paused for a second. "You realize this is dangerous territory?"

"Right, but why would someone else inside the CIA be looking to investigate Hasanović?" Boris asked.

Watson picked up a foam stress ball that he kept on his desk. "Oh, come on. Probably every sensitive document, every decision, every death warrant would have passed under his nose, including anything US-related, from Bill Clinton downward at that time."

"We've just given this guy Johnson a shot across the bow ourselves," Boris said. "I arranged for a friend of mine to give him a good kicking. Didn't quite go as planned, but I hope he got the message. You need to remember I can't afford for him to get far down the track either, not if he's a war crimes investigator. What else do you want me to do?"

Watson considered his options. "I'll have a think about it, but one thing you need to make sure of: Johnson cannot get his hands on those damn documents you've got. I warned you to get rid of them a long time ago; it's going to backfire badly."

Boris frowned. "Get rid of my insurance policy? I definitely won't. I'm not mentioned in there, and neither is Marco. But there are references that could lead to you. So they're going to backfire on you, not me. But anyway, they're secure. There's no way he can get his hands on them without blowing himself into the Adriatic and halfway to Italy."

"As I advised you a long time ago," Watson said, "I think you should give me the location where you've hidden them as a safeguard, you know, in case something happens to you."

Boris snorted. "You don't seriously think I'm going to give you that. Twenty years of asking, and you still haven't got the message."

"You don't get it," Watson said. "If this guy Johnson gets hold of them, I'm finished. And if that happens, I'll make damn sure I take you down with me."

Watson ended the call. "Damn it, damn, damn, damn it!" he muttered. He paced around his office a couple of times, then stood and stared out of the window.

He sat back down at his desk and rang another secure number, this time for his CIA colleague Alan Edwards.

"Alan, it's Robert. Listen, apart from that RUNNER job in Sinj, there's something else. Sorry, buddy, there's a lot going on here at the moment. This one is quite urgent."

He heard Edwards swear under his breath before answering. "Okay, what's that?"

"This goes back to '93 and the weapons supply arrangement we had with Izetbegović and his army," Watson said. "His office had records of that, a dossier, that we asked him to get rid of, but we don't think that happened. They sort of disappeared. I know who's had them, but I don't know where they are. Anyway, I've heard through the grapevine, from one of my moles, that another group at Langley, I think run out of the director's office, is trying to get their hands on the docs now as well. No idea why, but I will find out. I think, though, that someone's trying to do the dirty on me. We can't afford for anyone to get their hands on those papers. There's very good high-level political reasons why not. Understand?"

"So you want me to—"

"Yes, you've *got* to locate them," Watson said. "I need them. And if you do, there's a promotion in it for you."

"Okay, I'll give it my best shot. Where do we start?"

"Here's what I need you to do. You start in Split. I'm about to send you a secure email with the details and a photograph of the person working for the other Langley group whom you need to track. He may well lead you to the documents. The guy's name is Joe Johnson."

"Do you know much about him?" Edwards asked.

"Yes, unfortunately." Watson sent the email to Edwards and then gave him a brief summary of his dealings with Johnson in Pakistan and Afghanistan.

"Okay, read the message I've just sent you. And now listen." Watson spent the next ten minutes carefully going through a series of instructions with Edwards before ending the call.

* * *

Thursday, July 12, 2012
Mostar

Boris had just finished packing his small suitcase at the Hotel Mepas. He had been in a bad mood since late the previous night, when he had learned that Tomislav had come off worst in his encounter with Johnson.

He was still muttering to himself when Marco burst into the room.

"Job done. The American bastard's leaving for New York," Marco said.

"What?" Boris asked.

"That guy Johnson, he's booked himself on a flight back to the States, leaving Dubrovnik tonight."

"How the hell do you know that?"

"Just had a message from Tomislav. He says Filip again called in to see Omar, you know, Tomi's boss, to say he was heading back to Split and thanks for his help. Filip said— you'll like this—that Johnson had been attacked down near the Stari Most and was heading back to the States tonight. Filip is driving him to Dubrovnik Airport, apparently."

Boris grimaced as he tightened his leather belt, then let it out a notch from its usual position. His frame was becoming increasingly padded by surplus flesh now that he was into his late forties.

"Hmm," Boris said. "I doubt Tomi's responsible for his departure—he didn't exactly emerge from last night unscathed, did he?"

"Well, no."

"But anyway. If Johnson's going, then Tomi's probably earned his money. What about the woman?" Boris asked.

"Don't know about her."

"Hmm, we'll see. All sounds way too neat."

"If he's gone, he's gone," Marco said.

"Yeah, let's see. I'd like to keep a track on the woman, though, and on Filip. How can we do that?"

"Could get Tomi to do it, or one of his cronies."

"Yes, definitely, get him on it. I want to know what she does, where she goes. She's obviously working with him. Same goes for Filip," Boris said.

"Okay, I'll have a chat with Tomi."

"Now, what about those land mines. Have you spoken to the supplier? I want to get moving with them," Boris said.

Marco leaned against the doorframe. "Yes, I've talked to Ratko. It's all under control. He's going to have them in the next couple of days. He'll take them to the site, and we can meet him there. Shouldn't be a problem."

"Okay," Boris said. "As long as we get them before

Monday. Remember I'm flying back to London on Tuesday, so we either need to put them in place Sunday afternoon or make an early start Monday. I'm also going to have to do some work at your place for the next couple of days—research for the interviews I've got coming up."

"I'm more interested in what we're going to do about Johnson and Filip," Marco said. "My gut instinct is to have another go at eliminating both of them."

CHAPTER EIGHTEEN

Friday, July 13, 2012
Astoria

Johnson yawned deeply, feeling exhausted after less than three hours' sleep on the flight to New York.

He knocked at the battered green front door for a third time, then stood back and waited. The paint around the lock was partly scratched away by years of contact from fingernails and keys.

There was no answer.

Johnson grabbed the handle of the screen door, from which the protective mesh was missing, banged it shut, and went back through the rusty front gate. Aisha was nowhere to be seen.

Johnson had decided not to make contact in advance, for fear of being rejected before he could even meet her. Instead he planned to rely on the well-practiced doorstep charm that had served him well over many years.

He checked his watch. It was five in the afternoon. Maybe he should just sit it out.

Across the road, next to the graffitied steel door of a car repair company, stood a few cinder blocks. Johnson crossed the street, turned two of the blocks up vertically, placed another across the top to form a seat of sorts, and sat down to wait under the shade of a large tree.

He tapped out a long secure text message to Vic's private cell phone to update him on the inquiry and explain his visit to New York to see Aisha.

A few minutes later, Vic replied, expressing his surprise that Johnson was back on US soil but liking his progress.

Three doors down, where 38th Street met 34th Avenue, Johnson noticed a café, Ćevabdžinica Sarajevo, with a bright green frontage and a gaudy yellow and red sign. Maybe this Bosnia neighborhood in Astoria was as close as Aisha could get to a home away from home in New York.

A young couple emerged from the café, hand in hand, and passed him before disappearing into another house down the street.

Then, at just after six o'clock, a woman wearing sunglasses and with dark hair that fell past her shoulders walked around the corner past the café. She paused and peered inside, holding her hand above her eyes to reduce the glare, then continued down the road and turned into the gateway of number 12C.

Johnson sat up straight.

The woman removed a key from her jeans pocket, unlocked the door, and let herself in, closing the door behind her.

Aisha Delić. It had to be.

Johnson waited for ten minutes, smoked a cigarette, then turned on his phone's voice recorder, casually got up, and walked across the street.

The woman opened the door a couple of inches on a robust-looking security chain, almost before he had finished knocking. "Hello?" she said, raising her eyebrows. He could see her recoil fractionally, probably due to his somewhat battered appearance. Johnson had been focusing so hard on his task that he had almost forgotten his bruises.

"Hello, are you Aisha?"

She recovered her poise. "Yes . . . and who are you?"

"I'm Joe Johnson," he said. "Sorry to bother you, but I've just come from Mostar. I'm a war crimes investigator, and I was hoping you might be able to help me with something regarding an inquiry I'm working on, if you could spare a few minutes."

Her dark eyes scanned him up and down, a sympathetic look on her face. "An investigator? Did you get into a fight in Mostar?"

"There was an incident, as you can probably see, but it's a long story."

"Okay, well, tell me briefly what this is about. I've had a long day at work." She smiled for the first time.

"Yes, and I appreciate your time. I was hoping I could speak to you about someone you know, or did know." Johnson said. He hesitated, then added, "It's actually about your former husband, Franjo Vuković."

The smile vanished. Aisha stood motionless for a couple of seconds. "Can you show me identification or something?" she asked.

Johnson handed her a business card and explained that he used to work for the OSI but was now an independent investigator. He reached into his pocket and took out his passport, which he held up at the photo page.

She eyed him steadily.

"You'd better come in," Aisha said eventually. She unclipped the security chain and opened the door. He stepped inside and realized the scruffy exterior of the house belied its interior, which was tidy and minimalistic, with freshly painted walls and sanded wooden floorboards. Johnson glanced around approvingly. "Nice place you have here."

She nodded but said nothing, then walked to her kitchen table, next to patio doors that led to a small rear garden. She indicated to two chairs, and they both sat.

"How did you find me?"

"I bumped into an old friend of yours, Ana, in Mostar."

"Ana's in Mostar? Don't think so. She's in London."

"Yes, but she's in Mostar doing a project, on bridges, architecture, that kind of thing."

Aisha scratched the top of her head. "I think you're wasting your time, but go on."

"Why do you think I'm wasting my time?"

"He's dead, I'm certain of it. He vanished off the planet twenty years ago, and as far as I'm concerned, he can stay off the planet. What is this about?"

"Okay, I was approached by someone who asked me to investigate him for alleged war crimes. This man believes he's alive, that he changed his identity and is living another life somewhere," Johnson said.

Aisha raised her eyebrows. "*Alive?* Where? Is that true? Who told you that?"

"Well, I can't say who approached me, but I was hoping you might be able to help me with the other questions, like where he's living."

"Sorry, I can't. Anyway, which war crimes are you focusing on, out of his many?"

"The ones we think we can get him on involve the treatment of Bosnian Muslim prisoners at the Heliodrom. Several of them died," Johnson said.

"Yep, they did. I know all about the Heliodrom. Every

Bosnian does." She paused and swept her hair back, her eyes focused intensely on Johnson now. "It really was awful what they did to the Bosniak prisoners in there. We all knew what was going on."

Johnson could see that Aisha's eyes had moistened. She was visibly biting her bottom lip.

"I'm sorry. Bad memories," she said. "It just suddenly hit me."

"It's fine. I'm sorry for stirring them up."

"Is it just the Heliodrom, or other things? There were quite a lot."

"Such as?"

"How long do you have? What about the Old Bridge?" she asked.

"What about it?"

"He blew it to pieces. Nobody ever pinned that on him."

"Tell me more," Johnson said.

"He was in charge of the guys in the tank that knocked down the Stari Most. It all went out on worldwide television. I think he did it on purpose when the cameras were there—I wouldn't be surprised. They were on Stotina Hill, shelling the bridge for a day and a half before it finally collapsed. The cameras filmed the lot. Nobody knows about that but I know there are witnesses who would give evidence if he's ever found."

"That would be exactly what I'm looking for to build this case, assuming we find him," Johnson said. "I've heard a lot about the bridge."

"Everybody adored that bridge," Aisha said. "It was where I kissed him for the first time in 1987. It was the traditional meeting point between Croats and Bosniaks, Catholics and Muslims, west and east. There were lots of couples like us back then. We married two years later. But during that war my husband turned into someone else, a monster I couldn't even recognize. I hated him by the end."

Now a tear rolled down her cheek.

"I honestly think he's dead. No one has heard from or seen him since the end of '93. If he actually is alive and you find him . . . well, if you get to Franjo before I do, just let me know," she said.

"It must have been difficult. I'm sorry to bring it all up again," Johnson said.

Aisha shook her head. "I'll send you something I wrote. It's easier than me trying to sit here and talk about it. It's too hard, way too hard. I put it all down in words, in my journal. I'll send you a few pages. The only issue is, it's written in Croatian. I don't suppose you're going to be able to read it?"

Johnson smiled and broke into Serbo-Croat. "Well, I can speak some Croatian, so it's not a problem."

Aisha looked surprised, then replied, also in Croatian. "Very impressive. How did you learn that?"

Johnson, feeling somewhat self-conscious, switched back to English and explained that he had done a stint in Bosnia and Croatia in 1999 while working for the OSI and had studied hard to learn the language at the same time.

"Also, do you have any photographs of Franjo?" he asked. "I haven't got one, and I really need to see what he looks like. Doesn't matter if it's old. It will still give me an idea."

"There are a couple, tucked away in a box somewhere, that I can scan and email to you," she said.

"Thank you for that and for your time. Seems like a great little neighborhood you're living in here," he said, transitioning them to less emotional ground now that he knew she couldn't help him find Franjo.

"Yes, it is," Aisha said. "There were hundreds, thousands of us Muslims who came here from Bosnia in the '90s. I'm kind of grateful to the US government for making it happen."

"There's a couple of other things," Johnson said. "I've also been asked to try and locate some important documents that went missing at that time, ones that were linked to Alija Izetbegović's office in Sarajevo, where I believe your father worked."

Johnson detailed part of the background to his search and said that Ana had remembered Aisha being upset one day over some documents, claiming it was Franjo's fault. But he omitted telling her that the request to find the documents had come from the CIA.

Aisha folded her arms and looked at him unblinkingly. "Missing documents? Ha." She snorted. "Who asked you to find those?"

"Oh, just someone linked to the investigation I'm doing."

Aisha pursed her lips. "I haven't talked about this before," she said. "In fact, nobody's asked me. But my father's long dead, so I guess it doesn't matter. Ana's correct. One of the biggest arguments I had with Franjo was over some documents that I'm 100 percent certain he stole from my father's study in Mostar. That's another reason I can't stand him. It caused my father a lot of problems."

Johnson felt his heart rate pick up sharply.

"Franjo stole them from your father? How?" Johnson asked.

"We were fairly certain it was one day when he came to my father's house looking for me, but nobody was in. He had a key because he was part of the family. He let himself in and probably just stumbled across them in my father's office. It wouldn't have taken a rocket scientist to work out what they were about."

Johnson stared out the window. "But why did your father have them in Mostar?"

Aisha shook her head. "Honestly, my father should not have had them. In fact, he took them, stole them, from

Izetbegović's office. They were foreign ministry documents that Izetbegović told him to destroy, but he didn't."

"Why not?"

"He realized their significance."

"And what was their significance? What were they about?"

"That I can't tell you—for a couple of reasons, one of which is that my father swore me to secrecy after they disappeared. But they are dynamite. Politically explosive."

"Dynamite? In what sense?"

Aisha leaned back. "Well, if the contents of those documents came out, half the White House from that time, from the president downward, would be hit by flying shit, and we Bosnians living here would be scapegoated."

She pointed toward an American flag hanging on her kitchen wall next to a nighttime photograph of a floodlit Stari Most. "And I don't want to have to leave here—I like it. It's home, despite all the sectarian anger that certain politicians, like Patrick Spencer, keep throwing around."

Johnson sat up straight. The story was slowly unravelling like a ball of wool.

"How do you mean? Tell me—what's in these documents that is so damaging?"

But Aisha just shook her head. "Another time."

Johnson furrowed his brow. It was time to change the subject. Maybe he could get her back to the documents later.

"That's fine. I appreciate all this, especially after you said you had a tough day at work. Who do you work for here?" he said.

"What's that got to do with it?" She glanced at her watch and stood. "You're going to have to go now. I've got a date this evening, and I need to get ready."

"But hang on—"

"No. No, we'll stop there." She stood and motioned toward the door. The discussion was over.

She ushered Johnson out into the street and said a brief goodbye.

He wandered back along 38th past the café, now feeling extremely uneasy, yet energized. So she believed Franjo was dead and that he'd stolen a set of politically explosive foreign ministry documents from her father.

What the hell? Could they be the same documents that Vic's looking for?

CHAPTER NINETEEN

Saturday, July 14, 2012
Manhattan

"How am I doing? Well, I found her last night, at her house. I think I've made a big breakthrough regarding the documents. She told me that Franjo stole a highly politically sensitive dossier from her father's study, which he in turn had taken from Izetbegović's office. But then she wouldn't give me the details of what was in it," Johnson said.

"Dossier? Could it by chance be the same set that Vic's asked you to track down?" Jayne asked.

Johnson leaned back on his bench in the southeastern corner of Central Park, near the zoo. "I've no idea. I mean, how many dossiers and documents would there have been in Izetbegović's office at that time? But she did say that these documents are dynamite and politically explosive. She says if the papers surface, all the Bosnians living here would be scapegoated and half the White House from that time would be hit by flying shit, from the president down."

"*What?* That all sounds very over the top."

"Yes, I know, I know. That's what I thought. She wouldn't or couldn't tell me what was in the actual documents, and she says she doesn't know where they are. So we're not much further forward. She also seems convinced that Franjo's dead."

"But she doesn't know for certain?"

"Correct, she doesn't know. Just guessing, as he's been off the radar since '93."

It had taken Johnson fifty minutes to walk from his hotel, the Vetiver in Astoria, across the Queensboro Bridge into Manhattan, and along East 60th Street to the park.

He propped his phone between his shoulder and his left ear, wincing at the pain that kicked in from the bruise on his torso. He took out the pack of cigarettes from his jacket pocket.

Johnson said, "She said she's going to send me a copy of her journal or something, where she wrote it all down. She said it would be easier to explain it all that way," Johnson said.

"Do you think she will?"

Johnson put a cigarette in his mouth. "Highly unlikely. I'm probably going to have to go back and see her again."

"Okay," Jayne said. "How are you feeling? Any better?"

"Still feeling bruised, and the forehead is still a mess, but the walk made me feel better—I'm in Central Park."

Jayne told him that she had been in touch with one of her old SIS colleagues in London who had ideas about how to track down Hasanović, but it would probably take her a couple of days at least.

"Hmm. All right, I'm not going to stay here long," Johnson said. "Hopefully I can get on the plane back tonight, in which case I'll be back there on Monday. Have you heard from Filip?"

"Only a text to say he's still in Split with his father."

"Okay. Let me know if there's any more developments. Talk soon." Johnson hung up and kicked the pavement in front of him.

He leaned back on the bench and finished his cigarette, then took out his phone again and checked his emails. He had been wrong. There *was* something from Aisha.

Johnson sat up and tapped on the email. The pain from his bruises seemed to suddenly recede. She had written a short note.

Thanks for visiting. As I said, I think Franjo is most likely to be dead. But I agree that if you think otherwise you should try and track him down and make sure justice is done. He got away with more than you'll ever know about. Therefore, I'm sending you a few journal pages, as promised. They tell a story. I think it is best that I do this—I would just cry if I tried to sit down and say it. There's not much, but maybe there's information in here that could help you.

She also included her cell phone number.

A PDF document and a photograph were attached in Aisha's email. Johnson clicked on the PDF first.

As it opened, Johnson could see it contained a black-and-white scanned copy of a handwritten journal entry, scribbled in untidy handwriting in a spiral-bound notebook. He flicked through it and realized she hadn't sent the entire journal, just selected entries from various days.

With occasional assistance from the online translation app on his smartphone, he slowly began to read the Croatian text.

Sunday, April 30, 1989. Strange but beautiful to think that Franjo and I will be married in another three months. He came around for lunch today. It's one of those weekends when my father is here at home, not working in Sarajevo. My mother treats Franjo like a son now. They don't mention the Muslim-Catholic thing, at least not to me. Funny that he still tries to call them Mr. and Mrs. Delić. "You'll be part of the family soon, so just call us Erol and Mirela," my father says with a smile. It's become a game. Zeinab thinks it's hilarious. She'll have her turn when she comes home with a fiancé. I'm learning English. My lessons are going well, and I'm becoming more and more fluent. My father's idea—he says he did the same thing when he was my age, and it was the best thing he ever did. I guess it paid off because he has an interesting government job where his English is so useful. Maybe I can do likewise in television one day!

Friday, July 27, 1990. Beautiful day today in Pobrežje. It's difficult to believe it's only 15km from Dubrovnik. It's a different world, so rural and peaceful, such wonderful views across the hills to the sea. We are going down to the beach tomorrow to swim and have a picnic. I'm spending today making two dresses, so relaxing. Franjo's stepmother used to be a dressmaker and has all the equipment here—a big sewing machine, even proper mannequins. He is so lucky to have a family holiday house here to escape to, and I'm so lucky to be married to him. Little passing traffic, just a few farmers driving tractors and trucks, that's all.

Thursday, April 15, 1993. I don't know where this is all going to end. Mostar is divided now and our marriage feels divided too. The Croats are in control of the western side of the river, and we still have the eastern side. Several Muslims going out to buy food were killed last week by snipers up on Hum Hill. I used to be at school with one girl who was hit. Franjo says we can't carry on, and he's going to leave. He's sure he'll get killed by Muslim mobs. It's impossible to talk to him now. He just speaks over me and looks at me with eyes that don't see and ears that don't listen. I can't even trust Franjo anymore. My father's certain he stole important documents from his study, and Franjo can't look me in the eye and tell me he didn't do it.

Monday, November 8, 1993. The worst day. The shelling of the Stari Most started today. I could hear it from our house: the whining, crashing, banging. It went on for hours and only stopped a short while ago, at 9pm. If this goes on much longer, the bridge will go down. I know it's Franjo's tank down on Stotina Hill that is bombarding the bridge that we all love. How can he do it? That was where we kissed for the first time, only five years ago.

What has happened to him? The man I loved became a military robot, acting without thinking or feeling, like so many other people around here. All of them fighting a senseless, illogical war that will achieve nothing.

Once we were married: lovers, friends—a Croat Catholic man and a Bosnian Muslim woman. Now he's gone and we're enemies. What nonsense.

This city is destroyed, a wreck. Not much food or water. People are scared to go out in the streets in case they get hit by Croat shells or snipers from the west, on Hum Hill.

There are only 25,000 people left here in East Mostar. We are all under siege now. I guess if the bridge falls, the fight that is left in the people here will disappear. It is the only link we have to the front line. Many of the boys I grew up with are now soldiers with the Bosnian army. They trained as dentists and accountants. Now they shoot to kill Croats. And me? Three times now I've done things I never thought I'd do and will never talk about. Never. We all have.

We will have to keep fighting here, because if we don't, we will die. There is only one choice. We fight to survive.

Johnson suddenly felt thankful that he hadn't grown up amid such turmoil and carnage. He tried to imagine what it would have been like but struggled.

He lit another cigarette and then flicked through the other pages. The next two entries were for a few weeks later.

Wednesday, December 1, 1993. I still can't write about how I feel. I've talked with my friends, some of whom have also lost their families. We get angry together, we get drunk together, then we grieve together and cry together.

Monday, December 20, 1993. Yesterday I left Mostar, maybe for the last time. I don't think I will go back. I have left my old life behind. The loss of my father, my sister, and now my mother has been too much to bear. I can hardly write about it. I feel guilty about leaving so many of my friends and neighbors in the hellhole that Mostar has become, but I feel I have no choice.

So, I'm alone now with my guilt.

The journey out was a difficult one. We first traveled on foot at night through a gap in the Croatian front line, and then after a long trek across the mountains in freezing weather, we got a lift on an aid truck.

I am fearful of writing down on paper exactly how I got out, in case this is read by somebody in the Croatian army. Others will follow me, I know, tomorrow and in the next few days, probably until the Croats realize what is going on and fill the gap.

I am now across the Croatian border near Imotski, and tomorrow I hope to get to Split. Then after that, who knows? I will definitely seek refugee status somewhere, maybe in America or Britain.

Thank God. Thank God. It seemed like a miracle that I got through the front line without being killed, raped, or robbed. Really a miracle.

That was it, six journal entries. Six snapshots of a life, spanning the gulf between happiness and tragedy, Johnson thought.

He clicked on the photograph. It was a picture of a young man, tanned, with dark curly hair and brown eyes, but with a distinctive thin black line running down across his iris from his pupil. So that was the coloboma that Petar had mentioned.

Johnson pocketed his phone and leaned back on the bench. An old man carrying a takeout sandwich shuffled past.

What to do next? Johnson sat and gazed across Central Park.

Come on, think it through.

What was Aisha trying to tell him from the select diary entries she had sent?

There was her bitterness toward Franjo over the way the war had torn them apart, plus her tremendous sadness at the loss of her family. Johnson wondered what had happened to them.

But she had also done, or had to do, things she was ashamed of. In that situation, it didn't take much to imagine what, Johnson thought, but she didn't seem the sort to take someone's life. Or perhaps she had. Maybe she didn't have a choice.

Looking at it in detail, she and Franjo had seemed happy in the beginning. It was clear she was close with the family she'd lost. The couple had tried to live a normal married life; Franjo's family had kept a holiday house near Dubrovnik where they'd had good times. He might want to check out that house; it was definitely a fresh trail to pursue.

Then there had been more affirmations that Franjo had destroyed the bridge. Then more tragedy, overwhelming loss, and finally, escape.

The hope in her final pages hinted at why she refused to risk the exposure of the documents' contents. She felt it threatened the life she'd built after the tragedy of war.

And yet, the excerpts from her journal raised almost as many questions as they answered.

Johnson found himself revisiting Aisha's words from the previous day. He took out his phone and flicked to the recording of their conversation, then pressed the play button.

"Honestly, my father should not have had them. In fact, he took them, stole them, from Izetbegović's office. They were foreign ministry documents that Izetbegović told him to destroy, but he didn't."
"Why not?"
"He realized their significance."

And then . . .

". . . half the White House from that time, from the president downward, would be hit by flying shit . . . "

Dynamite, indeed, Johnson thought. *Assuming it's true.*
He knew he had to find the documents. But how?

* * *

Saturday, July 14, 2012
   Astoria

It had taken Johnson multiple text messages and two phone calls—for which he took the precaution of using the relatively secure Skype service, given the CIA's interest—but finally he had persuaded Aisha to meet him for coffee that afternoon at the Ćevabdžinica Sarajevo café.

"Is this as close as it gets to home, this café?" Johnson asked.

"I guess so. There's quite a few Bosnians who live in this area, and we do meet here. That's why I rent that house just down the road. It's convenient. We go to mosque together, eat together, socialize."

Aisha stirred sugar into her coffee. "In fact, it's been fine here, at least until that Republican clown Spencer started stirring things up. He needs to keep his mouth shut; he's giving Muslims a bad name, causing a lot of bad feelings toward us. Perhaps there's been a tiny minority, whom we wouldn't even acknowledge as Muslim, that uses the Koran to try and justify their violent ways. But if Spencer carries on like this, he's going to generate so much hatred and resentment among a much wider group of Muslims, you know . . ." She left the sentence unfinished and shook her head.

Johnson cocked his head. "Do you find that people in the mosques here, even in New York, attempt to radicalize you?"

She pursed her lips. "Seldom, but I'd be lying if I said that never happens. There are groups and certain individuals who act as enablers, or leaders, and do that. Very much in the tiny minority."

"So has anyone tried to radicalize you?" Johnson asked.

Aisha sipped her coffee. "Not really."

She checked her phone for messages.

Johnson took advantage of her distraction to turn on his phone voice recorder and then got to the point. "I'm planning to fly back to Dubrovnik tonight. I would like to resolve this issue regarding Franjo and the documents—"

"Tell me why you're so determined? I told you, I think he's dead. If he's not, he's likely impossible to find. And all of this was twenty years ago, and it didn't happen to you, so why do you care?"

Her abrupt inquisition interrupted Johnson's flow and took him by surprise. "It's my job to track down those who have committed war crimes and bring them to justice, for one thing. Especially where there's been crimes against large numbers of people, such as human rights abuses or genocide. Far too many people across this planet have done awful things and are still running around free when they shouldn't be."

"Yes, it's your job. But why do you care?" She was insistent.

"It's a long story. One of my biggest influences stemmed

from my mother's experiences when she was in a Nazi concentration camp during the Second World War. She suffered a lot at the hands of SS commanders and guards, and that inspired me to do something. It was one reason I joined the Office of Special Investigations in DC. But it was also partly just because of the way I am, the way I think. These charismatic national leaders—like Hitler in Germany, or maybe Slobodan Milošević and Radovan Karadžić in Serbia and Bosnia—who somehow seize the moment, they create a movement against a minority in their own country. Frankly they've done things they should pay for. But it's also the hundreds, thousands of others who blindly follow them."

"Like Spencer, you mean?" Aisha said, cupping her chin in her hand and looking obliquely at Johnson.

"Spencer? Well, I don't think he's killed anyone or sent armies to drive people out of their own country, has he?"

Aisha shrugged. "Probably only a matter of time."

"Let's hope not. The real point is the people I've mentioned had people further down the chain who did the dirty work through choice, usually for their own gain, and who also need to be held accountable—like Franjo, if he's as guilty as you say."

"Yep, he is."

Johnson paused, debating how to get the conversation back on track. "There was a lot in your diary, and in what you said yesterday, that might help. I'd like to go take a look at this holiday house of his near Dubrovnik. How do I find it?"

Aisha took a paper menu from a holder, flipped it over, and took out a pen. She drew a rough map of a road heading inland from the sea. Then she drew a small square right on a hairpin bend.

"Ah, I see. You think he might be there? I really can't imagine so, but that's it. Pobrežje. A tiny place. The house is right on a sharp bend like that. I don't think you'll miss it.

There were five big pine trees in front of it, so unless they've cut them down, that's your landmark. It was a rough old road up to the village, though: single track with passing places. You'll need to go slowly. Mind you, that was twenty years ago."

"Okay, thanks," Johnson said. "So the house was Franjo's family holiday house? They all used it?"

"Yes, various family members. When I was there, Franjo said his stepsister, Natasha, had been visiting the previous week, before we came, with her little boy. I've forgotten his name."

"A stepsister? Really? Did you meet her?" Johnson asked.

"No, I never met her, but Franjo talked about them often. I remember he showed me photographs of her and the boy once; he resembled Franjo a lot. Natasha used to live in Dubrovnik. She was the secretary to the harbormaster in the port there. But she was a single mother, no father around, Franjo said. A difficult life, I guess. I've no idea what happened to them."

"Franjo's parents, both dead?"

"Yes, Goran, his father, and Mira, his stepmother, both died during the war. His brother, Šimun, and his sister Elena both died too."

"Hmm. Interesting. How did they die?"

"I don't know," Aisha said.

"I was sorry to read about your parents and sister. Can you talk about them? What happened?"

Aisha's eyes moistened again. She wiped them with the back of her hand and shook her head. "What's the point? Too painful. Lots of people lost their families."

Johnson nodded. "Also, I don't like to ask, but the things you did that you wrote about, that you can't talk about, were they—"

"No. They were not war crimes. It was wartime, Joe.

Everyone did things they don't want to talk about. People who were ordinary—fathers, mothers, children—went from their normal everyday lives to killing people to defend themselves and their communities, their friends, their families. After the war, they reverted back again, or tried to. That's war, what it does to people. I might be angry and bitter about things, but I'm not a hypocrite—I'll admit I did things, like we all did, to survive, but I'm not stupid. I know the difference between that and war crimes. I'm not a person of interest in the cases you're building."

Johnson felt stunned by her candor. "I didn't mean it like that."

"Then what did you mean?"

"I was going to ask if you've ever . . . talked about it with anyone. It's a burden to carry on your own."

She glared at him. "That's my business."

"Okay. I won't mention it again. And was it in character for Franjo to have just taken the documents from your father's study?"

"Sadly, yes," Aisha said. "He was an opportunist and dishonest."

"And now you really think he's dead? And you've no idea where the documents could be?"

"I've no idea where they are. And yes, he's got to be dead. There's been no trace of him anywhere. I did a lot of searching online, a few years ago. There was nothing."

* * *

Saturday, July 14, 2012
New York City

The plane climbed steeply out of JFK Airport. Johnson, in a

window seat, relaxed in readiness for the long flight back to Europe.

He was belatedly about to switch his phone into flight mode when the secure text message arrived from Vic.

Joe, some bad news. Watto is chasing those documents too, separately from me. Don't know why but will try and find out. Will call you as soon as I can. Vic

Johnson didn't hesitate. He dialed Vic's number and ducked down behind the seat in front of him in an attempt to get out of the flight attendants' line of sight.

Come on, answer it, answer it . . .

The line picked up. "Vic, I've just taken off and I've got about ten seconds before we're out of phone range. I'm heading back to Dubrovnik from New York. I'll update you later. Now, just tell me, what the hell—"

"I don't know, Joe, but I'm hearing Watto wants those documents very badly. You know how many pies he's had his fingers in over the years. It could be related to some current operation or could be something from the past."

Johnson wanted to ask for specifics but was mindful that first, all the passengers around him could hear every word, and second, the call would cut off any moment.

"So you're telling me two factions are competing for the same thing?" Johnson asked, hoping he was being vague enough. "That's damned typical."

"Sums it all up," Vic replied. "But I don't know if he knows I'm also after them."

"Come on, Vic, if you know about him, then what're the odds of him not knowing about you? Let's get real."

"Yeah, you're probably right, but I'm not sure. Anyway, I've got a few sources I can go to internally to find out a little more."

"Well, get onto it, quickly, can you?"

Despite his efforts to stay out of sight, Johnson caught a glimpse, between the seats, of a flight attendant waving her arms in his direction, in an attempt to get him to turn off his phone.

He deliberately shifted his eyes to the plane window and pretended not to notice.

"When you said it could be something current, what do you mean?" Johnson said.

"Well, the biggest issue in that part of the world is Syria. And Watto heads Syrian operations. A ton of weapons are being funneled to the rebel forces there by various routes—mainly through Saudi Arabia, Turkey, and so on—and they're coming from various places, of which Croatia is clearly one. Now, whether Watto might have an interest in that, I've no idea, but—"

"You think it's related?"

"Well, it could—but—" Vic's words became fragmented and broken as the call quality deteriorated. The aircraft climbed into cloud cover, and the lights of New York, now far below, disappeared.

"Hello, Vic, hello?"

The signal disappeared completely, just as a flight attendant appeared at the end of Johnson's row of seats, her hands on her hips, staring at him.

Johnson shrugged, held up his phone, and put it on his lap.

That bastard Watto is messing with my investigations again . . . There's just no escaping the damned guy.

CHAPTER TWENTY

Monday, July 16, 2012
 Port of Dubrovnik

"Natasha? Yes, she works here. She just went across the road for a coffee break a few minutes ago," the white-haired man said from behind his computer screen.

Johnson nodded and walked out of the old stone harbor-master's office at the Port of Dubrovnik, a mile and a half north of the Old Town. Three seagulls squawked and fought over an old sandwich that lay on the ground in front of him.

Johnson walked a short distance to his right until he could see Jayne, who sat on a bench under a tree on the street corner, seemingly buried in a novel. She spotted him, but a slight shake of his head, followed by a nod in the other direction, indicated to her that he was heading elsewhere and that she should wait. She returned to her reading.

On the large tree-lined island separating the north and southbound roads past the port, he saw a snacks and drinks kiosk with a group of tables and chairs on the pavement, shaded by an expanse of large blue sun canopies. Behind them, dominating the port, were three enormous cruise ships moored at the quayside. They stood in a neat line, towering high above the modern passenger terminal.

Johnson crossed the road and walked casually to the kiosk. The tables were largely occupied by groups of tourists: families and backpackers as well as smartly dressed older couples.

At the back, sitting by herself, was a tall woman in a white blouse and a navy skirt, reading a newspaper and sipping a latte.

Johnson drew nearer and watched her for a few moments. Her hair was slightly gray, and bags were visible under her rimless glasses.

She seemed about the right age. Johnson walked up to her. "Excuse me, are you Natasha?"

Her head snapped up sharply. "Yes, that's me."

"I'm really sorry to interrupt your coffee break. I'm Joe Johnson. I'm hoping you might be able to help me with something. I'm a war crimes investigator, and someone pointed me in your direction."

Natasha raised her eyebrows. "War crimes? What's that got to do with me?"

"Nothing to do with you directly, you don't need to worry," Johnson said. "Do you mind if I sit down, so I can explain? It won't take long."

The woman put down her coffee. "Okay, as long as it's brief. I really don't have long before I need to get back to work."

Johnson slid onto the chair opposite her. "That's fine, I understand. Now, it might come as something of a surprise, but I've been trying to trace your stepbrother, Franjo. I'm actually following up a lead relating to things he might have been involved in during the war in Mostar, in 1993."

"*Franjo?*" Natasha asked, leaning forward. "What sort of things do you mean?" She pushed her glasses up on her nose.

"Allegations that are probably quite similar to those leveled at many other war criminals in these parts: unlawful killings, torture, destruction of monuments, that kind of thing. Theft of important documents, possibly. He seems to have vanished, and I'm just speaking to those who were close to him—including family, where possible."

"I doubt I'm going to be able to help," she said. "I haven't seen him for nearly twenty years."

Johnson felt his face fall. Aisha must have been correct, then. Franjo *was* dead.

"How did you get my name and where I work?" Natasha asked.

Johnson tried to smile. He usually didn't reveal his sources of information, but in this case, he needed to quickly establish credibility with Natasha and hopefully get her talking.

"Franjo's ex-wife, Aisha, gave me your name," he said. "I saw her in New York. She went to the States after they split up, which must have been in '93. She only mentioned you in passing. In fact, she said you'd never met."

Natasha nodded. "No, we never met. It was difficult."

"I see. So you didn't even go to their wedding?"

"No."

"So you haven't seen Franjo for twenty years. Many people assume he's dead. Is that what you also think?"

"Oh, no," Natasha said. "He's definitely not dead."

Johnson felt a jolt of adrenaline. Natasha's voice was strong and certain. "He's not dead? You're sure?"

"Of course," Natasha said. "He's been in contact, very occasionally. Once a year, usually. Never says where he is or what he's doing. It's always quick; how are you, is work okay, that kind of thing. One-way conversation. He's not a nice man, unfortunately."

Johnson fingered the old wound in his right ear. This was a breakthrough.

"So why does he call, then? Is there a reason?"

Natasha glanced around the other tables. "I'm sure he has his own reasons. But he doesn't tell me."

"How does he sound? In good health?"

She shrugged. "Yes, same as he always did."

"And you've never seen him in all that time?"

"No."

"Do you have any idea where he is?" Johnson asked.

"No. I haven't got a clue."

Johnson's attention was caught by a dark-haired woman wearing sunglasses and a navy blue T-shirt who was sitting at a table in the corner nearest to the kiosk. He saw her glance in his direction, then immediately look away.

He refocused on Natasha and lowered his voice a little. "So just by way of background, can I ask, was it your mother or your father who remarried?"

"My mother, Mira, got remarried to Goran, who was Franjo's father, when I was about six. My own father died of cancer." She stopped and picked up her coffee. "Do I have to answer all these questions? Is it necessary? I do my best to put him out of my mind every day, so this sort of thing doesn't exactly help."

Johnson pursed his lips. It was interesting that Natasha had such an intense dislike for Franjo but took his call every year.

"No, you don't have to. I'm not police, just a private investigator. It depends whether you would like to see justice done in this particular case or not. Of course, depending on how the investigation proceeds, it may well end up being passed to the authorities."

Natasha said nothing.

"Did you have a good relationship?" Johnson asked.

She gazed toward the expanse of water to her right that formed the bay of Gruž, a natural inlet that housed the port and sheltered Dubrovnik's fleet of vessels from the Adriatic's winter storms.

"No, we didn't," she said. "We had a relationship once. We lived in the same small house. Now we don't have a relationship. Can I ask, are you making any progress with your inquiries?"

"Slowly," Johnson said. "I've traveled from here to Split, to Mostar, to New York, and back here again. I've tracked down three women, including you and Aisha, and I've made only marginal progress. I've no idea where he is, if he's living under a false name, or even if he's still alive. But a sniper tried to take out a man while I was standing next to him. Another man I was with has been murdered. I've been beaten up in the street. So something tells me to keep going." He gave her a wry smile.

She raised her eyebrows. "Doesn't surprise me, not at all. Not in this country. Sorry, I need to get back to the office. My boss, the harbormaster, has a busy afternoon, and so do I." She drained the remains of her coffee and stood up.

"Have you been working here a long time?"

"Yes, I've seen several harbormasters in that time, but I've stayed in my job, somehow. I like it, mostly. It's crazy busy in summer, quieter in winter."

Johnson got up. "I'll walk with you. I need to go that way. Do you have a phone number I could take, just in case?"

She stopped and studied Johnson. Then she took out a card from her purse and handed it to him. "My cell phone number and address are on there. I don't know why I'm giving you this, but I am."

Johnson read it. "Jukić? Is that your maiden name, or have you been married?"

"I've never married."

They walked across the road and back toward the harbormaster's building. Its old stone frontage, with green shutters upstairs and metal barred windows downstairs, formed a sharp contrast to the modern terminal building across the road. A few mopeds stood outside near some large flower tubs.

"You have a son, yes?" Johnson said.

She turned her head sharply. "Yes. He's grown up now."

"What's his name?"

She exhaled hard. "I'm sorry, I really don't want to answer any more questions."

"Just one more, sorry," Johnson said. It was something he'd deliberately left until last. "Did Franjo ever mention anything to you about important documents or a dossier of government papers?"

Now they were outside her office. "He did once. He said they were hidden," she said.

"Hidden? You know about them, then?"

"Yes. They were hidden somewhere secret. I don't know if they still are. That was a long time ago. He mentioned them once to me, I think by accident when he was drunk one night."

"Do you know where they might be hidden?" Johnson said, consciously keeping his voice from rising.

"You said that was the last question."

Natasha turned and walked into her office, closing the door firmly behind her.

Johnson thrust his hands into his pockets. He stood still for a moment, debating whether to go into the harbormaster's offices and try to continue the conversation. It was understandable that Natasha needed to get back to work, but he felt that that she was brusque because she didn't particularly want to be questioned further. There had to be a reason for that.

He thought better of going into the office and instead walked toward the bench where Jayne was still sitting. He parked himself next to her.

"Well? How did it go?" Jayne asked.

"One big breakthrough," Johnson said, "which is that Aisha was wrong: Franjo is alive. He contacts Natasha occasionally, but she has no idea where he is. He doesn't tell her. She doesn't like him."

Jayne leaned forward. "Alive! That's a big step forward," she said. "And the documents?"

"Well, I asked her at the end if she knew anything about a dossier of documents, and she said they were hidden. That's all. Then she walked off." Johnson threw up his hands. "Anyway, we have another port of call, don't we?"

The previous day, after Johnson had arrived back from New York, they had agreed they would head to Franjo's old holiday house in Pobrežje village once he had finished talking to Natasha.

He took out the small map that Aisha had drawn for him and glanced up, just as the woman in the blue T-shirt from the kiosk got up and walked to one of the mopeds outside the harbormaster's office. She removed a white helmet from the security box on the back and sat on her machine.

Johnson found himself wondering why Natasha had been so evasive about her son that she wouldn't even give his name. Maybe she thought Johnson might seek him out and give him the third degree.

Johnson took out a cigarette, offered one to Jayne, who declined, and lit it. And he realized he'd also missed a trick when she had talked about Franjo's periodic calls to her. *"He's been in contact, very occasionally. Once a year usually. Never says where he is . . ."*

Damn, why didn't I ask when he calls each year? When's the next one due? Christmas? Easter? A birthday?

* * *

Monday, July 16, 2012
Mosec, Croatia

Marco pulled his black Lexus off the narrow single-track road right at the top of the horseshoe-shaped bend and put it into first gear. He turned right and slowly edged the car up behind some rocks, then continued for a couple hundred meters until he reached some trees, out of sight of the road.

"Doesn't look like he's here yet," Marco said.

Boris put on his sunglasses, then got out of the car and walked across the baked dry earth until he got to the nearest tree. There he sat down, leaned back against its trunk, and lit a cigarette.

The sun was already high in the sky, and the ground felt warm to the touch.

Marco climbed out of the driver's seat and walked over to Boris. He looked at his watch. "He won't be long. I said between eight and quarter past, so there's a while yet." He also sat down next to the tree.

They waited in silence, both men taking long drags from their cigarettes.

Just then, there came the sound of an engine from the direction of the road, out of sight beyond the rocks. Its tone lowered and faded, then picked up again, remaining at a high pitch as it drew nearer.

"Here he comes," Boris said. "Just remember I'm Stefan to this guy. It's arms business, okay?"

Marco nodded. "Don't worry. I know."

An old long-wheelbase Land Rover Defender emerged from behind the rocks, steered around the row of trees and parked next to the Lexus. A man got out and limped slowly to them, a khaki green baseball cap pulled over his straggly gray locks.

He nodded at them unsmilingly. "Marco, Stefan. Thanks for bringing me out here. It's the asshole of nowhere."

Both Boris and Marco stood up, and the man reluctantly shook hands.

"Ratko, we're here precisely because it's the asshole of nowhere. Nobody lives around here. That's why I chose it," Boris said. "Is it all in the Land Rover?"

"Yes, all there, Stefan. Shall we unload?"

They walked across to the vehicle, and Ratko opened the rear door to reveal a number of rigid cardboard boxes of different sizes.

"It's split between the PROM-1s, which each include two rolls of trip wire—they're in the bigger boxes—and the PMA-3s, the flat ones, in these smaller boxes," Ratko said. "You'll need to intersperse them, probably in a ring around your target . . . wherever that is."

"Okay. Just show us the goods, so we're sure what's there," Boris said.

Ratko began to unload the boxes, and Boris and Marco joined in.

After they were all on the ground, Ratko opened the cardboard boxes, flapping back the lids so that Boris could see inside. He checked the contents.

"Okay, all there. Come with me," Boris said. Ratko followed him to the Lexus, where Boris took out a small black leather pouch, from which he removed a large envelope.

"All in euros," Boris said.

Ratko removed two bundles of banknotes from the envelope and counted them swiftly, flicking them between his finger and thumb in a well-practiced manner.

"Good, all there," he said. "I wish you good luck, and be

careful." Ratko shook hands with the two men and jumped back into his Land Rover.

Once he had driven off, Boris said, "Now down to work. We'll need to carry this lot to those trees, down the safe path, and then we can begin digging."

After half an hour, the pair had carried all the boxes to some trees further into the scrub.

Sweat dripped from each of the jowls under Boris's double chin. He took the map from Marco, scrutinized it, then walked over a ridge and into a natural bowl in the terrain that was roughly circular in shape.

At the base of the bowl, about eighty meters away, stood a small, low-slung stone barn in a poor state of repair, with a rusted red corrugated iron roof.

Just to their right, there were traces of what had once been a vehicle track to the barn. Two twin tire tracks fashioned from crushed stone and brick were largely overgrown with bushes. But Boris ignored the track and instead led the way, in a seemingly random fashion, between a few straggly olive trees and clumps of lavender, until they got to the barn.

The solid oak door stood in contrast to the ramshackle nature of the rest of the building.

Boris took a set of keys from his pocket and first undid a large main lock, then did likewise with a smaller latch-type lock. The door swung open and they walked in.

The walls of the barn were just a shell; there were no interior walls, just a rough floor made of square concrete slabs, and no proper ceiling. When Boris looked up he could see straight through the joists to the rafters, to which the corrugated iron sheeting was fixed.

There were four glazed windows, two at the front and two at the back, with no openings. Four thick iron burglar bars crossed each of the windows.

"Has your friend Drago finished repairing that safe yet?" Boris asked.

"He said he'd be finished with it last week," Marco said. "But then he called me to say he'd be a few more days. He's done his bit with the welding, but he needs to get his locksmith to refix the combination lock."

Boris grunted. "Well, tell him to get a move on. He's had it for nearly three weeks now. I don't like leaving the documents here if they're not in a safe. I want to get it back in here as soon as possible."

"That reminds me," Marco said. "Drago sent me an invoice for the safe repair." He reached inside his pocket and pulled out a folded sheet of paper. "Here you go, this is it. Three hundred euros. Actually a damned cheek, given he's not even finished yet, but we'll need to pay him in cash. I'll sort it, but perhaps you can refund me."

Boris took the sheet and scanned it. "He sent it to your workshop address? How does he know that—I thought you kept that secret?"

"Yes, I do. But he knows I'm sometimes there, because his own workshop is just down the road. He just dropped it in by hand, he didn't post it."

"Okay, then," Boris said. "Thanks. If you can pay him, I'll pay you."

Marco stared at his friend. "I really think you should just keep all those documents in a proper bank vault."

"Some of them are in a vault. But I don't trust the banks, never have, especially not after the raid in Zagreb."

It had been a near miss for Boris. Fifteen years earlier, he had been close to opening a safety-deposit box account with one of the large banks in Zagreb. But he had abandoned his plan after its vault had been raided by a gang who took tens of millions of euros' worth of jewelry, gold, and cash, as well as valuable documents.

He had considered storing the documents at his old family holiday cottage in Pobrežje but had decided against that; it would be too obvious a place to search if anyone ever learned he had possession of them.

Instead, he had then bought the old barn in the wartime minefield, 240 kilometres northwest from Pobrežje, under a false name, for a cheap price. Now his documents were split between the barn in Moseć and a bank vault in Dubrovnik. He also had scanned electronic copies stored in his password-protected online Dropbox account.

"It's safer this way," Boris said.

Marco shook his head. "I don't think so, especially now that they're demining the area."

"Yeah, but by putting our own mines in, we get around that, don't we?"

Marco shook his head. "Don't know. I don't like it."

Boris ignored him and walked to the wall, then withdrew a small crowbar from a narrow fissure between two stones. He strode to one of the paving stones near the far right-hand corner of the barn.

He placed the hook of the crowbar under the slab and levered it up until he could get his hands underneath, then slowly heaved it up and pulled it sideways.

There, under the slab, was a large cavity, roughly a meter square and fifty centimeters deep, lined with sheets of steel that were pocked with rust marks. Four large steel bolts lay loose in the bottom of the cavity, along with a cardboard document box.

Boris bent down and picked up the box, flipped the lid open, then shut it again.

"All okay. Still there," Boris said. "If your friend Drago gets a move on, we can get the safe put back in this hole, and everything will be secure again."

He replaced the box in the cavity and moved the slab back into position.

"Okay, let's go and get the real work done," Boris said.

He replaced the crowbar in the wall cavity and led the way back out of the barn and up to the ridge, where he stopped next to the pile of boxes containing the land mines.

Boris looked back toward the barn, then down at the ground. He stroked his chin thoughtfully. "We'll put the first one here."

He picked up one of the boxes containing the PROM-1 mines and removed a pack. He unwrapped the packaging and took out a dark green bottle-shaped device with a long gray neck and three short prongs at the top.

"Lethal," Boris said. "I saw a super-slow-motion film of how these little bastards work in a documentary that came into our studio," he said to Marco. "At that speed, you could actually see how, when the trip wire's pulled, the first small charge pushes the mine half a meter up into the air. Then the main explosive goes off and blasts metal around 360 degrees. If you're within fifty or sixty meters, it's game over. In real time, it all happens so quickly you can't see anything."

He grimaced, then gingerly handed the device to Marco and picked up a tool with a special blade for digging circular holes. "Have you got the detailed map? We need to mark exactly where we put each one and where the trip wires go, including the distances the wires run so we can find our way in when we need to."

Marco nodded and held up a clipboard on which was a large-scale map, with a ring drawn around a cross in the center. He sighed. "I don't know, this is going to be a lot of damn hard work."

"Yes, but it needs to be done."

Boris made a mental note to scan in and upload the

updated mines map to his Dropbox folder once they had finished.

Using the circular digging tool, he made a neat circular hole into which he placed the mine, so that only the prongs at the top were visible. Then he carefully pushed a small amount of dust and soil around it so it was scarcely visible.

Boris undid the two packs containing trip wires. He attached one end of the first wire to the top of the mine and then walked fifteen paces in one direction before fixing the thin wire, now pulled almost taut, to a metal rod that he stuck into the soil. Then he did likewise with the other trip wire in the other direction.

After that, he returned to the mine and carefully removed the safety collar around the top.

Boris stood. "One done. That's covering thirty meters, so I think we'll need roughly another twenty or so to put a full ring around the rocks. Then we'll put the PMA-3s near to where the trip wires are tethered. So if by some fluke somebody spots the trip wire for the PROM-1 and tries to pull it out, they'll get taken out by the PMA-3 instead."

"Neat," Marco said.

Boris handed the digging tool to Marco. "Here you go, your turn. Just be damn careful with these trip wires."

* * *

It took them some time to finish the work and move the remaining boxes to Marco's Lexus. Boris leaned against the back of the car and closed his eyes momentarily. The early afternoon heat was unbearable.

"That's a good job done," Boris said. "We only have a handful of the PROM-1s left and I think just three PMA-3s. Worked out well. I'm exhausted now. I need a beer."

Marco threw the digging tool into the back of his car, and

Boris heard him mutter something about how it would've been unnecessary if they'd used a bank vault instead.

"What did you say?" Boris said, turning around.

"You heard me. But it's done now, so it doesn't matter." Boris gave him an annoyed look.

Marco's cell phone beeped. He took it out of his pocket. "I'm surprised we get a signal out here in the middle of nowhere. It's showing one bar of reception."

He read his messages. "Shit, it's from Tomi. He's in Dubrovnik. The girl he's got tailing Johnson's helper has contacted him to say she saw her picking up Johnson from Dubrovnik Airport this morning. He's back in town. I think we should head straight down there."

Boris paused. "Yes, I think you're right. We'll have to. That's 250 kilometers. Three and a half, maybe four hours, I guess. We just need to make sure the girl tailing him stays there until we arrive then. Does she know what she's doing?"

"Yes, I'm told she does." Marco said.

Boris swore loudly again. "That didn't last long. He must have been in the States only a couple of days. I don't like this at all."

CHAPTER TWENTY-ONE

Monday, July 16, 2012
Pobrežje village, near Dubrovnik

The new paved road, dynamited and carved out of the steep rock cliff, twisted in a series of hairpin bends high above the bay of Gruž, where the late evening sun reflected off the shimmering Adriatic.

Two of the three cruise ships that Johnson had seen earlier that afternoon at the port were still there, way below them, but now looked like toy boats at their moorings.

As Johnson drove the car around the next sharp turn, a moped came into view as it navigated the corner below him; the low-lying sun glinting off the rider's helmet.

"It's a few more kilometers up here," Jayne said.

"Okay," said Johnson. "They must have upgraded the road to Pobrežje since Aisha was last up here. She said it was a rough single-track road with passing places."

They were now climbing high into the hills surrounding Dubrovnik.

In his mirror he again glimpsed the moped behind him, but it disappeared from view as he rounded another hairpin.

They passed a yellow sign marked Pobrežje, then a couple of run-down houses on the left. "This place isn't even a village," Jayne said.

"There's a row of pine trees up front," Johnson said. "Five of them, behind that old stone wall on the next hairpin. That must be it."

He pulled over to the side of the road some distance before the bend and waited for a few minutes, glancing occasionally in his rearview mirror to see if the moped rider was going to come back into view.

It was probably an unnecessary precaution, he told himself, but the rider had a similar white helmet to that of the woman he had noticed near the harbormaster's office after talking to Natasha.

But the moped didn't reappear. So Johnson restarted the engine and drove the remaining short distance to the bend, where he parked on a piece of rough ground.

The road cut left around the hairpin, but ahead of them, leading behind the pine trees, lay an unpaved single-track lane.

Johnson reached underneath the driver's seat and took out Filip's Beretta that Jayne had kept while he was in New York.

He dropped the magazine and racked the slide to make sure there were no live rounds in the chamber, then made sure the magazine was full, reinserted it, and checked the safety catch. He pushed the gun into his waistband and let his shirt hang over it.

Jayne unzipped her small backpack and pushed it toward him, its flaps hanging open. He saw a Walther lying inside.

"Where did you get that gun?" Johnson asked.

"A contact in Dubrovnik. An old SIS agent who I used to

deal with years ago when I was working here. I got in touch with him while you were in New York. He gave me a few other bits and pieces as well, stuff that might be useful to me while I'm here."

Johnson got out of the car. "I don't think you'll need it up here somehow. But that said, there was a moped tailing us for most of the way up. It disappeared just before we stopped."

"Maybe someone just coming home from work."

"Maybe. It must have turned off the road, but I don't know where. I just thought it was odd."

Johnson walked several steps back down the road and stood, watching and listening for a minute or two. There was no sign of any movement.

He rejoined Jayne. "Okay, let's take a walk," Johnson said.

They moved up the side of the road and started down the lane, which had tall grass growing in the strip between the two tire tracks on each side. Clearly it hadn't been used much recently.

Johnson's phone vibrated in his pocket as a message arrived. He took out his phone and read it. "It's Filip, wanting to know how we're getting on. He's still in Split. Not much use to us there, is he?"

Jayne grunted in response. It was now half past eight, and the sun had almost set over the Adriatic to their right. A glittering yellow path of gold ran all the way from the horizon to the shore.

There was a long paddock to the left, with grass that looked as though it hadn't been cut at all that summer. In the center, a few ducks waddled around near a pond that was almost dried up.

Ahead of them was a high stone wall, and to its right was an open gate that the lane passed through. A long wooden ladder was leaning against the wall.

Johnson and Jayne stopped when they reached the gate.

He took the diagram that Aisha had drawn for him from his pocket and examined it. "That must be the house up front there," he said.

About a hundred yards further along, just left of the lane, was a large, neglected two-story stone cottage; chunks of the cement rendering were missing, the walls were cracked, and there were holes in the roof where tiles had fallen off. To the right of the house, next to the lane, a garage had been built against the side wall, and to the left there was an outhouse.

A framework of rusty scaffolding, with planks at the first-floor level, ran along the front of the property. An old cement mixer stood near the front door, next to a pile of sand.

"One of the guys at the war crimes conference told me it was around this area where the Yugoslav army, the Serbs, were based when they were bombarding the Croatians in the western areas of Dubrovnik in 1991," Johnson said.

"Definitely looks like this house has been in a war zone," Jayne said.

They continued walking down the lane until they reached the house. Johnson went over and peered through a window. "Here's the kitchen. There's still some equipment in here: a fridge, a microwave. Looks filthy, though."

He moved to the next window. "There's even a TV in there, an old one. I think we should try and get inside, now that we're here. It crossed my mind that if Franjo has chosen to disappear, he might want some sort of bolthole in this country he can use as a base if he does return occasionally. Who knows? This is remote enough to probably tick all his boxes."

Jayne walked to the front door and pushed it firmly. "It's locked. The windows look secure as well."

"What about upstairs," Johnson said. "We could get up on that scaffolding and see if there's a way in there."

He climbed a wooden ladder that was propped against the

scaffolding and swung himself onto the planks that were fixed to the metal frame. He checked the road, watching carefully for any sign of movement, then walked the length of the building and tried each window.

"They're all secure. Unless . . . oh, hang on, what have we here. I might be able to pry this one open. It looks like a storeroom." Johnson picked at the window frame with his fingernails but couldn't get it to open outward. He took a Swiss army knife out of his pocket, flipped open a blade and worked it into the crack between the frame and the pane.

After several minutes, the window finally swung open with a rusty creak. Johnson turned around and looked down at Jayne on the ground. "We're in. Come up."

Jayne nodded. She pulled herself up onto the wooden planks and followed Johnson through the window.

The room had makeshift shelving on one side, stacked with old paint cans, brushes stiff with dried paint, and other decorating equipment. Johnson flicked the light switch by the door, and the single bare bulb hanging from the ceiling came on. "Someone's still paying the electricity bills," Johnson said and turned the switch off again.

He walked out of the room, along the upstairs landing, which had bare floorboards, and poked his head into the next room. It was empty apart from a small table on which sat an old computer processor unit with a chunky square monitor, covered in dust, and next to it a paint-splattered white router box.

Jayne followed him into the room. "Looks like a museum piece. See if it works," she said.

Johnson peered under the desk and turned on the plug switches to the computer and router, then flicked a switch on the side of the machine. A small orange light lit up on the side of the processor, and the monitor began to hum. After half a minute, the screen burst into life.

"What operating system's on there?" Jayne asked.

"It's got Windows XP . . . old but reliable," Johnson said.

"A bit like yourself," Jayne said.

The machine finally finished booting up. Johnson checked the hard drive. "There's nothing on here, only a copy of Microsoft Word, but no documents saved or created, no photos. That's strange," Johnson said.

"Is there a web browser on there? An internet connection?" Jayne said. She looked over Johnson's shoulder at the screen.

"Yes, Internet Explorer. And there's broadband. The router works. That's odd too—doesn't look like anyone's used the machine for years, yet they have a broadband connection. Weird," Johnson said.

"Any favorite websites saved, any browsing history?"

Johnson clicked a couple of times at the top of the screen. "No favorites. Browsing history . . . let's see, just one. Dropbox. That was accessed February 20, 2008, almost four and a half years ago. That's it."

He stood and folded his arms.

"Might as well try the Dropbox link if it's been used," Jayne said. She leaned over the machine and clicked on the link in the history list.

Slowly, the web page loaded. "Unfortunately, it's not saved the login and password," Johnson said. "Sometimes it does. Too much to hope for."

He was interrupted by a massive bang as the window pane exploded and fragments of glass flew across the room. There was a whining sound, and two large chunks of plaster fell off the wall next to the computer.

Before Johnson could move, there came another bang, a whine, and the plastic side and screen of the computer monitor shattered into pieces.

"Get down!" Jayne screamed and threw herself to the

floor.

Johnson hit the floor a second later.

Two more bullets smashed into the computer, which fizzed and then threw out a bright electrical flash, followed by a small bang.

"Let's get out of here," Johnson said. He crawled flat on his stomach across the wooden floorboards and through the doorway onto the landing.

Jayne followed. "Get into one of the other rooms," she said tersely.

They crawled down the landing to the next doorway. Johnson twisted to look at Jayne. There was enough light to see that blood was running down the right side of her neck from a cut, and then he noticed another cut on her ankle. He pulled out a handkerchief from his pocket.

"You must have been hit by some glass," he said, pressing the handkerchief to her neck. "And your ankle."

Jayne put her hand to her neck and then looked at it. It was covered in red. "Shit," she said. "I felt something hit me when the window went." She took the handkerchief and pressed it to the wound.

Blood from the cut on her ankle left a trail on the landing where she had crawled along.

"I'm going to put the light on in this room, so they think we're in there, then we'll move into the next one," Johnson said.

He reached up and flicked on the bedroom light switch, then ducked straight down again. Two bullets immediately smashed through the now illuminated window and the lace curtain hanging in front of it, then hit the wall, causing another hail of broken glass and plasterwork. The light bulb popped and went out.

"They're going to pepper anything that moves," he said. "We're sitting ducks in here."

CHAPTER TWENTY-TWO

Monday, July 16, 2012
Pobrežje

"Don't think I hit the bastard, but I got the computer," Marco said from the top of the ladder.

Boris removed the pair of binoculars from his eyes. Above him, Marco had his Zastava M76 propped on the top of a stone wall near the lane that led to Boris's old family holiday house in Pobrežje village.

"Good job. It's been years since I used that PC," Boris said. "I don't think there's anything on there, but I'm not taking the risk. I couldn't see Johnson or the woman. Could you?"

"Too damned dark," Marco said. "All I saw was the PC monitor, so I went for that. Then I hit the second room when the light went on. If they come out and break cover, we'll pick them off."

Boris glanced at Tomislav, who was sitting on a cinder block next to the wall, and Monika Kovač, who was perched on her moped. She had done a good job tailing Johnson while waiting for them to arrive from Moseć, he thought. As soon as she reported back to him that Johnson was at Pobrežje, he had known what they were there for. It seemed like a good opportunity to take care of the American and his helper while they were out in the country, well away from the city crowds.

Marco put his eye back to the scope mounted on top of the Zastava, which rested on a folded sweater.

"Nothing, no sign of them now," Marco said.

"Just keep watching," Boris said. "They'll show themselves at some point." He reapplied the binoculars to his eyes.

The group fell silent. Darkness was rapidly descending. An owl called from some trees to the left of the house.

Suddenly a light flicked on in the window nearest to the lane, at the opposite end of the house from the room with the computer.

Boris focused his binoculars on the window. He saw the thin net curtains in that room were pulled closed. A shadow flicked across the curtain, and a hazy image appeared behind it. Maybe an arm?

Then the clear silhouette of a head appeared briefly from the left-hand side and moved back again. Another silhouette appeared on the right side of the curtain and moved back immediately.

"See that, Marco? They're in there. Can you hit them?"

"Yes," Marco said. "I'm seeing shadows on the curtain."

The light remained on. Then the shadow of a head appeared again on the left, followed by another shadow from the head on the right.

Boris squinted through the binoculars. "Hit them," he said.

There was a loud bang. Through the binoculars, Boris saw the window glass explode inward, the curtain move, and the head jerk backward. Marco immediately fired again, and the other head disappeared.

"Got the bastards," Marco said in a calm voice. "Got both of them."

Boris was startled by a cracked, reedy voice from behind him, beyond where Tomislav and Monika were sitting. "Who are you and what are you doing with that gun? I heard shots. Are you shooting at that house? My husband is calling the police right now."

Boris turned to see through the gloom a small white-haired old lady standing on the lane, a walking stick in her right hand.

"It's actually my house," Boris said to the old lady. "We've had terrible problems around here with foxes. They've been killing our ducks."

He went over to her. "The only way we can get rid of the foxes is to wait until it's dark, when they come out to chase the birds, and then try and shoot them. I don't like killing animals, but sometimes it's the only way."

The old woman frowned at Boris and said nothing. She screwed up her eyes and furrowed her brow. "I'm not sure . . . You really shouldn't be doing that. You'll have to explain it to the police. They'll be here soon." Then she hobbled slowly back down the lane into the darkness.

Boris watched her go. "We'd better get out of here," he said to Marco. "The job's done anyway. I don't want to explain to the police why we were shooting the shit out of my own house with a sniper rifle or why there's two dead bodies in an upstairs bedroom."

"Yes, let's go," Tomislav said. "I'm not getting into all this. Come on, Monika, we're out of here."

Boris surveyed the house. "Marco, can you shoot that light out in the house first. It's going to attract attention otherwise."

Marco raised the rifle to his shoulder, squinted into the scope and took careful aim through the bedroom window, where a bare light bulb was still shining from behind the net curtain. He pulled the trigger.

From the house came the distant sound of a minor explosion, and the light popped out.

"Right," Boris said. "Now let's get the hell out of here."

Monika started the engine on her moped, put her crash helmet on, and handed the spare one to Tomislav, who jumped on the back. They drove off down the lane while Boris and Marco jogged behind them back toward the road.

Marco climbed into the driver's seat of the Lexus. Near to it was a gray Opel Astra, which Monika had identified as Johnson's.

"Hang on a minute," Boris said. "I'm just going to let the American's tires down, just in case."

"What do you mean, just in case? I just shot the bastard," Marco said, his voice rising sharply. "Come on, leave it. We need to get out of here, quickly."

"Okay, okay, go then." Boris got into the passenger seat and checked his watch. "I think we should head straight to Split. I've got a flight back to London tomorrow for a meeting with my editor that I can't miss. He doesn't know I'm here."

Marco rammed the Lexus into gear and accelerated down the mountain road, his tires squealing.

As they rounded the first hairpin bend, they heard the sound of a siren from farther down the hill. The flashing blue-red, blue-red of a police car roof light came into view as the vehicle screamed up the hill past them in the other direction.

"That was close," Boris said.

CHAPTER TWENTY-THREE

Monday, July 16, 2012
Pobrežje

Johnson was on his haunches and about to stand up when another bullet smashed into the light bulb in the center of the room and continued into the wall, bringing down another shower of plaster fragments and dust. It went dark.

"My God," he muttered and flattened himself to the floorboards again.

Being under siege, the dilapidated state of the house, and the knowledge that one wrong move could mean taking a bullet—it all combined to give Johnson a momentary flashback to the shoot-out in Jalalabad, in 1988, that had marked the beginning of the end for his CIA career.

"I thought they'd fallen for it," Jayne said from the corner of the room. She held Johnson's blood-soaked handkerchief firmly to her neck.

"Yes, I thought so after he hit the second one," Johnson said. "Maybe he's realized."

He picked up one of the two decrepit, battered mannequins that were lying on the floor next to him and pushed it against the wall, then did the same with the other.

Both mannequins had holes in their heads where the bullets had gone straight through the moth-eaten cotton covering and the polystyrene underneath.

"Don't know," Jayne said. "Good thinking on your part, but we've still got to get out of here somehow." She shot Johnson a sideways look.

Johnson gave a slight nod. "Have to just sit it out for a bit. He's definitely going to have to come in. He won't leave thinking he's left two dead bodies up here."

"Agreed," Jayne said. "Best option is to take him when he comes up the stairs, probably from behind that wooden cabinet on the landing. I could get a shot from just underneath it as his head appears."

Jayne tightened the strip of cloth she had wound around her ankle. "Of course, that's provided I don't damn well bleed to death in the meantime."

She removed her Walther from its holster.

They lay on the floor in silence for another five minutes. There was the faint sound of an engine starting somewhere away from the house, followed by what sounded like the squeal of rubber on the road.

Johnson looked at Jayne. "Hear that? Think they've gone?"

"Doubt it. Must be someone else."

"I'm wondering if we can get out through the back of the house then away down the far side of the paddock," Johnson said.

"Yeah, there must be a back door downstairs, or a window."

They both crawled to the top of the stairs and only then stood up, when they were out of sight of the windows. The house was lit only by slivers of light from the rising moon that slanted in through the windows.

Johnson, his eyes now adjusted to the darkness, led the way slowly down the stairs, which emerged into the living room area.

He moved through the kitchen, then turned to Jayne, who was just behind. "Here, we can go out the back door; we'll just unlatch it. Are you okay to walk?"

"Yeah, just about. I'll hobble."

Johnson clicked the door open and stepped outside onto ground that was covered in broken pieces of brick and concrete. He flattened himself against the rear wall of the house and looked to his left.

"We'll have to go this way, not up the lane—they'll be waiting there. Then we can go down the other side of the paddock. We can get behind that hedge. Nobody's going to see us there."

Jayne nodded.

They moved behind the hedge to the far side of the paddock, then kept inside the line of a long row of trees that ran down the eastern perimeter of the property as they made their way through the long grass back past the tall stone wall toward the road.

"There's nobody around. I think they've gone," Johnson said.

Then came the unmistakable wail of a police siren farther down the hillside. "Oh hell, somebody's heard the gunshots," Johnson said. "We'd better get out of here, or else we'll be hauled in for burglary."

Now they moved at a fast pace to the end of the paddock, just as a police car flew around the corner. Its roof lights flashed and its siren screamed as it sped down the lane toward the house, its suspension squealing at intervals.

"They'll check the house first. Can you run?" Johnson asked.

"I guess so. I'm not feeling too great, to be honest, Joe. And I'm leaving a trail of blood behind me. That cloth bandage has come off my ankle."

Johnson studied her with concern. "Okay, let's give it a try. If we can just get to the car, you'll be fine. Tell me if you need supporting. Let's go."

He broke into a jog through the long grass, Jayne stumbling behind.

When they reached the lane, Johnson glanced back. The lights on the police car strobed across the front of the house, the siren still blaring.

They jogged along the lane and within half a minute were back at the Astra. Jayne was looking ashen. The handkerchief she clutched to her neck was covered in blood, as was her shirt.

Johnson let out the clutch and shot off down the moonlit road. It was only when he was out of the village and around the bend that he turned on his headlights.

They had gone around the second hairpin bend when Johnson saw Jayne move out of the corner of his eye. She had slumped against the passenger door. Her head lolled sideways, and her eyes were closed.

PART THREE

CHAPTER TWENTY-FOUR

Monday, July 16, 2012
Dubrovnik General Hospital

Jayne winced as the needle pierced her skin.

"I think you'll need about six in here and a few in that ankle," the doctor said in his heavily accented English.

He pulled the thread through and slowly tightened it. "You were fortunate this cut in the neck just missed the artery. That will teach you to be more careful next time you try such a tricky repair job."

She had told him that the injury had occurred while she and Johnson were trying to mend a glass greenhouse at their holiday house. A pane of glass had broken and slashed her neck as it fell, catching her ankle as it hit the floor, she had said.

The doctor looked skeptical but said nothing.

Johnson buried himself in a magazine he had picked up from the waiting room.

"Your friend here says you passed out in the car," the

doctor said. "You'll need to take it easy for the next couple of days." The doctor finished stitching her neck, then moved on to her ankle.

Johnson stood up. "Jayne, I'm just going outside to make a call," he said. She nodded without looking at him.

He walked out of the doctor's cubicle into the reception area, took out his phone, and pondered for a few seconds.

Which one to try first?

On a hunch, he dialed a number.

"Hello?"

"Hello, Natasha, it's Joe Johnson. You'll remember me from this morning. I'm sorry to call late—"

"Thanks for the apology."

"Well, I—it's just that I need something urgently, and you probably can't help with this, but I'm a bit desperate, so I'm calling just on the off chance that you can."

There was a pause on the other end. "What is it?" she said.

"It's to do with the inquiry, about Franjo. Have you ever received an email from him?"

"No, never."

"Nothing at all? Ever?"

There was silence for a couple of seconds. "You want to try and contact him, I suppose. Several years ago I did get one about a bank issue. That must have been at least ten years ago."

"Could you find the email?"

"You'll have to wait. I need to look."

There was a long silence, followed by a thud, then the rhythmic clicking of a computer keyboard. Presumably Natasha was scrolling through her old emails.

After what seemed like an interminable period of time, Natasha came back on the line and gave him an address: blackbrown186543@hotmail.com.

"That was it," she said. "But it was in 2001, so I've no idea whether he still uses that address. Unlikely."

She was probably correct, Johnson thought as he took out his notebook and wrote it down. The address looked designed to be disposable and anonymous.

He sighed. "One reason I need it is because there's a website, Dropbox, to which I need access. I have a strong hunch Franjo might have used it to store information, but it requires an email log-in and a password. Obviously, people choose passwords based on places, names, and so on that are important to them. I was hoping you might be able to think of something he might have used."

Natasha gave a half laugh, then went silent. "You've really got nerve," she said eventually.

"Well, I need access for very good reasons, relating to probable criminal activity. Listen, we're not having this conversation, and you're not giving me any information. We can think of it that way."

Another silence. "I've no clue, really. I've only got one suggestion: Luka."

"Sorry, Luka?"

"Yes, Luka. The name. L-U-K-A. Luka."

"Is that it? Four letters? Any other letters or numbers attached to it?"

"I really don't know . . . I suppose you could add the number ten after it. I actually haven't got any idea. I'm guessing."

"Okay, I can try that. Luka10. Any other ideas? Is there a particular reason why it might be Luka?"

"It's just a name that might be meaningful, and no, I can't think of any others," Natasha said.

"Okay, thanks, I really appreciate it," Johnson said.

"All right," she said and hung up.

Johnson went back to the doctor's cubicle to find Jayne

standing, a wraparound bandage now covering her ankle and a large rectangular one taped to her neck.

"I'm extremely hungry. Can we get something to eat?" she asked.

Johnson nodded. "Yes, I'm feeling starved too. Let's do that."

"How was the call?"

"Informative. You know that Dropbox account, the one we saw on the machine in the house?"

"Yep."

"I've got a possible password, and an old email address for Franjo."

"A password and an email? Where from?"

"I just had a hunch to call Natasha. She really doesn't like Franjo."

* * *

Tuesday, July 17, 2012
  Dubrovnik

It was after midnight by the time Johnson finally checked himself and Jayne into a hotel, the Neptun on the Lapad peninsula. It was just down the road from the hotel where his Croatian visit had started twelve days earlier, the Valamar Lacroma.

Now, half an hour later, having taken a shower, he sipped a whiskey on the balcony overlooking the nighttime blackness of the Adriatic Sea and the Elaphiti Islands, the outlines of which he could just about make out under the moonlight across the water.

Johnson opened his laptop, which he had placed on the wooden outdoor table, navigated to the Dropbox website, and keyed in what he hoped were the correct email address and password.

Jayne walked out on the balcony past him wearing just a skimpy white camisole, with no bra underneath, and a pair of equally skimpy pajama shorts.

Johnson groaned. "Do you have to do that?"

"Do what?" Jayne said.

Johnson motioned at her body.

Jayne laughed. "It's a warm night. I thought the look would be spoiled by these bandages, so I didn't really worry about it."

"For the record, it'd take more than a few bandages to spoil the look . . ." Johnson muttered. Now he was having another flashback, this time to Islamabad in 1988 and the apartment where most of his brief affair with Jayne had been conducted.

Johnson shook his head, trying to refocus. The details Natasha had given him weren't working. "Damn, this password is no good."

"What did she give you?"

"Luka, then the number ten."

"Are you trying upper and lower case?" Jayne asked.

"Let's try with a lowercase first letter," Johnson said. "Nope, no good. To be fair, she did say it was just a guess. She didn't actually know."

He leaned back in his chair and sipped his whiskey. "We don't even know if the email is correct."

Jayne put her hands on her hips. "Just try it with the number first, then lowercase and then uppercase. Try all combinations."

Johnson turned back to the keyboard. "All right, digits in first, then uppercase . . ."

Five seconds later, Johnson whistled softly. "Well, I'll be . .

. how the hell did she know? She hasn't seen the guy for twenty years. Or so she said."

"So she said," Jayne said as she came around the back of his chair and looked over his shoulder at the laptop screen. Johnson felt her nipple rest on his right shoulder as she leaned in close.

He groaned again. "Jayne, I'm not complaining, but don't start a fire if you're just going to put it out again."

She chuckled. "How do you know I'm going to put it out?"

Johnson shook his head. "Okay, there's not much here, just a folder marked Moseć with a few documents in it. A couple of maps and a Word document."

"Moseć?" Jayne said. "That's north of Split. I went through that area once. Let's see those maps."

Johnson opened the first map. "What's this? A CROMAC MIS portal map?"

"Ah, CROMAC. They map and clear land mines. The Croatia Mine Action Centre. I dealt with them when I worked here, when they started."

"Looks like a map showing mined areas; presumably these areas marked red are the danger zones?"

"Yep, I'd guess so. Mines are a major problem around here. Loads of farmers, kids, walkers, and so on were getting blown up regularly in rural areas. I'm sure it still happens," Jayne said.

Johnson opened up the next map, which was much more detailed and showed an area just outside the village of Moseć. There was a circle marked around a dot in the middle, which Johnson estimated was several hundred yards off the road.

Jayne again leaned in behind Johnson again to look at the screen.

The third document was just a text file, comprising a set of short instructions.

Park behind trees down rough track, follow path past mini cairn to right of rock. Twenty meters straight to large bush, right ten meters to barbed wire.

It continued in a similar vein for four further paragraphs, describing what was very obviously a precise route through a minefield.

Johnson accidentally caught his laptop keyboard with his thumb and typed a Z at the top of the document. Jayne immediately noticed what he had done and pointed it out.

"You'd better erase that," she said.

He pressed the delete key. "You know what I think this might be?" Johnson said. "Those documents that Franjo stole from Aisha's father—the place where they're hidden. What else would it be?"

Jayne stood up straight. "Possibly. But it doesn't say that. And in this part of the world, who knows? Could be guns, ammo, whatever. Can you copy those documents to your laptop? Let's have another look at them in the morning. We need to talk to Filip about these."

Johnson turned back to the keyboard and copied the documents to his hard drive, then logged out of the Dropbox account.

She checked her watch. "It's half past one. Let's get some sleep. I'm absolutely exhausted."

"Sleep?" he asked casually, intending it as a joke.

Jayne eyed him steadily and raised her eyebrows. "Now who's starting a fire?" She paused and glanced at her bandages. "I'm too wounded, can't you see? And I'm not sure you quite know what you want from me, Joe . . . Is that a fair comment?"

With that, Jayne stepped into her room in the suite they shared.

She's right, Johnson thought. *Maybe I don't know.*

* * *

Tuesday, July 17, 2012
  Heathrow Airport

Boris was striding through the Heathrow arrivals hall when his phone rang. He read the number—it was Marco.

"What's going on?" he asked. "I just got off the plane."

"I was wondering if you'd heard anything from the police yet?"

Boris had thought it odd that there had been nothing in the Croatian media about the discovery of two bodies in a house in Pobrežje. He'd been checking all the news websites on his phone since his plane from Dubrovnik had landed.

But one thing was certain: police wouldn't be contacting him very quickly.

"That's unlikely," he said. "Remember I transferred the ownership of that house to an offshore company registered in Mauritius. There's no easy way for them to get contact details."

"Okay. So that means we won't have any confirmation?"

"No. The best thing is to keep checking news websites. It's bound to be reported at some stage. Don't worry about it."

"I'm not worried about it. It's just that I have this feeling—"

"Relax, Marco. We did well down there. You did a good job. Sorry, I've got to go. I'll call you later."

He hung up.

* * *

Wednesday, July 18, 2012

Washington, DC

"Why am I so keen to help Joe?" Vic said. "Well, first, I hired him for this particular job. Two, he saved my life once in Afghanistan. And three, Watto hates him. And anyone who Watto hates is my buddy."

"Fair enough. I was just wondering," Helen Lake said. She leaned her head on Vic's shoulder and lowered her voice to a whisper. "Nice to be having a lunch out with you."

Vic smiled. "You bet it is."

They sat in a neatly maintained Victorian garden adjoining the intricate brown-gray stonework and balconies of the Heurich House building, also known as Brewmaster's Castle.

Helen sighed. "Actually, you know, I don't know how much longer I can keep working for Watto. He's such a dog. Rude, unreasonable, never says thanks, always criticizes."

Vic nodded and snaked his arm around Helen's shoulder. "You put up with him remarkably well and don't grumble, usually. That's one of the many things I like about you—you're discreet with everyone at Langley, apart from me. I feel privileged you share the truth with me, and that's no lie."

Vic paused. "So what have you picked up that might help our friend Joe?"

"Well, it looks complicated," Helen said. "Watto has spent a lot of time talking to the guys in Croatia, Bosnia, and also Turkey and Saudi. He's had phone calls, teleconferences, you name it. He was in Turkey for a visit only a couple of months ago. An odd bunch of contacts he's got there in Istanbul, I can tell you. From what I can gather, he helps smooth the path for arms of various kinds to be shipped out of Croatia to Turkey and Saudi. From there, they go onward to help the Syrian rebels who want to bring down Assad."

Vic pursed his lips. "Just smoothing the path? Making sure they don't get interfered with? Is that what you mean?"

"No. More than that. I've seen paperwork that talks about a 10 percent cut to the facilitator, as they call it. Now, this is 10 percent of a multi-hundred-million-dollar contract, so we're talking a large amount of money. At the bottom of the sheet is an account number where the 10 percent should be sent. Some company registered in Bermuda."

"What's wrong with that?" Vic said.

"Nothing obviously wrong," Helen said. "It's just a gut feeling I have. Watto just seems to take an oddly hands-on approach to his Syrian responsibilities for someone at his level. He delegates far less than other senior people I've worked for. Not always, but just in some areas."

"Hmm," Vic said. "But he's not got a house that's out of line for someone of his age who's ridden the housing market up over the decades and has been regularly promoted, even if it is a government job. His lifestyle doesn't invite suspicion."

"Of course not. He's not stupid," Helen said. "I've never said anything to anyone. I don't have any proof. If I did say something and I was wrong, I'd be out of work. In fact, I wouldn't say it to anyone other than you."

Vic remained silent for a few moments. "Okay, so you're suggesting that the reason Watto is after the same set of documents that Joe's chasing for me is because it might throw light on something that he'd rather keep in the dark?"

"Like I said. It's just my woman's intuition based on what I see him doing, the meetings he has, and the way he operates. I could be wrong. But if large amounts of money are being funneled to him through some arms deal, I wouldn't be surprised."

Vic shook his head. "Shit. I don't know. But I'd best warn Joe what we suspect might be going on. He'll need to watch his back. Is it okay if I tell him?"

"Yes, you'd better do that, provided you can absolutely trust him."

"Yes, we can trust him all right. No problem with that."

"Good. Now, shall we go for that drink?" Helen asked. "You owe me one."

CHAPTER TWENTY-FIVE

Wednesday, July 18, 2012
London

"I've got the studio guys at CBA to confirm your plan," David Rowlands said. "So, you're all set to interview Patrick Spencer on Friday the twenty-seventh, at their headquarters in New York. They're happy for us to use their facilities near Penn Station. I think they hope we can do the same for them in London sometime."

"Excellent, well done for sorting that out so quickly," Boris said. "We haven't got long to plan this, so I'll make a start this morning. I'll get a couple of the researchers to pull together all of Spencer's recent speeches and stuff from his website. Then we can start building a grid of potential questions in different topic areas. I really want to nail him on a couple of things."

"Yes, absolutely," David said. "One thing I'd like to focus on is what he thinks the impact of his anti-Muslim rhetoric is going to be across the States. All the evidence says it's divisive and that it's triggering aggression among non-Muslims."

"Yes, so then if he tries to deny it, we hit him with hard evidence and make him seem either ignorant of what's going on or just an out-and-out liar," Boris said. He scribbled in his notebook.

David's secretary came into his office and put a latte in front of Boris and a tea next to her boss. "There you go—some refreshments."

"Thanks, Vicky," David said without looking up from his notes.

When she left the room he said, "We'll need to get the New York studio up to speed on what we want on the technical side. They've already asked if they can have some footage of your previous interviews so their set designer and lighting director, a guy called Tim Burroughs, can prepare."

David spooned sugar into his tea and stirred it, then glanced at the bank of monitor screens at the end of his desk, which showed their own SRTV programming as well as satellite TV news programs from the BBC, Sky, and CNN.

"So what's the plan for marketing the interview?" Boris asked.

He sat back as David talked him through the strategy, which, as he expected, was to market the interview just to advertisers over the next few days. They'd push it hard and sell as much airtime as possible but otherwise keep it quiet.

Then, for maybe three or four days prior to the event, SRTV would run some ads to grab the attention of viewers. It was a well-trodden road.

David sipped his tea. "Actually, with that marketing plan in mind, it would be useful to have some big exclusive story about Spencer a day or two before the interview, to generate some headlines and get some publicity."

Again, this was a proven formula. It had worked spectacularly well in the run-up to an interview Boris had conducted with the German Chancellor Angela Merkel in Berlin. The exclusive story that SRTV had run about her and the German presidential corruption scandal two days before the interview had doubled the forecast audience, and the company had sold a huge volume of advertising.

David tapped the desk. "Thing is, Boris, the ratings have slipped over the past year or so. We're getting fewer viewers per show on average. Things like the Owen interview definitely help, but the trend is down. If that continues, we'll be in trouble with the powers that be here. Funds are tight. We've been very generous with your contract both in terms of money and also the amount of time you get off between shows. If you want that to continue and to keep your profile, we need to deliver something really special."

David leaned back in his chair.

Boris sucked the end of his pen. "Hmm, I've been thinking along the same lines myself, actually. There is one thing we might be able to do. I've picked up wind of some documents that go back to Bill Clinton's time at the White House, when he screwed up US policy toward Bosnia during the war in the early '90s."

"That's your part of the world, isn't it, originally?"

"Yes, originally. But anyway, these documents, as I understand it, could throw Clinton in quite a bad light. He supported the Muslims in Bosnia and offered a lot of them refugee status or asylum in the US when they were being shelled to pieces by the Serbs on one side and then the Croats. That was when the Bosnian Croats and the Bosnian Muslims—the Bosniaks—were fighting each other."

"So how is that relevant now? And how's it relevant to Patrick Spencer? I don't get it," David said.

"It's partly the refugees. Spencer is bound to start ranting about immigration policies in that regard. And it's also how

Clinton, a Democrat, supported the *Islamic* government of Izetbegović. It'll get Spencer all heated up about his Christian principles and how Democrats are too liberal, helping Muslim countries and Muslim refugees that only want to destroy the States. See where I'm going? He'll lose it."

David shrugged. "You mean, to get Spencer worked up, you'll use these documents detailing how a past president supported an Islamic government in a war and then took in their refugees? Is that it? Do we really need the documents to do that?"

"No, we don't. But if we do it this way, it would be a good one to discuss with Spencer, given that Clinton's lovely wife, Hillary, is clearly thinking of running for president in 2016. He's bound to take some outrageous jab at Hillary. Republicans hate her. Democrats will defend both her and Bill. A double whammy, potentially."

"Yeah, that could be good," David said. "We'll just need to make sure we get the toughest possible story angle from these documents, then. Can I ask what your source is?"

"Not at this stage," Boris said. "I'm still waiting to get the documents, but it sounds promising. Dodgy practices at the highest levels—it's all in there and it's copper-bottomed, believe me. I need to go to Croatia to sort it out. I'll probably go tonight."

He paused. "If what I've got in mind comes to fruition it'll be an absolute blockbuster story. It'll go global. I'm not going into exact details now just in case it doesn't all pan out."

* * *

Wednesday, July 18, 2012
Split

. . .

Johnson and Jayne were on the outskirts of Split, heading toward Antun Simic's house, when Vic called from one of his burner phones.

"Vic, you're going to have to be quick—I'm driving," Johnson said.

"Don't worry, Doc, this won't take long. On a completely confidential basis, my friend Helen has come up with some info—on Watto."

"Your *friend* Helen?"

Vic ignored the jibe. He outlined what he'd heard about Watson's unusually hands-on approach to the Syrian arms sales, as well as the facilitator payments.

"We don't know for certain," Vic said, "but it's possible there's a link between those payments and why he's also chasing the same set of missing documents from Izetbegović's office that we are. Maybe if the documents surface, they could prove and therefore threaten the payments."

Johnson let the information sink in. "Okay, thanks, Vic. Don't worry, I'll take care of things at this end. I'm going to make damn sure he doesn't get to those documents before I do. I'll bust a gut to make sure of it. You know, it's about time someone blew the whistle on Watto. He thinks he's the Don Corleone of Langley."

"Yeah, you're not the first person to say that, Joe. But you'd be the first to do something about it—and then you'd have to hope you're not the last."

Johnson snorted. "Don't joke about it. He doesn't need an excuse, and I've been shot at too much lately. There's something I need you to do, though. When you spoke to me originally about this job, you gave me the name of the CIA man in Split, a guy called Alan Edwards. I haven't contacted him and don't intend to if I don't need to. But it would help to know on which side of the fence he sits. Is he in Watto's pocket?"

There was a pause. "I don't know. Good question. I do

know that Watto's worked with him, but whether he's put him on the payroll, so to speak, is another question. Leave it with me and I'll try and find out."

"Okay, talk soon. Thanks." Johnson ended the call.

"Get the gist of that?" he asked Jayne.

"Yep, I did," Jayne said. "And I've just had an email from one of my ex-SIS friends in London. They've been trying to track down what happened to Franjo Vuković during and after the war here. They think he went to Germany, but after that there's absolutely no trace. It's as if he disappeared off the planet."

"That's almost the exact phrase that Aisha used. But the thing is, unless he was killed and someone buried him in a hole somewhere, he would have had to change his identity. And doing that in Germany after the war here wasn't easy . . . Doing that anywhere in Europe wasn't easy."

Jayne nodded. "No, not easy. Unless, of course he had some high-level assistance in getting false papers, a false passport, and so on."

"High-level assistance?" Johnson said. "Maybe from some intelligence service well known to both of us, you mean, like the CIA?"

* * *

Wednesday, July 18, 2012
Split

Filip looked slightly disbelieving. "So, we're in for a game of Russian roulette, then. A minefield. Let me see that map."

"Okay—I just want one promise, Filip. There are no scoops, no exclusives. It's confidential until we have this resolved. Then you can write something afterward," Johnson said.

"You've got my word on that," Filip said. He turned the laptop around and scrutinized the Croatian Mine Action Centre map carefully. "Yes, these maps are updated regularly by CROMAC, so as it shows, there will be a lot of live mines there. We'll need a mine detection expert with us."

Johnson tugged at the old bullet wound at the top of his right ear. "Do you know anybody who could do it at short notice, like tomorrow?"

Filip sat and thought for a while. "There is an ex-Croatian army guy I know who's good. But whether he's available, I don't know."

Johnson told Filip to go check and watched him disappear inside his father's house to make a phone call.

He turned to Jayne. She had removed the large white dressing on her neck but still had a flesh-colored bandage covering the stitches that held her wound together. A large wraparound bandage was still taped to her ankle. Meanwhile, the area around his left kidney still ached from the beating he had received in Mostar. They made a good pair, he thought.

Filip reappeared. "Okay, my man can help us—his nickname's Mino, for obvious reasons. He doesn't like his real name to be known, understandably. He can do it tomorrow, if that suits you. But he's going to charge three thousand US dollars in cash for the day's work. It's up to you."

Johnson whistled. "Three grand?"

He raised his eyebrows at Jayne, who nodded. "Probably the going rate," she said. "We're not going down the DIY route with this. Charge it to your expenses with Vic."

"Okay," Johnson said. "Tell Mino we'll go with that. We start early tomorrow. I'm assuming he's trustworthy, and I hope you haven't told him exactly what we're looking for."

"No, I've not given him any details, and he's rock solid," Filip said. "He'll get us through, don't worry."

* * *

Wednesday, July 18, 2012
Split

Alan Edwards pushed his sunglasses up onto the top of his bald head and casually slipped a brown envelope across the counter of the Go-Cro car rental office. "See if that makes a difference," he said to the office manager, who wore a name badge that read Mate Glavas.

He swiftly slit the envelope open and peered inside, then closed it again. Then Mate carefully scanned the customer waiting area. Only one other person was there, and he was engrossed in a newspaper.

"Okay, just give me a minute," Mate said. He sat at his computer and tapped away for a few minutes.

Then he stood and returned to the counter. "It's a gray Opel Astra," he said in a low voice. "Right now, according to my GPS monitor, it's parked on Marasovića Street, about half way up. You're in luck—that's not far from here. I'll write down the registration number for you."

Mate scribbled on a piece of paper and pushed it across the counter.

"Like I said, we haven't had this conversation," Edwards said. "You've been very helpful." He nodded and walked out.

Edwards breathed a sigh of relief. After a day spent trawling around various car rental company offices in Split's city center and at the airport, he had almost lost patience. He would have put money on an American using one of the big international chains, Hertz or Avis, so he'd placed them at the top of his list.

But no. He'd tried all of them. Instead, Johnson appeared to have opted for the smallest outfit, a two-man operation with a fleet of just twenty vehicles, the company's website told him. Go-Cro had been the second to last on the list that Edwards had compiled.

The CIA man jumped into his black Audi and accelerated along Split's seafront toward Marjan, the hill overlooking the city at the western end.

Five minutes later, Edwards was making his way up Marasovića Street. "Gotcha," he muttered to himself when he spotted the Astra.

He pulled over underneath the shadow of a tree, waited five minutes, then got out of the car, and wandered up the road. While bending down to tie a shoelace, he managed to place a small magnetic GPS tracking device under the chassis of the rented Astra.

Then he returned to his Audi and settled down to wait.

* * *

Wednesday, July 18, 2012
   London

Boris sat in the departure lounge at Heathrow Airport and flipped open his laptop. His plan was to make a few notes to send to David confirming his intentions, at least in outline form, for the Spencer interview.

He checked his watch. He had forty-five minutes before his flight to Split. Time to write the email and then slip into the bar for a quick gin and tonic.

Boris started to type and then realized he already had

some outline notes that he had put into his work Dropbox account for access anywhere.

He logged onto the work account and downloaded the notes. Then he remembered he also needed to upload the revised minefield map from his laptop to Dropbox for safekeeping, so he logged onto his personal account.

He dragged the revised map into the folder marked Moseć. Just as he was about to log off again, he realized he also needed to update the accompanying Word file with brief instructions on how to negotiate the pathway through the minefield and to the barn. He had written the document over a year earlier and hadn't touched it since.

He was about to click on the document to edit it, but then something about the list of files caught his eye.

Alongside the title of the Word document, the next column read *Last opened on 17/7/2012 00:43 AM*.

Boris read and reread it, just to make sure. Then he opened the document. Nothing had changed.

But someone had clearly opened it. And it wasn't him. *Who the hell?*

Boris swore under his breath.

CHAPTER TWENTY-SIX

Thursday, July 19, 2012
Moseć

"Middle of nowhere," Johnson said as he braked to a halt. "Four miles of single-track road and one house. Not a single car."

"Welcome to Šibenik-Knin County," Filip said. They were high in the hills overlooking a plain on one side and a valley on the other. The ground was parched and rocky, with only a handful of larger trees.

Johnson examined the minefield map that he had printed out. "This is it, no doubt about it."

He slipped the Astra back into gear and drove slowly up a track that led off the road, the car's undercarriage catching occasionally on the uneven surface, and then parked next to some trees. Mino followed in a blue Jeep.

Johnson put his Beretta inside his belt, got out, and approached Mino, a barrel-chested man with a deep tan who wore a long-sleeved checkered shirt.

"We'll need to work as quickly as we can, but safely of course," Johnson said. "There's also a risk we could end up with company, given the way things have gone on this trip so far."

There came a series of loud, deep-throated barks from the rear of the Jeep. "That's my vital piece of equipment—Slobodan," Mino said. "It's his job to get us through the minefield today. You'd better go and make friends." He handed Johnson two doggie treats.

"A dog? Is he safe?" Johnson said.

Mino nodded. "Of course."

Johnson walked around the back of the car and opened the trunk. An enormous German shepherd jumped out, grabbed the treats off Johnson's outstretched hand, and immediately sniffed his crotch.

"Hello, boy," Johnson said. He started stroking the dog's ears.

Jayne walked around the back of the Jeep, and Slobodan repeated his crotch-sniffing routine. Johnson laughed. "That's a better option than mine."

Mino, who also had a gun in a holster at his waist, said, "Slobber's my best. He was trained in South Africa, and I've had him for a year now. He's a machine once he gets going—absolutely loves this job."

He reached into the back of the Jeep and removed a cardboard box, which he handed to Johnson. He gave Jayne another box and threw a backpack over his shoulders. "I'll go up front. You carry these and Filip will be the rear gunner, just in case."

Mino took the maps and printed instructions out of Johnson's hand and studied them. Then he rolled up his shirtsleeves, revealing muscly forearms. "Just a few words on safety. You all need to follow precisely where I walk, so we'll move slowly. Concentrate hard. If you somehow find that you've strayed off the path I'm setting, don't move, stand still, and call to me. I'll come and get you back on track. If that happens, it's important that you all stand still. If you've any doubts, just ask me. Okay?"

Everyone nodded.

"Okay, let's go," Mino said.

He led the way down a faintly marked path, with Slobodan in front of him in a red harness on a lead, nose to the ground. "Most dogs get confused in high-risk areas like this if there are too many mines. They like to keep it simple and sniff one at a time. But Slobber here doesn't have that problem. He concentrates well."

Johnson followed him, with Jayne and Filip behind.

"Footprints here—see? Someone's been through not too long ago," Mino said. He pointed to a series of large boot-prints in the dust. They passed some more trees and approached a ridge.

Suddenly, Slobodan stopped dead and sat. He looked at his master.

"Uh-oh, what have we here," Mino said. He stepped forward and carefully surveyed the ground in front of them, looking right and left.

Mino took a treat from his pocket and gave it to Slobodan. Then he got down on his haunches and continued to look. "Bastards," he said in a low tone. Then he pointed to the base of a bush to his left. "See it?"

After staring for several seconds, Johnson saw, sticking slightly above the ground, a three-pronged fin shape. Mino edged closer and pointed again for the benefit of the others.

Then Johnson also saw a minutely fine trip wire that ran from the top of the mine at shin height across the path and into some bushes. It would have been almost impossible to spot without the early warning given by Slobodan.

"I see it—just," Johnson nodded.

"The shitheads have put down PROM-1s," Mino said. "Can you believe it? They're nasty little bastards. If we'd walked through that trip wire, we'd be crows meat by now. They're a nightmare to disarm, so I'm not going to even try. I'm going to find where the trip wire goes and remove it."

Johnson gave a slight involuntary shiver. He knew about PROM-1s from his time in the region in 1999.

Mino turned off the path at right angles, then inched his way with Slobodan leading as he followed the trip wire. Then Slobodan suddenly stopped and sat again.

"These guys have done a proper job here," Mino said. "They've mined the ground next to the trip wires as well as the path. That's a nasty trick. If you follow the trip wire to pull it out at the other end—bang! Okay, we know their tactics now. I can work around that."

He carefully stepped around the half-buried mine and slowly pulled out a thin metal pole to which the trip wire for the PROM-1 was attached. Then he walked back to the mine and placed the loose wire on the soil near the visible prongs. "Okay, let's keep going."

They continued another twenty yards to the ridge. An old, decrepit-looking single-story stone barn with a rusty corrugated iron roof was visible at the bottom of a natural bowl in the terrain.

They had gone only another ten yards when Slobodan stopped dead and sat down again. Mino swore, then went through the same procedure. "Another damn PROM-1." Again he moved the trip wire out of the way.

This time, once Johnson, Jayne, and Filip had passed through, Mino carefully replaced the trip wire, which led to a mine five yards left of the path. Johnson asked why he had done it.

Mino pursed his lips. "Security. You said some guys might show up while we're here. You never know. If they have to disarm one or two of the mines, it'll slow them down and give us a chance to get out, or at least prepare." He patted the handgun in the holster at his waist.

Mino studied the map again, then drew Johnson's attention to a line on it which marked the edge of the circular ridge that ran around the bowl-like area in front of them.

"I think the spot we want is that barn. Has to be," Mino said.

Jayne folded her arms. "Yes, you're right. It'll be in there or nearby. Hopefully that's not booby-trapped."

Mino shrugged. "We'll go and find out."

Johnson stared at the stretch of ground between them and the barn, which was at least seventy yards away. There was certain to be another bundle of mines before they got there. He hoped that Mino and Slobodan continued to work with the same surgical precision as they had done so far.

* * *

Thursday, July 19, 2012
Moseć

Edwards walked slowly up the track, following the tire marks left by Johnson's Opel and the blue Jeep, until the two vehicles came into view, parked behind some trees.

The Zagreb chief of station placed his hand on the Beretta M9 that was holstered on his belt and surveyed the trail of footprints around the cars until he had worked out where the group had gone.

There were four sets of prints. One set must belong to Johnson—whom Edwards had seen emerging from the house on Marasovića Street in Split; he had recognized him from the photograph sent by Watson. The other two must belong to the woman and the man who had been with Johnson as he left the house. The fourth set must belong to the driver of the Jeep, whose identity Edwards also didn't know.

There were also animal prints, unmistakably those of a large dog, which must have been in the back of the blacked-out Jeep.

Edwards stopped to think. He had taken extensive precautions to avoid being spotted as he tailed Johnson's Astra out of Split. He knew that Johnson would be watching out for surveillance.

The Astra had stopped at a service station until the Jeep had arrived. Edwards had parked at a truck stop across the road and had waited until the two vehicles got back on the road again. He had gotten a brief glimpse of the Jeep driver but had no idea who he was.

He had trailed them as they continued north for around an hour up the D1 and then the D56 roads until they turned left down a single-track lane.

After parking, Edwards made his final approach on foot through some bushes. He enjoyed both surveillance and countersurveillance activity and was equally adept at both. Here, the prints in the dust made his task easy in one respect.

But his concern mounted after he passed two signs, written in Croatian, which left no doubt as to the main danger in this particular stretch of countryside.

Both had a skull and crossbones logo within an inverted red triangle with a message underneath that could not be clearer: *Ne Prilazite: Na Ovom Području Je Velika Opasnost Od Mina.*

He had seen similar signs elsewhere in the Balkans and had no need of the Croatian learned in his biweekly classes to know the meaning.

"Keep Out: Danger From Mines in This Area."

Edwards halted. He knew Johnson was trying to find

some highly sensitive papers that had been hidden for some time. That was most likely the reason he was now wandering into an extremely dangerous remote minefield.

Given there were four people to contend with, all presumably armed, and a big dog, the odds were not stacked in Edwards' favor.

But what was it his boss had said?

We can't afford for anyone to get their hands on those papers . . . There's a promotion in it for you.

Watson had been very clear that Edwards should do whatever was needed to retrieve those papers.

He stood and scratched his chin. He had been stuck in Zagreb, something of a CIA backwater, for almost three years. Thoughts of a bigger job, maybe in Moscow or a large European capital, went through his mind. Maybe Paris or Berlin.

He couldn't afford to upset Watson at this juncture.

Almost without making a conscious decision, he began to walk slowly up the poorly defined path where the trail of footprints led.

* * *

Thursday, July 19, 2012
Moseć

It had taken them some time to cross the ground to the barn. Mino had carefully dealt with four more PROM-1 mines, coiling the trip wires and placing them at the side of the path.

Johnson put on a pair of thin rubber gloves and handed pairs to the others. Then he banged his fist on the large oak door to the old barn. "We could just blow it in, but I don't particularly want to leave a calling card."

He scrutinized the battered old corrugated iron roof, which came down to just above head height. "Could we get in through the roof?"

"We could try," Mino said. "We could unscrew a couple of those metal sheets at the bottom, then wedge them up enough to get through. I just need some wood or something to hold them up."

He dipped into his bag and took out a screwdriver and a few attachments; then he walked around to the back of the barn and came back a minute later holding three lengths of wood. "These'll do the job."

Jayne eyed an iron drainpipe attached to the wall at the corner of the barn. "I think we can shimmy up that pipe."

Johnson nodded. "I think best I go in there with Mino. You and Filip had better wait here. Just knock on the door twice if you see anyone."

It took Mino several more minutes to clamber up the drainpipe and unscrew the roofing sheets. He eventually managed to prop them up sufficiently with the wood to create a two-foot gap through which he could climb.

Johnson followed, feeling glad that he had made some effort to keep trim at the gym. He clung to one of the horizontal wooden purlins that stretched across the rafters from one side of the barn to the other. Then he reached down and grabbed a length of climbing rope that Mino had knotted to one of the joists. Johnson used the rope, which had knots at intervals, to lower himself. He landed on his feet next to Mino in the gloomy interior of the old building.

The interior walls, like the outside, were composed of a rough unplastered stone surface. The floor consisted of concrete slabs laid over crushed brick.

Johnson looked around. "It's basic, that's for sure," he said.

Mino grinned. "There's hundreds of these old semi-abandoned barns and cottages all over rural Croatia. Most of them were wrecked during the war. You can pick one up for a pittance if you want a restoration project."

"Or somewhere to hide something," Johnson said. "We'd better go over this place quickly. If there's anything in here, it has to be in a wall cavity or maybe under the floor. There's nowhere else. I'll do the walls, you do the floor."

He took a small flashlight from his pocket, turned it on, and went to the other end of the barn. Then he began to sweep the beam slowly and deliberately over the rough surface of the wall.

After fifteen minutes, the only thing he had found was an old crowbar that had been wedged deep into a crack between two of the wall stones. They carried on searching.

About five minutes later, Mino called to him. "Hey, Joe, come over here. Check out this paving stone. It's been moved. See, there's tiny scrape marks around the edge. They look recent."

Johnson joined him and examined the floor slab on which Mino's torch was focused. He was right: there were minute signs of activity.

He scoured the room, then picked up the crowbar, which he had extracted from the wall crevice. "Let's see if we can lever it up with this," Johnson said.

But then it crossed his mind that the slab might have been booby-trapped. "Pity we can't get Slobodan in here to check this out," Johnson said.

The two men stood silently for a short time, weighing the risk.

"Frankly, I doubt they'd have booby-trapped this slab," Mino said. "If it went up, the whole house would be blown up with it."

That was true. But Johnson felt his stomach turn over as he maneuvered one end of the crowbar under the slab, then pushed down on the other end of the bar. The slab rose enough for Johnson to get his fingers underneath and lift it.

Mino shone his flashlight into the cavity below.

The unexpectedly large hole was lined with metal sheeting. At the bottom lay four large metal bolts and a document box made of thick cardboard.

"Surely that can't be it? Or maybe it is. I was expecting something more secure," Johnson said. He had envisaged a steel vault or a safe or something similar, not just a hole in the ground.

Johnson picked up the box, then flipped its lid open. Inside was a bundle of yellowing papers, some of them bound together with lengths of string. Most were typewritten.

"These are all in Serbo-Croat. What's that say, at the top? Bosnia Ministry of something or other, isn't it?" Johnson pointed to the header of one of the documents.

"Yes. Bosnia and Herzegovina Ministry of Foreign Affairs," Mino replied.

Johnson flicked quickly through the papers. He looked at Mino and grinned. "This has got to be it. Let's get out of here."

* * *

Thursday, July 19, 2012
  Mosec

The path led through bushes and past a couple of trees. The footprints continued, but there was still no sign of anyone. Working on the assumption that if he planted his feet where the fresh prints were, he should be safe, Edwards continued toward a ridge ahead of him.

Suddenly, Edwards heard the very faint sound of voices drifting on the breeze that blew toward him.

He crouched next to a bush, then edged forward until he reached the top of the ridge. There he cautiously lifted his head until he could see what lay beyond.

Roughly eighty yards ahead, at the bottom of a natural bowl in the terrain, stood an old stone barn.

At the right-hand side of the barn, one of the iron roofing sheets was curved up at the bottom, supported by lengths of wood.

Outside the barn door stood the man and the woman he had seen with Johnson when they emerged from the house in Split. A large dog, probably an Alsatian or a German shepherd, lay next to them.

It was obvious to Edwards what was going on. He remained there for some time, just watching. The man, woman, and the dog outside the barn hardly moved.

Then at the top of the barn wall, from underneath the iron roofing sheet, a man appeared. It was Johnson. He straddled the top of the wall, swung his legs over, then lowered himself to the ground, using a drainpipe as support.

Then the Jeep driver also appeared from under the roofing sheet, clutching a small box. He passed it down to Johnson on the ground. Then he reached behind him, pulled up a length of rope that he threw to the ground, then lowered himself down the drainpipe.

Surely, Edwards assumed, the box contained the set of documents that Watson wanted.

He scrutinized the ground in front of him. A variety of bushes, olive trees, and other undergrowth dotted the ground between him and the barn, but he could see a clear, narrow trail of footprints in the dust.

Edwards calculated that provided he stuck closely to the prints, he could continue at a crouched walk through the bushes and probably get quite close to the barn without being seen.

There was a sizable clump of scrub between him and the barn. From there, Edwards was very confident that given the cover and the element of surprise, he could accurately take out all four of them with his semiautomatic.

The unknown factor was the dog. Would it smell or hear him? The wind was blowing toward him, which reduced the likelihood, but Edwards was uncertain.

He half stood and started to edge slowly forward until he drew near to the clump of bushes, ahead of the ridge.

Just then, he heard the dog bark. The sound made him instinctively look up. He saw the dog was on its feet, facing his direction, its tail in a rigid curl over its back. It let rip with a series of loud, aggressive, deep-pitched barks, interspersed with snarls and growls. The damn animal must have either smelled or heard him.

Edwards cursed to himself, and in a moment of confusion, involuntarily stepped forward, his focus on the dog rather than on the trail of footprints in the dust and his foot placement.

Through his trouser leg, he felt some resistance against his shin as he moved forward.

There was a small explosion just to his left.

Edwards had just whipped his head around in reaction to it when there came a much greater, deafening blast.

It was the last thing Edwards heard.

CHAPTER TWENTY-SEVEN

Thursday, July 19, 2012
Moseć

The three men and Jayne were left momentarily stunned by the ear-piercing blast that echoed around the bowl-shaped depression, sending shrapnel ripping through the bushes and grasses to within yards of where they stood.

Johnson was the first to recover his faculties. His mind flashed back to his conversation with Vic the previous day about Watson also chasing after the set of documents.

Surely it isn't Watson himself up there. Could it be Marco or Franjo?

"Shit! Whoever triggered that will be fox supper," Mino said, visibly shaken. "We'd better go check."

Again letting Slobodan take the lead, he went back along the path, carefully making sure he didn't stray from the trail of footprints they'd made earlier. When he reached the bush, he stopped.

Johnson caught him up, then saw the mangled and bleeding body lying on the ground. "My God," he muttered. The man's face was pulped and almost unrecognizable, while the upper torso oozed blood from a series of large puncture wounds.

After taking a few seconds to compose himself, Johnson handed the document box to Mino and carefully stepped over to the body. He put on his rubber gloves.

In the corpse's right hand, still being grasped firmly, was a Beretta.

Johnson bent down and went through the man's pockets. There was a set of car keys, which were undamaged, and a thin wallet, which had a hole ripped through it by shrapnel. There was also a spare magazine for the Beretta and a cheap cell phone.

Inside the wallet was a bank card and a handful of notes. Alan R. Edwards was the name embossed on the card.

"Unbelievable," he said. "CIA. It's their damned Zagreb station chief, Alan Edwards."

Jayne stood, hands on both hips, staring at the body. "Bloody hell. Watson must have sent him," she said.

Johnson nodded. "I'd guess so."

He turned on Edwards's phone and scanned the call register, which was empty. There were no contacts stored and no messages. A burner phone. He gave a thin smile.

Johnson replaced the phone and wallet in Edwards's pocket and put the car keys in his own pocket. He momentarily thought of taking the Beretta, which was standard issue for CIA operatives in the field, but decided not to. It would probably be traceable and maybe even had a built-in GPS tracker.

He removed his rubber gloves, took the documents box back from Mino, and placed it carefully into his bag. "We need to get moving, quickly. If someone comes, we're in trouble. You do realize this is going to cause a diplomatic nuclear war. Langley will go ballistic."

"Hang on a minute," Mino said. "First we need to screw that roof panel back as we found it. Then I'm going to replace the trip wires as we leave. All of you stay still."

Mino handed Slobodan's lead to Johnson, walked back to the barn, shimmied back up the drainpipe, and used his screwdriver to restore the corrugated iron roof panel to its original state.

On Mino's return, they retraced their steps along the narrow path and to the top of the ridge. Every so often, Mino paused and replaced the trip wires that he had removed earlier.

As they drove back down the track, they passed a black Audi, which had clearly belonged to Edwards. Johnson stopped, put his rubber gloves on again, and used Edwards's keys to open the Audi. He gave it a quick search, but the car was immaculately clean and contained nothing of interest. Johnson locked the vehicle and threw the keys underneath.

They drove on, back to the main road, the D56. About fifteen seconds after they turned onto it, a black Lexus 4x4, traveling far faster than the speed limit, flew past them in the other direction.

Johnson, surprised at the Lexus's speed, glanced in the Astra's mirror just in time to see the car brake hard and swing left with a squeal of tires onto the narrow lane from which they had just exited.

* * *

Thursday, July 19, 2012
   Mosec

. . .

Boris stood at the top of the ridge and surveyed the scene below him. "What the hell's gone on here? Someone's trodden on one of our mines. There's body bits everywhere."

He took a few steps forward, then turned to look at Marco. "It's either some idiot hiker, or someone chasing our documents. It must be whoever owns that black Audi parked on the road."

Boris walked down the shallow incline to where the mangled remains of a human body lay. He edged his way carefully around the corpse and stood, hands on hips. That was when he noticed the gun in the man's hand.

"Hikers don't normally carry Berettas, do they?" Boris muttered. He prized the gun from the man's hand and checked that the gun's chamber was empty and the safety was on.

Marco scanned the path in both directions. "I don't know what the hell's been going on. Several people have been along here. You can see different footprints. And a dog's paw prints."

Boris went through the man's trouser pockets, which were soaked with blood, and pulled out a phone and a wallet, which he flicked through. "Alan Edwards. Who's he? I think I've heard the name somewhere."

Boris pocketed the gun, the wallet, and the phone, then continued on toward the barn at the bottom of the dip, carefully stepping over the trip wires as he went.

At the second one, Marco bent down. "Someone's moved this wire," he said. "It's not as taut as when we left it, and the pole's in a slightly different spot."

When they reached the barn, Boris unlocked the door. He strode to the far wall, retrieved the crowbar, and used it to open the underfloor cavity.

Then he uttered a kind of primeval roar, jumped up, and kicked the floor. "Bastards! *Bastards!* The papers have gone."

Marco walked to the cavity and looked down. After several seconds, he said, with some finality, "It's Johnson."

"It can't be, you shot—"

"I don't know, I don't think I did," Marco said. "I had a strange feeling. The way those bodies fell back when I shot them through the window—there was something not quite right. I tried to tell you on the phone."

Boris glared at him. "What the hell are you talking about? There was nobody else in the house."

"They just didn't look right. I don't know how to describe it. I didn't like to say at the time because I felt a bit stupid."

"I was watching that window through the binoculars, and you definitely hit them," Boris said.

It was then that Boris remembered: his mother's old dress-making mannequins had been stored in that room.

But surely not?

Marco shrugged. "I might be wrong—I hope I'm wrong—but it's my gut feeling."

Boris grimaced. "Either way, I *told* you, it's that damned safe. If that idiot Drago had finished the repair on time and we'd got it back in here, this wouldn't have happened."

"You've got copies of the documents."

Boris stood up. "Yes, I've got electronic copies, but that's not going to be any good for what I've got in mind. I need the *originals*. And I need to be able to prove they're originals, otherwise they're worthless. And more to the point, if it *is* Johnson, what's he going to do with them? That's my concern."

Marco spread his hands. "I think it is Johnson."

Boris was about to rebuke his friend again, when another thought struck him. "There was an odd thing. Last night at the airport, I found someone had been into my Dropbox folder and read the instructions on how to get into the minefield. But if that was also Johnson, how the hell did he get into it?"

Marco folded his arms. "The 'how' of it isn't really important anymore—it's done. Is there anything in the documents that could blow your cover? Will he be able to track you down in the UK?"

Boris bowed his head. "Just trying to think it through. There's no mention of me or you in there, nothing that incriminates us or references any involvement. And there's no onward trail that could lead to any of our addresses. I've made sure of that. So the answer is no. But I don't want to take the chance, so we'll have to try again to get rid of Johnson. He's got to go. There's too much at stake."

"You're certain there's nothing on either of us in those documents?"

"Absolutely certain. One hundred percent."

Boris bent down and replaced the slab over the floor cavity. Then he returned the crowbar to its spot in the wall. "Come, we've got to get out of here," he said. "I don't want police coming here and linking us to the death of that guy out there."

"All right. Where to next?"

"First we need to check if Johnson really is alive."

CHAPTER TWENTY-EIGHT

Thursday, July 19, 2012
Split

"Aisha was right. These are pure dynamite," Johnson muttered as he leafed through the documents in Antun's living room.

Still wearing the dust- and mud-covered clothes from the minefield expedition, he sipped his coffee and passed the papers to Filip.

"I've got the gist of these, but can you translate all the detail?" Johnson asked him.

The bundle consisted of several dozen slightly yellowed papers, nearly all of which were official documents, on Ministry of Foreign Affairs notepaper. Many of them were dog-eared and bound together with pieces of string running through holes punched in the left margins. Most were type-written memos, although a few were roughly handwritten. A couple were in some form of shorthand.

Johnson pointed to one handwritten document, headed IRAN. "Let's do this note first."

Filip placed it on the table. "It's from someone in Izetbegović's foreign ministry. Looks like briefing notes or something." He began to read out loud.

Army ill-equipped vs. Karadžić, Serbs.
Arms from Tehran—go.
USG/POTUS will not interfere with flights. Unofficial
CONFIDENTIAL—against UN/US policy.

Johnson leaned forward. "So weapons were coming in from Iran to help Izetbegović and his Muslim government? From *Iran*? My God."

He paused. "And it basically says that Bill Clinton's crew gave them the green light, behind the scenes. Is that right?"

Filip nodded. "Yes, it sounds like a tacit go-ahead. There's another list detailing various weapons—automatic rifles and ammunition, antitank missiles, land mines, and other gear—with prices. And there's a final note: it says Izetbegović okay to all."

Johnson shook his head. He was certain that if the US had opposed such a transaction with Iran, it wouldn't have happened. That would be the same Iran that, if he recalled correctly, Clinton once described as a state sponsor of terrorism. He knew that Clinton had given Iran a tongue lashing for sending arms to terrorist organizations, including Hamas on the West Bank.

"I don't believe this. It sounds like Clinton told the Bosnians and the Croatians he didn't have a problem with them importing weapons from Iran?" Johnson asked.

"The White House just looked the other way, according to this," Filip said.

Johnson nodded. "That figures. They would never put that kind of thing down on paper."

Jayne tapped her fingers on the table. "I can see why that CIA guy was after these documents. They must be petrified of this lot getting into the public domain. *The Washington Post* would have a complete bloody party with these."

Filip picked up another sheet, this time typewritten. It was from the Bosnian ambassador in Iran and detailed how he and the Croatian ambassador, who was also working in Iran and was also a Muslim, had arranged to create a pipeline that enabled the delivery of weapons and heavy artillery from Iran to Bosnia through Croatia.

Filip turned over the page. "Listen. This states that there were a number of people in both Croatia and Bosnia who facilitated the delivery of the weapons. And in the absence of cash payments, they were given clearance to take a portion of the weapons delivered."

"Go on," Johnson said. "Does it name them?"

"No, but it does say that these payments to individuals ranged in value between two and three million dollars each. Oh, wait a minute, it says there were eight individuals involved."

Johnson stood up, his hands on his hips. "Between two and three million dollars," he repeated slowly. "I'm just wondering whether our friends Franjo and Marco were among the recipients of this arrangement. There has to be some closely linked reason why they've been keeping these documents under such close guard? Does it say what these individuals did in return for the payments?"

Filip shrugged. "Doesn't say exactly. Facilitated the delivery, whatever that means. But a note at the bottom says that according to information received from Erol Delić, these eight people were suspected of removing far more weapons than the quota value allocated to them. They were thought to have creamed off as much as 30 to 50 percent of the total amount. So, basically, those bastards have filled their boots."

He glanced at Johnson. "Might explain how Marco made his money. And it might add another nail to his coffin if police catch up with him over Petar's murder."

Johnson tugged at his chin. "Yes, it certainly would. Interesting. Well, if that's the case, we can perhaps do our bit to pile on the evidence. I'd say if that kind of arrangement had been agreed, with payments of that size in the shape of weapons, it might also have been noted by the Bosnian spooks. They had people at high levels in every ministry, every government office—I know that."

He knew from his time in Bosnia previously that the government and military intelligence organizations were unlikely to have let that slip through without recording who had benefited. They were quite scrupulous over that type of thing. He made a mental note to check in with his old intelligence service contacts.

Filip continued to read. "This goes on to say that an unnamed US Pentagon defense adviser requested that all written documents referencing Clinton or other White House officials should be destroyed because of the implications. It says there are more details in appendix C, and in brackets is the word *mujahideen*. But there's no appendix C to this document."

He pointed to an identical stamp on the front of several documents over which someone had scribbled a signature. "See that stamp? It says 'Urgent: Shred Immediately.' The person who signed them is Haris Hasanović, foreign ministry secretary."

"Haris Hasanović?" Johnson said. "That man again."

Filip turned over to the last page in the pile, which was a single handwritten sheet. "This is an odd one," he said. "It refers to additional documents which are held in a safe-deposit box at the Dubrovnik branch of an Austrian bank. And it names the keyholder."

"What's the key holder's name?" Johnson asked.

"It just says Luka."

"Luka?" Johnson said. He jerked up. "Did you say *Luka*?"

* * *

Thursday, July 19, 2012
Split

Before leaving Split, Johnson wrote two encrypted emails. One went to his old Bosnian intelligence contact, Darko Beganović, whose job now came under the Intelligence-Security Agency of Bosnia and Herzegovina. The other was to Bogdan Novak, now at the Military Security and Intelligence Agency in Zagreb.

Both emails asked the same question. Was there anything in the files of either organization that might corroborate and confirm the importation of arms into Bosnia and Croatia from Iran during 1992 and 1993?

In particular, Johnson asked, was there anything that might confirm whether two individuals, Franjo Vuković and Marco Lukić, had been among those rewarded for facilitating such transfers by being allowed to skim off a portion of the weapons?

Johnson added in the emails that it would be worth checking locations such as the Croatian State Archives in Zagreb, where the *Zbirka Dokumentacije o Ratu u BiH*— the "Collection of Documents on the War in Bosnia and Herzegovina,"—were housed.

Both archives had proved useful to him in the past. They had been relocated from Split to Zagreb after the war and included a large number of HVO records. In addition, Darko, he thought, might be able to worm his way into the top-secret classified files at the Ministry of Defense archives in Sarajevo.

To Johnson's relief, Darko replied almost immediately.

Hi Joe, good to hear from you. And good that someone's finally investigating the free-for-all that took place when the stream of aircraft carrying arms from Iran started arriving in the '90s. It was like kids in a sweet shop at that time. I promise I'll get onto this for you as soon as I can. Good luck with it! Darko.

Twenty minutes later, Johnson was at the wheel of his Astra, Jayne in the passenger seat, accelerating onto the highway that led south to Dubrovnik.

"There's something about that Natasha woman," Johnson said. "She gives me a password that gets me into Franjo's Dropbox account—and what is it? Luka. Then we get a bundle of documents with a note about more documents in a safe-deposit box, and who's got the key? Someone called Luka," Johnson said.

They had left Filip behind in Split, as he said he needed to see his lawyer to resolve some paperwork relating to his release from prison.

"It's a pity we don't have someone to tail Filip, frankly. I'm still worried about his intentions toward Marco," Johnson said.

Jayne reclined in her seat. "Agreed, but we don't have the resources, so that's it." She paused. "How about if, first thing tomorrow, when Natasha's gone off to work, we pay a visit to her house. Check it out."

"Yes, that's not a bad call," Johnson said. "From my meetings with her, I don't think we're going to make more headway by a direct approach. She was pretty reluctant, even if she did help. Also, we don't have much time. Once Franjo realizes those documents are missing, he's going to be after us —along with Marco, I'm sure."

Johnson glanced over his shoulder at the pack of papers sitting on the seat behind him and pushed his foot down harder on the accelerator.

* * *

Thursday, July 19, 2012
Astoria

Aisha sat on a mat at the back of the mosque with Adela and listened intently as the imam got into the meat of his speech.

"The enemies of Allah are plentiful, especially in this country, but there is one more than most who has been in the public eye recently," he told the rows of men and women who had turned up for Thursday evening prayers.

"I don't want to name names," he said, "but he seems keen to label all Muslims as terrorists. You all know whom I'm talking about. Well, this is what I say. It's the role of Muslims to accept peaceful offerings, peaceful thoughts, and peaceful actions when others offer them to us."

The imam paused and thumped the side of the wooden minbar from which he was preaching. "But when our families, our communities, our faith, and our Allah comes under attack, then it is our role to fight back and to fight back hard."

There were several murmurs among those sitting on the floor in front of him. People were shaking their heads.

Aisha and Adela exchanged glances. The mosque, just off 31st Avenue in the middle of Astoria, was fuller than normal, Adela had told Aisha.

The imam continued, "If they want to call us Muslim terrorists, then fine—let's show them what Muslim terrorists really are. Let's be good Muslims and be good terrorists. You might as individuals think you are all unremarkable people—but you're not. You are worthy, fine Muslims who can become great in the eyes of Allah. Go, do it."

Two men near the front suddenly got up and walked out. One of them called back over his shoulder as he left. "You're wrong. You'll give us all a bad name with that talk. It's not what Allah wants us to be."

Several others rose and followed them out.

Aisha's immediate thought was that they were right. And furthermore, the imam was taking a considerable risk, given that the FBI and police were known to have cultivated informers in some mosques.

But the imam seemed unworried, and his talk continued for another half an hour in a similar vein. By the end, only about a third of the original congregation remained. Aisha noticed that many of those who remained frequently muttered to their companions and shook their heads at some of the rhetoric. In her experience, that was a fair reflection of the views of the Muslim community in which she was involved. The vast majority, like her, were against violence.

At the end Adela said, "See, I told you it would be worth coming along. Inspirational, isn't it? Makes you feel proud to be a Muslim in the face of that spite that Spencer keeps throwing in our direction."

"Up to a point. Not what most people in there were thinking, though," Aisha said.

Adela shrugged. "That imam's having a few smaller meetings at his home over the next couple of weeks, and you can come if you want to. The discussions get a bit more, um, advanced and practical, in terms of how we can fight the fight, if you know what I mean."

"What are you trying to tell me?"

"What I'm saying, Aisha, is that you should come along and see how you can best serve Allah in this community when, like the imam says, we are all coming under attack at the local level and national level."

Aisha raised her eyebrows.

"There will be people at these meetings who will be able and willing to obtain whatever equipment any of those attending require," Adela said. "They'll not only obtain the equipment, but they will give you all the help and tuition and expertise and encouragement you need if you want to learn how to use it. Do you understand what I'm saying?"

Yes, Aisha knew what her friend was saying. "So, would you do anything to help this imam's cause, if someone pushed you?"

"You know me," Adela said. "It's my cause too. It wouldn't take much. What about you? You weren't exactly an angel during the war back home, were you? You've been there, done that, sort of?"

An angel? Nobody Aisha knew had been an angel during the war. It was more a question of doing whatever was necessary to keep herself and her family alive. She had lived with the consequences since, though, and tried not to think too much about it; otherwise she tended to sink into bouts of blackness that sometimes continued for weeks at a time. In her mind, the acts of violence she had committed in the distant past had been for personal reasons, not religious. Her family, her neighbors, her friends, and her city had been under attack, and she had retaliated.

"It was war. We all did things," Aisha said and averted her eyes. "But at the moment I've no interest in going down that route again. I feel strongly that we must do something to counter the poison Spencer spreads, but I don't want to get involved in violence—not again."

"Well, if you change your mind, let me know."

They walked out of the mosque and into the lingering summer evening sunshine outside. It was still warm. New Yorkers were milling about in cafés, restaurants, bars, and parks to enjoy one of the best days of the summer so far.

CHAPTER TWENTY-NINE

Friday, July 20, 2012
Dubrovnik

The one-way street lay high above Dubrovnik's Old Town, whose red roofs and church towers, all surrounded by colossal stone walls, were laid out below him. Johnson wished he'd brought a decent camera.

He parked next to a pair of pine trees down the street from the address written on the card that Natasha had given him, put on his sunglasses and his baseball cap, and settled down to wait.

He turned on the radio and found a local news bulletin in Croatian, of which he could understand enough to make sense of most of the stories. One report was about a man who had been killed by a land mine in the Moseć area the previous day. He had apparently parked his car in a remote area and had gone for a walk through terrain that was clearly marked with warning signs about mines. A farmer had found the body after spotting the man's car.

What made Johnson sit up was the final sentence of the report, stating that no identification had been found on the man's body and efforts were ongoing to find out who it was.

Who took the wallet? Probably not the farmer.

Johnson turned the radio off and focused on the house. It was the left one of three that were joined together, wedged onto a small plot set into the hillside. It was built of white-painted brick, narrow at the front, but it went up three stories and stretched back some distance.

An old stone wall and a pine tree marked the left boundary. Between that and the house was a small terrace with a wooden arbor and trellis, over which sprawled a large vine plant, giving plenty of cover, Johnson noted with relief.

At about half past eight, he saw a woman emerge from the front door, close it quickly behind her, and descend the steps to street level. It was Natasha.

She checked her phone, put it in her handbag, and crossed the road to a parking bay, where she climbed into a white Volkswagen Golf. A minute later, she drove up the road and out of sight.

Johnson waited another twenty minutes, did several checks up and down the street for any sign of local activity or surveillance, then strode confidently to the house and up the steps.

For the plan he was about to put into action, he and Jayne had agreed he should go solo. She would remain on standby in a café, and if he didn't return by half past ten, she would come and track him down.

Over the years, Johnson had acquired many skills; not all were legal, but they were useful when deployed with a moral motive. At least, that was how he justified their use to himself.

One of those skills was opening door and window locks.

Natasha's front door was a typical modern plastic

composite-style affair—solid, yes, when correctly secured. But based on the speed with which she exited the house, Johnson suspected she hadn't locked it properly with a key but had merely clicked it shut.

He removed a pair of thin rubber gloves from his pocket, put them on, and tried the door handle. Sure enough, when he pulled it up and down, he could hear the hook bolt mechanism moving inside. It was secure enough to stop a normal person getting in but not a burglar with a modicum of knowledge.

Johnson pushed down the handle to disengage the bolt then took out a thin bladed tool from his bag, inserted it between the door and the frame, and wiggled it until the latching bolt pushed back.

The door swung open.

Johnson walked in, checked that his handiwork had left no mark on the door or the frame, and clicked the door shut behind him.

Natasha's house was immaculately tidy, but the long rug covering the hallway floor was threadbare, and the walls were in need of a lick of paint.

He moved into the kitchen at the rear of the house. It was clean, but there were no luxury appliances, just a basic microwave and a kettle, an old stovetop coffee maker, and a battered old dishwasher. Clearly the harbormaster's office wasn't paying her a fortune.

Similarly, the living room contained a bulky, outdated widescreen television instead of a modern flat-screen model. There was no satellite TV box. On the walls were a few landscape prints and a couple of faded black-and-white photographs of what looked like Dubrovnik many decades earlier. But no personal memorabilia was on display at all.

Odd, Johnson thought.

He went back to the hallway and up the stairs. There were

two bedrooms and a bathroom. The first bedroom, the largest, was clearly Natasha's. A pair of jeans sat neatly folded on top of a chest of drawers, a folded ironing board stood up against a wardrobe, and a bookshelf in the corner contained a few novels. It also had two framed photographs.

Johnson walked over to take a closer look. The first photograph appeared to be of a school athletics team: ten boys and a couple of girls who looked as though they were probably all in their mid-teens. There was no label to give any indication of who they were, but Natasha must have had a reason for having this picture in her room.

He picked up the picture frame and turned it over. There was no label. Johnson sighed, replaced it on the shelf and glanced around the room.

The other photograph showed a youngster with short dark hair, a confident broad face and a firm, slightly pointed chin. Johnson looked back at the athletic team photograph. The same boy was standing in the middle of the back row.

Johnson had a sudden thought, remembering his own children's school photographs. He picked up the framed team picture again, flipped back the four clips that held the image into the frame, removed the cardboard back, and took the photograph out of its enclosure. Now a line of tiny print at the bottom of the white border was visible—the photographer's indexation code. There was a school name, Gimnazija Dubrovnik, followed by a seven-digit number, and then two words: Jukić, Luka.

Johnson felt his scalp prickle as he read the name. *Is Luka her son?* He must be. She had never married, or so she had said. So he must have taken her surname, Jukić.

Johnson stared out the window.

Further documents in a safe-deposit box . . . it names someone who has the key . . . Luka . . .

He replaced the photograph and moved into the second

bedroom, which was also quite tidy. A couple of posters of the Jamaican sprint stars Usain Bolt and Yohan Blake hung on the wall, together with a picture of the Hajduk Split soccer team. A pair of running shoes lay on the floor, and a few CDs were scattered on the desk. This must be Luka's room, then.

There was a chest of drawers and a bedside table. He squatted on his haunches next to the table and opened the top drawer slowly. He found a few banknotes, a pair of headphones, a Swiss army knife, a compass, an English-language dictionary, and a passport.

Johnson picked up the passport and opened it. The name read Luka Jukić. The photograph looked as though it had been taken in his late teens.

Johnson realized he hadn't gone through Natasha's room properly. He walked back through and opened the chest of drawers, but it contained only clothing. The top drawer of a bedside table contained a Bible, a well-thumbed English phrase book, and an iPod with headphones. Natasha clearly lived a sparse existence.

At the back of the second drawer was a velvet-covered box. Johnson took it out and looked inside. There was a gold ring and also a flat brass key, engraved with a six-digit number on one side and *Erste Credit Bank* on the other.

Johnson had seen a few of these in his time. It was a bank safe-deposit box key.

He placed it on the bedside table and used the camera on his phone to take pictures of both sides of it from several angles. Then he removed a small box containing a soft wax material from his bag and made an imprint of the key in it.

He carefully replaced the key in the velvet box and stood up.

Johnson decided he had what he needed. Or did he?

He scratched his chin. He could get a copy of the key

made. But how would that help if ID was required at the bank, as it almost certainly would be?

And now he remembered that access to deposit boxes always necessitated a second key, held by a bank official, to be used simultaneously alongside the one held by the box owner.

The longer he thought about it, the more it became obvious there was only one way around the problem.

* * *

Friday, July 20, 2012
  Dubrovnik

At around half past six that evening, Johnson parked outside Natasha's house for the second time that day. He tucked his bag of tools under the driver's seat. Then he strolled up to the door through which he had entered illegally just nine or so hours earlier and this time rang the doorbell.

Natasha, who was still wearing her work outfit, almost jumped backward when she saw who was standing on her patio. "What . . . what are you doing here?" she asked.

"I'm sorry to bother you again," Johnson said. "I wasn't intending to come back to you, but I'm finding myself in quite a difficult situation and . . . well, it's just that, at the moment, I don't have anybody else to go to. You're the only person who's been remotely helpful. It seems to me as though your stepbrother's done a lot wrong, and I'd like to sort it out. I was really hoping that you might spare another ten minutes so we could have another chat."

Natasha's eyes dropped to the doorstep. "I don't know," she said eventually. "What good will it do?"

"It'll help me to build evidence," Johnson said. "Either

he's done things for which he should go to court, or he hasn't. You would be a real help to me as I try to work that out."

After a few seconds, she nodded. "Come in. We can have a quick chat."

She led the way to the living room that Johnson had seen earlier and pointed toward an armchair. She sat on the sofa.

"First, I'd like to thank you for your help with that password and the email address. Believe it or not, it worked," Johnson said. "Since then, I've seen another document that Franjo had, and that indicates there's more important papers being held in a bank safe-deposit box here in Dubrovnik. It also said the key could be obtained from Luka. I'd like very much to see those documents."

Natasha sank back into the sofa. "A key? From Luka?"

"Yes, that's what it said."

"God, what am I getting into here?" she muttered. She gazed up at the ceiling.

"So do you know anything about a key for a safe-deposit box?"

Natasha eyed him steadily. "Maybe."

"Well, do you have access to the box?"

She exhaled and looked at the floor. "I don't know."

Johnson ignored the gesture and continued to press her. "Have you opened the deposit box before?"

She finally gave in. "No, I haven't. Franjo asked me not to. He *ordered* me not to." Natasha looked at Johnson and held her hands out, palms upward, as if to say she had no choice but to comply.

"Would you mind if I come with you to the bank so we can open it together? Do you need any special identification?"

"It's in Franjo's name, but he gave me power of attorney so that I could open it if necessary. He told me it was in case any thing ever happened to him, so either of us can open it.

But not unless it's a real emergency. I need to take ID with me, and the key. I'll think about it, okay?"

Johnson hesitated. "Can I ask you a question?"

"You've done nothing but ask me questions since you found me at my office."

"What I'm wondering is . . . I'm assuming Luka is your son, correct? How old is he?" Johnson asked.

She ran her hand through her hair. "What does it matter to you? He's about to turn twenty-five now, if you must know."

"Okay. Can I ask who's his father? You haven't mentioned him."

"I don't really want to talk about it."

"Well does Luka have any kind of relationship with Franjo, then?" Johnson persisted.

She laughed, a false, sardonic kind of laugh. "You could say that. Luka is Franjo's son."

"His *son?*"

"And his step-nephew."

"His son *and* his step-nephew?" A light went off in Johnson's head. "You mean—"

"Yes. That's what I mean."

Johnson sat silently for a few seconds.

Of course. Why does it take me so long to clock these things . . .

He soon regained his composure. "So when did your relationship with Franjo start? Did it last long?"

Natasha snorted. "It lasted about two weeks—in the sense you mean. It was back in the autumn of 1986. I was twenty, and he was a couple of years older. We got very drunk one night. We were both feeling frustrated, I think. Neither of us had partners. We watched a film on the sofa, and afterward, it just kind of happened. It seemed natural at the time, though we both knew we shouldn't be doing it."

She paused. "It wasn't . . . it wasn't incest. We weren't

blood relatives, obviously. Just stepbrother and stepsister. But you know, we'd lived as brother and sister for a long time before that. We both felt *extremely* guilty. I *still* feel guilty about it. We knew it was wrong. So we stopped after a couple of weeks."

"But two weeks was enough?" Johnson asked.

Natasha shrugged. "Yep."

"Must've been difficult. Where's Luka now?"

"He works in Split. He's got an apartment there, but he comes back here fairly often, so he has a room here, upstairs. He'll be back on Sunday, which is his birthday. He always comes for that. In fact, that's the only time we ever hear from Franjo. He calls on Luka's birthday."

Johnson sat up. "So that's the once-a-year call you talked about the other day? He always calls this house number on that day?"

"Yes. It's always a quick call, ten minutes maximum. I don't know if he's worried we're going to trace his call and track him down or something. I don't know what he thinks. But that's all he gets. That's the only contact he has with his son." Natasha seemed close to tears.

Johnson stood up and walked around the room. "Hang on a minute, he's going to call here on Sunday, on Luka's birthday?"

"Yes, always in the evening. That's when he calls. If he doesn't, it would be a first."

"Okay, you've just given me an idea."

CHAPTER THIRTY

Saturday, July 21, 2012
Dubrovnik

A casual passerby wouldn't have given it a second glance. The discreet brass plaque on the stone pillar next to the gate read Erste Credit Bank, Austria. It was one of several similar plaques on the pillar, all relating to various law firms, finance houses, and banks.

Behind the ten-foot-high green iron fence, with its sharp-tipped spikes designed to dissuade intruders, was a four-story brick mansion. A security guard sat in a small kiosk at the entrance.

The bank was on Vukovarska Street, just outside Dubrovnik's Old Town, in an area of the city frequented more by businessmen and financiers than tourists.

Johnson drove underneath the vehicle entrance archway and parked in one of the visitor's spaces behind the green railings. He picked up the small backpack containing the documents from the minefield, which he had brought in case they were needed for cross-checking with the ones they were now hopefully going to view. Then he stowed his Beretta in the glove compartment and firmly closed the door.

"Shall we go in?" he asked Natasha. She patted her handbag, where she had placed the safe-deposit box key, and nodded.

They entered the building and approached the security desk, where a uniformed guard directed them to the first floor.

The Erste Credit Bank offices were protected by a thick glass frontage and a security-controlled revolving door. Once they were through that, Natasha explained the reason for their visit to an owlish bank official with round steel-rimmed glasses and showed him the key.

"You'll need to sign an admission slip. Then I'll obtain the corresponding security key and escort you to the vault," he said.

The man disappeared into a back room while Natasha filled in the form, including the six-digit key number, 581482. Two minutes later he returned, scrutinized the form and Natasha's passport, and led them through double doors he opened with an electronic security pass.

The bank vault, which the official accessed through a thick steel door with multiple security codes, was a narrow rectangular room lined floor to ceiling with square and rectangular deposit boxes of different sizes.

The official checked the number on the key that he held, then stepped to the corresponding box, inserted the key into one of the two locks on the front, and turned it. "You unlock yours," he instructed Natasha. She did likewise. The door clicked open.

"I'll leave you to it. Press that button over there when you've finished, and I'll let you out," the bank official said. He left the room.

Natasha looked at Johnson. He nodded. She removed a large brown paper envelope from the box and sat down on one of two chairs at the end of the room. "Okay, let's have a look," she said.

At first glance, the papers looked very similar to those that Johnson had retrieved from the minefield. There were only a handful this time, however. Johnson flicked through them: more official typed memos and unofficial handwritten ones from the Ministry of Foreign Affairs in Sarajevo, most of them brief.

"My Serbo-Croat is slow. Can you read through these quickly for me?" Johnson asked. She nodded.

The first one was a handwritten sheet. Johnson pointed to it. "Okay, let's start with this."

Natasha picked up the sheet and read aloud in a quiet voice.

July 23, 1993
ACTION
MEMORANDUM FOR THE PRESIDENT:
Haris Hasanović—detail of meeting with Alija Izetbegović.
AI approved plan to allow mujahideen to continue entering and remain in Bosnia, supported by Iran special ops forces.
Current estimate: 3,000–4,000 in country (Afghanistan, Turkey, Iran, Pakistan, Sudan).
AI believes mujahideen presence vital to ARBiH survival. ARBiH will help arm mujahideen.
HH advised AI that go-ahead to be implemented immediately.
Mujahideen presence to assist Islamic fundamentalist sentiment in Bosnia/Croatia and help AI objective of building Balkan Islamic influence.
In-country CIA operative advises POTUS opposition highly unlikely.
Pentagon military adviser in-country gave similar advice—no

personal opposition nor advising US to oppose. But no formal US
approval to be given.
AI advised mujahideen forces are good fighters, particularly as shock
troops, and to be given full access to weapons imports from Iran. AI
advises mujahideen presence will help encourage and funnel in
funding from supportive Middle East/Gulf regimes.

"A CIA operative," Johnson said. "That's astonishing, effectively giving a go-ahead to violent Islamic fundamentalist mujahideen in Bosnia."

He turned to Natasha. "Thanks for translating that. Do you mind if I see the sheet?"

Natasha handed it to him, and Johnson was able to make out enough of the content to be certain that her translation was on point. He didn't want to offend her by asking, and he knew he would have to verify it later, but it was clear that this document was shocking.

"My God, I can see why they kept these in the bank vault," Johnson said.

But who was the CIA operative in Sarajevo at that time? Must have been some hard nut. That would have been a dangerous posting.

There was no name in the document. Johnson knew that the ARBiH was the Army of Bosnia and Herzegovina, Izetbegović's forces, but the Pentagon military adviser was also not identified. That, and the identity of the CIA official, would be something he would need to ask Vic to help with.

He leaned back in his chair. "Can you read the next one, please?"

July 29, 1993
ACTION
MEMORANDUM FOR THE PRESIDENT:
Haris Hasanović—detail of meeting with Alija Izetbegović
AI confirmed go-ahead for Mr. B to receive Bosnian passport to facil-

itate travel to and from B-H. To be processed immediately via Bosnia embassy in Vienna.

AI advises note of thanks for military assistance and training services supplied to accompany passport.

AI confirmed regular schedule of future meetings with Mr. B at Sarajevo office to be arranged and put into diary.

HH confirmed this to be processed.

USA in-country representatives from CIA and Pentagon now informed by HH. Objections unlikely, they advise.

"Is that it?" Johnson asked.

"Yes, just a short one."

"It doesn't say who this Mr. B is?"

"No."

Johnson paused. "Okay, go on to the next one."

Natasha turned to the next sheet. "This is another short one," she said, and began to read again.

August 3, 1993

ACTION

MEMORANDUM FOR THE PRESIDENT:

Haris Hasanović—detail of meeting with Alija Izetbegović

AI instructed go-ahead for mujahideen training camps be given. To be set up in Poljanice (Bila valley), Travnik, Zenica, and Orasac (also Bila valley).

Fighters from training camps to be allocated to ARBiH 3rd Corps or 7th Brigade.

Possible visit by Mr. B to training camps.

US in-country representatives from CIA/Pentagon to be informed by HH. No objections expected.

Johnson had Natasha run through the other documents, all of which related to activity involving mujahideen in Bosnia, the supply of weapons from Iran, and other similar issues.

Then Johnson took out his phone and photographed each of the sheets, including those from the minefield. "Just in case," he said.

Once he had finished, he put them back in the brown envelope. "Okay, I think we're done," Johnson said. "I have an idea. You said Franjo always calls on Luka's birthday, to your house number, right?"

"Always."

"We'll trace the call; I know someone who can arrange that. Then we should be able to get the address."

He walked over and pressed the call button to summon the bank official.

When he arrived, Johnson asked the man if there was an alternative exit other than the front door. The man didn't ask why and, in fact, seemed utterly unsurprised at the request.

"There is a way, down the back staircase," the official said. "Follow me." He led the way through two sets of secured double doors, nodded at a security guard manning a desk near the second of them, and then went down an uncarpeted staircase to the ground-floor level.

The official steered them along a corridor until they came to a steel door that opened into a small courtyard at the rear of the property. "You can go out here and turn left along the path, and that will take you onto a road that leads to a parking lot at the side of the building, not the front. Less chance of being seen, which I assume is the objective. Good luck."

Johnson, who clutched his backpack containing all the papers from the vault as well as the minefield, looked at Natasha. "Doubtless it's unnecessary, taking the back door, but you never know who's watching."

They took the path until they reached the side road and

then made their way behind a brick wall to a corner where the wall stopped and the green iron railings began.

Johnson paused and leaned against the wall of a small Tisak newspaper kiosk while he checked his wallet, scanning carefully up and down the road as he did so.

All seemed quiet, and he could now clearly see his car at the other end of the parking lot, around eighty yards away. The lot was full, but there was nobody anywhere near the gray Astra.

"All looks fine," he said. "Let's go."

Now Natasha was visibly nervous. "I'm not used to this kind of thing."

They walked up to the Astra. Next to it, on the far side, was a black Lexus 4x4 with blacked-out windows.

Something stirred at the back of Johnson's mind when he saw the Lexus, but events then unfolded too quickly for him to process his thoughts.

He clicked his remote to unlock the Astra and was just about to open the driver's door when the front passenger door of the Lexus, right next to him, jerked open sharply and smashed into his ribs and hip.

Winded by the impact, he looked up just as a man dressed in black jumped out and pressed a hard, cold metal object into the base of his skull.

"Don't say a word, get in the back of your car, stay silent." The voice was English with a hint of a local accent.

"Franjo. Shit! What the *hell* are—"

But Natasha's exclamation, in a high, panicky voice, was cut short. Johnson saw that on the other side of the Astra, another man had clapped his gloved hand over her mouth and pushed her into the rear seat.

"Get in, now," said the man whom Johnson now knew to be Franjo Vuković. He dug the gun harder into Johnson's skull.

Johnson, stunned, complied and climbed into the back
seat, realizing as he did so that there was nobody in the
immediate vicinity to see what was happening.

"I'll take that," Franjo said. He grabbed Johnson's backpack and tossed it into the front of the car. "And I'll have
that, too," he said, grabbing the car key from Johnson's
hand.

"Hands behind your back and keep them there," he said,
continuing to level the gun at Johnson's head.

Franjo opened the glove compartment. He looked unsurprised to discover the Beretta, which he put into Johnson's
backpack.

While Franjo pointed his gun at Johnson, the other man
stuffed a rag in Natasha's mouth, secured it with duct tape,
and tied her hands tightly together behind her back with thin
cord. He then moved on to Johnson and did likewise.

Once Johnson and Natasha were trussed and gagged, the
two men closed the doors of the Astra.

Johnson cursed inwardly. He had failed at a fairly basic
level to carry out sufficient surveillance detection measures
upon returning to his car and had now paid the price.

Franjo jumped into the Astra's driver's seat; the other man
slid into the passenger seat, from where he pointed his gun
straight at Johnson.

"Do you want to blindfold them as well?" the man asked
Franjo.

"Not necessary."

Within seconds, the car shot out of the parking lot and
sped down the road.

Johnson, who interpreted the lack of a blindfold to mean
his end was now very near, nevertheless instinctively followed
training received many years earlier and recorded in his mind
the route they took.

He resigned himself to a trip out into the country where,

he assumed, the inevitable would follow in a dark forest somewhere.

But instead, the journey was over inside ten minutes. Rather than heading out of the city, Johnson recognized the route toward the hotel he and Jayne were staying at, the Neptun on the Lapad peninsula.

Just before reaching the Neptun, the car doubled back down a road that ran parallel to the sea; after what Johnson estimated was no more than half a mile, the car pulled up outside a large black steel gate that slowly slid open.

Franjo steered the car through and down a short, steeply sloping driveway that zigzagged left, then right; he stopped in front of a double garage door, which also opened automatically.

The car edged into the garage and stopped. The electronic door closed behind them.

Franjo, without speaking, opened the Astra's rear doors and indicated to Johnson and Natasha to get out. He then opened a door at the rear of the garage that led into the hallway of a house.

"Go, move, down the hallway, then down the stairs," Franjo ordered. He pointed the gun at them and waited until they were on the stairs, then followed them down.

The house was sparsely furnished, almost unlived in, based on the glimpses Johnson had of a few rooms through open doorways.

Franjo grabbed Johnson by his shirt collar, the other man steered Natasha, and they then pushed both of them into a room that was carpeted but otherwise completely empty, as if it were waiting for new occupants to move in. Franjo removed Johnson's phone and wallet, turned off the phone, then placed the items into a plastic bag along with Natasha's phone, and threw it into a corner of the room.

Through a window, Johnson briefly glimpsed the sea,

probably no more than thirty yards away through some bushes, before Franjo pushed him onto the floor next to what looked like a steel heating or water pipe that ran along the bottom of the wall.

Franjo held Johnson's hands in place, still behind his back, next to the pipe while the other man used more thin cord to tie him to it. They repeated the process for Natasha, who audibly sniffled behind her gag. Franjo used more cord to lash Johnson's feet together, and the other man did the same to Natasha.

Unable to speak because of the rags in their mouths, Johnson and Natasha could only exchange glances. Her eyes, now red-rimmed and teary, had taken on a haunted, desperate aspect.

Johnson hoped for her sake that his own eyes were telling a more positive story. But he didn't feel as though they were.

Franjo stood, then left the room with the other man. The last thing Johnson heard as they closed the door was Franjo muttering something about fetching the Lexus.

CHAPTER THIRTY-ONE

Saturday, July 21, 2012
Dubrovnik

It had been a relaxed start to the day for Jayne. But by one o'clock in the afternoon, she had become quite concerned.

She spent the morning sitting on the balcony of the two-bedroom suite she was sharing with Johnson at the Hotel Neptun.

She read several chapters of her novel, a spy thriller by John le Carré, then went for a long swim in the large roped-off area of sea next to the hotel.

After that she rented a Jet Ski and went for a fifteen-minute spin around the bay. When Jayne, wearing a chic one-piece blue swimsuit, returned to shore, she even got a couple of wolf whistles from a group of youngsters in their early twenties. It made her laugh a little.

But once she had toweled herself dry, her concern about Johnson and Natasha deepened.

The arrangement had been that Johnson would call and

update her as soon as he and Natasha had finished at Erste Credit Bank.

But now, four hours later, he still hadn't called.

Very unlike him, she thought.

But what to do? She wasn't sure.

At two o'clock, Jayne made a decision. She took a taxi to the bank branch, where she knew Johnson would have driven with Natasha.

There was no sign of the gray Astra in the parking lot. She went into the bank offices, where she found a bespectacled official who was extremely reluctant to give her any information other than to confirm that nobody by the name of Ms. Jukić or Mr. Johnson was currently on the premises.

Jayne mentally ran through her other options. The only other obvious location she could check was the address Johnson had given her for Natasha's house, high on the hill overlooking the Old Town. While the taxi driver waited, she went up to the house and knocked several times. But it was clearly empty.

Jayne knew that if she really needed to, she could get Alice or one of her other contacts at GCHQ in the UK to attempt a trace on Johnson's cell phone. But that would involve potentially opening a whole new can of worms.

"You have a problem, lady?" the driver asked when she returned to the taxi.

"Maybe. I was trying to find someone, a traveling friend of mine. He's got a rented car and was meant to return to the hotel in it, but he didn't turn up and hasn't called. It's a bit odd," Jayne said.

"You worried about him?"

"Possibly." She tried to understate her concern, but the driver seemed to pick up on it.

"GPS," the man said. "Some of the car hire companies have it these days so they know exactly where the vehicles are. They don't like them going cross-border without them knowing about it. If it's urgent, that's your best bet. Try the rental company, and with luck you'll get someone helpful."

Of course. Why didn't I think of that?

Jayne nodded. "Good idea, thanks."

* * *

Saturday, July 21, 2012
Dubrovnik

Johnson struggled to see how he and Natasha were going to extricate themselves from the mess they were in.

He surveyed the room. There was nothing he could use to free his hands, which had been expertly trussed to the heating pipe behind him. He couldn't communicate with Natasha verbally because of the gag, and he struggled to breathe properly.

The pipe dug painfully into the base of his spine, and his feet felt increasingly numb from the tight cord that bound them together and limited his blood circulation. He could see the bindings were cutting hard into the flesh around Natasha's ankles as well.

Franjo's sudden attack and the method of it had left Johnson in little doubt about his intentions. The fact that Franjo hadn't even bothered to blindfold him told him all he needed to know.

And when he tried to put himself in the Croatian's shoes, he could see the logic. Johnson now knew too much, had seen too much. In reality, there was probably little time left.

Johnson knew he wasn't far from the Hotel Neptun, where, he imagined, Jayne was probably relaxing on a sun lounger, drink in hand, awaiting his return.

Surely she would realize after a while, though, that something had gone wrong. But the chances of her locating him were minimal.

The plastic bag containing his phone was tantalizingly close. He could see it just a few feet away in the corner of the room.

But he had seen Franjo turning it off, making it extremely difficult to trace, and there was no way of reaching it.

He was out of options.

* * *

Saturday, July 21, 2012
  Split

It had been a frantic morning for Mate Glavas. His small car rental company only had twenty cars, but eleven of them had been returned, cleaned, and rehired in the space of five hours.

The usual Saturday morning influx of tourists on early flights, together with others heading home after a couple of weeks in the Croatian sun, made for a stressful burst of activity in the office.

Now his plan was to lock up for a half hour and walk to the delicatessen down the road to get something to eat, drink an espresso, and take a breather.

Then the phone rang.

Mate would normally have let it go to voice mail at a time like this. But he could see from the +44 international prefix it was a British cell phone number, and a good slice of his summer business came from that direction.

So he picked it up.

"Hello, Go-Cro, how can I help?"

He listened as the female British caller identified herself

as Jayne Robinson, the partner of an American, Joe Johnson, who had hired a car from Go-Cro on the tenth of July; he had gone missing after a trip from their hotel into Dubrovnik. Could he help her?

When she described the gray Opel Astra, Mate didn't need to ask for the registration number.

He had been keeping an eye on that particular car, with some rising degree of concern, ever since he had received a visit from a man asking him to locate it in exchange for an envelope full of US dollars.

Of course, his vehicles were well insured with a company that paid out when they were stolen or involved in accidents, as inevitably they occasionally were. But the hassle and paperwork involved, not to mention the drain on his precious time, made it something that Mate dreaded dealing with. So he kept a particularly careful watch on his vehicles that didn't stick to normal tourist driving patterns.

"I have to say, madam, I've been a little worried about that car."

"Why is that?" Jayne asked.

"It's been to a few locations that I would describe as high-risk," Mate said.

"Ah, so you're able to track where your vehicles are?" she asked. "That might be useful."

"Like many of the rental companies, I've got a GPS system here. Yes, of course."

Mate had seen the car parked some distance off-road in an area where land mines were known to be a danger, in the countryside north of Split, near Moseć. It had also traveled across the Bosnian border to Mostar, which was forbidden under Go-Cro's rental terms without an additional payment. It had also been driven at speeds significantly higher than the legal limit between Split and Dubrovnik, although no police notices had come in so far.

"So you have GPS," Jayne interrupted. "Would you be able to pinpoint where it is right now for me?"

"No, madam, we have client confidentiality rules."

"Okay, I appreciate that," Jayne said. "But I have a strong feeling that my partner has possibly encountered some difficulties. I'd make it worth your while."

It was too much to resist. Two hits on the same car. "There is a cost attached to providing those details, madam," Mate said. "It's a service I do sometimes provide, but I would require payment of one hundred and fifty US dollars."

He waited. Jayne said nothing for a few moments. Then he heard her sigh heavily. "I'm in Dubrovnik, and you, I assume, are in Split. So how would I pay you?" she asked.

"I would take a PayPal payment to my personal account," Mate said. He gave her the details, waited for her to confirm the transaction, and then told her to remain on the line.

A few minutes later, he'd checked that the payment had gone through and had run a search through his GPS system. "The car currently appears to be parked right next to a house in the Babin Kuk area of Dubrovnik," he said. "It's right next to the sea and down the road from a hotel complex, the Neptun and—"

"The *Neptun*?" Jayne asked.

"Yes, you know it?"

"We're staying in it."

As soon as he had given her the address, she thanked him and hung up.

Mate stared at the phone for a minute. Then he shook his head and went back to his computer screen. Perhaps he should just double-check the position of that Astra, he thought. It seemed worryingly close to the water.

He flicked on the screen, refreshed it, and then waited while the GPS map showing all his vehicles scattered across Croatia loaded up once more.

A minute later, the refresh was complete. Mate zoomed in on Dubrovnik until he was focused on the point where the Astra had been. It had gone.

"Shit," Mate said. He zoomed out and spotted it about a kilometer or so away, clearly moving, because each time he refreshed the screen it had gone farther up the road.

Mate watched it until it stopped outside a building marked as a bank. He wondered briefly whether he should call the woman back and tell her the car had moved on but decided he couldn't be bothered. She would have to work it out. He shrugged and turned off the screen again.

CHAPTER THIRTY-TWO

Saturday, July 21, 2012
Dubrovnik

"I really hope Johnson and Natasha are shitting themselves," Boris said. "You know, I thought I could trust her, but it seems I was wrong. We can chat and decide what we're going to do with them."

He brought Johnson's rented Astra to a halt on the road outside the Erste Credit Bank parking lot.

Marco nodded. "All Americans are the same. Stuck their noses in here twenty years ago, backed the wrong side, and what happened? It backfired big time. And now they're still at it. Never learn their lesson."

"Correct, that will be the subtext of what I'll be saying when I get the story on air about those documents. It's going to be a huge story. That should be my bonus in the bag for this year. It'll earn the commercial guys an absolute fortune."

"We'll dump this car here instead of keeping it at your

house," Boris said. "They might have a tracker on it or something. I don't want to take the risk."

They left the Astra, then Marco drove the Lexus back to his house.

"I just need to be clear what to do with Johnson," Boris said. "I've got the documents back, but I can't just walk away and leave him. He might not know where I live or what my cover is now, but when I break that story, he'll see it for certain."

Boris paused as Marco navigated a roundabout.

"So, either I drop the story," he continued, "or we finish him off. It's the biggest damn story I've ever had my hands on. I've been sitting on it for years waiting for the right moment, and now I've got this interview with Spencer. So I've got to go for it. There's no way I'm giving it up or having it ruined by some American investigator."

His face flushed a little at the thought of it. "The other problem is Natasha," Boris said. "I can't begin to decide about her. To be honest, I think I can frighten her enough to put her back in her box. I'll threaten Luka. She'll shut up if she thinks something might happen to him."

Marco shrugged. "It's your call. To me, the whole thing sounds like one big unnecessary risk. You can drop the story, and that'll be the end of all of this. It's an ego trip. But you're not going to listen."

Boris knew that there was some truth in what Marco had said. But then again, he'd never experienced the adrenaline rush of breaking a big story on international TV, so he'd never really understand.

The Lexus pulled into the gated driveway of the house overlooking the Adriatic in Babin Kuk. Marco unlocked the front door and they stepped inside. "Feel like a beer?" Marco asked. "It's a hot afternoon, I could do with one. Let's just go and check that our two guests are still safe first."

They walked across the hallway of the house, which was at first-floor level, and then down the stairs to the ground floor.

Boris opened the door of the storage room and leaned against the doorframe. He studied Johnson and Natasha, who were half lying, half sitting, their backs against the wall, hands tied behind them to the pipe, legs trussed in front.

"You Americans need to learn to keep out of our business in the Balkans," Boris said to Johnson. "You've never understood us and you never will. We've been fighting each other here for a thousand years, and we'll probably still be fighting in another thousand. So when you and your presidents, Clinton, Bush, and all the others, come here thinking you're going to solve everything, well, forget it. You know *nothing.* You didn't twenty years ago and you don't now."

Boris walked across the room and spat on the carpet in front of Johnson. "Enjoy your last few hours in Croatia, Mr. Investigator." He glowered at Natasha. "And when I've finished with you, you won't want to ever cross me again."

He walked back upstairs into the kitchen, Marco close behind.

Boris took two beers out of the fridge and went into the long living room that ran across the front of the house, with spectacular views over the sea through floor-to-ceiling windows. It was stiflingly hot. He opened the three large skylight windows above him, which allowed some slightly cooler air to flow in, then sat in an armchair and placed the beers on a table next to him.

Two armchairs and the table were the only furniture in the room.

Marco sat next to him and grinned. "Those two down there must be shitting themselves." He sat in the other armchair and picked up one of the beers.

"Yeah, well, they won't need to worry for much longer, so makes no difference." Boris took a swig from his beer.

Despite his love of London, Boris was quite envious of Marco's lifestyle in Croatia. The house his friend had bought in Dubrovnik five years earlier had been a good investment. Since then, several new hotels and bars had been opened nearby, and prices had rocketed. The location was idyllic, and Boris couldn't understand why Marco didn't use it more. He hadn't even bothered to get the place properly furnished.

Boris took another long drink of beer, settled back in his chair, and closed his eyes.

Marco was reading a car magazine from the table. "Seen this, about the Jaguar F-Type? They're launching it next year. I think I might put a deposit down on one when they come out. It'd go well with the Lexus as a fun car for weekends."

Boris ignored him. "I want to get everything finalized here tonight. This has dragged on long enough. Johnson's got to go tonight," Boris said. He closed his eyes again, his breathing now deeper and steadier.

As he did so, a loud rattle and a clunk came from the skylight window above them, then a loud hissing sound and a thud as something heavy landed on the red-tiled floor next to Franjo, who opened his eyes at the sound, then jumped like a startled dog.

"What the hell's that?"

In front of him was a large silver aerosol-type canister, which was hissing loudly and throwing out clouds of dense white gas at high volume straight toward him and Marco. It instantly reminded Boris of the fake smoke that his producers sometimes used in his TV studios for atmospheric effect.

But this wasn't fake smoke.

A second smoking canister flew through the next skylight window, nearer to the door, also throwing out white gas.

Boris leapt to his feet. "Shit, shit, tear gas. Quick, get out of here," he shouted.

But Marco was already clutching his face. "Aaargh, my eyes," he yelled.

Then the gas from the second canister caught Boris in the face. He instantly felt an agonizing sting in his eyes, which automatically closed up; then, as he breathed in again, the gas reached the back of his throat. He felt his mouth and his airways immediately start to tighten, causing him to gulp in more air and make things worse. Within seconds he felt as if he were drowning.

Marco staggered into Boris, who had now completely lost his sight. He felt suddenly dizzy and fell onto the floor. As he fell, his foot flicked sideways and caught Marco's ankle, causing his friend to also trip over.

Both of them lay on the floor just a couple of meters away from the two canisters, which continued to spew white smoke. By now the room was full of gas.

Boris tried to crawl toward the door, but an uncontrollable, rapidly rising nausea in his stomach overwhelmed him. He retched and threw up violently over a red Persian rug that lay in front of the armchairs.

His throat felt as if it were on fire, his sinuses burned, and his eyes streamed water. He could see virtually nothing, but he heard Marco also loudly vomiting next to him.

Then came the sound of a sharp and extremely loud explosion from the floor below.

* * *

Saturday, July 21, 2012
Dubrovnik

Johnson could hear the muffled sound, coming down through the floor, of two men talking in subdued tones in the room directly above. Presumably it was Franjo and Marco.

But suddenly there were two loud thuds as objects fell onto the floor above him, followed by a few shouts and a scream, and then a large thump on the floor, followed by another.

A minute or so later, through the wall immediately to his right, Johnson heard an explosion so loud it hurt his eardrums. He heard a crash as something heavy fell to the floor, and a vibration ran through him.

What the hell's going on?

Seconds later, Jayne opened the door of the room, strode over to Johnson without saying a word and, using a Swiss army knife, cut the cords that held his wrists and feet. Then she cut the duct tape that was wound around his head and removed the piece of cloth in his mouth.

"Jayne, thank God. What—"

"Ask the questions later. Let's go," she snapped.

Johnson struggled to stand, his leg muscles failing to obey the instructions he was trying to send to them after hours tied in one position.

Jayne bent down and freed Natasha, who seemed utterly shell-shocked and barely able to move. She stood, but Johnson could see deep indentations in her ankles where the bindings had dug into her flesh.

"Come on, up, let's go," Jayne said, more urgently now.

Johnson picked up the plastic bag containing his phone and followed Jayne.

She led the way out the door, and along the lower hallway where Johnson saw the wooden external door lying flat on the floor, its single pane of glass shattered, hinges broken. The plasterboard next to the door was also smashed and had burn marks close to ground level.

Natasha hobbled behind him, struggling to keep up.

"We need to run. Just try," Jayne said. "I've knocked those guys on their asses with tear gas grenades, but we haven't got long before it wears off. Five minutes, ten maximum. Let's go."

She led the way across some wooden decking, down a short flight of steps, past a thick clump of bushes and pine trees, and onto a concrete pathway that ran parallel to the sea, which lay a few yards below them over some rocks.

A number of tourists, some just wearing bikinis and swimming shorts, licked ice cream cones and held their children's hands as they strolled past. Surely, some of them must have heard the explosion when Jayne had blown in the door just minutes earlier, Johnson thought. But none of them appeared concerned.

Jayne turned right. "The Neptun is only about five minutes this way," she said. "If we run, we'll be there by the time those guys can breathe again."

She broke into a jog. Johnson did likewise while Natasha, whining with pain, fell in behind them.

They had gone no more than a hundred or so yards when it hit Johnson.

"Shit, the damned documents," he said. "They're still in the house. All of them, in that backpack."

Jayne stopped running momentarily. "Seriously, Joe, you can't. You just can't. If those guys happen to come around while you're in there, you'll be a dead man. Don't worry about it. Leave it."

She turned and jogged onward.

They passed the Cave Bar, where Johnson had drunk a beer after the war crimes conference that now seemed so long ago, and continued until they came to a beach bar area to their left and, finally, the Neptun.

They had only run three-quarters of a mile, Johnson estimated, but Natasha was gasping. She held on to a metal rail outside the rear entrance to the hotel. "Sorry, I'm struggling," she said.

Johnson felt relieved to have escaped, but once that emotion had subsided, his mind automatically refocused on the task in hand.

By the time they reached their third-floor room, Johnson could feel the anxiety building.

"We can't let this slip now," he said. "We've got Franjo just down the road, and he's got the documents we need to nail him. Let's just think this through."

"You mean you didn't photograph them?" Jayne asked.

"Yes, I did, actually," Johnson said, holding up his phone. "All of them. But I need the originals back if we're going to take him to trial. And Vic wants the originals—he's not going to be happy with some photos."

Jayne stood, hands on her hips. "Just take a breather for a second so we can think. You and Natasha have just been kidnapped. Just take a while to cool off, or try to."

"Okay, okay," Johnson said. "You're right. And thanks for saving my ass—again. I screwed up badly when we left the bank, like a rookie. I owe you."

Jayne gave a thin smile. "I'm sure my turn will come. It works two ways. But I seriously don't think we should walk near that house where Franjo is right now. If anything, let's drive and have a look from the road. There's a car rentals place at the other side of the hotel. I've got a Golf waiting on standby—I reserved it just earlier when I found out where you were."

Johnson nodded his approval. "Good. Let's go, then. If we could somehow block the gate, we could get the Croatian police in. Though would that work? Do they take a vested interest if it's a Croatian involved in war crimes from twenty years back?"

"In my experience from when I worked here, it'll be difficult," Jayne said. "It'll be too complicated for a small-minded local cop. They'll refer it upward. You'll get procrastination, delays, red tape. They'll want to know what we're doing and won't like it if we're seen taking the law here into our own hands—especially if they find out I've been throwing tear gas grenades around and blowing in doors. Also, if you get a senior cop involved, you don't know which side of the conflict they were on during the war. Unless you get lucky, it could make things worse. Frankly, the best bet is to get him outside Croatia, then get the authorities involved. But how we do that, I don't know."

Johnson tugged at his ear. "Yes, that's true in Franjo's case. But what about Marco? He's murdered Petar, and that has to be a local police matter."

"I agree. But how do we separate the two? You get the police in to deal with Marco now, then our strategy for Franjo goes out the window."

Johnson shrugged. "Fair point. But we don't even know where Franjo's based, where he lives," he said. "And if he does live abroad, what name does he use? Obviously not his real one. It feels like two steps forward, three back. And he's still got the original documents, after all that work we did."

"Let's go have a look anyway," Jayne said. "If they're still there, I've got more in my bag of tricks than just those two tear gas grenades and the plastic explosive."

"Yes, where did you get that gear?"

"Same place I got the Walther," Jayne said. "From one of our old SIS agents in Dubrovnik. He's a former Croatian Defence Ministry guy. I told you—he's a useful man to know. His place is like an Aladdin's cave. I've also asked him to do a bit of work and find out where Haris Hasanović lives."

Johnson nodded. "That's useful. Aladdin, eh? Maybe he can rustle up a magic lamp as well. It might come in handy for this job."

He eyed Natasha, who was sitting on the couch and looking shell-shocked and disoriented. "Are you okay, Natasha?" he said. "I need to apologize to you for the way I bungled things when we left the bank. I put you at serious risk, and I take full responsibility for that."

"It's fine," Natasha said, her face ashen. "Don't worry about it."

Johnson sat next to her. "You're not going to be able to go home tonight, unfortunately. But I'm sure you realize that. You can stay here and we'll figure something out. Just make sure you don't leave the hotel, okay?"

"Okay, I get it," she said. "Thanks."

"I did think that if Franjo were going to call your house to speak to Luka on his birthday we could trace the call and find him," Johnson said. "But that's obviously not going to happen now."

"I've already texted Luka and told him not to come tomorrow," Natasha said. "I don't want him caught up in all this. I'll celebrate his birthday with him another time. He's going to be very upset, as I am too."

Johnson nodded. "I'm really sorry about that, but I do think you've done the right thing. That's sensible." He told Natasha to wait in the hotel room while he and Jayne went to the car rental office and picked up the Volkswagen Golf she had reserved.

As soon as she had signed the paperwork, they collected the car, drove back down the road past the Cave Bar, and slowed outside the house where Johnson had been captive.

The black gate was open.

"Stop there," Johnson said.

He raised himself up in the car seat and poked his head out of the sunroof. "I can just about see the house. They were driving a black Lexus 4x4, but there's no sign of that. And no sign of our Astra, either. They must have gone."

CHAPTER THIRTY-THREE

Sunday, July 22, 2012
Dubrovnik

Johnson had a fitful sleep. He woke at just after two o'clock, then again at four thirty, both times after the same dream: that he was chained to the pipe in the house down the road and that Franjo was slowly choking him by force-feeding him the documents.

After waking again at six thirty, Johnson gave up and went to make himself a strong coffee. He then sat on the hotel balcony, looking out to sea. He felt frustrated. He'd had a brush with Franjo, but now the man seemed to have disappeared again.

He was still thinking of his next steps ten minutes later when the door to the other bedroom opened. Jayne appeared, followed by Natasha, who had slept on a sofa bed.

"Morning, Joe," Jayne said. "Natasha's had a thought about how we might find out where Franjo is based. And I've got something for you as well."

Johnson nodded at Natasha. "Hope you managed to get some sleep after all that," he said. "What are you thinking?"

"I had some but not enough," she said. "Listen, I don't actually know if it's going to help find out where he is, but I recall Franjo talking about an arms company, based in Sarajevo. It makes ammunition, shells, mortars, rockets, that kind of thing. He was very pleased with himself because he had bought shares in it before the war, when the price was low. Then, of course, it supplied all sides during the war and I assume did well. But afterward, I've no idea. I don't follow these sorts of things."

"Do you know what it was called?" Johnson asked.

"I think it was something like VVM Sustavi. Means 'VVM Systems.' Maybe VMV, I don't know. You'd have to check it. But I was thinking, if he is a shareholder, maybe it has a record of his details somewhere?"

"It would have to so it could send him shareholder information, dividends, and so on," Johnson said. "Good thought. Thanks for that, Natasha. You've been very helpful—I really appreciate it."

"I told you," Natasha said, "I don't like Franjo—since the war, I never have. I'll help how I can."

Johnson nodded, took out his phone, and did an internet search. "Here we are: VMM Oružje Sustavi, based in Sarajevo, listed on the Sarajevo Stock Exchange. Would that be it? It makes artillery and ammunition, all sorts of stuff."

"Yeah, that must be it. Definitely," Natasha said.

Johnson frowned. "The thing is, how do we get hold of the shareholder information? I'm certain the company wouldn't disclose it. That's only done for major shareholders with a significant percentage of the stock. We need someone with access to those kinds of financial records. Let me think on it, but let's park that one for now. Jayne, you mentioned something?"

"My old SIS friend here in Dubrovnik, Bernard Djokovic, has sent me an address where he believes Hasanović is currently living," Jayne said. "He got it from someone he knows in the Bosnian government pension fund, an administrator, who has access to their databases. The address is in Split."

Johnson rolled his eyes. That would be yet another three-and-a-half-hour journey. "He's confident it's the same guy?"

"Oh, yes, he's confident. Hasanović is apparently one of the very few ex-government officials who's not on a pension ten times what it should be. Bernard says most of them set their own pension payments and they're all loaded now. But this guy, apparently, is trustworthy."

Johnson snorted. He had realized long ago, during his stint working in the region in 1999, that certain people had actually been sorry to see the civil war end. While a hundred thousand people died during the fighting, including those killed in high-profile massacres at places such as Srebrenica, others had somehow managed to walk away from the carnage having siphoned off small fortunes.

Some estimates by international observers had put the total amount missing from public funds during and after the war as high as a billion US dollars. Significant amounts of international aid money had also vanished.

"He's one of the few honest ones, then," Johnson said.

Jayne nodded. "I think you're right."

Johnson leaned back in his seat. At least there were still a few slender leads to go on. In that moment Johnson realized that amid the chaos of the previous couple of days, he hadn't updated Vic on developments regarding the documents found at the minefield and in the bank safe-deposit box.

He stared out the window. *A CIA operative and Pentagon military adviser involved in enabling arms imports into Bosnia from Iran and arranging mujahideen training camps in the country.*

On many levels, the revelations did not surprise Johnson. But who the hell were those people?

Then he stood up. "I just need to go and make a phone call to the US. I'll be right back."

Johnson left Jayne and Natasha on the balcony and went to his bedroom.

First, he needed to inform Aisha that Franjo was definitely alive. He tapped out a message on his phone summarizing the situation, although omitting details of their recent encounter, and asked Aisha to let him know if anything else came to mind that might help him, as he still had no idea where Franjo was based, what he was doing, or what alias he might be living under.

Then he dialed Vic's cell phone number. It was answered after several rings.

"Vic, it's Joe."

"Doc—where are you?"

"In Dubrovnik. Listen, I've got some good and bad news. The good is we found those documents." He gave Vic a summary of their adventures in the minefield and, after extracting a promise to keep it quiet, described the demise of Edwards. However, Vic had already heard whispers in the Langley rumor mill about the Zagreb chief of station's death.

"You can't worry about that," Vic said. "He shouldn't have been there. You've done a very good job with the dossier. I'm pleased. But you said there was bad news as well?"

Johnson paused. "Yes, I'm afraid so. We've lost the documents again."

"*What?*"

Feeling somewhat embarrassed, Johnson told Vic of his incarceration at gunpoint and the debt he now owed Jayne.

"We've got copies of the papers, but I know you'll need the originals. We're working on getting them back. There were actually a few bombshells among those papers," Johnson said. "Listen to this: a senior CIA operative and a Pentagon military adviser in Sarajevo were involved in fixing arms import deals to Bosnia from Iran in '93. Can we find out who they were and who was stationed there?"

"Interesting. Yeah, I'll get onto that," Vic said. "From memory, I don't think we had a station chief in Sarajevo at that time—it was too dangerous—only one in Zagreb. So it must have been someone operating informally, I'd guess."

Vic hesitated. "By the way, given Watto's interest in the documents you had, I've arranged for his phones to be tapped. Had to get one of my NSA technical guys to do it on the sly. There's no way I'd have got official clearance for it, not for Watto."

"Smart move. I hope it doesn't backfire," Johnson said.

"Yes. But also just to warn you, Watto's working on plans to nail you."

"How do you mean?"

"I gather he's already decided you're responsible for Edwards's demise. He was Watto's blue-eyed boy. He's apparently livid."

* * *

Sunday, July 22, 2012
Langley

"It was bad enough to lose my top guy in Croatia and you're now also telling me that Johnson got hold of the documents?" Watson asked, his voice rising.

Despite the rather crackly encrypted phone line, he heard Boris take a deep breath, then mutter something that sounded vaguely insulting.

"What? What did you say?" Watson asked.

"SILVER, I'm in a roadside café halfway between Dubrovnik and Split. So I can't talk, there are people about. But the bottom line is, you sent one of your guys after my documents when I warned you not to, and he's paid the penalty. I'm sorry, but that's your responsibility and his. It has nothing to do with me."

Watson seethed silently.

"Also," Boris said, "although Johnson had the documents briefly, we've got them back again now. You kept telling me Johnson's an incompetent, but frankly, he and that woman helping him are not proving easy to handle."

Watson felt a heaviness in the bottom of his stomach. He was still trying to piece together the story coming from Croatia, but it seemed as though he had seriously screwed up for the first time in many years of running off-the-books operations such as this one. After receiving a phone call from someone in the Zagreb station to tell him about Edwards, he had swiftly called Boris to get his version of events. But he certainly hadn't expected to hear that Johnson had gotten to the document cache first.

Now he was fire-fighting on two fronts: first to make sure his boss, the deputy director of the National Clandestine Service, didn't suspect that Edwards was involved in any unauthorized off-the-books activity when he died; and second, to stop Johnson or Boris from doing any damage with the documents.

"So how long did Johnson have the documents for?" Watson asked. "I'm guessing long enough to read them, so what will he know?"

"The really vital ones were in the safe-deposit box. He had them for hardly any time. We caught him as soon as he came out of the bank, trapped him, and tied him up at SUNMAN's house here. They were in a bag with the others from the minefield. I grabbed his Beretta, too," Boris said.

"So you caught him. He's still in SUNMAN's house, then, I assume. When will you dispose of him?" Watson asked.

There was silence for a few seconds.

"No, he's not in SUNMAN's house," Boris said. "Not anymore. Someone teargassed me and SUNMAN, then blew in the door and rescued Johnson. He had some woman with him, who we were also holding. My gut feeling is it was the other woman working with him who must have teargassed us and got them both out."

Watson tried to process what he was hearing. This was the problem with dealing with amateurs. It was like trying to herd cats. He mentally counted to ten.

"Dammit, man. So he's escaped. What happens now if he's read those documents? What does he know? Do the documents identify anyone—me or anyone else?" Watson asked.

"Unlikely. They're vague."

Watson's breathing became heavier. "Is there any way Johnson could work it out?"

"Only if he gets to Hasanović, which he'll struggle to do. At least I think—"

"Don't think," Watson said. "Make sure. You'll have to get to Hasanović before Johnson does. He's now obviously a risk, so get rid of him and Johnson. I would suggest you or Marco hire someone else to do the Hasanović job. Don't take the risk of doing it yourself. That would be foolish at this point. Get someone good, though."

"You don't need to spell it out. Marco knows people."

"Well, we can't have any information that points to me made public. Got it?" Watson said. "This is the most almighty screwup."

"Understood."

"And do the documents name, or say anything about, a

former Pentagon military adviser who was in Bosnia?" Watson asked.

"The papers do mention someone from the Pentagon, yes, but they don't name the person. Who is that, anyway?" Boris asked.

Watson tapped his fingers on the side of his chair. "Never mind. If the documents don't mention his name, you don't need to know."

Thank God I've kept all these people's identities hidden from each other, Watson thought.

"I need to get going now," Watson said. "I've got a plane to catch."

"Where to?"

"Where do you think? I've lost my top man in Croatia, and there's an arms lift about to happen out of Sinj, which he was supposed to oversee. So I'm flying to Split to sort it out."

Boris paused. "Okay. But calm down. Threats aren't going to help. Just remember I've got a system in place if you do anything that harms me. Details about you will go to a number of key people in the States. Okay?"

"So you've said before." Watson wiped his brow with the back of his hand. "I'm not threatening anything. I just want to get this fixed."

Watson hung up. He realized his hand was shaking a little.

CHAPTER THIRTY-FOUR

Sunday, July 22, 2012
Manhattan

Aisha knew the instant she saw the picture of his naked eye. She felt a little light-headed and groped for a chair. It was a slightly grainy photocopy, but there was absolutely no mistake.

It was him all right. The man whom, until that morning when she woke up to the text from Joe Johnson, she had assumed had been dead since 1993.

Aisha had arrived early at the CBA television studios for her Sunday news shift. She'd had time to pick up her internal mail and actually read through it, for once.

One of the items was a memo in an envelope from the station director in advance of the forthcoming interview with Patrick Spencer at the studios.

The interview was going to be with *Wolff Live*, a British show she'd never seen. Attached was a color picture of the interviewer, a Boris Wolff, together with a short biography, a list of other people he had interviewed, and a couple of photocopied profile interviews with British media and broadcasting trade magazines.

Aisha first flicked through the biography, then glanced quickly at the two magazine articles about Wolff. The second of the articles had a large main photograph of him in action, interviewing the German Chancellor Angela Merkel. But it was the second photograph on the following page that made her snap to attention. It was a close-up picture depicting a makeup artist preparing Wolff prior to one of his shows.

He was glancing sideways at the camera, and at that angle, she could see it—the defect in his right eye, the one that all those years ago she had found so endearing. It was a black line running from the bottom of his pupil across his iris, making it look almost like a keyhole. A long time ago, Aisha had loved the absolute uniqueness of it. Now she stared at it and she knew.

This wasn't Boris Wolff. It was Franjo Vuković.

She studied the photos again.

If it hadn't been for the eye, she definitely wouldn't have recognized him. His thick beard had gone, he had lost most of his hair, and rather than the flowing dark locks that he had been so proud of twenty years earlier, what little was left was tightly cropped to his scalp. His face was significantly fatter, with two fleshy jowls under his chin, and his nose was a little crooked in a way it hadn't been before, as if it had been broken at some point.

Whereas in his youth he had been thin and tall, now he was far more heavily built and quite imposing.

But in the other photos the eye defect wasn't visible. How did he hide it? She found the answer in the article, three paragraphs from the end. "On camera, Wolff normally wears a colored contact lens in his right eye to hide a defect of the iris . . ."

Aisha set the papers down on her desk.

Of course. What did Vuković translate as in English? Son of the wolf . . . the wolf's son.

So Johnson was correct. Franjo was alive.

Aisha picked up the picture again and stared at it. So, he had interviewed various political leaders, a rock star—even the England cricket captain.

But how the hell had he managed to do it? From an upstart trainee broadcast journalist in Split to, seemingly, a top political interviewer in London? She had no answer.

His English back then had been little more than decent school standard. Presumably now he spoke like a native Brit. And he must have completely reengineered his entire identity to do it.

But one thing she did know. The same anger she had tried to push to the back of her mind for the previous nineteen years now surged back up inside her, as it had done every time she thought about him.

The bitterness continued to eat at her, no matter how much she prayed to Allah for it to go away, and now the thoughts and memories tumbled around her mind yet again. Aisha closed her eyes.

On the eastern side of the bridge, she waits, her blue dress flapping in the wind. Her father and sister are out of sight, still on the way back from the front line. It's taking forever. Another tank shell screams in and crashes into the center of the bridge; dust and black smoke rise up, masonry falls into the river, people scream.

Then, at last, through the gloom, they appear on the other side: her father, her sister, and two others. They're carrying a stretcher to the arch, an injured, bandaged man on it. She's relieved at seeing them alive. "Hurry, hurry, quick, come over, before the next shell," someone yells. Nearby, another man is speaking fast into a walkie-talkie.

But before they can move, a shell detonates right next to them. She screams and screams and runs over the bridge, up the slope and down the other side, through the scaffolding and the broken stones and the rubber tires and the tarpaulins and old blankets and piles of debris.

People shout, "Stop! Stop! Stop!" But she keeps going until she sees what was her family but is no more. Her father lies bloody and motionless, his legs mashed and ragged, his face destroyed; her sister's body is torn and red and limp. She wails and lies with her head on her father's chest, feeling his last warmth, clutching her sister, telling her she loves her. And she feels shredded and empty and alone and frightened and angry.

Aisha opened her eyes. She could not forget, and no matter how hard she tried, she could not forgive, either. She swore and threw the briefing pack into her bag.

She felt very unsure about what to do next. She sat at her desk and tried to think. Should she give Johnson a call and tell him? But that was no guarantee of justice. What proof did he have? Indeed, what physical proof did *she* have, other than what she had seen and knew for certain? No, she needed a concrete guarantee. Maybe there was a different way.

She left her desk and headed into Studio One, just down the corridor from Studio Three, where she was scheduled to work that day on the main news program. Her colleague Olly was there, fiddling with the scenery hoist panel.

"Olly, have you read the memo about the Spencer interview? You working on that one?"

He frowned at her. "You all right? You're not looking great."

"Yeah, I'm okay."

"You sure?"

"Yes."

"Well, yeah, I'm working on Spencer. I thought I'd take a chance to see the big man close up. Speaker of the House today, who knows, he could be president in four years' time. You doing it?"

"I'm not listed to do it, no," Aisha said. "But now I'm

thinking that maybe you're right, it could be interesting. Which studio is it slated for?"

"Studio One, of course, here. If you want to do it, go and speak to Steve now. He's sorting out the roster. I think he still needs one or two people."

Aisha nodded. Studio One was the largest of the three CBA studios, with an extensive array of lighting equipment, all on motorized hoists suspended from the overhead grid, the crisscross of metal walkways high above the studio floor.

Her specialist role was to program and operate the lighting desk that controlled all of the fixtures and other special effects in the studio.

Aisha worked closely with Tim, who, as lighting director, was in charge of the look of the show.

Studio One had seating for an audience of up to four hundred people. It was rarely fully utilized, but Aisha knew all the seats would be occupied for the Spencer interview.

Aisha strolled over to Steve Abrahams, who had wandered in to see what was going on.

"Steve, just a quick question. You still need a couple people for the Spencer interview with that British team that's coming over?"

"Yeah, certainly do. Had one or two dropouts, including Will, the other board op. You up for it?"

"Sure, put me down."

"Great, you're down. Thanks, Aisha. There'll be a few meetings coming up with the studio director and with Tim. We need to get this one absolutely right, make a good impression, and show the Brits what we can do, right?"

Aisha nodded, her face serious. "Creativity's my bag, you know that."

She walked away. Then she sat in one of the audience seats and stared up at the lighting rig, almost in a trancelike state.

Several minutes later, Aisha took out her cell phone and texted Ana, telling her simply that she now knew Franjo was alive but giving few other details. Ana had been following up with her ever since Johnson's visit, and Aisha felt compelled to tell her.

Then she began to tap out another message, this time to Adela.

CHAPTER THIRTY-FIVE

Sunday, July 22, 2012
  Split

Johnson took a mental snapshot of Haris Hasanović's home as he and Jayne Robinson walked through the gate and up the path toward the front door. Hasanović might have been one of the most honest members of Izetbegović's inner circle of government, but he had still clearly done pretty well.

"Not bad for a civil servant. It would definitely require a salary supplement of some kind," Johnson said. He stopped and studied the large three-story stone house, which sat on a landscaped plot, fifty yards wide, that ran from the road right down to the water's edge.

The property stood less than a mile west of Split's marina and not far from Antun's far more modest house.

"Yes, perhaps it's old money. He's left Bosnia and taken the Croatian waterfront option for his retirement. Ironic, isn't it," Jayne said. The property, flanked by pine trees, looked slightly in need of some love and care, as many older people's homes do.

Johnson glanced over his shoulder toward the road. He had taken extensive measures to ensure he hadn't been tailed on his way to the property, including a stop-start journey with detours through various parts of Split, down side streets and around the perimeter of the Old Town. It wasn't quite as elaborate as one of the surveillance detection routes he had run in his CIA days, but it wasn't far off. He had then parked out of sight of the road, in a recess behind some bushes, down a narrow alley at the side of Hasanović's property.

A set of curved stone steps rose from the path to a decorative oak front door. Johnson pushed the old brass door bell.

The silver-haired man who answered the door opened it no more than a third and peered at Johnson from behind metal-framed glasses.

"Mr. Hasanović?"

"Yes. Who are you?"

"I'm Joe Johnson, an American war crimes investigator. Sorry to bother you on a Sunday, but I was hoping you might be able to help with something I'm working on. I was directed to you by the family of one of your former colleagues years ago. I was wondering if you could spare a few minutes."

Hasanović gazed at Johnson. "War crimes? I thought they were being handled locally, not by overseas investigators. What is it you're working on?"

"I'm searching for someone who's suspected of mass murders of Muslims in your Bosnia, twenty years ago, and who stole important Foreign Ministry documents that originally came from Alija Izetbegović's office."

Hasanović straightened his shoulders slowly, his dark eyes now gazing steadily at Johnson. "Documents? From Alija's office?" He furrowed his brow at Jayne. "And who are you?"

"I'm Jayne Robinson, from London. Also an investigator. I'm working with Joe."

Hasanović stood still for a few seconds. His thick glasses lenses magnified his eyes and gave them a slightly surreal look.

"So who sent you to me?" Hasanović asked.

"I'd rather not say while standing on your doorstep," Johnson said. "It's quite sensitive." He checked over his shoulder.

Get a move on.

"I understand. Come this way," Hasanović said. He led the way through a wood-paneled hallway into a library lined with oak bookshelves, its leaded window looking up the garden path toward the road. He pointed Johnson and Jayne to a pair of leather armchairs and sat himself down behind a large polished wooden desk.

"I can tell you that intelligence sources sent me to you," Johnson said, hoping that a little frankness on his part might help pry open Hasanović's defenses.

"But you can't say exactly who?"

"No."

Hasanović sighed. "Okay. Tell me more about those documents. Are you looking for the person who stole them from Alija's office?" Hasanović asked.

"No, they were taken from Izetbegović's office by someone, and the person I'm looking for stole them from that person," Johnson said.

Hasanović paused. "You know, you may be confusing me with someone who still cares about this sort of thing. Twenty years ago I did, but now I'm enjoying my retirement. However, just tell me—these documents, is there a Mostar link involved?"

"Um, yes."

"Would it have anything to do with a man called Erol Delić, by any chance?" he asked.

"Kind of. I think he was the man who removed them from Izetbegović's office in Sarajevo."

"Okay, I know what you're talking about," Hasanović said. "A lot of documents went missing at various times, but this particular bundle was especially sensitive. I remember them clearly. I'd stamped them for shredding because we couldn't afford for them to get out. It would have wrecked things for the Bosnian government in Sarajevo. For a while, I dreaded waking up every morning in case the headlines were suddenly all about Iran delivering a load of arms to Izetbegović despite the arms embargo that the cowardly European governments had put in place. Thankfully that didn't happen. But it would also have seriously upset certain people from outside Bosnia if those details had been made public at the time . . . including some from the other side of the Atlantic, I might add."

He tapped the wooden desk with his forefinger and then continued, "I'd have killed Erol if I'd known at the time that he'd taken them. But he covered his tracks, and actually, I think the Croatian army, the HVO, did the job for me. Killed him, I mean. What I don't know is where the documents ended up. Not that it matters now."

Johnson tugged at the hole in his right ear. "Well, that's the issue. After a long struggle we got the documents from two Bosnian Croats, both from Mostar. One was Franjo Vuković, the other Marco Lukić. And we wanted the documents for the reason you said. They're sensitive. Explosive even. But then things went wrong and those two got them back again. It's not just the documents—they are both men that I want to nail for the war crimes I mentioned."

Hasanović shrugged. "From what I recall of those documents, if they found their way into the press now, they'd be a lot more damaging to certain American politicians and other officials than they would be to low-level Croatian army guys. That's where I would focus. I mean, unless you've got cast-iron proof about war crimes, trying to get convictions is going to be a tall order. If not, I'd forget it."

Johnson couldn't help but raise his eyebrows. "No, I disagree. Wrongdoing is wrongdoing, no matter where the person is on the seniority ladder. Justice should be done, whether it's war crimes or corruption."

"I'm not sure where this is taking us," Hasanović said. "Is there anything else I can help you with? I'm not going to be able to somehow conjure these documents back for you, unfortunately."

"There are a couple of things," Johnson said. "Some of the documents referred to a Mr. B. They talked about him being given a Bosnian passport, and they also said he was involved with mujahideen training camps in Bosnia, and CIA and Pentagon advisers were not expected to raise objections. Who is this Mr. B?"

A faint smile crossed Hasanović's face. "You're telling me you haven't worked that one out?"

"No."

"I can tell you now that he's dead."

"Who was it?"

"It was Osama bin Laden."

Johnson fell back in his chair. "*Bin Laden?*"

"Yes, it was him. For us in Sarajevo, hmm, I have to admit, it wasn't our finest hour. And I told Izetbegović so at the time—I warned him. But he would have none of it. He thought having Bin Laden in the tent pissing out at the rest of the Western hemisphere, the Catholics and the Orthodox Christians, would be a good thing. He said it would help us hold our own against the sadists from Serbia who were massacring every Muslim they could find, and it would help promote Islam in this region."

Hasanović's face had turned from a grayish white to a healthier-looking pink. He seemed energized again. Then in a lower voice he continued, "But for your all-knowing CIA, for your Pentagon military advisers, and for your former president Clinton, the decision to look the other way when Bin Laden arrived and to set up camp in Western Europe was in a different class altogether. It was a goddamned disaster. It put Bin Laden on a launchpad. It armed him. When the Americans finally killed him last year in Pakistan, they were eighteen years too late. They let the horse out of the stable doors in '93."

Johnson took a minute or two to process what he was being told. There were the other names he needed, too.

Come on, Joe, think this through.

"There was also a CIA operative mentioned in the papers but not named. Do you remember who that was?"

Hasanović pursed his lips. "It was a man called Robert Watson. Yes, that was him, Watson. I met him a few times—didn't like him."

"*Watson?*" For the second time in a couple of minutes Johnson felt utterly incredulous.

"Yes, Watson. Arrogant man, treated us all like shit. I remember him well."

Johnson nodded. "Now it makes sense," he said quietly.

"Makes sense? What does?" Hasanović said.

"Nothing. He's someone I know, that's all."

"Another thing you should check out is arms smuggling out of Croatia to the Syrian rebels," Hasanović said. "The weapons being exported now are mainly the same ones that were imported twenty years ago and skimmed off from the plane loads that came in from Iran. I've heard they're shipping them out of Sinj, on night flights. They've got the local police in their pockets."

"Sinj?" Johnson asked.

"Yes, a small airfield near the Bosnian border."

"Who's behind the shipments?"

"I don't know, exactly."

Johnson frowned. "Okay. I'll take a look at that. Just to go back to the documents I saw, the other person who's not identified is the Pentagon military adviser who also turned a blind eye to the Iran shipments and effectively let it happen. The documents mentioned him a couple of times, but there was no name. Do you know who—"

"Oh, yes, I know who it was all right," Hasanović broke in. "He's—"

But then it was Hasanović's turn to be interrupted.

A loud, sharp double rap came at the front door. Not the sound of knuckles on wood, but rather, hard metal. It was a bang, not a knock.

Hasanović stood and walked into the hallway. Johnson and Jayne followed. The old man stood still, watching the front door. There was another loud rap, then another, this time harder and louder.

Johnson reached swiftly for Hasanović's shoulder. "Wait, don't. Just wait a minute. I've just got a feeling—"

He was interrupted by another rap, followed by three loud bangs.

Through the small frosted window in the door, Johnson could just about make out the opaque outline of two figures, both wearing black tops of some kind, both with black hair.

"Don't answer it," Johnson said. "Can we move to a different part of the house?"

Hasanović turned and walked stiffly down the hallway to the stairs, then began to climb. He beckoned Johnson and Jayne to follow.

They had all reached the first-floor landing when the first bullet smashed through the front door. Then came another immediately afterward. One of the bullets hit the wall at the far end of the hall, making a large hole in the plaster.

Hasanović beckoned Johnson through a doorway to the left, which he shut and locked behind them. Now they were in another paneled room with a huge television in the corner, an array of DVDs, and a couple of long sofas.

The sound of more gunshots came from downstairs, then a series of loud thuds, as if the door was being hit with a heavy implement. Finally, there was a louder blast that sounded to Johnson like a shotgun, and a crunch as the door gave way. Shouts came from downstairs.

Hasanović walked to a drawer, opened it, and took out two identical pistols. "Have you got a gun?" he asked Johnson.

Johnson shook his head and glanced at Jayne, who had already removed her Walther from her linen jacket pocket.

Hasanović gave one of the weapons to Johnson. "Zastava M70. It's good to go. Follow me."

He looked over his shoulder as he strode through another door, which he again closed and locked behind him with a key.

They passed through to a small landing from where a narrow staircase with uncarpeted wooden steps went up and down.

"We go up here. Servants' staircase," Hasanović said. His voice sounded unsteady, and Johnson could see the old man's hands were trembling.

"Let's get out of here. You go up the stairs," Hasanović said. "I'll follow."

He waited until Johnson and Jayne had gone up a flight and then followed.

Hasanović had climbed a quarter of the way up when he swore loudly; there was a heavy thud and a clattering sound below him. Johnson looked down and saw the old man had somehow dropped his gun on the wooden stairs. The weapon bounced hard off two steps, then fell between the banisters and down to the ground floor below.

"I'll go and fetch it, I'm sorry," Hasanović said.

Johnson held up his hand. "No, leave it, just leave it. I'll—"

But the old man ignored him and began walking down the stairs.

"Shit. I said leave it. Come up here," Johnson said, raising his voice sharply. Hasanović waved his hand dismissively and continued down.

He had picked up the gun and was heading back up the stairs when two loud shotgun blasts in quick succession crunched through the door between the TV room and the staircase, leaving splintered holes in the woodwork. Then came another two rounds.

Johnson took careful aim and loosed two shots at the door, which were immediately followed by a shout and a low-pitched yell from the other side. He continued to aim at the door as he edged backward up the stairs to the top landing.

"Quick, come up here," Johnson shouted to Hasanović.

The old man obeyed. He was halfway back up the stairs when a door crashed back against a wall on the ground floor below.

Hasanović turned momentarily to look below him, then tried to accelerate up the stairs, but he was far too slow. There was a sharp crack, the whine of a ricochet, and then another shot.

Almost in slow motion, Hasanović's head jerked forward. Johnson saw a plume of blood spray out from the front of his head, and then he toppled, his arms and legs spread wide, down the flight of stairs he had just climbed.

Instinctively, Johnson launched himself toward Jayne, who

was standing in an alcove in front of another door. "Go," he yelled.

She opened the door behind her and went through. Johnson followed right behind. He whipped around, pulled a bolt across the door, then followed her along a narrow corridor that ran the length of the back of the house. On the left were doors leading off to other rooms, on the right were windows overlooking the garden.

At the end was a white glazed door. Jayne sprinted toward it, pulled the handle down, and pushed it open. In front of them was an external metal spiral staircase that led down to the garden.

As Jayne clattered down the staircase, Johnson turned just as the men behind him pumped shots through the woodwork next to the bolt that secured the door at the other end of the corridor.

Johnson jumped down the stairs, taking them two at a time. At the bottom, Jayne sprinted toward a brick wall around twenty yards away that marked the edge of the property, then went around a tree and through an arched black gate that stood slightly ajar.

Johnson took off after her and threw himself through the gate just as a bullet zinged into the brickwork a few inches to his left.

Now they were in the narrow alley, paved with concrete and lined by high brick walls on both sides, where they had parked the car earlier.

Jayne ran hard up the single-track lane, Johnson just behind, his lungs aching, his legs pumping, and he cursed inwardly the number of cigarettes he had smoked in the past couple of weeks. He felt in his pocket for the car key as they reached the Golf, clicked the car open, and dove into the driver's seat, while Jayne jumped into the passenger seat.

Then he shoved the key into the ignition and started the engine, putting the Zastava on his lap.

Johnson accelerated out of the recess where he had parked and up to the top of the alley, the tires squealing in protest on the concrete.

In his rearview mirror, just as he was about to turn left from the alley onto the street, Johnson glimpsed a dark-haired man—who he was certain wasn't Franjo or Marco—emerging from the black gateway into the alley. A second later, there were two successive bangs as bullets flew into the bodywork at the rear of the Golf.

Johnson flinched reflexively but rammed the car into second and floored the accelerator as he turned, the engine screaming. In his mirror he noticed a silver Mercedes saloon farther up the road. Then two dark-haired men appeared at the end of the alley; one of them leveled his gun toward the Golf.

But Johnson was too far away by then and moving fast. He pushed into third gear, his foot still hard on the pedal. His head was hunched over the steering wheel, and his hands gripped it so tightly his knuckles turned white.

Just before he turned right, Johnson checked the mirror again. He saw the two men open the doors of the Mercedes and jump in. The Zastava on Johnson's lap fell to the floor and slid under the seat.

After a couple of sharp turns, Johnson headed onto Marasovića Street and accelerated up the hill. He glanced in his mirror. There was no sign of the silver Mercedes.

He reached Antun's house, and again the tires squealed as he turned sharply off the street and down the sloping driveway behind the row of conifers that shielded the house from the road.

Johnson braked hard to a halt just yards from the house, next to an azure Subaru Impreza with a large exhaust pipe, which was obviously Filip's newly acquired car. He turned the engine off. It was then he realized he was sweating profusely after the escape from Hasanović's house, his hands shaking. Jayne, also visibly sweating, sat still and momentarily leaned her head back against the headrest.

Johnson bent down and grabbed the Zastava from under the seat, then got out and took cover behind the front wing of the Golf, from where he could see up the driveway. Jayne crouched behind a bush near the front door, from where she could also cover the entrance to the property, her Walther at the ready.

Ten seconds later Johnson heard the deep whine of a high-powered engine coming fast up the road and glimpsed the silver Mercedes as it flew past on the other side of the conifers.

They waited another five minutes before Johnson stood and walked to Jayne. "They obviously don't know Filip lives here. Don't know who that was, though. Definitely not Marco and Franjo."

She nodded. "No, but just as bloody dangerous."

The front door behind them opened. There stood Filip. "I heard the car, then looked out and saw you."

"Yes, we've just had a slight skirmish with two gunmen," Johnson said. "We were at Hasanović's house, not far from here, and they got in and shot him dead. We're lucky to have gotten out of there."

Filip's eyebrows rose. "Marco and Franjo?"

"No, not them," Johnson said. "Other guys. Never seen them before."

"And they've killed Hasanović?" Filip asked. "This is crazy. Most likely men working for Marco, then."

"It must have been," Johnson said. "But I feel like a damned idiot, frankly."

Filip shook his head. "You'd better get inside. Go through

to the kitchen. I'll make you some coffee. I didn't even know that Hasanović lived near here. Tell me what happened."

"Those two assholes burst in while we were talking to him and gunned him down on the stairs of his own house," Jayne said. "It would have been us as well if we hadn't moved so fast."

"My God," Filip said. "How did they get in?"

As they walked to the kitchen, Johnson described how the two men had shot their way through the front door and a couple of internal doors.

"Haris gave us some useful information," Johnson said, "but he definitely had a lot more. So we're still no closer to knowing where Franjo is based or what his alias is or where Marco is. Have you heard any more from the police?"

"No," Filip said, as he prepared coffee. "I've actually just finished a phone call with the police detective running the inquiry into Petar's murder. He keeps telling me they can't find Marco. Trouble is, he knows I'm a convicted war criminal and won't take me seriously."

"You're right," Johnson said. "The police should have him behind bars by now. Our problem is I'd prefer to have Franjo arrested outside of Croatia or Bosnia—I think there's more chance of pinning him for his war crimes that way. And unlike with Marco, who's obviously going to have to answer for Petar's killing, I don't really want to get the local police involved. So it's tricky."

"So you don't have any leads at all?" Filip asked.

Johnson paused. "One, possibly. Not from Haris, though. Have you heard of an arms company called VMM Oružje Sustavi, based in Sarajevo? It's listed on the Sarajevo Stock Exchange."

Filip filled three cups with coffee and pushed two across the kitchen countertop to Johnson and Jayne. "Actually, yes, I know it quite well. What's the connection?"

"I heard Franjo is still a shareholder in the business," Johnson said.

Filip whistled. "Is he? Interesting. If he bought low and put a decent amount in, he's probably made a fortune in the past five years. The stock's gone up around tenfold."

He told Johnson that VMM had supplied weapons to the Croatians during the war, then went through a bad time afterward. Corruption had been a major problem, and VMM struggled with that, he explained. A lot of the managers had been siphoning off equipment and selling it to black market outlets all over the world, resulting in huge losses for a few years. But they had gotten rid of the corrupt managers, recovered well, and were now globally exporting weapons, ammo, mines, blasting caps, and other equipment.

"Fine," Johnson said. "If it's doing well, then it will probably be paying dividends to shareholders. So how are they paying Franjo? The company must have a shareholder register, with addresses and contact details, and it must pay dividends by bank transfer or check."

"And you want to know how to get those details?"

"Correct."

Filip sipped his own coffee and thought for a moment. "There's Viktor, a friend of Petar's from Moscow. He called my father last week after he heard about the shooting, and I had a word with him. I hadn't seen him since '95 but we had quite a chat. He's a miserable bastard, but he was extremely angry about what happened to Petar, so he might help."

He went on to explain that Viktor, a former defense-industry computer engineer, had gone to the "dark side." He was part of a group of software specialists that worked for a shadowy Russian outfit specializing in the use of Carbon and Turla software tools. They were infiltrating the systems of defense companies and selling their secrets to whichever state defense departments were prepared to pay for information that might give them an advantage when it came to the procurement of missile systems, weapons, ammunition, and other equipment.

Johnson grinned. "He told you all this?"

Filip looked out the window. "Not on the phone."

Johnson decided not to ask any more questions. If Filip thought his friend Viktor—whether that was his real name or not—might be able to get the information needed, then he wasn't going to argue about the methodology. *Think of the greater good.*

"Okay. When can you get in touch with him? If you like, I can speak to him. I'm fluent in Russian," Johnson said.

Filip leaned against the kitchen counter. "Let me speak with him, and we'll see what we can arrange. Have you wondered if Marco also invested? He and Franjo did everything together back then. I want to nail that bastard for what he did to Petar. You talk a lot about Franjo, but you need to remember that asshole Marco as well."

"Don't worry," Johnson said. "We haven't forgotten him. They're both going down together."

Johnson put the phone back in his pocket. "The other thing Hasanović mentioned was something about an airfield at Sinj. He said arms are smuggled out of there at night to Syria—the same weapons that came in from Iran in the early '90s. I'd like to take a look."

CHAPTER THIRTY-SIX

Monday, July 23, 2012
  Sinj, Croatia

Watson kicked one of the cardboard crates that stood in a corner of the darkened warehouse, then sat on it and lit a cigarette. A woman handed him a mug of coffee, which he took without speaking. He ran a hand through his white hair and stared at the floor.

A few dim light bulbs lit the interior of the small building, its corrugated steel walls pockmarked with rust. A pallet was already loaded on a small forklift. Its driver sat checking his phone. A few other men lounged around, waiting.

Watson checked his watch. It was half past one in the morning. He yawned deeply and took a sip of his coffee. He had slept only intermittently on his overnight flight from Washington, DC, to Split, via Vienna, and he already just wanted to be home.

A few days earlier, he had been relaxing at his home in

Wolf Trap when he had received news from Zagreb about the demise of his Croatian chief of station. Then there had been the subsequent call from RUNNER during which he learned that Johnson had somehow gotten his hands on documents that could potentially blow the whole lid off of a scheme Watson had kept quiet for two decades.

What a shitstorm.

Following the death of Edwards, the trip had been an easy one to explain to his boss, the deputy director. There were a lot of loose ends to tie up, and he needed to work out a replacement for Edwards as well as ensure that staff at the station in Zagreb were on top of arrangements for repatriation of the body.

After he'd done that, Watson had rented a car in Split and had driven the twenty-five miles to Sinj to ensure there were no hiccups with the arms sale agreed between "Stefan" and Mustafa for onward transit to Syria.

The CIA had secretly been playing quite a significant role across various countries, of which Croatia was one, in helping Syrian rebel commanders and their supporters shop for weapons that could be used to help bring down Bashar al-Assad, the Syrian president.

This had given Watson the perfect cover for his side operation. For a long time he had taken special measures to ensure not only that Boris and Marco got the deals ahead of other suppliers but that loading and transporting them went through without any interference from Croatian authorities.

There would be no local police patrols anywhere near the airfield this evening. The police chief in Sinj, whom Edwards, with some assistance from Watson, had finally recruited after almost a year of effort, had made sure of that.

The logistics were a hassle, but after years of smoothing the way for many deliveries of weapons, Watson had almost

$10 million in a numbered bank account in Zürich, which he had opened specifically to store his portion of the proceeds— of which Boris and Marco took by far the lion's share. The Zürich account was one of several Watson held in tax havens to quietly accumulate the proceeds of such off-the-books operations.

Not that the deputy director knew anything about the personal payments, the bribes, which Watson had received from Boris and Marco in return. Of that, Watson was certain.

Now Watson stood and walked over to the large double doors of the warehouse and stepped outside. He peered into the darkness.

Sinj was a small airfield, known locally as Piket, with a smooth 1,200-yard grass strip normally used only by private aircraft enthusiasts, businessmen, and small commercial planes.

Watson felt the burner cell phone he had purchased at Split Airport vibrate in his pocket. He never took his security for granted: he had removed the SIM card and battery from his CIA phone before leaving Split and had also taken the precaution of having the device checked for bugs.

He answered the call.

"SILVER."

"SILVER, it's SUNMAN. Are we ready to go? The plane's coming in."

"Yes, we're ready to go," Watson said. He had arranged for the road to be blocked in both directions by a supposed water leak. There were two local water-company vans and barriers out on the road at both ends of the airfield, including diversion signs, to prevent any passing traffic.

"Is RUNNER with you?" Watson asked.

"No, he had to head back to Split," Marco said. "He has a few jobs he needs to do there."

"Okay, we're good to go here. I'll confirm when the job's done," Watson said.

Watson could hear a faint drone coming from the darkened sky to the east. The Antonov An-72, a nimble twin-engine cargo jet, which could operate using short grass runways, was on its way in.

* * *

Johnson braked to a halt in front of the red and white workmen's barrier and large white van that blocked the road.

"What's this?" he said.

Jayne pointed at the green and blue logo on the side of the van, which was illuminated in the car's headlights. "Hrvatske Vode . . . that's Croatian Water," she said. "They must be repairing a leak or something. Bit odd at this time of night, don't you think?"

She took out her phone, clicked onto her maps app, and scrutinized it carefully. "The airstrip starts over there. You can just about make it out," she said. "Looks like the airport buildings are a bit farther up this road, on the left."

Johnson wound down the window of the Golf and peered out. "We'll have to park and walk, then. Might be a good thing for us. If the road's blocked, there'll be no passing traffic to see us."

He killed the Golf's headlights, then turned around. After a short distance, a rough track led off to the left past what appeared to be a timber yard, with piles of logs and wood stacked up inside a mesh fence enclosure.

Johnson edged cautiously down the track, then turned again and parked behind some bushes so the car was out of sight from the road.

He leaned over and removed the Zastava from the car's glove compartment. Then he pushed it into his waistband

and put two spare magazines, which Filip had acquired for him, into a small black backpack.

Next Johnson reached behind his seat and picked up his Olympus mirrorless camera, with its 40–150 mm zoom lens, and also placed that into the backpack. He switched on the camera and confirmed that the shutter click sound effect was disabled. "Right, let's go and check it out."

Jayne also put her gun in her waistband and shoved two spare magazines into her jacket pocket, then got out of the car.

From that point on, they both knew they wouldn't speak unless there was an operational need.

They walked back down the track toward the road. The water company van stood side-on behind the barrier, silent and unattended, its lights switched off. Drainage ditches on either side made it impossible to drive a vehicle past—the van completely blocked the road.

Johnson peered through the van window, then put his hand on the hood. It was still warm; the van had probably only been placed there very recently, he guessed. There was no sign of activity.

Jayne pointed silently toward the airfield, indicating to Johnson that they should walk there behind the hedge rather than on the road.

They scrambled down a small ditch and up the other side, onto a mown area of grass, then made their way eastward, sticking tight to the cover afforded by the darkness of the hedge. In the distance, the black outline of the hills surrounding the tiny town of Sinj was just visible against the slightly paler sky.

Gradually the silhouette of two buildings came into view ahead of them, both of which had lights shining dimly from inside.

Johnson stopped.

On the night air, the faint drone of an approaching plane was just audible. Then to their left, in the middle of the grass airstrip, a light flicked on, its narrow beam shining into the sky. The sound of the plane's engines grew louder, and the light flicked off and on three times.

Hasanović had been correct. The aircraft wasn't visible, though. Johnson scanned the night sky, trying to spot it.

Jayne pointed and he tried to follow her line. Then he spotted it: a black silhouette visible against the sky for a few seconds before it dropped below the level of the surrounding hills.

The water company van was clearly just a decoy to prevent casual passersby from getting close. Johnson began walking again.

They hugged close to the hedge and approached the rear of what appeared to be a small hangar, made of corrugated steel.

An engine started inside the hangar, and a small orange forklift emerged, carrying a pallet on which rested several large cardboard boxes.

The low, insistent drone of aircraft engines grew nearer, and then, through the gloom, Johnson saw the aircraft touch down and run three-quarters of the way down the grass strip before turning and heading back toward the hangar.

It stopped thirty yards short of it and the engines shut off, the whine dwindling gradually until the aircraft stood in silence.

Johnson took out his camera, turned up its ISO light sensitivity to the maximum, and took a few pictures of the aircraft and the hangars. There was just enough peripheral light to give an exposure. He pointed silently to the back of the hangar, where he could see a few rust holes in the metal, and then to his camera. Jayne nodded.

They crouched and shuffled behind a grassy bank until they reached the rear of the hangar.

Johnson flattened himself to the ground and crawled the last ten yards until he could see through a sizable rust hole in the hangar wall. Inside, a few men stood around several boxes on pallets.

He carefully raised his camera's zoom lens to the hole in the metal sheeting and pressed the shutter release halfway down to focus the blurred image.

What appeared in his viewfinder caused Johnson to nearly drop the Olympus.

The figure was shockingly familiar; angular shoulders, a white mop of hair with a well-shaped cut at the back, an open-necked shirt with a blue and red checkered pattern.

The man turned his head so his face was visible. It was Robert Watson, sitting on a cardboard box.

Johnson turned to Jayne and pointed in Watson's direction. She nodded, having peered through another hole and also recognizing him.

He reapplied his right eye to the viewfinder. The cardboard box on which Watson was seated had a white sticker on the side marked Fragile: Microwave Ovens. He was reading a sheaf of papers.

So this was how one of the CIA's top dogs earned himself extra pocket money. Unbelievable. First he arms Bin Laden and his boys. Now it's the Syrian rebels.

With his lens at a full 150 mm, equivalent to 300 mm on his SLR, Johnson zoomed the camera in as tightly as he could on Watson and the papers, pressed the shutter release, and silently clicked off a few frames. When Watson's face was visible again, Johnson clicked a few more.

The forklift sped back into the warehouse and picked up another pallet of boxes. Johnson took a few pictures of the forklift, which then turned and took its load out to the waiting aircraft.

Johnson clicked on one of the photographs of Watson on the camera's viewing screen and magnified the sheaf of papers he was reading.

He couldn't read the actual writing, but it appeared to be a list of some kind, running vertically down the page. It was probably a list of the weaponry that was being loaded onto the aircraft, Johnson surmised.

Microwave ovens, my ass.

Johnson turned off the display and looked through the viewfinder again, then pressed the camera lens back up to the hole.

As he did so, he moved his right knee out, which threw him off balance a little. He recovered his position, but as he did, the end of the zoom lens banged gently against the metal wall of the warehouse.

* * *

Maybe it was some kind of sixth sense, a self-protection mechanism, of the kind that had enabled Watson to be a survivor rather than a victim over his four and a half decades of service with the CIA.

It had kept him alive through a series of gun battles, including, in late 2001, the battle of Tora Bora in the deadly maze of caves in eastern Afghanistan. At the age of fifty-five he had been the oldest member of the team and had injured his knee in the process. That was when the CIA's National Clandestine Service, together with Special Forces colleagues, had unsuccessfully hunted for Osama bin Laden.

And perhaps it was partly because now, at an age when most men were retiring, he had experienced no loss of acuity in hearing or eyesight.

Whatever the reason, Watson heard the faint metallic noise behind him, despite the hustle and bustle going on around him in the warehouse and the clattering of the forklift truck returning from the Antonov aircraft outside.

He immediately turned from the papers he had been carefully scrutinizing and rapidly scanned the back of the warehouse, about twenty yards away.

In the corner, not far above the ground, he caught no more than a flicker of light reflecting from something shiny in a hole in the steel hangar wall.

But it was enough.

Watson stood and took a few slow paces toward the source of the reflection. Immediately he realized what the shiny element behind it was. But it vanished and the hole went black.

Watson swiveled and limped quickly over to a security guard who stood next to one of the piles of cardboard boxes, an AK-47 hanging against his back on a shoulder strap. A second rifle rested on the floor, leaning against the cardboard boxes beside him.

Johnson stood up and stuffed the camera into his backpack, which he swung onto his shoulders. He could see that Jayne had realized immediately from his speed of movement that something had happened.

She pointed back to the road, turned, and ran ahead of Johnson in the direction they had come, across a rough area of ground littered with pieces of timber and old bricks that were just about visible in the faint glow of light being thrown from the warehouse.

Johnson took off after her as she veered left toward the hedge. He looked over his shoulder and glimpsed a figure emerging from the side of the warehouse to their right. The silhouette was clear enough for Johnson to see that he was raising a rifle to his shoulder.

Johnson grabbed the Zastava from his waistband and had no choice but to call to Jayne, five yards ahead of him. "Down!"

She ran around a stack of railway ties, dived to the ground, and rolled into the bottom of the hedge that separated the airfield from the road. Johnson dived a fraction of a second later, just after a rifle shot had rung out, followed by another two.

Johnson half cried out as he felt an impact on the side of his left shoulder. As he landed, he instinctively put his right hand to the place and found his jacket was ripped. He'd been hit, but it seemed like a glancing blow that he hoped was more coat than flesh. He found he could still move his left arm freely, albeit with a little pain.

Johnson raised the Zastava and fired a couple of shots toward the silhouette at the side of the warehouse. The man hit the floor as Johnson's shots ricocheted with a loud clang off the metal wall of the building, just to the right of his target.

There were two flashes to his left as Jayne also fired shots at the guard, who was now invisible, flat on the grass.

Johnson pointed to the road, then jumped up, bent himself double, and ran through a small gap in the hedge.

But in the darkness, he miscalculated the depth of the drainage ditch at the side of the road. As the ground fell away beneath him, Johnson went headfirst into the grassy bank on the far side of the ditch, certain as he did so that he heard more bullets hissing through the hedge above his head.

His left shoulder hit the ground as he landed. "Shit," Johnson muttered involuntarily.

"Stay in the ditch," Jayne said as she landed next to him.

Additional shots whined just above their heads; then came fire from a second semiautomatic weapon.

Johnson gestured along the ditch in the direction of their car. They began to move, crouching as low as possible as they left the protection afforded by the stack of wooden ties.

Johnson risked raising his head slightly, looking from behind the hedge toward the warehouse.

Now there were two figures visible, one behind the other. Johnson realized the guard was in front, almost completely blocking his view of Watson.

Johnson raised his pistol carefully and took aim, resting his right arm and gun on a small rock at the base of the hedge.

He fired two shots, causing both men to dive to the ground again. Johnson's instinct was that he hadn't hit them.

"Run," Johnson muttered. "They're both on the floor."

From behind him, near the warehouse, came the deep-throated roar of a diesel engine firing up, followed by a squeal of tires as the clutch on the vehicle was let out quickly.

Johnson and Jayne jumped up and began sprinting hard down the road toward the Hrvatske Vode water company van. Johnson could now feel wetness down his left arm, coming from the shoulder wound.

There was another squeal of tires behind them, louder now.

Johnson and Jayne drew near to the van. Behind them came the high-pitched whining of a diesel engine being thrashed at high revs.

They sprinted around the back of the white van, Johnson to the left, Jayne to the right, just as a bullet smashed into the metal bodywork.

Johnson turned and crouched behind the van's rear

bumper, then took two shots at the rapidly approaching vehicle, a Land Cruiser. One bullet hit the windshield, and the Land Cruiser veered right, straight into the ditch where it came to an abrupt halt, tilted at forty-five degrees.

Johnson made sure he was shielded from the direct line of sight of the men in the Land Cruiser by the body of the van, then made his way toward Jayne, who was heading for the Golf. He followed her around the corner of the timber merchant's compound to the car, which was just a little farther up the track behind the bushes.

As they reached the car, there was more gunfire from behind them.

Johnson jumped into the Golf's driver's seat.

Jayne opened the passenger door. "Do you want me to drive?" she asked.

"No, let's go," Johnson said. He screwed up his face in pain, started the engine, and shot off down the lane toward the van.

"Go, go for it," Jayne said, her voice level.

Johnson could see the driver of the Land Cruiser had reversed out of the ditch and onto the road, but the man's route forward was completely blocked by the van and the twin ditches on either side.

As Johnson approached, he got a clear view of a man holding a gun who climbed out of the Land Cruiser's passenger door. It was Marco Lukić.

Johnson floored the accelerator and looked in his rearview mirror to see Marco aiming the gun in his direction. The Golf sped down the road away from the airfield, its rear end swinging slightly as he steered around a bend.

For the second time in two days, the rear of the rental car took a couple of bullets, one of which smashed into the rear window.

Johnson groaned as he shifted into third but said nothing. Quickly, they were out of range and into the outskirts of Sinj.

"I'm going to have to fix that shoulder for you," Jayne said. "We can't exactly go into a local hospital here. That SIS emergency aid training of mine might finally come in handy. You'd better find somewhere we can park and sort it out."

Johnson nodded. He turned down a side street, cut another left down a narrow road, and pulled up under a streetlight.

Jayne pulled a small first aid kit from her bag and removed a small bottle of rubbing alcohol, two bandages, some tape, scissors, and a curved needle and thread and set to work.

Johnson removed his shirt, gently peeling away the material from the wound, to which it had already begun to stick.

The bullet had nicked the side of Johnson's shoulder, leaving a shallow gash, an inch and a half long, which was bleeding steadily.

"You're lucky it's just clipped you. Very lucky. Another inch or two and it would have shattered your shoulder. I can fix this," Jayne said confidently.

She splashed some alcohol over the wound, which bit into Johnson's nerve endings and made him clench his teeth.

"I can't stitch this, it's too wide. But it's shallow, so I'll pack it with gauze to stop the bleeding. I think it'll be fine. If it's sore in the morning we can go to the hospital and come up with some explanation," she said. She packed a square bandage over the top of the injury and wound the gauze over Johnson's shoulder and under his armpit to hold it in place.

"That's the best I can do," Jayne said. "I'm going to drive now. We'll go back to Split and head for Filip's house. We'll have to get another car. The rental company will go bloody crazy when they see this one, so I'm not going to take the risk. I'll just hire another and leave this at Filip's. We can sort this one out later."

"Maybe we could borrow Filip's Subaru?" Johnson said.

"No. He's told me the starter motor's playing up. I don't want to risk it."

They swapped seats and set off.

Johnson groaned as the car went over a pothole and jarred his shoulder. "At least I've got the pictures of Watto."

Jayne nodded. "He's screwed, frankly."

CHAPTER THIRTY-SEVEN

Monday, July 23, 2012
  Split

When the effects of ibuprofen and a generous slug of brandy wore off, Johnson awoke on Antun's living room sofa, where he had insisted on sleeping so Jayne could use the spare bedroom. He looked at his watch. It was eight o'clock, just three hours after he had finally gotten to sleep.

He dropped his head back on the cushion and stared at the ceiling. He assumed from the slightly reduced throbbing in his shoulder that it had thankfully not become infected during Jayne's makeshift repair operation.

Johnson moved his left arm and winced. He looked at the bandage. The bloodstains on the bandage had dried and there was no evidence of fresh seepage coming through.

Johnson grabbed his phone and tapped out a secure text message to Vic.

Got injured in a shootout with Watto. Unbelievable. He was overseeing arms shipment from Sinj airfield, near Split. I have photos. Any progress with checks on his bank accounts?

Then he remembered it was still only two o'clock in the morning in DC and swore to himself.

Filip poked his head around the door. "How you feeling, Joe?"

"Shit."

"Not surprised. Jayne told me what happened before she went to bed."

"Did you hear back from your friend Viktor?" Johnson asked. "Can he get Franjo's address from the VMM share register? Is Marco's address on there?"

"He's working on it," Filip said. "VMM is one of the companies they've penetrated with Turla. They've been in there for over a year, but their focus has been on the weapons technology and sales and marketing side. He said they need a bit of time to get into the investor relations directories. And then they need to work their way through a lot of shit. But it's moving."

Johnson nodded. "Good. Tell him it's really urgent. It's the vital missing cog."

Then his phone pinged as a text message arrived from Ana.

Joe, I've been exchanging messages with Aisha and I'm worried. Can you give me a call as soon as you can?

He used his Skype app to call Ana's cell phone.

"Ana, it's Joe here. Are you still in Mostar? I got your message."

"Yes, still here. Something's going on with Aisha. She sent me a message saying she now knows Franjo is still alive, but—"

"Correct, Ana," Johnson interrupted, "he is alive. I told her that was true. The issue is we don't know where he's based." As with Aisha, Johnson decided not to tell Ana about the almost deadly recent encounters he'd had with Franjo and Marco or the fact that he had come frustratingly close to the two men but hadn't been able to have them arrested.

"But you see," Ana said, "that's worrisome. I always wondered why she hated him quite so much after the war. She never really told me. Yes, they split, but so did many couples back then. It was more than that. But I've talked to more people here while I've been doing my research on the bridge. I've been given a few hints about what happened the day the Old Bridge was destroyed."

Johnson sat up and winced again at the pain in his shoulder. "What hints? What did he do?"

Ana hesitated. "Listen, I'll let you know, as soon as I'm sure of what I'm saying—there's one more person I need to speak to later today."

"Come on, Ana. Can't you give me a clue?"

"No, not yet."

"Okay, but you know I need to get Franjo on trial for the war crimes he's committed. Better to give me information than withhold it."

"Sure, but if what I'm hearing is true, you need to make sure Aisha doesn't learn where Franjo is before you get to him."

"Why do you say that?" Johnson asked.

"Because if she got to him first, I think there's a chance she might just kill him."

"*What?*"

"I can't explain now, but let's say that I'm starting to think her hatred of him is more complicated. I promise to explain as soon as I understand it all myself, but I wanted to warn you. Don't call her."

Johnson suppressed a groan. "Okay, I won't."

"Thanks, Joe, talk soon."

Ana hung up and Joe fell back onto the couch. *What's going to crawl out of the woodwork here?*, he wondered.

* * *

Tuesday, July 24, 2012
New York City

"You've been spending a lot of time in Studio One recently, Aisha. Everything okay?"

Aisha jumped and looked up to see Olly standing in the doorway, hands on his hips.

"Yeah, fine," she said. "Just trying to get the DMX addressing sorted for the extra moving lights we've brought in for the Spencer interview. Tim's asked me to come up with some cues using this new fancy special effects light he's decided to bring in for the beginning and the end, so I'm just thinking it all through."

She paused. "We need to try and do something really good —make it as memorable as possible."

"Okay, good. Are you making progress?" Olly asked. It was only quarter to eight in the morning, and Aisha knew that Olly would be surprised to see her already in the studio.

"Yes. I'm just working out how to program this new fixture, because I've never seen it before. He wants to use it after the final question, when the interviewer guy, Boris or whatever his name is, wraps up and thanks Spencer for coming on the show. Anyway, I've been reading the manual, and I've got a few ideas."

Aisha scratched her chin and studied the rig above her head.

Olly stared at Aisha for a moment. "Okay, I'll leave you to it."

He opened his mouth and started to say something else but then stopped and walked off, shutting the studio door behind him.

Aisha climbed the stairs to the lighting gallery where the control desk was situated, along with the wall of monitors that allowed the crew to see all the different camera angles.

She sat down at the lighting desk. Then she opened the control panel for the lighting hoist system, which allowed the lighting bars to be lowered to the studio floor so the electricians could put the various lamp units in place.

Next Aisha glanced at the lighting plot, which mapped out the design of the TV studio set and the lighting fixtures needed for the interview.

She noticed that the new special effects light was to be rigged on a bar directly over the set where the interview would take place.

Aisha then looked out of the big gallery window into the studio and up into the blackness of the lighting grid. There, high in the ceiling, the lighting bar in question was almost invisible against the other black-painted hardware.

Should she do what she had in mind—or not? Aisha sat there undecided for a full five minutes, staring up into the darkness, her hands clasped together.

The feelings she had tried to bury for two decades had never gone away. Was now the time to put them to bed for good? Was this the only way? Or was there another way?

She visualized the studio audience sitting, eager, excited, listening. Mothers, dads, children, grandmothers, and teenagers.

Three times Aisha's hand hovered over a button on the control panel. Three times she withdrew it again.

But then she suddenly and decisively pressed it, and the bar, consisting of a large metal enclosure that housed cables, sockets, and other electronic equipment, slowly descended.

She exited the gallery and stepped down to the studio floor. The bar, on which two normal lamps and the big new special effects lamp had already been mounted, came to rest just above the floor. Aisha now stood right on the spot where she knew Spencer and Franjo would eventually face each other in two armchairs for the interview.

She walked over to the inner studio door, turned the lock, and pulled down a blind to cover the small window that looked into the area between the inner and outer studio door. Then she went back to the lighting bar and used a screwdriver to remove the side panel so she could see the space inside.

Aisha reached into her backpack and removed two small black metal boxes. The first was similar in size to a paperback book, with a clip on each corner; the second was the size of a cigarette pack, also with clips on each corner. Adela's friends from the mosque had not wasted any time in getting what Aisha needed once they heard about the possibility of an attack on Spencer. They had also showed her precisely how to use the equipment she now had in front of her.

She opened a flap on the larger of the two black boxes. Inside was a small slab of reddish-brown material. She closed it again, took eight screws from a small plastic bag, and used the screwdriver to attach both black boxes to the inside of the lighting bar enclosure. Then Aisha took a length of electrical wire with a plug on each end; she pushed one end into a socket on the larger box and the other into the smaller box.

Next, she took out her cell phone, called a number, and watched as it rang. After a couple of rings, a small green light on the smaller of the two black boxes started to flash. Aisha cut the call off immediately.

Then she screwed the side panel back into place on the lighting bar so it looked just as it had before, with the two black boxes fixed firmly in place on the inside but invisible to any external scrutiny.

Aisha returned to the gallery and clicked again on the button that drew the lighting bar back up into the rig. Then she unlocked the door and raised the blind to avoid any questions when the morning crowd arrived.

Next Aisha toggled the computer screen to the lighting desk software that CBA used to program its lighting cues, or changes, in advance for the various television shows that it produced.

Aisha selected the show file that the team had already created for the Spencer interview. A preliminary list of lighting cues had already been set up by Tim, the lighting director, which Aisha knew from experience she would need to modify and fix for the interview. She scrolled down to the end of the list.

Just before the last couple of cues, to dim the studio lights when the final credits started to roll, she inserted an extra cue that would lower the lighting bar on which she had just worked to bring it right down over the heads of Spencer and Wolff. It would bathe the two of them in an animated dappled white water effect against the blue of the darkened set behind them.

Aisha saved the new settings and closed the application.

Then she walked out of the CBA studios and across the road to a small park, where she sat on a bench by herself, took out her phone, and called Adela.

"Hi, it's me. I'm just calling to tell you I've done it," Aisha said quietly. "I found it hard to decide, but it's done."

There was a long pause. "You've done it, really? That's good, Aisha. I had my doubts, but I apologize. Allah is great."

* * *

Tuesday, July 24, 2012
  Split

"Now's the time, Marco," Boris said. "It's like I've always said. Now that we've screwed all we can out of the weapons cache, sold it off, why should I continue keeping the dossier quiet? We've got the cash. Now I'd like some career glory. It's a huge scoop for me, a payoff." Boris looked at his friend.

"Nice for you. No use to me," Marco replied. "And you're wrong, the cache isn't almost all sold off. There's enough left to make two more large loads. So while you go glory hunting, I'm going to be worse off because it'll be very difficult to sell more Kalashnikovs for a long time. You'll scare off all the buyers. They won't trust us."

Marco walked to the drinks cupboard in the hotel suite and poured himself a single malt.

"But we don't need any more money," Boris said. "And this is just too good to miss."

To him, the key revelation was still that the Clinton administration had effectively allowed Izetbegović to bring weapons to Bosnia from Iran—and that was a story that would shoot him to the top.

Marco turned around and took a large slug from the whiskey glass. "Quite apart from that, the more you put your head above the parapet the greater the chance of Johnson tracking us down and building a war crimes case against us. That's what he does—remember? And that's quite apart from what I did to Petar. You said before that either we finish him off or you drop the story. And we haven't finished him off."

Boris went out onto the balcony of the eighth-floor suite at Le Méridien, a tourist hotel and casino next to the beach at Podstrana, a few kilometers southeast of Split, and stood, thinking.

Then he leaned over the balcony, scanning right and left to check that nobody was eavesdropping. He turned back to Marco. "You're right, it's a risk to go ahead with the story. But I think it's a risk worth taking. The chances of Johnson getting to me are actually small. And even if he has photographs of the documents, he won't have the originals."

Marco rolled his eyes. "The other thing to remember is that if those documents go public, Watson's identity is going to come out, even if he's not named directly. Someone will work it out. Then he'll be after you as well as Johnson."

"It doesn't have to come out," Boris said. "He's not named. But I'm not that sympathetic to Watson. He's made about $10 million that should be ours, and he's not had to take much risk. It's purely been money in return for not putting obstacles in our way."

Marco nodded. "You don't have to remind me how much money he's taken. But without him covering things up for us over the years, would we have been able to do what we've done? Unlikely."

Boris knew that was true, but he still hated the feeling of someone else getting a cut that should be his. His journalist's instinct had for a long time also left him curious about the identity of some of the other people named in the Izetbe-gović documents, including the "Mr. B" who was referenced more than once and the anonymous Pentagon defense adviser. He had always felt that to find out, he would need to take risks that could blow his cover.

It was possible that running the Iran story might bring him further leads that could identify those people. Overall, this story was far too good an opportunity to let slip.

CHAPTER THIRTY-EIGHT

Tuesday, July 24, 2012
  Split Airport

The lounge at Split Airport was crowded, the year-round cohort of business travelers supplemented by a large number of peak season summer tourists.

Watson struggled to find somewhere quiet to have an important phone conversation prior to boarding his flight back to DC's Dulles Airport, via Vienna.

He poured a large Jack Daniel's on the rocks at the self-service bar, then made his way to one of the black club chairs in the corner near the window, overlooking the runway.

Watson dropped his bag on the floor, then clutched his left wrist, which he had sprained when he dived to safety during the firefight at Sinj. He knew that at his age he had gotten off lightly, but a tendon injury would take some time to heal.

Who the hell was that gunman with the camera? Watson suspected it might have been Johnson. But how would

Johnson possibly know about the Sinj operation? Only a very small, tight group of people were in the loop about the night flight.

He drank the whiskey in one gulp, picked up his bag in his right hand, and strode out into the terminal building again. There was so much noise there that it was actually a safer location from which to make a call than the hushed lounge, where fellow passengers could eavesdrop.

Watson dialed a number with his Croatian burner phone. "RUNNER, I need to talk to you urgently," he said as soon as the call was answered. "I'm still extremely worried about Johnson having read those documents."

"I told you, we got them back," Boris said.

"Where are they right now?"

"I have them on me."

"You're carrying the damned things around with you? You're going to keep them under wraps, I hope?" Watson asked.

"That's my business," Boris said.

There was something in Boris's tone. Watson was preparing to give him both barrels when the phone went dead.

Boris had hung up.

Watson cursed. He called another number, this time for a US cell phone. Doing so was a risk, but unusually, he was feeling a little stressed now, and the call couldn't wait until he was back on US soil. He would have to let the guy know.

"EDISON, its SILVER. We've got a problem."

"This had better be urgent. Go on, tell me."

"Something may be about to kick off in Bosnia. Some important documents have leaked, ones that came from Izetbegović's office back in '93. You know what I'm saying?" Watson said.

There was a long silence at the other end of the line. "I've been worried about this happening for twenty years. You'd better level with me. Do these documents name names?"

"No, don't think so. But people might add two and two together."

The man code-named EDISON muttered a stream of expletives. "So it's potentially career-ending?"

"Not necessarily. But potentially," Watson said.

"Sonofabitch. How long have you known about these documents? And who's got them?"

Watson said, "I've known about them for some time. But previously I've been fairly confident the person who had them wouldn't do anything silly. The guy who has them is a Bosnian Croat, an arms trader by night, with a respectable job by day. I'm worried he might make the documents public. He's not after you, I don't think, but the problem is that the trail could lead to you."

"Is there anything we can do?" EDISON asked.

Watson paused again. "Not obviously."

"Well, can we just pay off whoever it is who's had the documents?"

"It's complicated," Watson said. "Throwing money at the problem won't work. The person who's had them for some time, actually ever since '93, is difficult. He hasn't done anything with them, but I'm not certain how long that will last. Even worse, another person managed to get his hands on them for a short time—an American war crimes investigator. We've got them back, but I've been told this investigator guy is fully aware of the contents. I don't know whether he's copied them or not, but yes, he's another threat."

"This is goddamned awful timing for me. I've got a series of public events coming up," EDISON said.

"So what's new? Cancel them," Watson said.

"I can't. They're too big. Can't you just dispose of these people? That's what you do, isn't it, in your profession?"

"It's not that easy," Watson said. "If I take them out, there's some sort of mechanism in place to take me down as well. I'd most likely go to prison, that's if I didn't get a bullet first."

"So we're screwed?" EDISON asked.

"I wouldn't say that."

"Forgive me, but it looks that way to me."

CHAPTER THIRTY-NINE

Tuesday, July 24, 2012
Split

Out of the corner of his eye, Johnson saw Filip ambling out of his kitchen door carrying a printed sheet of paper and heading in his direction.

Johnson was busy on the phone with his son, Peter, who was at Amy's house; he was congratulating him on making the district basketball team. Peter had trained hard all year, and the selection was well deserved.

Filip stood waiting until Johnson finished the call. "Sorry, I didn't want to interrupt," he said, "But I've got something here that might be of interest. Viktor's come up with the goods."

Johnson forgot the two painkillers he had in his hand. "He's got it?"

The piece of paper that Filip held gave him his answer. "Share register for VMM. He's emailed a copy of the page we need."

Johnson put the tablets and glass of water down on the table. "Let's see."

Jayne looked up from her phone screen as Filip held the page so Johnson could read it.

"He got the whole list," Filip said. "There's nearly four hundred shareholders, nearly all of whom have addresses in the former Yugoslavia, mostly Bosnia and Herzegovina. But twelve are based elsewhere."

He pointed to the heading, which read "Non-Yugoslav Investors."

"These first nine are all investment houses, hedge funds, the usual suspects, based in New York, London, Zürich, and so on," Filip said.

He slid his finger down the page. "But then you've got these three—all individuals, not institutions. One has an address listed in Sydney, Australia, another in Johannesburg, and then this one in London, a Boris Wolff."

Filip went on, "Just look at that surname, Wolff. You can speak some Serbo-Croat. What's the significance of that?"

Johnson tried to reconcile the English surname with his somewhat rusty Croat vocabulary. "Tell me." But then, before Filip could speak, it dawned on him. "The Croat word for 'wolf' is *vuk*."

"Yes."

"So Vuković?"

"Exactly," Filip said. He momentarily looked impressed. "*Vuković* means 'the son of the wolf.' That's your man. It's got to be. Franjo Vuković is Boris Wolff. He has an address listed in Ennismore Mews, London."

Johnson let out a low whistle. He suddenly forgot his throbbing shoulder. "Filip, that's good work, if it's true. I mean, it's a different word, but there is a connection. I'm a bit surprised he didn't choose a name that's more obscure."

Jayne leaned over and studied the sheet. "Yes, but how

many times do you see this sort of thing? People are just too proud, too emotional about their roots. They can't sever family ties, geographic ties."

"There's the first name, too," Filip said. "Boris is an old Bulgarian name—not a million miles from Bosnia. In the old Bulgar language, which nobody speaks anymore, that also means 'wolf.'"

Jayne exchanged glances with Johnson. "If this is correct, we need to get to London," she said.

"Agreed," Johnson said. "But let's get it confirmed. Jayne, can you do an online check and see what you can find about Boris Wolff in London?"

"Sure," Jayne said. She took out her phone and began a Google search.

Johnson placed his hands behind his head and leaned back. "If that *is* him, we'll need evidence, of course. And if we could get him arrested on British soil, that would be perfect —far better in terms of getting the prosecution process under way in an orderly way than trying to do it from here."

"Bloody hell," Jayne said, staring at her phone screen. "Look at this. The only Boris Wolff I can find listed for London is a TV interviewer—a political and international affairs specialist. Works for a company called SRTV and has a show called *Wolff Live*. That can't be him, surely?"

"Is there a photo?" Johnson asked.

She tapped on the screen and held up the phone, which showed a photograph of a middle-aged man with neat short dark hair and a fleshy face, wearing a suit.

"That's him," Johnson said. "Can he really be doing that job?"

"He could," said Filip. "He trained as a broadcast journalist, remember. Does it say anything else?"

"There's some other stuff here," Jayne said. "One or two minor magazine interviews with him, a handful of newspaper articles. Surprisingly little, though. Looks like he's interviewed a few top politicians, most recently David Cameron. And it says he's got an interview coming up on Friday with Patrick Spencer, the US speaker of the House. There's a short biography, but it doesn't say where he's from, no mention of Bosnia or Yugoslavia. Just says he spent some time at the BBC World Service earlier in his career. Nothing about family."

"He wouldn't exactly be giving much background away if he's changed his identity," Johnson said. "Even your people at Six didn't find any trace of what happened to Franjo after the war, did they?"

"No, other than the vague Germany connection I told you about," Jayne said.

"Look," Johnson said. "he'll likely have those Sarajevo documents at his London house. I need to get them back as well as pick up any other evidence. There's only one way of doing that."

Jayne looked at him. "What? Get into the house?"

Johnson nodded. "Does it say where this interview with Spencer is taking place?"

"It just says it's happening in the US. No location given. Most likely DC or New York, would be my guess."

"I'll get Vic to check. That could help us," Johnson said. "If it's him, and he's interviewing in the US, his house will likely be empty. We could even have him arrested in the States. The key is getting those documents back as evidence first, though. I think I'll head over to London first thing tomorrow."

He turned to Filip. "The other question is over Marco. I assume he's not listed among the investors?"

"No," Filip said. "Unfortunately not. I'm putting feelers out in other directions among my network, though. Don't worry, I'll find him."

"When you do, tell us," Johnson said. "I don't want you to start taking revenge."

"No. I think you're forgetting I've done sixteen years in prison," Filip said. "I hated every day. So I want Marco to do life."

Johnson's phone beeped. He read the message and stood up. "It's from Ana. I need to give her a call."

"Okay," Jayne said, "You do that. Meanwhile, I'll go and phone Natasha at the Neptun and tell her she unfortunately needs to stay there for a day or two longer until we can make 100 percent sure it's safe for her to go back home."

"Yes, I agree. Just apologize to her again," Johnson said. "Tell her we'll cover the bill—I'll just add it to Vic's expense sheet, given she's only there because we're trying to get his documents."

Jayne gave a half smile and took her phone from her pocket. "Yes, will do."

Johnson walked from the patio into the house and rang Ana's number, again using Skype.

"Joe, hi, I've found out something," she said without preamble as soon as she answered the call. "It's about Aisha."

"Hi, Ana. Go on, then."

"I met with someone this afternoon. Listen to this. That day the Stari Most was destroyed was the day Aisha's father and her sister were killed, right? And you remember the bridge was destroyed by tank shells?"

"Yes."

"Okay. This person, who was an eyewitness that day, described to me how the tank had been firing at the bridge parapets but suddenly adjusted its line of fire to the archway on the western side of the bridge right at the moment Aisha's father and Zeinab, her sister, were there with a couple of other people. They were carrying wounded people from the front line back to eastern Mostar for treatment at the hospital. This person told me how someone with a walkie-talkie shouted instructions to the tank commander to adjust his aim. He yelled things like, 'Now, now, they're both there.' That kind of thing."

Ana stopped speaking for a moment, and Johnson thought he heard her sob.

"Sorry, Ana, take your time."

Ana hesitated, then continued, "The two of them were hit and killed immediately, together with the two others and a guy on a stretcher. Apparently, the guy with the walkie-talkie shouted that he'd got them and gave a bit of a whoop, a victory shout, or something like that."

Ana took a deep breath. "Joe, I'm very, very close to 100 percent confirmation that that commander was Franjo. And . . . it's true that Aisha's always been more bitter about Franjo than you would have expected, but all this does explain it. He's directly responsible for the death of her father and sister. Joe, she's never gotten over that loss."

Johnson stared up at the sky. The white cloud formation hanging over the Adriatic horizon west of Split had turned a vivid scarlet as the sun began to set. He realized as he watched that it was a metaphor for the Balkans: white to scarlet, a blood-red sky.

"Joe, are you still there?"

"Yes, I'm here. Sorry, just thinking."

"There's more. The guy I talked to said that the details of what happened were actually recorded during one of the international tribunal hearings in The Hague. One of the tank crew, who my source thinks is the only survivor, gave evidence as part of the prosecution inquiry into how the Stari Most was destroyed and referred to this incident. That's the testimony that would cement it. But my source said we would have to go to The Hague to look at the transcripts to check it out. I think we should go there and get them."

"Ana, thanks for all this," Johnson said after a few seconds. "It opens the door to a lot of evidence that we need to nail Franjo."

He went on to explain to Ana what he had discovered about Franjo's apparent alias, Boris, from the shareholder register, and that it now appeared Franjo was based in London and was working in TV.

"You've done well to get that information, then," Ana said. "You didn't share all that with Aisha, I assume?"

"No, of course not. Anyway, I only just learned it myself."

"Oh . . . but, Joe. The other reason for this call is that I received a text message from Aisha. It just said that she'd had a vision that Franjo would be dead inside three days."

"You serious?"

"Yes. It might be just her hatred coming out now that she knows he's alive, but it crossed my mind that she might have discovered his identity and location, too."

Johnson pursed his lips. "Was there anything in her message to suggest she had a plan?"

"No, nothing."

"*Three days?* Damn it," Johnson said. "Okay, I'm going to locate Franjo, but for the war crimes case against him, I need those files at The Hague. You've done some of the research on this. You're close to it. So I have a big favor to ask."

"You want me to go to The Hague?"

"Will you do it? I need to get to London." Johnson said.

"Yes, sure. Tomorrow morning?"

Johnson let out a sigh of relief. "Thank you so much. You get yourself on a flight, and I'll sort out the costs with you."

He ended the call, then tapped out a secure text message to Vic, who he knew was busy trying to get more detail on Watson's involvement with the Syrian arms sales out of Sinj, following Johnson's text detailing the shoot-out at the airstrip.

Urgent...two things. First, we think Franjo Vuković has an alias, Boris Wolff, and is a TV interviewer based in London for SRTV. He's apparently due in the US to interview Patrick Spencer on Friday. We don't know where. Can you find out? I'm heading to London ASAP to check out his house—hoping to locate your Sarajevo docs there and gather other evidence. Second, can you keep an eye on Aisha? She sent friend Ana a msg saying she had a "vision" Franjo would be dead in three days. That was two days ago. I'm worried about her intentions, especially if Franjo is heading to the US. Can you put tail on her ASAP? Will send address and details separately.

He sent the message, then forwarded, also by secure text, Aisha's phone number, email, and street address to Vic, then he checked through his emails.

At last, there was an encrypted reply from Darko Beganović at the Intelligence-Security Agency.

Having spent most of the previous day trawling through old Ministry of Defense files, Darko had found references to an F. Vuković and M. Lukić as being among those benefiting from the Iran arms imports. The documents stated that Franjo had received weapons to the value of $3 million and Marco to the value of $2 million. The details were in a scanned attachment.

Johnson couldn't help himself. He punched the air and immediately winced at the pain in his shoulder. But he didn't care. Now, at last, he was making progress.

The scan was a copy of an internal memo, typewritten in an abbreviated style not dissimilar to the Ministry of Foreign Affairs documents that Johnson had already seen. He skimmed through the file.

Under a single-word headline, "Iran," and a date, March 4, 1993, it stated simply:

Regarding facilitating delivery arms/ammunition from Tehran (air),
MoFA has given clearance for weapons allocation to eight persons:
A. Dizdar $5m
F. Vuković $3m
J. Pašović $1m
Z. Bouchnak $1m
M. Romanić $2m
N. Škiljan $4m
K. Gunić $1m
M. Lukić. $2m
Recommendation: set surveillance operations against the above
persons pending security and integrity clearances (Ref: 7619).

The email from Darko said:

Joe, this is all I could find, but it may be enough? There's no clear
sign that the surveillance operations recommended were ever set up.
Certainly there's no files relating to that. Sorry.

Too right it was enough.

Johnson picked up his glass of brandy from the patio table and turned to Jayne, who had finished her call with Natasha.

"How was she?" Johnson asked.

"She didn't take it well. She doesn't want to be in that hotel but accepts it's for her own safety," Jayne said, shrugging.

Johnson nodded and updated Jayne on the details Ana had unearthed of Franjo's role in Erol and Zeinab Delić's death.

Jayne started to ask questions, but Johnson interrupted her. "Wait," he said, passing over his phone so Jayne could read the email from Darko. "There's more. Take a look at that."

He watched as Jayne read it, her eyes widening. While she was reading, he put two painkillers in his mouth and washed them down with the brandy, completely disregarding the instructions not to mix with alcohol. *Who cares?*

"Bloody hell," Jayne said in disbelief. "So Vuković is Wolff. And Vuković deliberately killed Aisha's father and sister on the Stari Most, in addition to all the others he doubtless murdered. And now we have clear evidence of both Franjo and Marco landing a windfall of millions of dollars' worth of weaponry from Iran."

"That's one thing I love about you," he said to Jayne. "Your deadpan way of summing up the essentials."

To Johnson, an important factor was that details about the payments Franjo and Marco had received definitely wasn't in the dossier from Izetbegović's office.

Maybe Franjo doesn't even know these other incriminating documents exist? In which case I'm holding the aces.

Johnson suddenly started to feel as though the fog was clearing. But then a thought struck him, and he felt his scalp tighten. What was it Aisha had said to him in New York? *If you get to Franjo before I do, just let me know.*

He reached for his phone and tapped out a text message to Ana.

Do you think Aisha's actually capable of killing?

A couple of minutes later, a reply came back.

Aisha was normally never violent. But in the war she killed more than once. Grenades, I think. Yes, she could do it.

* * *

Wednesday, July 25, 2012
The Hague, Netherlands

Ana walked confidently into Churchillplein 1, the former Aegon insurance company building in The Hague that housed the International Criminal Tribunal for the former Yugoslavia.

A notice indicated the prosecution case against Ratko Mladić, the Bosnian Serb military leader captured in 2011 after sixteen years on the run, was continuing in Trial Chamber One.

Three lawyers wearing black legal gowns and white wing collars, deep in conversation, swept past. A pair of security guards, both in short-sleeved pale blue shirts, stood near the door.

Ana approached a man at the information desk who pointed her toward a court officer in the corner. "He will get whichever court transcripts you require. Go and take a seat."

Shortly afterward, she was poring over a bound file containing transcripts of a 2009 trial hearing for General Slobodan Praljak, the former commander of the Bosnian Croatian army, the HVO, and several others.

It took her more than an hour to find the witness statements she was searching for.

First, there was one from Praljak denying that he had anything to do with ordering the tank to fire on the Stari Most. And there was another from another soldier, Branko Perić, who claimed he was standing next to the tank on November 9, 1993, when the bridge went down.

Ana looked around her and spotted a sign that said no cameras or videos were permitted. But nobody was watching her. She quietly took out her phone and took pictures of the relevant sections of the files.

The first one, quoting Perić, read:

"The tank commander, Franjo Vuković, ordered the three men in the tank to keep firing at the bridge. He told them they had to destroy it and complete the job. So they continued to pound shells at the bridge most of Monday, the eighth of November, and then continued on Tuesday morning, the ninth. On Tuesday, the tank commander was very busy on his walkie-talkie, communicating with another man

who was near the Stari Most and who was giving him directions. I could hear what the other man was saying. At one stage, when they had stopped firing shells for a period for some reason, I heard the other man tell the commander that the man he was interested in was approaching the bridge, along with three other people, and they were carrying a man on a stretcher. They were standing near the archway on the western side."

She turned the page and photographed the next section, still quoting Perić.

"The commander immediately ordered the guys in the tank to adjust their line of fire by a number of degrees, I can't remember what, and to resume firing immediately. The next shells that were fired crashed into the bridge at the western end. A few minutes later the man called again on the walkie-talkie and told the tank commander that the target had been eliminated and others also killed. After that, the tank commander, Franjo Vuković, said something like, 'Well done, a good job,' and thanked him. Then they switched their fire back to the original spot. And soon after that, the bridge fell down into the river, at about ten o'clock."

The text corroborated exactly what Ana's informant had told her: that two of the five people killed that morning were definitely Erol and Zeinab Delić and that it had been done deliberately.

She left the building and sat on a bench next to a fountain, emailed the photographs of the files to Johnson, and then called him a few minutes later. He was already at his hotel in London.

Ana talked Johnson through what she had found.

"Okay, we've got what we need," Johnson said. "Well done."

"I would guess that Zeinab was unfortunate to be with her

father, who was undoubtedly the real target," Ana said. "So, what's next?"

"I need to get into Franjo's, or Boris's, house here tonight."

"Get in? As in break in?"

Johnson remained silent.

"I'll assume that's a yes. Good luck with it," Ana said.

"Breaking and entering's not my scene," Johnson said. "I hate doing it, but sometimes you just have to think of the greater good. Now that we know what's driving Aisha, we must move. I don't want some sort of street justice handed out here."

PART FOUR

CHAPTER FORTY

Wednesday, July 25, 2012
   London

After four hours, Johnson was certain no one was home. It was ten minutes to midnight, and he had been watching Franjo's home in Ennismore Mews since eight. And still there were no lights on.

He had left Jayne with Filip in Split to continue the search for Marco while he went after Franjo. She was less than keen on getting involved in breaking and entering in London, her home city, so she left it to him.

Johnson scanned up and down the street, which was lined on both sides by terraced homes and was lit only by the dim glow from a quarter moon.

Johnson's rented Mazda sedan was parked across the street from Franjo's house, but he had moved the car several times over the course of the four hours, switching between his current location and the neighboring Ennismore Gardens, from where he had instead patrolled on foot to keep an eye on the property.

The street was full of builders' dumpsters. Clearly many properties were being refurbished, including the house next door to Franjo's, which, like several others, had scaffolding up the front of the building and appeared empty.

At ten minutes to one, Johnson picked up a small canvas roll-up bag of tools that he had bought, and after checking carefully once again that there was no surveillance, got out of the car.

He could see that finding a way into the house would be tricky. There were no alleyways between the terraced mews houses and no easy access to the rear. He decided to try the empty house next door first, hoping to find a way into Boris's property that way.

The ground-floor windows were bolted shut; he would have to climb the scaffolding and try the upper windows. There was no ladder, so he levered himself up to the planks at first-floor level by standing on a window ledge.

He winced as he did so. Thankfully, his shoulder had improved significantly over the previous twenty-four hours, but it remained sore and he knew this break-in wasn't going to help the healing process.

Johnson glanced left and right down the street. There was still no movement. At the back of his mind he still worried that the house he was targeting might not be the right one, that it might not actually belong to Franjo. But he knew he only had one option if he wanted to be certain.

He peered through the first-floor bedroom window. The property looked completely empty. There were no carpets. Workmen's tools lay on the floor along with a couple of stepladders, bags of plaster, buckets, drills, hammers, and planks.

The window had an old-fashioned sash. Johnson checked

the latch fastener in the center, between the upper and lower window panels. It had barely been closed properly; the swivel latch clip was rotated only a fraction of an inch into the housing that kept the window shut.

From his tool bag, Johnson removed a long knife, which he slid between the two sash windows, and applied some pressure to the latch. After a few seconds, it unclipped.

Johnson slid the bottom window up and climbed into the property.

He climbed the stairs to the second floor, which appeared to be a converted attic, with skylight roof windows in three rooms. He climbed up an aluminum stepladder and opened one of the skylights, which led out onto a shallow sloping roof, and scanned his surroundings.

Johnson realized that the property he was in, and Franjo's next door to the right, had very similar shallow, sloping roofs, so he could easily climb across. They had virtually identical skylights.

Johnson levered himself up onto the roof, then scrambled down about three feet to a V-shaped channel between the properties that funneled rainwater to a drainpipe.

The nearest skylight on Franjo's property was three feet up on the other side. Johnson considered it, weighing his options. It was an old-style, single-glazed pane.

He took out his tool kit and removed a small diamond-tipped glass-cutting tool, similar to a drawing compass. He stepped onto the other roof and leaned against the tiles while he fastened the cutter firmly to the glass with a suction cup. Then he rotated the diamond tip around the suction cup, cutting a perfect circle in the glass, which he scored over several times.

Next, he attached two strips of duct tape across the etched circle; he removed the compass cutter from the suction cup, replaced it with a flat circular wooden disc, and banged gently on the disc with his elbow until the glass circle separated from the rest of the pane. The sticky tape prevented it from falling down.

Johnson waited five minutes to ensure there was no reaction inside the house, which was still in darkness. Then he removed the suction cup and the glass circle, and reached through the hole in the glass to open the skylight.

A couple of minutes later, Johnson was tiptoeing down the stairs of Franjo's house.

The third room he tried on the first floor was locked, but there was a key in the lock. Johnson let himself in. It was an office, with a desk, a computer, and three filing cabinets. Johnson closed the curtains, then turned on the small flashlight on his phone and looked around.

Where to start?

Johnson worked his way through the top drawer of the first filing cabinet, which contained mainly notebooks, reports, and background information on leading UK and European politicians: Ian Owen, Angela Merkel, the new French president François Hollande, and others. All were in labeled cardboard file partitions. There was no doubt now that the property belonged to Boris Wolff the TV interviewer.

The second drawer down contained a few yellow cardboard folders. The top one had a sticker on the front marked Patrick Spencer Printouts.

Johnson took it out. Inside were photocopies of some handwritten notes listing a series of questions about how Spencer viewed his role as speaker of the House; his future intentions toward the US presidency, his views on immigration, Muslims, foreign policy, Arab nations, domestic policy, poverty, religion, and so on.

He continued to flick through the papers.

Near the back was a folded sheet of paper that appeared

to be some sort of invoice, from a Drago Planić, for three hundred euros. The invoice, written in Croatian, said it was for "repairs to safe."

But it was the name and address at the top of the printed invoice that caught Johnson's eye: Marco Lukić. The address was Unit 6, Koplica Street, Split.

Johnson stared at it and breathed a sigh of relief. He definitely had the right man. The Marco connection proved it.

Better still, this might also lead him to Marco—was this address on the invoice where Marco lived? Unit 6. It sounded more like some kind of business premises. Either way, it could be crucial. He made a mental note to ask Jayne to follow it up.

The final document was a printout of an email titled "Patrick Spencer interview 27 July." It appeared to be from Spencer's press secretary, addressed to Boris Wolff at an SRTV email address, and consisted of one line, confirming the interview date. There was no reference to location or time.

That corroborated the details that Jayne had found from her Google search, then.

Attached to the printout was a photocopy of a return air ticket dated the previous evening, the twenty-fifth of July, from London's Heathrow Airport to New York's JFK.

Johnson pursed his lips. The interview must be in New York, then. It was now the early hours of Thursday morning, and Boris—or Franjo—was due to interview Patrick Spencer on Friday. Johnson would need to get the first available daytime flight to New York later that morning.

The next sheet was a printout of a brief email from a David Rowlands, whose signature at the bottom showed he was the editor of the *Wolff Live* program at SRTV. The email was headed "News schedule" and contained what seemed to be a shorthand list of news stories but with no further explanation.

Syria—Assad chemical weapons? Aug 3 (tentative)
   Afghanistan—US Military death toll nearing 2,000. Aug 6 (firm).
   UK—London Olympics analysis. July 28 (firm)
   Croatia/Bosnia—Sarajevo documents. July 26 (firm)

Johnson read the last line three times, then exhaled hard.

Sarajevo documents, scheduled for today.

This wasn't good. The last thing he wanted was for news organizations to start splashing the Bosnia story all over the world, just when he needed radio silence so his suspects wouldn't run for cover before arrests could be made.

The one thing Johnson hadn't found was any trace of the dossier of documents he so badly needed. He spent some time carefully going through every other potential storage location he could find in the office and the other rooms in the house.

But there was nothing.

* * *

Thursday, July 26, 2012
   London

Once Johnson had extricated himself from Franjo's house, it was past two in the morning. He walked back to his Mazda, opened the door, and jumped in. He placed the yellow folder containing the documents from Franjo's filing cabinet onto the passenger seat.

Then he accelerated away, turning onto Exhibition Road and past the Victoria and Albert Museum. He drove for ten minutes, following the satnav on his phone west through London toward Heathrow Airport. Only then, as he reached Hammersmith, did he pull onto the side of the road.

First, Johnson sent a secure text message to Jayne in Split.

URGENT, Jayne, I may have an address where you can find Marco in Split. Let's talk as soon as you're awake and I'll explain.

Then he made an encrypted call to Vic, giving thanks as he did so for the five-hour time difference that meant Vic would still be up in DC.

"Vic, it's Joe."

"Hi, buddy, where are you now?"

"London. I've just been into Franjo's house. Or rather, Boris Wolff's house, as he calls himself here."

"Did you find the dossier?" Vic asked.

"No. But I did find some other useful information which confirms his identity and that he's a TV interviewer, as I told you. He's definitely in New York now for an interview tomorrow with Patrick Spencer. Have you had any luck tracking down where it might be?"

"We think it's CBA, though it's not confirmed yet," Vic said. "The TV studios are very secretive about these things. Unfortunately, CBA just happens to be where Aisha works— we found that out after you told me to keep an eye on her."

"Shit—it would have to be that one," Johnson said. "I'm worried about Aisha. I've found out she has much more of a motive than I thought. Franjo apparently killed her father and sister with tank shells the day the Old Bridge in Mostar was destroyed in '93."

There was a pause. "Hmm. That's tough on her, if so," Vic said.

"Yeah, I know. You've got to assume the worst—that's she may be gunning for him still. We can't afford to have a dead Franjo. He's done too much. We'll need to get him to Sarajevo at some point so he can go in front of a war crimes court."

"Yeah, agree, 100 percent," said Vic. "I'll get my team to keep a close eye on her, in that case, and we'll talk to the studio. What else did you find at Franjo's house?"

"There was a list of news stories scheduled at his TV company, including one for today, the twenty-sixth, or tomorrow for you there, about some Sarajevo documents. I'm assuming that's got to be the docs that we want. So what's going to be in that story? I could take a fairly good guess. He's bound to be taking potshots at the US and at Clinton about the arms-from-Iran revelations. A news organization would dress it up as a smoking gun, the final proof."

"Well," Vic said, "It's not necessarily a bad thing if we want to have Franjo arrested. It lays a nice backdrop for that to happen."

"Yes," Johnson said, "but the other issue is Watto. He's not named, but the trail will lead to him, and the last thing we want is his name out in the media—not if we're gathering evidence and aiming to arrest him. All of his CIA friends, his political friends, and all of his carefully cultivated high-placed connections from over the years will just put the wagons in a circle, protect him, and cover it up, and he'll get away with it."

"Yes, but if he's not named, people won't make the connection immediately. Are there any other shocks in those documents?" Vic asked.

"There are two other people referred to who aren't named. I only just managed to get their identities from the Bosnian government official, Hasanović, before Franjo's cronies shot him dead. One of the two is a guy referred to as Mr. B in the docs, who helped with mujahideen training camps in Bosnia and was given a Bosnian passport. He was effectively given the green light by the US and its guys on the ground in Sarajevo, who didn't object. Guess who it was?"

"Tell me."

"You're not going to believe this—it's Osama bin Laden."

Vic was silent for a second. "*Bin Laden?*"

"Yes. One of the US guys on the ground who didn't object was Watto, and the other was a Pentagon military adviser. Hasanović was about to tell me who the Pentagon contact was, but then he got a bullet through the head."

Vic whistled. "A Pentagon military adviser? Interesting. I'll see if we can find out who was in Bosnia from the Pentagon at that time. Maybe Watto's the one person who has that information. I'm actually waiting right now for some recordings, transcripts of some of his phone calls over the past few days, since I put that unofficial tap in place."

"Okay, let's see, then," Johnson said. He yawned deeply and leaned back in his car seat. Now he felt the adrenaline that had kept him going in recent days suddenly drain out of his system.

"I'm feeling exhausted, Vic. Sorry, buddy, I'm struggling to think straight. I'm heading for Heathrow. I'll be on the next flight I can get to JFK, so should be there midafternoon your time. Hopefully I'll get a bit of sleep on the plane. Also, if the shit's about to hit the fan, doesn't the White House and State Department need to know?" Johnson asked.

"Yes, I'll sort it. And they'll go nuts, believe me. It'll be absolute panic there. Iran is the great unmentionable. You'll see."

* * *

Thursday, July 26, 2012
  Split

.   .   .

Jayne's alarm went off at 6:30 a.m., echoing around her bedroom at the Hotel Luxe, where she had decided to move from Antun's house for a night, prior to flying back to London.

The alarm woke her from a deep sleep. Half opening her right eye, she picked up her phone and stabbed a forefinger at the button on the front to turn it off.

Then she noticed a text message notification on the screen from Johnson. *URGENT*, it said.

She jerked up in bed and tapped on the message.

Ten seconds later, she was dialing Johnson's number.

Jayne found Johnson was at Heathrow, waiting to get a flight to New York. He talked her through the details of his nocturnal visit to Franjo's house, including the address that he had found for Marco. Jayne wrote it down on the notepad the hotel had left on her desk.

"Okay, I'm on it, Joe. Don't worry, we'll cover it. Leave it with me—I'll get down there with Filip. You get going to New York and deal with things at that end."

Jayne hung up and sat there for a moment, suddenly energized.

Her only issue was Filip. Could she trust him? She would have to. She sent a text message asking him to get to the Luxe as quickly as possible as she had abandoned her plan to fly to London. They now had an urgent job to do together.

By quarter to eight, Filip had arrived, dressed in a black polo neck shirt and black jeans. She spent a few minutes briefing him on what Johnson had uncovered at Franjo's house in London.

"Did you know that Marco has a business unit in Split?" Jayne asked.

"No, but I know that area, and it's rough as hell," Filip

said. "It's definitely not a business park. It's more like a collection of old shacks and car repair garages. The only business he's involved in, as far as I know, is trading weapons."

They agreed to go and check out the address. If there was any sign of Marco, they would immediately call the local police, who were still hunting him in connection with Petar's murder.

If there was no evidence of him being there, they would stake out the place for a period, and then Jayne would make a decision about whether to try to enter the building and search for any useful information.

She told Filip to wait for a few minutes while she went to the bathroom. After using the toilet, she cleaned her teeth, threw her toiletries into her small vanity case, and opened the door to her room.

Then Jayne stood still for a couple of seconds: Filip was no longer there.

Her first instinct was to open the door into the corridor and look out. But there was no sign of him.

Then she glanced at the desk. The sheet of notepaper on which she had written the address lay there, next to her phone. Then she realized, with a jolt, where Filip had most likely gone.

"Shit!" she said out loud.

She swiftly dialed Filip's number. But it went straight to voice mail.

"Bloody Filip," she muttered, as she grabbed her bag and ran out the door.

CHAPTER FORTY-ONE

Thursday, July 26, 2012
Split

Jayne sprinted out of the Hotel Luxe's main entrance and around the corner to the parking lot. On the far side, she spotted a familiar azure Subaru Impreza.

"Thank God," she muttered under her breath.

Filip was repeatedly trying to start the engine, which was turning over but not firing into life.

Jayne ran to the passenger door and flung it open. "What the hell are you bloody playing at?" she demanded, crouching down so she could look him in the eyes.

A Beretta was on the passenger seat next to him.

Filip glared at her. "What I'm playing at has nothing to do with you. But it's got everything to do with my brother."

"No," she said. "We're not playing that game, although it's not a game, is it? You saw that message, didn't you? The address?"

Filip shrugged.

"Listen to me," Jayne said. "We're going to nail him. We'll nail him for killing your brother. But we're also going to nail him for what he did twenty years ago, the details of which we now have."

Filip said nothing.

"And you're not going to get to him with that gun anyway, are you?" Jayne said. "Because your bloody car won't start."

Filip let out a loud huff. Then he nodded slowly. "Okay. Whatever."

"Good man," Jayne said. "We just need to solve the slight problem of transport."

She stood and surveyed the car park. An old maroon Mercedes stood against the wall. It had a cracked windshield, one hanging wing mirror and several dents in the bodywork.

"See that Merc. If we could get into the damn thing, we could hot-wire it," she said.

Filip climbed out of the Subaru and gaped at her, open-mouthed. "I've got a toolbox in the back of the Subaru—there's a set of slim jims in it. I should be able to break into it with those."

"Have you got a crosshead screwdriver and a knife in there as well?"

Filip nodded and strode to the back of the Subaru, opened the trunk, and took out the toolbox.

"Okay, bring that," Jayne said. "Let's run—we need to get out of here." She jogged across the parking lot, Filip following close behind with the toolbox.

The Mercedes looked at least fifteen years old. Filip put the toolbox down, opened it, and took out a long, flat piece of metal. Jayne could see a few people over near the entrance to the parking lot, near the street, but they were facing the other way.

"Nobody's watching. Go for it," Jayne said. Filip slid the thin metal slim jim down the crack between the glass window and the metal panel of the driver's door and wiggled it around in a well-practiced manner. Fifteen seconds later, the car door swung open.

"Great," Jayne said. "Give me the screwdriver and the knife."

Filip reached inside the toolbox and handed Jayne a small red army knife and a screwdriver.

"Right," she said. "You ring the police, give them the address we've got, and tell them who we believe may be there and that we're heading there too. While you're doing that, I'll get this car started up."

She used the screwdriver to remove the plastic cover over the steering column. Then she sifted through the colored wires that ran up the column until she found what she was looking for.

Jayne glanced at Filip, who was staring at her. "What are you looking at me like that for? Get on the phone," she said.

Filip obediently dialed the emergency services on his phone and began to brief the operator.

Jayne pulled the ignition and battery wires out of their housing, then used the knife to trim off the plastic coating and spliced the ends together. The dashboard lights lit up. Then she quickly touched the starter motor cable to the battery wire, and the Mercedes's three-and-a-half liter engine growled into life.

Filip finished his call and nodded his head in approval as she revved the engine. "Where'd you learn to do that?" he asked.

* * *

Thursday, July 26, 2012
  Split

. . .

The rough cinder block garage, with a rusty car outside propped on bricks, its tires missing, stood only four kilometers from the elegant and historic tourist center of Split. But in many senses it was a world away.

Marco nosed his Lexus 4x4 down Koplica Street, a fragmented collection of adjoining unmade gravel roads in the northern part of the city, which was situated only a few hundred meters from the back of the gleaming modern railway station.

Very conscious of the police hunt that was under way for Petar's killer, he had taken every precaution to avoid being followed.

Marco parked outside the garage, next to an abandoned industrial site surrounded by rusty barbed wire. As he climbed out of the car, he stepped over a plastic bag full of dirty used hospital syringes that lay in a puddle.

An old workbench stood outside the garage, which had a corrugated asbestos roof and a makeshift plywood door that failed to fit the frame in which it sat.

Next door, there were two similar run-down cinder block garages, also in a state of disrepair.

A man with a straggly, gray, tobacco-stained beard sat on the workbench and puffed a pipe. He had a frayed baseball cap on his head and wore navy blue oil-stained dungarees.

The smell of the tobacco smoke reminded Marco of when he was a boy and his uncle invariably had a pipe in his mouth whenever he visited.

"Drago, how's it going?" Marco said. "The safe. Is it finished?"

Drago sucked hard on his pipe and nodded. "Yes, all done." He indicated toward the garage immediately to his right. "It's in there, behind closed doors."

"Not that that's going to make much difference now," Marco said.

"How do you mean?" Drago asked.

"We got raided. While we didn't have the safe. Which was your fault, so you screwed up in a major way."

Drago stared at him. "Shit, you're joking?"

"No. Sadly not joking. My friend Stefan isn't happy, so you have a lot of making up to do. Otherwise . . ." Marco left the sentence unfinished.

Drago slid off the workbench and wiped his nose on his sleeve. "Well, I did the best I could," he mumbled. "It was a longer job than I thought. And the guy I got to sort the lock took longer than I thought, too. Was it cash that got taken?" He searched Marco's face for a sign of comfort but failed to get it.

Marco just shook his head.

Drago ambled to the neighboring garage, where he pulled on a steel bar that was holding the two doors closed. After some tugging, it came free, and he opened the doors outward.

There, standing on a wooden bench in the garage amid an array of oil drums, old tools, boxes, worn tires, and dirty rags, was a small but solid-looking metal safe.

"Okay," Marco said. "Let's load it up. I'm going to take it to my unit down the road for now."

"It's damn heavy. Are you going to manage it at your place?"

"Yeah, I've got a mechanical lift I can use."

"And you keep the safe there, do you?" Drago asked.

"No."

"So what do you use it for?"

"Too many questions. You don't need to know."

Marco took some used banknotes from his pocket and counted them out before handing them to Drago. "There, one hundred and fifty in cash. Should have been three hundred. So half price. You're lucky to get that, frankly."

Drago took the notes. "Okay, one hundred and fifty. The safe's yours."

Marco reversed his Lexus into the garage and right up to the bench. The two men slid the safe into the back of the car.

He nodded at Drago, then drove toward his own unit, half a kilometer down the road.

Marco had acquired the unit, a single-story building made from cinder blocks and a corrugated steel roof, for cash about eight years earlier. On the outside, it was in better condition than Drago's but not greatly so. And that was one of its advantages. Nobody would have suspected that goods worth millions of dollars sometimes passed through it.

There was little to differentiate the building from the others on the road.

The walls were covered in graffiti, and someone had tipped a pile of builder's rubbish on the concrete rectangle that was intended for parking.

From the outside, it looked a dump. Inside, there was a small bedroom, in case Marco needed to stay there, a shower room, and a surprisingly well-equipped kitchen, alongside the large storage area that comprised the majority of the floor space.

Marco had also ensured it was secure. Behind the rickety wooden doors were steel roller doors secured with large padlocks, and the windows were bricked up on the inside.

He was certain that nobody could possibly get in without drawing attention to themselves. However, he had never installed a burglar alarm. The last thing he wanted was for a false alarm to sound and for police to come poking around.

Marco parked the Lexus outside, took his keys, and let himself in through the kitchen door.

He flicked the kitchen lights on and was just about to close the door behind him and lock it when he glimpsed out of his peripheral vision a black-clad figure emerging from around the corner of the building to his left, on the side farthest from the street.

Marco didn't stop to see who it was. Instinct told him he needed to get out of the man's line of eyesight.

He ducked behind the left side of the doorframe and pulled his gun from his belt.

As he did so, there was a loud bang, and he felt a sharp impact at the top of his right bicep, followed by an indescribable pain. His arm froze and he involuntarily dropped the gun. He glanced at his arm to see blood spurting from beneath his T-shirt.

To his right he saw the woman who had been working with Johnson crouching next to a black trash can no more than ten meters away, pointing a gun at him.

Immediately, the black-clad figure appeared in the doorway, holding a pistol, also pointed straight at him. Now Marco recognized him.

"This is for Petar, you bastard," Filip said. "Get inside."

Marco slowly raised his left arm, his right dangling uselessly at his side, and backed into the kitchen, facing Filip.

"No. Don't shoot me," Marco said. "Listen, I just—"

"I should kill you. I really should. Get on the floor," Filip ordered. "Lie down on your front, and put your hands behind your back."

As Filip spoke, Marco saw the woman walk into view behind him. "Do what he says," she said. "Now."

"Fuck it," he said, as he got on his knees. "Fucking Franjo."

* * *

Thursday, July 26, 2012
  Wolf Trap, Virginia

. . .

Watson sat down on his favorite rock among the pine trees next to Difficult Run River and took out his burner cell phone. He winced as he caught his sprained left wrist on his belt buckle.

Watson's wrist had become a mosaic of purple, blue, and black as the bruising had spread over the back of his hand. He clasped his right hand to the spot. His damaged tendon was feeling a little better, but the improvement was only marginal.

After two long-haul flights within just a few days, being up most of the night supervising the Sinj arms transfer, then being injured and getting very little sleep, he felt utterly exhausted.

The flight delays in Vienna hadn't helped, and Watson had finally gotten home only at about five o'clock the previous afternoon. Then he'd dosed himself with Ibuprofen, gone to bed, and slept.

When he'd finally gotten around to watching the news over breakfast that morning, the Bosnia documents story had broken. Coverage was virtually wall-to-wall.

Now he carefully surveyed the area, checking for the habitual dog walkers or others who might have less legitimate reasons to be in the woods. Only when he was satisfied he was completely alone did he turn on the phone.

He was surprised to see he was getting five bars of reception, far better than the one bar he usually got outside his house, or even sometimes no signal at all. Maybe the phone company had put a new mast in somewhere.

"EDISON, it's SILVER," he said when the call was answered.

"About time. Where have you been? Have you seen the TV coverage? Going crazy out there. What the hell—"

"Yeah, I know, I know, I saw it just earlier. That's what I

warned you about a couple of days ago. These are the Sarajevo documents."

"Yes, but I wasn't expecting coverage like this. It's not naming me or anything, but it's getting close to the bone," EDISON said.

"That's why I'm calling, to calm things. Like I told you before, these documents don't actually name names. But they do talk about a CIA operative and a Pentagon military adviser in Sarajevo at that time who turned a blind eye to the Iran imports. The fact you were then working for the Pentagon seems to have escaped everyone so far, and I don't see why it should surface. It's not being mentioned in reports; all the focus is on Clinton and the White House," Watson said.

"Okay, as an old friend, I'll take your word for it," EDISON said. "But I've got a lot planned for the next few days—a few key appearances. It would look extremely odd if I suddenly scrapped it all. So I'm going ahead as if this has nothing to do with me."

"I don't think you'll get caught, but can't you cancel these events?" Watson asked.

"No, it also involves one of my donors. Anyway, how much have we got coming to us from that last shipment? Has it been finalized?"

"Yes, more or less," Watson said. "It's going to be about a quarter of a million US each. Peanuts in the scheme of things, but enough. It'll go straight to the usual account. Don't worry, the payments are all secure."

EDISON said, "Good. But what I want to know is, can we stop this coverage? And, if so, how?"

Watson said, "No. The cat's out of the bag. But look on the bright side—at least the cat doesn't have a name tag around its neck."

He wasn't going to mention to EDISON that the minute

he suspected his involvement might become public, he was planning to run. A private jet would be on standby at Lees-burg airport, twenty-five minutes from his house.

However, Watson knew that such an escape might be more difficult for EDISON, who wasn't seeing the bright side. "You'd better make damn sure the cat doesn't have a name tag, SILVER, or else my career's over, and yours will be over too. You understand me?"

EDISON didn't wait for an answer. He hung up.

CHAPTER FORTY-TWO

Thursday, July 26, 2012
New York City

Johnson saw it on the screens as soon as he got off the British Airways Boeing 777 and into the arrivals hall at JFK.

The morning TV news programs on the airport's monitors were running video footage of the Bosnian war from the 1990s as well as old speeches from Bill Clinton. Weapons experts were pictured holding Kalashnikovs and rocket launchers, and there was old film of an Iran Air jumbo jet taking off from Tehran airport.

He felt himself start to sweat. This was news coverage that he could instinctively see was already too big, out of control, unpredictable, and taking on a life of its own. There was no way of knowing where it would end up—just the kind of situation that Johnson hated.

He stopped and focused on one of the screens, which showed an international news segment.

There was a clip from SRTV News, which was being

credited with breaking the story. The ticker running across the bottom of the screen read, "US helped Bosnian Muslims import Iranian weapons, secret documents show." The next headline said, "White House turned blind eye as mujahideen flooded into Bosnia—proof." A third said, "Patrick Spencer set to condemn US Muslim policy in set piece TV interview."

The next clip showed some academic arguing that the US had put weapons into the hands of radical Muslims that were later used against Americans and Western Europeans in a series of terror attacks, providing the momentum for the 9/11 attacks on the World Trade Center and the Pentagon.

"Did the United States' policy throw fuel on the fire?" the presenter asked. "We'll discuss all this and more after the break."

There seemed to be no mention of any involvement by a senior CIA man named Robert Watson or of Osama bin Laden on any channel.

Johnson walked on. He had seen enough.

There were two text messages on his phone. The first was from Jayne.

Marco's just been arrested by police here in Split. Me and Filip held him at gunpoint at that business unit address you gave. Involved a little drama first, though. Will tell you more on the phone.

Johnson smiled to himself. *Thank God for that.* He knew he could rely on Jayne to deliver the goods.

The second text was from Vic, telling him to wait near Starbucks in the arrivals hall. Johnson continued through the concourse until he spotted the coffee shop.

There was a tap on his right shoulder. He whirled around to find Vic standing behind him.

Vic grasped his right hand and shook it firmly. "Come,

this way, Doc. You've set the cat among the pigeons here, buddy."

"Not me. It's that maniac Franjo who's done it." He followed Vic toward the terminal's pickup zone. "Have you confirmed if it's CBA who's hosting the interview?"

"Yes, it's them. Aisha's studio."

Johnson swore. "Any suspicious activity from Aisha?"

"No, none."

'Well, given the unknowns, it might be an idea to have Aisha pulled in for questioning, just to keep her detained until we have Franjo in custody, whether that's before or after this interview. We don't want factors we can't control in the mix. I can help with that if needed. I've met her. I'll go with you."

"I've already requested that," Vic said. "We're getting her in and we'll keep her for a while. She can't do any damage, then, if that was her plan."

Johnson breathed a sigh of relief. "Do you know where Franjo is staying?"

"No. We're finding out."

A black Chrysler sedan was waiting outside. Vic walked over to it and got into the rear seat, indicating to Johnson to do likewise.

Johnson inclined his head toward the driver and raised his eyebrows questioningly.

"He's fine. One of my people. Don't worry, we can talk," Vic said.

"Okay. Any progress on Watto's phone taps?" Johnson asked.

"A bit. There's some slightly odd patterns coming up. Not just in terms of who he's calling, but from where, which we've also been monitoring. There's a spot near his house where calls have been made from an unidentified cell phone number, so I'm getting that tracked. It may or may not be him, we're not certain. We should start getting call recordings and transcripts soon. In fact, our next job is to talk to the NSA telecoms engineer who's been helping us. Hopefully we'll get an update."

Vic gave Johnson a new, clean iPhone, still in its packaging, and a pay-as-you-go SIM card. "Use this. I've got one as well. I suggest we use these to communicate between us for the next couple of days. Watto's quite likely to have arranged taps on my phone and probably yours, too."

Vic then reached into a small backpack he was carrying and handed Johnson a Glock and four spare magazines. "Here, you might need that, given the way things are going."

* * *

Thursday, July 26, 2012
  Astoria

The Ćevabdžinica Sarajevo café was unusually busy for a Thursday. Aisha and Adela had taken the last available table, in the corner near the door. They simultaneously stirred sugar into their cappuccinos.

Aisha sipped hers and looked up from under her long black eyelashes.

"So where did you put it?" Adela asked.

"It's in a lighting bar directly above the seats where Franjo and Spencer will be sitting. I've set it to come lower than normal so it takes them out."

She hesitated. "I want to do this. He's burned me up inside for years. I can't tell you what he did to my family and me."

"No doubts?"

"No. Well, only the audience. There'll be a lot of people."

Adela pressed her lips together. "Yeah. But it's the cost of what we need to do. Spencer is inciting people. It'll be a lot worse if we don't stop him—there'll be more deaths, more Muslims killed for doing nothing more than living here. You'll never get another chance to get both of them."

Aisha nodded, her eyes hardening again. She lowered her voice to a whisper. "I'm going to trigger it right at the end of the interview, just as the main studio lights go down and the credits are about to roll. The idea is to bathe Franjo and Spencer, two bastards together, in blue light with some fancy effect going over them. And then the whole place will go up. That'll be some damn fancy effect for sure."

Adela stared at her. "You know, Aisha, I never thought, even a couple of weeks ago, that you'd ever get to this point. At least, not without a war to push you to do it."

Aisha shrugged. "Two weeks ago I felt quite at peace with myself. Two weeks ago I never dreamed that Franjo was still alive, let alone coming to interview that bigot Spencer in my studio. But this is *personal*. This is war, in a way."

She paused, then began whispering again. "It'll be live on television, just like the way Franjo destroyed my father and my sister. That was on TV, on the Stari Most. It was filmed and broadcast the same night. It might have taken nineteen years, but it'll be a very symbolic kind of justice. I *hate* him, and the glory will be Allah's."

Aisha tapped her fingers nervously on the wooden table and glanced around the restaurant. "I need a backup plan, though. The detonator's number is saved into my phone. But just in case something happens and I can't do it, can you stand by?"

Adela sat back in her chair and raised her eyebrows. "Why would you need a backup? Won't you be in the studio?"

"No," Aisha said. "I'm going to phone in sick tomorrow.

I'm not cut out to be a suicide bomber. I don't have the guts for that."

"Okay, then, a backup," Adela said. She scratched her head. "So I'd just have to ring the number?"

"Yep, just ring the number. It should ring four times, then you'll hear it connect. Job done. You can hang up then. About ten seconds later, the detonator will be activated and the Semtex goes up. Your guy from the mosque spent about two hours talking it through with me. All I had to do was install it. Very easy. Anyway, you'll be watching the show, won't you? If anything goes wrong and I can't do it, you can call."

"Yes, fine," Adela said.

Aisha took a piece of paper out of her handbag and scribbled a number on it. "Here you go. There's the number. Put it into your phone now, just in case. Put it under Franjo Vuković. That's the best place for it."

Her friend nodded. "The studio audience. How many will there be?"

"That's something I'm trying not to think about."

"Well, roughly how many?"

"I don't know. Probably three or four hundred."

"The glory to Allah will be great, then," Adela said.

Aisha drained her coffee, suddenly feeling deflated. "I think we'd better get going." She put on her sunglasses and they both left the café.

She said goodbye to Adela, who turned left to go around the corner, where she could catch a bus back to her house.

Aisha turned right along 38th Street toward her house. Then she saw the police car parked outside, a few doors away. Two officers were just going through her front gate.

Immediately she did a one-eighty and walked back in the direction she had come from. Once around the corner, she began running after Adela, who was about to climb onto a waiting bus at the stop just up the road.

She shouted, "Wait, Adela, wait!"

Her friend turned, saw her, and stood with one foot on the pavement, the other on the step of the bus.

Aisha caught up, now breathless, and pushed Adela onto the bus. "Go, go on, quick, I'm with you. I'll tell you in a minute," she said to Adela.

The two of them walked to the back of the bus, which set off and threw them both off balance. They grabbed hold of each other, then fell into a seat.

"Cops, outside my house," Aisha said. "Two guys going up to the front door as I got near."

"Shit, they're onto you, d'you think? I can't see how . . ." Adela said.

Aisha shrugged. "Me either. Nobody at work suspects a thing. At least, as far as I know."

But then in a flash, Aisha did know. It must have been what she said to Ana, who knew Johnson, who was searching for Franjo. How stupid of her.

"Do you think they'll work out what's going on?" Adela asked. "Would they get the detection machines and sniffer dogs into the studio, do all that?"

"Not sure. Your man at the mosque, Faisal, told me it was old Semtex with no odor. Apparently these days it has a scent built in for security reasons, but the old stuff doesn't. But I'd guess they have ways of detecting it if they suspect there might be something."

"Would they cancel the interview?"

"I just can't see it," Aisha said. "Not unless they were absolutely forced to. It's going to be a massive earner. They have tens of millions of dollars' worth of airtime booked by advertisers, and the market's been slow recently. So they're desperate for cash. There's no way they can afford to cancel it. Also, with all these stories about the US helping to get arms from Iran to Muslims in Bosnia, well, I wouldn't be surprised if they've been deluged with more requests today. It's a peak-time show. It'll go global. That guy Spencer's a massive draw now."

"Okay, we just sit tight, then. Hope it goes ahead. Less than twenty-four hours to go now."

"I'll just come and stay at your place, if that's all right?"

Adela's house was about a mile from hers, at the northern end of 30th Street.

"Yep, we'll do it all from there."

* * *

Thursday, July 26, 2012
Manhattan

The National Security Agency cell phone security expert and cryptographer, Alex Goode, focused on the computer screen as it went blank, then a log-on page appeared. He keyed in a password and a map loaded up.

Johnson sat in the swivel chair next to him. Vic remained standing next to him and opened a fresh pack of chewing gum.

"The address. That's Wynhurst Lane, Wolf Trap, isn't it?" Goode asked.

"Correct," Vic said. "I believe your guys put a new phone mast in there only a couple of days ago. My director had to kick up a stink about it before there was any movement. He called your CEO."

"He did," Goode said. "Although, to be honest, we don't need a better signal to do the monitoring. That doesn't make any difference. However, the better signal does mean the phone owner is more likely to make calls, so we've got more of a chance of picking up traffic from that person. Hang on. I'll just need to zoom in a little here."

The three men were sitting around a computer terminal in the back of a CIA van that was parked on a side street in lower Manhattan.

Goode enlarged the satellite image until a picture of a cul-de-sac, with large houses around it, appeared on the screen.

"What we do is superimpose the phone mast locations onto the satellite image," Goode said. "Then we can click on the masts to get a list of calls made using that particular mast, which we can narrow down using a variety of criteria: time, carrier, call destination, and so on. This is quite a rural area, so I doubt there'll be a very high volume. It's not like trying to do this in the DC metropolitan area."

He clicked on a button at the top of the screen, and an orange dot appeared to the right of the screen. "That's the new mast, about a third of a mile away."

Then he called up a list of the call traffic running through the mast. "If he's used the tower, we can get him on here."

"How does that work?" Johnson asked.

"I won't go into the technicalities," Goode said, "but we're basically taking advantage of a telephony signaling protocol called CCSS7, for short. Common Channel Signaling System Seven. It's used to switch calls between different networks, but there are weaknesses in it that we can take advantage of. We can also decrypt the calls or text messages, if they happen to be encrypted."

Vic nodded. "Okay. And the numbers?"

Goode pointed to a list of phone numbers that had appeared down the left-hand side of the screen and to another set on the right. "These are the numbers local to the mast on the left, and those on the right are the remote ones. As you can see, there's only about fifteen local ones registering for yesterday and another nineteen today. That's nothing."

He looked first at Johnson, then at Vic. "We've been recording all the calls since this mast went live. Most of them are just women chatting, kids calling their buddies, husbands checking in, that sort of stuff."

Johnson began to tap his fingers on the desk. "So which are the relevant ones? Sorry, I don't want to rush you, but we're a bit limited for time."

Goode nodded. "Sure. There was one number that stuck out like a sore thumb. Long calls, some international, which are expensive from a pay-as-you-go cell phone, probably a burner. That's why we focused on it. Listen to this call from that number, which was just earlier today." Goode clicked on a button, and a list of calls popped up. He double-clicked on one, which began to play.

"EDISON, it's SILVER."
"About time. Where have you been? Have you seen the TV coverage? Going crazy out there. What the hell—"
"Yeah, I know, I know . . ."

Johnson and Vic exchanged glances at the first use of cryptonyms. Goode let the conversation run, and Johnson listened intently. The first voice was quite clear, the second somewhat muffled.

Johnson sat up when the topic of conversation changed and glanced again at Vic.

"But I've got a lot planned for the next few days, a few key appearances. It would look extremely odd if I suddenly scrapped it all. So I'm going ahead as if this has nothing to do with me."
"I don't think you'll get caught, but can't you cancel these events?"

"No, it also involves one of my donors. Anyway, how much have we got coming to us from that last shipment? Has it been finalized?"

"Dead certain that SILVER is Watto," Vic said, when the recording ended. "What do you think, Joe?"

"Yes, no doubt. The old boy's getting very careless—he should have retired years ago. I think they're discussing that situation I told you about, the one where I took the photos of Watto." Johnson felt constrained in what he could say in the presence of Goode, whom he didn't know.

"But I've no idea who EDISON is," Vic said.

Johnson shook his head. "No. But just one thought—did you make any progress on checking who from the Pentagon was stationed in Sarajevo in the early '90s?"

"No, we're still checking," Vic said. "We haven't seen anything obvious in the records so far."

"The voice quality isn't as good for EDISON," Goode said. "We haven't been able to trace the number yet. I think that's a pay-as-you-go cell phone as well. But give us a bit of time, we'll get there."

"Yeah, okay, that's good," Vic said. "Can you put these calls onto a memory stick for me? I'll take them into the office. Thanks a lot, Alex, that's good work you've done." Vic patted Goode on the shoulder. "Just keep on doing the same. If any more calls come through from that number, let me know immediately."

Goode copied the voice files and slotted a memory stick into the computer's USB port, then transferred them.

Vic picked up the memory stick and got up.

On the way out, he said to Johnson, "The second person, EDISON—his voice is familiar, definitely. But I can't place him. Has to be someone well known, based on the conversation."

"Yes, I know. It'll come to me. I'm going to listen to it a

few more times. That bit about the key appearances and donors." Johnson gave his friend a sideways glance.

"Let's get a voice analysis done," Vic said. "See if we can clean the recording up a bit. Might help."

Johnson shrugged. "Yep, give it a try."

"What about Aisha? Have you had her pulled in yet?" Johnson asked.

"Last I heard, NYPD had gone to her place. We'll leave it to them. Shouldn't be a problem. We have an ongoing conversation with the people at CBA as well. They've got no concerns about Aisha, said she's been a dedicated employee and has done a good job. She hasn't been promoted, but otherwise would have no reason to do anything that would harm the studio. So they're a bit bemused by it all."

"I'm thinking we should talk to them about postponing this interview," Johnson said.

"We've done that. They point-blank refuse. They say this interview is their biggest earner in two years. There's tens of millions of dollars riding on it. They can't afford to. The director whom I talked to said their debts are sky-high, they have the banks on their back, and if they cancel they're worried a couple of them will call in their loans and torpedo the business. It's high-stakes stuff."

"The other way around it is to pull in Franjo," Johnson said. "That would solve it. I've got a hell of a job to process the info before we could compile a charge sheet covering the war crimes stuff, but we could maybe hold him temporarily?"

Vic shook his head. "Yeah, we could if we knew where he was. His office in London claims they don't even know where he is staying. There's no trace of him so far at the major hotels. He can't be far away, but he seems to have vanished as well."

"Yes, well, he's rather good at that."

CHAPTER FORTY-THREE

Thursday, July 26, 2012
Manhattan

"Come over here, Boris, meet Sabrina."

Franjo turned, glass of champagne in hand, to Edvin Matić. His old friend from Mostar, with whom he was staying in New York, was standing in the door with a slim blond woman who towered at least three inches above him.

"She's got some stuff to keep you happy and help you relax before that big interview tomorrow. Come this way," Edvin added.

Franjo glanced out the window of the fourth-floor apartment overlooking St. John's Park, in Tribeca, and the Hudson River, then back at Edvin. He had certainly made a success of his move to the States.

"Okay," Franjo said. He drained his champagne, stood, and followed Edvin and Sabrina into the adjacent reception room.

On the table was a silver tray with twelve lines of white

powder. Next to the powder lay three rolled-up hundred dollar bills. Two other women were sitting on the sofa beyond the table, wearing outfits that left little to Franjo's imagination.

"There you go," said Sabrina. "Welcome to New York. Start on a high, end on a high." She laughed.

Franjo felt as if he did need something to relax him, to take away the anxiety he had been feeling. The champagne had helped; now he needed something more.

"I don't usually do this before dinner," Franjo said, "but as it's here, why not?" He picked up one of the rolled-up bills and snorted up two lines, one into each nostril.

The news coverage after the SRTV News revelations about Clinton and Iran had been massive and global, even more impactful than Franjo had expected. Now there would be a laser-like scrutiny of the interview with Spencer, because everyone would be expecting him to comment on it.

With only eighteen hours to go before the interview—which was due to take place at one o'clock the following afternoon to fit in with UK prime time television schedules—Franjo was starting to wonder if he hadn't gone one step too far.

Sabrina leaned over and picked up one of the other hundred dollar bills. Her hand brushed against Franjo's thigh, and she let it linger for just a couple of seconds.

Then she also snorted two lines and went to sit with the other girls.

Edvin picked up the final bill and snorted a line, then he burst into laughter. "Come on, Boris, let's refill that glass of yours, then you can join these three girls for an hour or two. If that's not good preparation for an interview, I don't know what is."

He led the way back into the room where they had

started, picked up a bottle of Cristal champagne, and refilled Franjo's glass.

"I'll do the white stuff but not Sabrina," Franjo said.

"Not your type?" Edvin asked.

"No. Definitely not. In any case, I've got a girlfriend in London, Hayley—so I might feel guilty afterward if I did. She was going to come here but couldn't make it in the end. Her mother was ill so she's gone to visit her in Edinburgh."

"Fair enough. Now, how's it going? Seriously, good to catch up with you. It's been a while," Edvin said. "Everything going okay, you know, on the Syria front?"

Franjo sighed and told Edvin about the events of recent weeks and the arrival of Johnson. "We've had a few run-ins— exchanges of fire, shall we say. Literally I mean. It's the last thing I need."

Edvin rolled his eyes. "Hope he doesn't get on my tail as well, then. The shadow of the Heliodrom never goes away, does it? Bad days."

Edvin had been one of the others in the same HVO army unit as Franjo and Marco in 1993. Their secrets of those days were literally sealed in blood.

"Well, like I said before, if you ever need my plane, it's at LaGuardia, a Gulfstream G280. That'll get you as far as South America, say Lima or Bogotá, no problem. Then you're out of here. They won't touch you. It's yours if you need it, my friend. You can go tonight if you're worried—do you want to just forget the interview? I don't know why you do this, anyway. It's not like you need the money."

Franjo drained his glass. "I know, I know, you're not the only one to say that. Marco keeps telling me the same thing. It's actually got nothing to do with money—it's professional pride. This is my biggest interview in the States. I mean, I've done a few prime ministers and presidents in Europe, but it's my biggest over here."

"Too big an ego, buddy. That's your problem: pride. It'll bring you down, like it has every proud man."

Franjo shook his head. "Nah. I just don't like throwing in the towel. It's taken me a long time to get Spencer on the hook for this one. But I tell you what, I actually would like a plane out of here the minute that interview finishes tomorrow. Could you get me a fast car straight from CBA to LaGuardia, then the plane? I'd owe you one, seriously."

"What passports you got?" Edvin asked.

"Canadian, German, Argentinian. All different names."

Franjo's phone pinged as a message arrived. He pulled it from his pocket and read it.

"Shit. It's from Watson. Says he's had an alert from Customs and Border Protection telling him that Johnson arrived in New York this morning. Although that doesn't mean anything—Johnson doesn't know my identity."

"How do you know?"

"How could he?"

"Still, you should pull this interview, I'm telling you," Edvin said.

Franjo shook his head. "Nah. It's in less than twenty-four hours. Then I'm out of here."

His phone began to ring. It was Watson. But Franjo declined the call.

* * *

Thursday, July 26, 2012
  Wolf Trap, Virginia

Watson rarely watched foreign satellite TV channels, but now, given the widespread coverage the Bosnia documents story was getting, he was flicking through all of them, checking for any new developments. In particular, he wanted to know if there was speculation over the identities of the CIA and Pentagon officials.

So far, to his relief, there appeared not to be.

But then Watson clicked onto SRTV, the British channel that had originally broken the story.

As he did so, the news program reached a commercial break, and an advertisement began.

"This Friday, SRTV's award-winning current affairs show, *Wolff Live*, will be in New York for an exclusive interview with the speaker of the House of Representatives, Patrick Spencer," the narrator said. "The 56-year-old, a controversial Republican, is seen by some as a future presidential candidate. It will be a unique chance to hear our star interviewer, Boris Wolff, talk to Spencer about his controversial views on immigration, Muslims, and many other issues."

But Watson didn't absorb any more of the advertisement. His mind raced into overdrive as he computed the implications of what he had just heard.

After four days out of the loop, traveling to Croatia and back, then trying to recover, he felt as though he were desperately playing catchup.

Cursing to himself, he reached for his phone and dialed RUNNER.

No answer. The phone rang out and eventually clicked over to voice mail.

Watson punched out a text message instead.

Just seen you're interviewing Patrick Spencer. Are you crazy? Do you realize who he is?? Cancel it now. Call me immediately. I'll explain.

Thirty seconds later, a reply came back.

Can't cancel. Too much at stake. It's my biggest interview ever.

Either the guy was drunk or on drugs, Watson thought, to be taking this so lightly. But at least he had responded. He redialed Boris's number. But now his phone seemed to be switched off, and yet again the unanswered call went to voice mail.

"What the hell," Watson muttered. He dialed another number, this time for EDISON, who answered after three rings.

Before the recipient could speak, Watson jumped in.

"EDISON, you fucking asshole. Why didn't you tell me you were going to be interviewed by Boris Wolff?"

"Calm down, what—"

"Shit, man," Watson interrupted, "You *have* to cancel. Do you realize he's the guy who fixes our arms sales out of Croatia? He effectively pays your goddamn bribes." Watson put his hand on his forehead, which was now clammy with sweat. He hadn't even bothered to go to Difficult Run River for this call. "That's not his real name, by the way. His real name is Franjo Vuković, and he's currently being hunted for goddamned war crimes."

There was a pause as Spencer took in what he had just heard.

"Dammit, Robert," Spencer said. "Why would I think to tell you? You're the half-assed fool for keeping me in the dark —all of us in the dark—trying to keep everybody separate from each other with your code names and compartmental-izing everyone. I don't know him and he doesn't know me— after twenty years! That's 100 percent your fault, not ours."

He's right, I'm damn stupid, Watson thought.

"I never dreamed, and why would I, that Boris Wolff would one day end up interviewing you, Patrick, of all people," Watson said. "Not once. The only thing on my mind has been security, and need-to-know is the biggest part of that."

Now he was furious. The use of cryptonyms had gone out the window.

"Well, you created this situation. Now you're going to have to sweat it out," Spencer said. "There's no *way,* absolutely no way, I can pull out of this interview. First, politically, it's a golden opportunity. Second, the guy who owns CBA is one of my biggest donors."

"How much is he in for?" Watson asked.

"Christopher Goldberg has put in more than one and a half million dollars over the past year and a half. I can't afford to lose that kind of support, especially not if I'm going to run for president in four years. Just as important, Christopher's business is on a knife edge right now. The loans could get called in any day, the bankers are getting mighty twitchy. He's had the toughest of years. This interview is going to be a big payday for him. I cancel, and I guarantee you that's the end for him. So, sorry, no way."

Watson picked up a baseball that was lying on his desk and threw it so hard against the opposite wall in his study that it rebounded at head-high level. He ducked out of the way but caught his injured left wrist on the side of the desk as he did so. A spasm of pain shot through him.

"Sonofabitch," Watson said. "Boris is saying he can't back out. You're saying you can't either."

He stood up and paced across the room, thinking furiously. "Okay, we're going to have to rig the interview, then. He's going to have to spoon-feed you questions. If he goes all guns blazing on this Iran arms thing and who knows what else, then we're all going to come across as utter assholes *and* wind up in the slammer."

Watson shut his eyes, propped the phone between his ear and his shoulder, and ran his hands through his white hair. "Oh, and that's not all. That idiot Johnson is on Boris's trail and mine as well. He's likely to come in and try to have him arrested or something tomorrow either before or after the interview. Then you'll be next, eventually, when they figure all of us out, and where does that leave you and your campaign?"

There was silence on the other end of the line.

Eventually Spencer spoke. "I just can't back out of this. There's too much at stake. It's down to you now. You got us into this mess. You can get us out. Do what you have to, Robert, but *fix* this."

Before Watson could reply, Spencer hung up.

CHAPTER FORTY-FOUR

Friday, July 27, 2012
Manhattan

Johnson was up and dressed by quarter past six in the morning, having slept little. He was about to call the concierge at his hotel, the Pennsylvania, to check when breakfast was served when Vic called.

"Sorry, Doc, it's early, but you have to listen to this. Alex Goode at the NSA's just sent it to me. It's a call last night between Watto and someone else. You'll know straightaway who it is."

Johnson groaned. His shoulder was still a little sore. "Hang on a minute." He sat in an armchair and sipped some water. "Okay, go on, then."

"Here you go. First voice you'll hear is Watto," Vic said. A somewhat crackly recording began to play.

"EDISON, you fucking asshole. Why didn't you tell me you were going to be interviewed by Boris Wolff?"

Johnson jerked forward, feeling as though he'd just had a double espresso.

"Shit, Vic. It can't be, surely?"

"EDISON *is* Spencer."

"Unbelievable," Johnson said. "So—"

"Wait, you need to hear the rest."

The recording came back on, and Johnson heard it all the way through.

"So Spencer's the third man in all this, the Pentagon adviser, in for a cut of the arms deals," Johnson said. "He must have been in it all along. You heard what he said—twenty years."

"He's finished. He's toast," Vic said.

"I agree, Vic, he is. But what do we do now? We could wade in and have both him and Franjo arrested before this interview, but it would look ham-fisted. They could play it that way with their media friends as well, given we're still building evidence. That'd be a big call. I'm happy to play a slightly longer game. Right now I'm more worried about Franjo being snuffed out by Aisha. Any word on where she is?"

"No. She didn't go home last night, which is seriously worrisome," Vic said. "We checked out her mosque, but no sign of her there. She must be at a friend's place, but no idea whose. The police are doing everything to track her down. She's due at work at half past seven for the interview, so let's see if she turns up. There's also been no sign of Franjo. He definitely didn't check into a hotel last night, so he must be with a friend or something as well."

"We've got to go over that studio with a fine-tooth comb," Johnson said. "Can we get sniffer dogs down there and say we're worried about security at Spencer's interview given all his anti-Muslim comments?"

"Yep, I'll get onto it."

"Okay, I want to get to the studio as soon as possible, so I'm going to have a very quick breakfast and hoof it. It's only a few blocks away on the other side of Penn Station. The TV studio's bound to be open. You can meet me there. Okay?"

"Yes, fine, but be careful," Vic said. "You're pissing off some powerful people here."

"I've already been shot at about three or four times on this job. What else is new? But I hear you."

"Okay. I'll see you outside the West Side Jewish Center. It's an old stone synagogue in front of the TV studio entrance. Forty-five minutes, right?"

"Okay. See you then."

Johnson grabbed his jacket, his wallet, and two spare magazines for his Glock. Then he pulled on a baseball cap and sunglasses and headed for the elevators.

Two New York Police Department cars, sirens wailing, screeched past Johnson as he made his way along Seventh Avenue after leaving the Pennsylvania.

He crossed 33rd Street, breaking into a run briefly to avoid a yellow cab, then continued past the melee of people that were swarming into the subway, the deli shops, offices, and banks.

At the junction of Seventh Avenue and West 34th Street, opposite Macy's department store, he turned left, the Empire State Building behind him.

Now the CBA TV studios were only two blocks away. Johnson continued past the array of glass and steel offices and shops until he reached the West Side Jewish Center on his right, next to an open-air parking lot.

There he paused. He checked the map on his phone. CBA was in a gray six-story glass-fronted building right behind the synagogue.

It was now almost quarter past seven, but there was no sign of Vic. Johnson pulled his baseball cap further down, leaned against the old wooden door, and waited.

After ten minutes, Johnson saw him. Vic strode across the parking lot and pointed urgently to his left, toward the TV studios. "The two sniffer dogs have just arrived. They brought them straight here from JFK. There was a bomb scare there during the night."

They crossed the lot toward the rear entrance of the TV studio in the corner. The huge doorway of the studio's loading bay was on the left, leading off the parking lot, and a pedestrian entrance, heavily branded with CBA logos, was on the right.

Outside the loading bay stood an unmarked white van, out of which climbed a woman and a man with two black Labradors, both wearing harnesses. The handlers took the dogs into the building, accompanied by two policemen.

"I've had a chat with the dog handlers already," Vic said. "They're going to comb the place. We've got a bit of time before the production team arrives. The lighting, sound, and camera crews are already there, doing their final checks. I gather Franjo is due here a bit later. But—"

"Is she there? Aisha, I mean?" Johnson interrupted.

"No. That's what I was coming to. She phoned in sick. Apparently it was a short call. She didn't speak to her manager, just left a message with a girl in the office. And we still haven't traced where she is. She's not at home, and her phone's now switched off."

Johnson grimaced. "Shit."

Vic led the way into the building. "They're going to be in Studio One, the largest one." He nodded at the reception desk and produced his CIA identification. "Can you sign this man in, please. Joe Johnson's his name. I'm vouching for him."

The security man took Johnson's proffered passport, photographed his face, and produced a visitor's badge.

Three other men approached. They were tall, heavily muscled guys who wore long-sleeved black shirts.

"My staff," Vic said. He beckoned them over. "You guys, just make sure nobody else comes in here without my say-so, okay? No CIA, no police, nobody. All right?"

The three men nodded. "No problem boss," one of them said.

"Okay, let's see what the dogs do," Vic said to Johnson. He led the way through the lobby and across a corridor toward a door marked Studio One.

Inside the studio the dogs were already hard at it with their handlers, who were systematically working their way around the set. Johnson watched as the woman handler steered her dog around two black armchairs that were placed at right angles to each other, a coffee table in the center, and four TV cameras that stood on the floor.

The other dog handler was working his way up and down the rows of audience seats.

Johnson stared up into the ceiling of the cavernous studio, which housed a crisscross maze of rails, cables, and lights. The room was already busy. Cameramen and sound crew were performing checks on the cameras that stood on the studio floor and at the rear of the room, while one of the lighting crew was using a multi-section pole to make adjustments to the overhead rig.

Johnson looked at a couple of guys who were busy working on a lighting bar. He approached them.

"Sorry, but can I interrupt you for a moment?" Johnson asked the men. "I'm Joe Johnson, an investigator working alongside a colleague of mine from the CIA over there, Vic Walter." He pointed to Vic, who was standing a few yards away. "We're just a little concerned about a couple of security issues, given we're going to have Spencer in here and the tone of what he's been saying about Muslims in recent weeks."

"Not now, buddy, not now," one of them said. "Can't you see we're trying to get this finished? We're behind with this already. It's urgent."

"I appreciate that, but this is urgent too."

"Right," the man said, visibly struggling to quell his irritation. "I'm the lighting director, Tim Burroughs. What do you want?"

"I'm just interested in the role Aisha Delić plays in the team here: what she does and her part in preparations for today's production, for instance. I know she's out sick today, but over recent weeks?" Johnson asked.

"There's no problem with Aisha. Her job has different parts to it—some planning, some technical, and some creative. She normally programs the lighting desk that controls all the lights in the studio," Tim said. "She also stood in for me yesterday and set all the lighting during rehearsals because I wasn't around. She did a decent job. Now, I really need to get a move on. Is that okay?" He turned his back on Johnson without waiting for an answer.

Johnson walked up to the dog handler in the seating area and introduced himself. "I assume you're not finding anything?" he asked.

"Nothing so far," the handler said. "We'll give these two dogs a while, then do the technical storerooms and production galleries as well if nothing shows up." He strode away, leading the dog to the rear of the studio.

Twenty minutes later the woman handler strolled up to Vic and Johnson. "It's clean," she said. "These dogs have found nothing at all. We've been over it twice."

"Okay, good. Let's hope we have nothing else to worry about," Johnson muttered. He felt slightly relieved.

* * *

Friday, July 27, 2012
  New York City

Franjo's head felt dense and heavy under the weight of the previous night's champagne, not to mention the lines of cocaine, of which he didn't often partake.

He put his hand on his forehead, which felt clammy to the touch.

Despite declining the invitation from Sabrina, it had been a very long way from the normal, professional, sober routine he followed prior to big interviews.

He knew where it was all headed. He knew he'd have to disappear again.

Screw it, this is the last one. I'll go out with a bang.

Franjo stared at the ceiling, then climbed out of bed and stepped into the bathroom. There was still plenty of time. He could get into the studio by ten o'clock, and the interview would start at half past twelve.

For months he'd planned and plotted to get this interview in the bag, then he'd been completely pumped when he finally landed it.

Then came the American, Joe Johnson, dragging up the dirt from his past.

Now he just wanted it to be over.

Edvin's right. I should just get out, get on the plane, and go . . . Screw the career, screw the TV company, screw them all.

Franjo rummaged in his toilet bag until he found a pack of painkillers. He removed two, filled a glass with water from the tap, and swallowed them.

Then he wandered back into the bedroom and picked up his phone, which he had turned off the previous evening. He turned it back on.

That was when he remembered the text messages the

previous night from Watson, telling him to cancel the interview. *What was that all about?*

Franjo noticed five lines of cocaine remained on the silver tray on the table. He picked up one of the rolled-up hundred dollar bills that also lay on the tray and stood staring at the white powder, wondering if he should.

Then the phone rang. It was Watson.

"RUNNER, it's SILVER. Where the *hell* have you been? I've been trying to call, but your phone's been switched off."

Franjo paused. "It's all under control, don't worry."

"No, it's not," Watson said, his voice low and monotonic, but with a threatening edge. "It's a very long way from being under control. Listen to me. I wanted to explain to you last night, but you wouldn't speak to me. Patrick Spencer, who you're interviewing today, is the other man in our arms ring."

Franjo furrowed his brow. "What are you talking about?"

"He was the Pentagon military adviser in Sarajevo, in the early '90s. He's been in it all along. I should have told you but—"

Franjo always felt irritable after drinking alcohol. Now, as he fully took in what Watson was saying, he could feel the underlying rage building up through his neck, into his head, until he exploded. "You sonofabitch. What the hell are you playing at? It's too late to cancel it! It's my biggest interview, and tens of millions are riding on it."

"I know, I know . . . Listen, I'm apologizing. It's my fault, I tried to keep you all separate on a need-to-know basis," Watson said. "We'll just have to manage it—"

"Manage it? How do you mean, *manage* it?"

"You'll have to rig the questions, go easy on him, keep to his strengths; immigration, Muslims, that lot. Keep it domestic, keep it US-focused. Don't ask anything about Iran, nothing about Bosnia, nothing about arms to Syria, nothing about foreign policy. Keep it simple." Watson stumbled over his words.

Franjo snorted. "You've no idea, have you? Absolutely no idea. I'm going to have my editor talking in my ear feeding me questions for the whole of the interview, all forty-five minutes of it. And you're telling me to completely ignore him. You idiot."

"Pretend the earpiece doesn't work or something," Watson said. "I don't know. You don't have an option. If it's a disaster, it's a disaster—but that's better than landing us all in the shit. I've spoken to Spencer, and I've told him that's what you'll do, so you'll just have to do it, okay? Then get out as soon as the interview's over. Can you talk to him before the interview? Give him a call now."

"Watson, you're history if I ever catch up with you. You might think you're a CIA hard-ass. You might have helped me make money in the past, but you've screwed up big time now. Send me Spencer's phone number. I'll call him."

Franjo hung up. Suddenly, he felt sober again. His phone beeped with a text message from Watson, containing Spencer's phone number.

He decided to ignore it for now.

Instead, he took his time with his morning routine, showering and dressing at leisure. He watched the news and greeted Edvin. Only then did he pick up his leather briefcase and leave. He'd get some breakfast, and then, on the way to the studio, he'd call Spencer.

CHAPTER FORTY-FIVE

Friday, July 27, 2012
  Manhattan

There was still an hour to go before the interview began when Franjo strode into the CBA TV studios green room, the usual preshow lounge area for participants. He knew from his earlier, very brief phone call with Spencer that he would be waiting for him.

There he was at the other end of the long room. Franjo watched the speaker of the House for a second. He was taller than he appeared on television—probably six feet—and had square shoulders. He was sipping an orange juice, flanked by two uniformed officers and two other men who Franjo guessed were probably PR flunkies. Spencer's neatly coiffured gray hair and pristine white collar and charcoal suit gave him an elegant, old-worldly aspect.

Speaker of the House today, maybe president-in-waiting in a few years, or so he doubtless thought.

Franjo grimaced, then walked up to Spencer and quickly

introduced himself. He noticed that the uniformed officers with Spencer were from the United States Capitol Police.

The two men eyed each other silently for a second.

"Let's get this over with . . . in private," Franjo said.

Spencer nodded and glanced at his colleagues, one of whom, sure enough, wore a badge identifying him as head of communications. Then he turned to Franjo and pointed toward the corner of the room. "We'll go over there. Come."

One of the Capitol Police officers stepped forward and spoke to Spencer. "Would you like me to come with you, sir?"

"No, I'm fine, thanks," Spencer said.

The two men began to walk toward the other side of the room.

The head of communications took off after them, but Spencer put his hands on his hips and said, as if admonishing a schoolboy, "No. This is a private chat; you don't need to be involved. Go and wait over there."

The communications man raised his eyebrows. "I really don't think that's a good idea. Are you sure you don't—"

"I said *no*," Spencer said flatly.

The man blinked, then obediently did a U-turn and returned to his colleague.

As soon as they were out of earshot of the others, Franjo spoke. "I'll cut the crap," he said in a low voice, "because time is short and we both know the score. At least now we do."

"Yes, now we do," Spencer said, his voice also low. "What a joke. Watson's well and truly screwed this up. But too late to do anything now. We'll have to go through with it. I hope you've carefully thought through your questions?"

Franjo nodded. "We can discuss that asshole and his games afterward. But let me tell you what I'm going to do in this interview."

He started to outline his plan.

CHAPTER FORTY-SIX

Friday, July 27, 2012
New York City

"There's something not right. I don't know, I've a gut feeling, Vic, just a gut feeling." Johnson tugged hard at the small hole at the top of his right ear and scrutinized the monitor in the production gallery.

Vic stood next to him, hands on hips.

The interview was about to begin. Johnson glanced to his right at the program's editor, David Rowlands, who wore headphones and spoke into a stalk microphone that was linked to Franjo's wireless earpiece.

The production gallery, at the rear of the studio, had a long floor-to-ceiling plate-glass window that allowed the producer, the editor, and other staff a clear view of what was happening in front of them.

Franjo sat in one of the black leather armchairs with his back to a large, modernistic *Wolff Live* logo. At a right angle to him, in the other armchair, sat the familiar figure of

Spencer, his hair swept neatly across his forehead, his gray sideburns clipped, his suit perfectly pressed.

The whole set was raised slightly on a plinth a foot above the level of the studio floor.

In front of them, the four hundred seats in Studio One were completely filled with selected guests, journalists, and VIPs who had been invited by either SRTV or CBA TV.

Standing at the right of the studio, backs to the wall, were two United States Capitol Police officers who Johnson knew were responsible for the speaker of the House's security. Another two Capitol Police officers stood at the left-hand-side wall. He had noticed a few others, together with New York Police Department officers, in the foyer.

Johnson's sense of foreboding was something he couldn't shake off, even though the security team, at his request, had taken the precaution of a further sweep of the studio by the sniffer dogs. There had also been additional personal searches of all guests and their bags. He was increasingly wishing he had asked Vic to have police hold Franjo and Spencer before the show, despite the possibility of it backfiring in terms of media reaction. But it was too late now.

The atmosphere on the studio floor was noticeably tense. The audience was unusually chatty, and the floor manager could be heard telling them to quiet down.

"Four, three, two, one, zero, we're live . . . Boris we're coming to you in thirty," the production assistant said.

As the title music faded, Franjo faced the camera and started his scripted introduction.

Johnson glanced at the teleprompter monitor in the gallery, on which the text of Franjo's words rolled up.

"Hello, and welcome to *Wolff Live*, today coming from New York City, where I'm interviewing Speaker of the House of Representatives Patrick Spencer, considered by many to be a presidential candidate of the future," Franjo began.

"Thank you, Boris, it's a pleasure to be here," Spencer said. Johnson noted that Spencer did not deny his presidential ambitions.

"Now, before we touch on the more personal aspects of your career, Mr. Speaker, I thought we should look at one of the key issues that's been at the center of focus both in the United States and internationally, and that's immigration and racial tension. Unrest in the States has been on the rise. Why do you think that is?"

David swore and tapped his fingers on his desk. "What the hell. He's already gone off script. He was meant to start with foreign affairs," he said.

On the set, Spencer moved quickly into a long answer to the question.

"Unrest has been on the rise, for sure, and there's one good reason for that," Spencer said. "The increase in immigration, the increase in unemployment this brings for our existing citizens—African-Americans, Latinos, and others—and the attacks we've seen on police, innocent citizens, and even children, are all clear evidence that our American way of life is under threat. Immigrants, many of them illegal, including a significant number of Muslims, have come to our shores and are a key factor behind a huge increase in homicides . . ." Spencer said.

The tirade had begun. *All very predictable.* Johnson had heard it all before, and Franjo was handing Spencer the questions on a silver platter, served up with a bow wrapped around them. A gift for a skilled politician.

So they probably know who each other is.

Johnson stood and watched for twenty minutes or so as the interview continued, the questions virtually exclusively focused on domestic US issues. He then walked into the lighting gallery where three of the CBA TV team, including

Aisha's last-minute replacement, sat intently watching the monitors, while Vic stood in a corner.

He turned to the lighting crew, trying hard to quell his concern and appear calm. Tim, the lighting director, was concentrating hard on the monitor in front of him.

"Excuse me, Tim," Johnson said. "I know you're busy, but I'm getting increasingly concerned."

Tim scowled. "What now?"

"It's Aisha. Over the past couple of days, have you noticed anything out of the ordinary with her? Anything unusual about what she did?"

"No, not really," Tim said. "She's been programming a new special effects lighting fixture I've brought in for this show. She's done a good job."

"Okay, so what does it do? Just briefly."

"It's for the closing sequence at the end, just to give it a bit of pizzazz," Tim said. "It'll throw an animated multibeam pattern all over the floor, just when Wolff and Spencer are bathed in a soft blue light as the credits start to roll."

"Is that normal for a straightforward political interview? That kind of fancy lighting effect?" Johnson asked.

"No, but I just wanted to do something different."

"Fair enough. So she did her job properly, from your perspective?"

"Yeah."

One of the other lighting team members turned around and looked at Tim. "Actually, Tim, I didn't mention it earlier, but she screwed up that goddamned bar over the set that's got your special on it. I had to reset it this morning."

"What was that?" Johnson asked.

"Nothing major," Olly said. "I came in early this morning to check everything and found she'd put the bar holding the special effects light quite a lot lower than I knew Tim wanted it, so I had to move it back up."

Tim grunted. "Thanks for telling me that, Olly. That would have screwed things up. I'll speak to Aisha about it when she's back tomorrow."

Tim turned back to Johnson. "So apparently she only did an okay job, then. But my opinion stands. Sorry, I have to concentrate on this now." He focused on his monitor.

Johnson nodded. "Okay, thanks." He walked back through to the production gallery, followed by Vic. Both men stood, arms folded, gazing out of the big glass window at the audience immediately in front of them and the stage beyond.

"What do you think?" Johnson asked his friend. "These guys have got too much going on to even think about Aisha. But it doesn't seem right to me."

"No," Vic said. "I agree. I think we're just going to have to be a bit insistent. Let's ask a few more questions. That guy Olly mentioned the lighting bar. Seems odd, somehow. Maybe ask him why she might have lowered it."

Spencer was still in full flow on the set.

" . . . So far all we've seen from the Democrats is immigration out of control, lawlessness, and a situation where American citizens are feeling completely overwhelmed and helpless. I want to change all that," Spencer said, his voice rising steadily. "That's why I'm suggesting we put up the barriers and make much closer checks on who's coming into our beloved country. Anyone with links to countries that harbor or foster terrorism can forget it . . ."

There was loud applause from the studio audience.

Franjo appeared to be struggling to get his questions in. In the production gallery, Johnson could hear David speaking to Franjo through his earpiece, instructing him to ask questions about the Iranian arms news coverage, the potential damage to Clinton's reputation, and his wife Hillary's prospects. But Franjo ignored him.

David threw his pen across the room and started swearing. The director turned around and looked at David, equally confused. "What the hell's going on out there? Didn't you discuss the question list? Is his earpiece working?" he asked.

Johnson went back to the lighting gallery once more.

"Sorry, Tim. One more question. Which is the special effects lighting unit you just mentioned that's going to be used at the end of the show?" Johnson asked.

"For God's sake," Tim said. He snatched a large paper plan from the desk and stabbed at its location with his finger. "It's bar forty-five, right there. You might just be able to see it if you look out the window, up in the rig. Not easy to spot, though. It's dark as an elephant's asshole up there."

The lighting team member who had spoken earlier, Olly, interrupted again. "You'd better leave Tim be. He's really busy. I'll talk to you. If you're asking about out-of-norm behavior, I did find Aisha in here on her own one morning really early."

"What was odd about that?" Johnson asked.

"You're not supposed to be alone in the studio for safety reasons."

Tim chimed in again. "Olly reported that to me, and I was going to talk to Aisha about it but didn't in the end. I figured it was a one-off since we were prepping for this."

Olly leaned forward. "Right, except, ten minutes later, I walked back past the studio, thinking I would check to see if she was okay, but the blind was down over the door window, and the door was locked, which was very unusual."

"You never told me that," Tim said, facing Olly.

Olly shrugged. "I was too busy. When I walked past and saw it, I'd already told you about her being in there alone, and I forgot about it."

"Why would she pull the blind down and lock the door?" Johnson asked.

Olly scratched his head. "Don't know. And there was that

bar I mentioned earlier. I told her twice about putting it too low. But she still put it in the wrong place, which was very unlike her. She's a pro."

Johnson exchanged glances with Vic, who raised his eyebrows. "Vic, I've had a gut feeling ever since we came in here that something's not right. And you know what my gut's telling me?"

"I can take a guess."

"We need to clear the building, get everyone out." Johnson addressed Tim. "How long is it until the end of the program? How long do we have?"

Tim checked the clock. "I'd say about three and a half minutes till we come off air."

Johnson felt his body go tense.

He spoke decisively to Vic. "I know this is a big call, but I'm saying it: let's clear the studio. Go tell the director we've had a bomb alert, and get security to sound the fire alarm. That'll do it."

"Yes, I agree," Vic said. "I'll tell my security guys to get out there and clear the audience through the fire doors."

"Get Spencer and Franjo out," Johnson said, "but keep them secure, and hold them tight. Don't let those bastards run. Let's go."

* * *

Friday, July 27, 2012
  Astoria

Aisha yawned. Her eyes ached, and she felt as though her head were slowly being squeezed in a vise.

"I couldn't sleep last night. I'm struggling," she said. "I

kept trying to focus on what this is about. It's for my father and Zeinab, that's what I tried to think of," Aisha said.

"So why didn't you sleep?" Adela asked. She glanced sideways at her friend, who sat next to her on the faded old blue sofa.

"Because every time I tried to relax and focus on justice for my father and sister, all I could see in my mind was a sea of other faces in that studio."

Aisha shuffled toward the edge of the sofa, the cell phone clutched tightly in both hands.

On her phone screen, the number she had already tapped out was showing.

Adela ran her fingers through her hair and stared at the television screen in front of them.

"Listen to him," Adela said. "Listen to this monster Spencer. I tell you, between him and Franjo, there's not much to choose from: the hatred they've stirred up, the damage they've done. You'll never have the chance to do this to both of them again."

Adela picked up the TV remote control and increased the volume a little further to listen to Spencer speaking.

"We've seen murders in our communities by Islamic terrorists," Spencer said. "We've seen attacks in many corners of our country. Our security forces have repeatedly uncovered evidence of plots, bomb-making equipment, clear intentions to kill innocent people. I say, enough of blood, enough of tears. It's time to keep them out—"

Then Spencer suddenly stopped speaking.

A loud repetitive squawking sound, like a siren, pierced the air, and a bright red strobe light began to flicker continuously across the *Wolff Live* studio set.

The TV camera showed Spencer as he looked at his interviewer, and the microphone picked up his question. "What's going on here? We're not finished."

The camera focused on Franjo, and then the shot widened to include Spencer. Both men were sitting up rigidly in their chairs, visibly alarmed. Then the picture faded and a commercial break began.

Aisha's eyes widened. "Something's wrong there, I don't know—"

"Sounds like a fire alarm's gone off in the studio or something," Adela said, a note of urgency in her voice. "That's why the red light was flashing. You'd better trigger it now, quick, before they all go. They'll evacuate the place. Come on. Press that button."

Aisha looked at the television screen, then down at the floor. She thought of Franjo and what he'd done to her family, to her father and to her sister, and all that he had stolen from her, on the Stari Most, with his tank shells and his war-fueled hatred. She raised her phone in front of her and her forefinger hovered over the green dial button.

But somehow the vision of her family was overridden, pushed to one side, by the image of Studio One, full of mothers and fathers and children and grandparents. And a crew of people she had worked with for a long time who were like family to her. She put the phone down on the sofa next to her, leaned back in her seat, and gazed blankly at Adela.

She couldn't do it.

"What the hell are you doing, Aisha?"

"I can't. All those people." Her face crumpled and a tear wound its way down the side of her nose and over her upper lip.

Adela's hand snaked out and snatched the phone from the sofa.

"Adela, no—"

But Adela jabbed her finger down hard on the dial button, then shoved the phone behind her, where Aisha couldn't reach it.

CHAPTER FORTY-SEVEN

Friday, July 27, 2012
Manhattan

A wave of alarmed chatter broke out among the audience in Studio One as soon as the fire alarm started wailing. The TV studio security guards shoved open the audience exit doors at the right- and left-hand sides of the set and ushered people out as quickly as they could.

As Johnson ran out of the lighting gallery, the initial wave of surprise among the audience rapidly escalated to panic, and people began first walking, then running, toward the exits. He saw an old lady fall over, only to be immediately trodden on by two teenagers who were jostling hard behind her. A young girl screamed, which set others off. Two men exchanged punches after they collided in an attempt to get through the increasingly packed doorway. The crowd pressed up hard behind each other at both exits as they headed for the open air.

The security guards were yelling at people to remain calm

and move smoothly but to little effect. There was too much noise now for their voices to be heard.

An irritated-looking Spencer and Franjo were now standing, bathed in a flickering red strobe light from the fire alarm system. Two of the Capitol Police officers were standing next to Spencer, conferring with him and gesticulating urgently. Three NYPD officers were striding toward them.

Johnson went up to Vic, who was in an animated discussion with two of his CIA colleagues. He raised his voice in order to be heard above the noise.

"Vic, can you talk to Spencer's security detail and work with them? Don't let either of those guys get away—it's crucial. And do it *now*. I'll follow."

Vic nodded at the two CIA men, who set off in pursuit of Spencer and Franjo. The two men were now being herded by the Capitol Police officers toward the right-hand door at the back of the studio, which led into the cavernous loading bay next to the parking lot.

Johnson and Vic followed right behind, while the security guards by the doors tried to speed up the evacuation process with urgent go-go-go motions to the exiting studio guests.

Just as Johnson got through the doors and out into the loading bay, a massive explosion erupted in the studio behind him.

The force of it knocked Johnson to the ground. He banged his chin hard on the floor, which forced his jaw sharply upward and sent a wave of intense pain through the side of his head. Flashes of bright light exploded in his eyes, and he felt a numbness run up the back of his skull.

The large door Johnson had just exited through was blown off its hinges. Part of the studio wall collapsed outward into the bay, sending pieces of plaster, cinder block, and cement to the floor. The air was filled with dust and smoke.

Everywhere people were screaming.

Johnson knew instinctively that although a good portion of the studio audience would have made it out, some would not have. There were too many.

He lifted himself onto his hands and knees but was immediately hit on the back of the head by another piece of plaster.

Johnson raised himself again and instinctively looked right, just in time to see Franjo, his dark suit covered in plaster dust, stand and run straight toward the huge vehicle exit doors.

One of the CIA men whom Vic had instructed to detain him lay motionless, a large chunk of cinder block next to his head, which was bleeding heavily from a long gash. Next to him lay both of the Capitol Police officers, one of them seemingly unconscious, the other groaning and clutching his head.

Somehow, Johnson got to his feet, feeling slightly dizzy as the blood drained from his head. But he forced himself to pursue Franjo.

"Sonofabitch," Johnson muttered.

Somebody had opened the vehicle entrance doors into the parking lot. Franjo charged straight through the gap toward the daylight outside.

Johnson ran after him, his legs feeling as though they would give way at any point. But as he moved through the bay, the dizziness started to clear.

Now he was a good ten yards behind Franjo, who crossed the parking lot in the direction of the West Side Jewish Center and the busy chaos of 34th Street.

Johnson saw a black Jeep 4x4 waiting at the curbside. Someone opened the back door, and Franjo altered course slightly to head straight toward it.

"Stop him," Johnson screamed.

As he shouted out, a car reversed rapidly out of a parking space, forcing Franjo to change tack yet again to get through the rapidly decreasing gap between the reversing car and a van that was parked against the wall of the synagogue.

The car then moved forward, but by the time Franjo recovered his momentum, Johnson was just two yards behind him and gaining ground rapidly.

He reached out, seized Franjo's collar, and pulled back as hard as he could, causing the TV interviewer to overbalance and crash heavily to the ground, his legs collapsing under him.

Johnson, his lungs now bursting, landed on top of Franjo and pinned him down. He pulled Franjo's right arm sharply behind his back and wrenched it hard. Franjo let out a yelp of pain.

From behind him, there was a burst of gunfire and Johnson saw through the shattered car window the Jeep driver's head jerk back in a spray of blood.

Within seconds, two NYPD officers ran up to them, one of them clutching a semiautomatic pistol. "That guy in the car had a gun, he was about to drop you," he said to Johnson.

Vic, who was behind the NYPD officers, flashed his CIA identity card at them. "We need to hold this guy," he said, pointing at Franjo. "Can you keep him near the studio door? I'll explain everything in a few minutes."

The officers seized Franjo, one on each arm, and frog-marched him back the way they had come.

As they passed Johnson, Franjo spat straight into his face. "You'll pay for that, you bastard. You'll pay," Franjo said.

Johnson and Vic trailed the two NYPD officers as they propelled Franjo back toward the television building, then forced him facedown to the ground just outside the loading bay, where one of them knelt on his back and restrained his arms.

Four more NYPD cars plus three fire engines arrived in convoy and screeched to a halt outside the building. Officers and crews piled out and ran in. Ten seconds later, ambulances began to arrive.

The scene that unfolded in front of Johnson as he made his way back through the loading bay and into the corridor behind was one of utter carnage.

Six dead bodies, disfigured and bloody, lay in the corridor, covered in debris.

In a corner, flanked by two security guards, a dazed Capitol Police officer, and four armed NYPD officers, was Spencer, sitting on a chair. Blood streamed from a large cut on the side of his head, his clothes were covered in white dust, and his hair was disheveled. He looked shell-shocked. One of the NYPD men was gesticulating at the speaker of the House, clearly trying to get him to move, but Spencer was shaking his head.

At least he's alive, Johnson thought.

That was more than could be said for a number of audience members for whom the evacuation had not been rapid enough.

One glimpse through a hole in the wall of the now wrecked Studio One confirmed to Johnson what his instincts had told him earlier. Several bodies, contorted beyond belief—many of them covered by the debris of plaster, mangled lighting bars, fixtures, steel poles, and other metalwork from the overhead grid—lay near the two audience exits.

Handbags, briefcases and backpacks were strewn across the whole area. Johnson could hear several cell phones ringing.

The sound of more sirens came from outside.

Johnson and Vic walked to the police officers who were standing next to Spencer. One of the officers stepped forward and barred their way.

Vic again produced his CIA identity card. "I know you

need to get Mr. Spencer to safety," he said, "but we also need to speak with him."

The officer nodded. "Noted," he said. "Talk to my superior." He pointed at another NYPD officer who was making his way across the parking lot toward them.

Johnson glanced at the officers holding Franjo, who was now sitting on the ground, his hands handcuffed behind his back. Johnson walked over and squatted down before him.

"Do you know who did this?" Johnson asked Franjo, indicating with his thumb over his shoulder toward the wrecked TV studio.

Franjo stared at him and shook his head a fraction.

"It was your ex-wife. She works at this TV studio."

"*Aisha?* Did *this?* No."

"That day you destroyed the Stari Most, what else did you do? Who did you target deliberately with those tank shells?" Johnson asked.

The corner of Franjo's mouth curled upward. "You have no idea what it was like back then. If your father-in-law gave the go-ahead for your brother and friends to be tortured to death in a rat-infested Mostar dungeon, you might feel differently, asshole." Now Franjo was snarling.

"*What?*" Johnson asked.

"Yeah, that's the truth. Erol ordered it. In the basement of the Fourth Primary School in Mostar. That was where the Muslims locked up the Croat prisoners. I was so angry. You ask me why I used that tank the way I did. Well, I'm telling you now. That's the war crime you should be chasing."

Johnson shook his head, realizing in a moment of clarity that Franjo had just summed up precisely why the war had escalated so violently on both sides and why the peace continued to be such a difficult one.

"Make no mistake," he said. "I would have chased him just as hard as you—if you hadn't killed him first."

CHAPTER FORTY-EIGHT

Friday, July 27, 2012
  Manhattan

Fifty minutes later, the chaos at the CBA TV studios building and in the parking lot outside was starting to abate.

Johnson would have liked to have had a conversation with Spencer. He wanted to tell him about the documents from Bosnia and the evidence of his actions to allow mujahideen into the country; to question him about his hypocritical stance on Muslims and immigration; and to explain exactly why his career was now over.

But before he could do so, the NYPD and Capitol Police officers, predictably, whisked him away.

To Johnson's intense satisfaction, he was in handcuffs and was swearing loudly—but in vain—at the surrounding officers. By that stage, a couple of television news camera crews had arrived, together with a posse of newspaper photographers, and they were able to capture the entire scene.

If it hadn't been for the carnage in the studio behind him,

Johnson would have been tempted to grin. The evening news headlines and opening footage were in the can, together with the following morning's front pages.

He knew Spencer would have to explain himself publicly and in court, probably on charges relating to corruption, trafficking in arms, and whatever else the FBI uncovered. Before that, though, he would have to face an absolute media frenzy. His life, at least in its previous form, was shredded, and he deserved everything he got.

Meanwhile, Franjo had been taken to a nearby NYPD station for questioning. The process had begun, and Johnson was very confident that the ending would be quite predictable.

A man in a black suit approached Vic, who greeted him warmly, then introduced him to Johnson as Dirk Hassbender, from the FBI.

Hassbender said, "Some good news. We've traced Aisha Delić. She was at a friend's house in Queens. We've just picked her up. She still had the phone on her that was used to trigger that bomb, although there's some confusion about whether she or her friend triggered it, so we've brought them both in. We'll run the fingerprints, but either way, it seems as if they both played a part in this chaos." He gazed at the studio entrance. "We think there's at least sixteen dead in there. Many others are injured, so the death toll is going to rise."

Johnson stepped forward. "Vic, does Dirk know about Robert Watson?"

"Yep, we're on it," Hassbender said before Vic could reply. "We've had a trace on him for the past twenty-four hours. Got a whole team on him."

Hassbender paused. "By the way, you might want to know about this. We found it near the set inside the studio. It's

Boris Wolff's briefcase." He held up an old leather case and opened it.

Inside, Johnson could see a crumpled folder stuffed full of slightly yellowed papers bound together with pieces of string.

"The Sarajevo dossier," Johnson said. "I owe you, Dirk. I think you've just salvaged my fee for this job." He grimaced at Vic. "That's what you wanted me to get. There it is."

"Is that it?" Vic asked. "The papers? The ones Franjo got back off you?"

Johnson nodded.

"We'll need to keep that in case it's needed as evidence," Hassbender said. "I'll arrange for copies to be made if you need them immediately."

"I certainly do," Vic said. "There's someone I need to get them to extremely urgently, so if you could get the copies done now, that would be great."

Hassbender nodded and walked off.

"Perhaps you can tell me now," Johnson said.

"Tell you what?" Vic said.

Johnson pressed his lips together. "Who asked you to track down the papers and why."

Vic looked away. "It's difficult."

"Difficult?"

"Yes. I'll tell you one day. But you've done a great job here, and they'll be grateful, despite all this shit." Vic looked over his shoulder toward the chaos behind him. "At this rate the director will be offering you your old job back."

Johnson almost managed a smile. "Just remember I'm going to need those documents to put my case together for the prosecutors in Sarajevo, so make sure your man Hassbender keeps them safe. They'll need the originals."

"No problem, that's fine," Vic said. "I'll work all that out."

Johnson nodded. As Vic checked for messages on his phone and then took a call, Johnson paced slowly away from

the TV studio building, past a tangle of police cars and ambulances, and across the parking lot to the side wall of the old
stone synagogue.

Then he turned, squatted on his haunches, and surveyed
the chaotic scene before him. He knew he needed to take a
few moments to think through the situation clearly. Was
there anything he was missing? What about Watto?

But instead of thinking clearly, Johnson bowed his head.
*Sixteen dead. Why didn't I see this coming? Why didn't we
catch it?*

He started running through the events of the previous
couple of weeks in his mind.

The self-blame game—my favorite. Aisha's reluctance to talk
about the death of her father and sister that day and his
unwillingness to press her harder about it . . . his reluctance
to have Franjo taken into custody at an earlier time . . . Had
he overplayed the problems around getting Croatian police
involved earlier?

Should have done more, should have moved faster . . .

At the end of the day, wouldn't a bullet into Franjo's head
a couple of weeks earlier have saved dozens of other people's
lives? What was this obsession with proper justice, real
justice? Was it always the answer?

Is it all worth it?

The answers he heard, in the voice of his dead mother,
were the same as ever.

Truth and justice, truth and justice, truth and justice.

The words spun slowly inside his head like a vortex of
water in a whirlpool, all congregating in the center.

Johnson stood. His phone rang, and he fished it out of his
pocket. It was Jayne. The sight of her name on his phone
screen jerked him out of his self-absorption. He pressed the
answer button.

"Jayne, how—"

"I've just seen a newsflash, Joe. It sounds awful there." Her voice was stressed.

Johnson exhaled. "Yes, shocking. It's hard to describe."

There was a pause. "Did you get Franjo?" she asked.

"Yes, we got him. We got Spencer, too. And you've got Marco—"

"We got him, yes, but only after I just managed to stop Filip from running off and killing him first," Jayne said. "I stupidly let him see the address of Marco's business unit that you sent me. I went to the bathroom at the hotel, came out, and he'd vanished. It was only because that Subaru of his wouldn't start that we've got a live Marco to take to court rather than a dead one. I then talked him out of the revenge option."

"*Shit*. Well done. I had a feeling that might have been the reason he was tagging along with us so closely. So we have the main guys, though I'm still waiting to hear about Watson. But as for the carnage here, we were just too late. Sixteen dead, so far. I don't know, Jayne, this thing. It's beyond terrorism in some ways—it's a whole different ball game from hunting down solitary Nazis. I'm having a hard time landing on the side of right."

"Listen, Joe, don't beat yourself up. Sounds as if you did a great job."

"You too, but it doesn't feel much like it right now." Johnson walked back across the parking lot toward the TV studio as he spoke, his phone clamped to his ear. "By the way, you need to call Natasha and tell her she can go back home now. I think it's safe, given both Franjo and Marco are being held."

"Yes, will do."

As Johnson drew nearer to the CBA building, he saw Vic with a group of men, including the FBI agent Hassbender.

Vic turned and spotted him. "Joe, we've lost Watson. He's gone off radar. We missed him."

Johnson spoke wearily into his phone. "Hang on, Jayne, I've got Vic here trying to talk to me."

He lowered the phone and looked first at Vic, then Hassbender, a blank expression on his face. "What d'you mean, lost him?"

Hassbender shook his head. "My guys arrived just in time to track his car from his house in Wolf Trap all the way up to Ronald Reagan Airport. We were certain he was in it—had a positive visual ID on him, even tracked his cell phone, everything. But then when we pulled him over, near the airport, it wasn't him. It was some look-alike, a stunt double, almost a spitting image. But not him."

"A *double*? So where the hell is he?" Johnson asked.

Hassbender shrugged. "We've no idea where he is."

"Jayne?"

"Yes?"

"I'm going to have to call you back."

* * *

Friday, July 27, 2012
Leesburg Executive Airport, Virginia

Watson wiped the mud off of his shoes as he got out of the black BMW sedan. The rainstorm had left the path through the woods next to Difficult Run River something of a quagmire. But a short trek across country from the rear of his house to the waiting car had been a small price to pay for a safe escape.

Once in the vehicle, the CIA veteran had a thankfully uninterrupted half-hour journey northwest from Wolf Trap to

Leesburg Executive Airport, just three miles south of the town of Leesburg.

Now Watson gazed across the airport's apron at the twin-engine Learjet 60 that stood on the tarmac, its taillights flashing.

He gave a brief wry grin at the thought of the look-alike he had sent in his own car, carrying his own cell phone, southeast to Washington's Ronald Reagan International Airport, a similar distance in the opposite direction from his house, pursued by the FBI's finest.

Bunch of amateurs, he thought.

Although, to be fair, time had been on his side. He was gone by the time the FBI had arrived; if they'd gotten there half an hour earlier it would have been far more difficult.

From his jacket pocket Watson took out a brand-new, deep navy blue Canadian passport. He glanced inside. There was his photograph, with the name Warren Smithson under-neath. He replaced it in his pocket. Then he picked up his bag and walked across the tarmac to the steps of the aircraft, where the pilot, Carlos Herrera, was waiting.

"Evening, Carlos," Watson said. "Good to go?"

"Yes, sir," Herrera said. "We're sticking to the original plan? Costa Rica?"

"Yep, same plan. We can get going as soon as you're ready. I don't want any delays getting off the ground now. It's urgent."

"Noted, sir. Should be about nine hours' flying time to San José. I've got food and drink on board as requested. I'll be good to go in a couple of minutes."

Watson nodded and climbed into the cabin, where he chose one of the eight comfortable leather seats.

Herrera put his head around the cabin door. "We're cleared for the flight to Juan Santamaría Airport. Takeoff in two minutes. Buckle yourself in." He retreated back to the cockpit.

A few minutes later, the Learjet's twin engines increased in pitch, and it began to taxi toward the main runway. Watson buckled his seat belt and sat back. He couldn't get his mind off Joe Johnson. Quite how he had been outfoxed by a man he viewed with such disdain was something he was struggling to come to terms with. But of one thing he was certain, he would have the last laugh.

Johnson, I'm going to screw you next time, he thought. And there would be a next time, he would make sure of that.

The engines roared as Herrera pushed open the throttle. The plane accelerated down the runway and took off into the darkness.

EPILOGUE

Friday, August 3, 2012
  Mostar

Johnson glanced down at the sliver of gleaming white on the stonework as the four of them walked over the apex of the Stari Most. The damage from the sniper's bullet was still clear for all to see, three weeks after their narrow escape.

He, Jayne, Filip, and Ana continued down the slope to the eastern bank of the Neretva River, past the tourist souvenir stalls and bars.

They had just come from a meeting with two officials from the War Crimes department of the Prosecutor's Office of Bosnia and Herzegovina, based in Sarajevo, who wanted to get their investigation under way as swiftly as possible.

Their next stop was another meeting, this time with detectives who had driven from Split. The officers had Marco in custody and wanted to carry out further interviews with Johnson, Jayne, and Filip.

The Bosnian authorities had offered to pay his and Jayne's expenses, so just two days after being reunited with his children in Portland, he had felt obliged to travel again.

Johnson had already briefed the others on the events of the TV interview between Franjo and Spencer, who had resigned with immediate effect as speaker of the House in an attempt to limit the political fallout. Vic had privately told him that CIA financial forensics teams had already uncovered a paper trail of payments into Watson's and Spencer's bank accounts relating to arms deals, dating back twenty years.

Ana stopped. "But what about Aisha? I mean, I know she didn't actually press the button in the end, but she did set up the whole bloody thing and put the explosives in place. She was going to do it. I keep thinking about that comment she made to me about having a vision of Franjo's death."

Johnson scratched the old wound at the top of his right ear. "I can't explain it any better than you can. I think she was a very bitter person. I don't think it was a case of being radicalized—the fact that she herself didn't push the button in the end tells you that much. It was more just personal anger. She'd not been able to forgive. FBI and police are trying to get to the bottom of who supplied the explosive. It's tragic. She's bound to do a stretch in prison, even if she didn't actually commit the final act in it all. And her ex-husband will too, almost certainly, for his war crimes. It kind of sums everything up."

He focused on Ana. "The Bosnian prosecutor's office will need to put together a dossier of evidence against Franjo. He's going to be in front of the court in Sarajevo, and we need to make damn sure the case is watertight. I've got some new cases that have come in, and I'll likely be starting one of them soon. So I could use some help compiling the dossier. I thought with your research background and the fact that you've done so much work on the Old Bridge already for your book, including finding eyewitnesses to Franjo's actions with the tank, it would be right up your alley. It might even be helpful for your book and give you more material to write about. Would you work with me on it?"

Ana nodded. "Of course."

"At least you've got Patrick Spencer behind bars as well as Franjo," Jayne said.

"Yes, he's done a lot of damage, and he'll pay for what he's done. But you can't penalize him for free speech. My worry is that somebody else will just come along and fill his shoes," Johnson said.

He gazed over the river and the Old Bridge. The waters of the Neretva seemed to Johnson like a metaphor for many of his investigations over the years. There were many twists, no clear path forward, and rarely a clean ending.

The death toll at the CBA TV studios had climbed to nineteen since the previous Friday but now looked unlikely to rise further, although a couple of victims remained in critical condition.

The biggest achievement, though, was that Franjo and Spencer, their careers in tatters, were facing time behind bars —as were Aisha, Adela, and Marco—and if Johnson had anything to do with it, they would be staying there for a long time.

The media coverage of the entire operation had reflected all that: it was hugely positive toward Johnson. And in turn, the publicity had brought in a whole string of potential investigative jobs to consider. The previous day, a query had arrived about republican terrorists in Northern Ireland, there was another one relating to Afghanistan, and various others.

"Penny for them, Joe," Jayne said.

Johnson realized he had become lost in his own thoughts.

He turned around. "You know, there was something that Franjo said to me when I was trussed up like a Thanksgiving turkey in that house in Dubrovnik. He said something like people have been fighting each other here for a thousand years and will be in another thousand. So when we Americans come here thinking we're going to sort things out, actually, we know *nothing*. We didn't twenty years ago and we don't now. That was the gist of what he said."

He paused. "I think he was right. We're going to get justice for some. But a whole bunch of people have died in a New York television studio as a result of what went on in Bosnia in the '90s. So what *do* I know?"

It struck Johnson that the other thing he didn't know, and the biggest outstanding mystery, was how his nemesis Robert Watson had escaped the FBI net and where he had gone to. Even a week after his disappearance there was no further clarity.

Yes, it was true that Watson's CIA career was over, just as he had ensured Johnson's was more than two decades earlier. However, that wasn't enough. Johnson knew that he wouldn't be satisfied until his old boss had been properly brought to justice. Exactly how and when and where he would achieve that was very uncertain, but Johnson knew he wasn't just going to let it lie. He was going to find a way. He would have to.

Johnson turned and kept walking across the Old Bridge.

* * *

BOOK 3 IN THE JOE JOHNSON SERIES: BANDIT COUNTRY

If you enjoyed **The Old Bridge** you'll probably like the third book in the Joe Johnson series, **Bandit Country**, which is another investigation into dark crimes from the past. It is available on Amazon—just type "Andrew Turpin Bandit Country" into the search box at the top of the Amazon sales web page.

To give you a flavor of **_Bandit Country_**, here's the blurb:

The murky underside of a terrorist war . . . A British police chief joins the list of high-profile Northern Ireland serial sniper victims. Tension rises as the US president visits. And the 29-year mystery around an IRA killer's gruesome death deepens.

Ex-CIA war crimes investigator **Joe Johnson** is called in as the sniper's body count rises. But with the motive unknown, the clock is ticking down as the president and UK prime minister prepare for a G8 world summit near Belfast.

Eventually, Johnson and his ex-MI6 colleague Jayne Robinson uncover historic hidden files, documents and dark secrets from three decades earlier that certain high-flying public figures would rather remained unread.

Johnson's investigation climaxes with a helicopter drama in the skies over Belfast.

Bandit Country—the third book in the Joe Johnson series—dives into the murky depths of historic conflicts between British security forces and the IRA, as well as the illegal US-based fundraising and weapons smuggling operations that armed the terrorists.

* * *

ANDREW'S READERS GROUP AND OTHER JOE JOHNSON BOOKS

If you enjoyed this book, I would like to keep in touch. This is not always easy, as I usually only publish a couple of books a year and there are many authors and books out there. So the best way is for you to be on my Readers Group email list. I can then send you updates on the next book, plus occasional special offers. There's no spam and you can unsubscribe at any time.

If you would like to join my Readers Group and receive the email updates, I will send you, **FREE**, the ebook version of another Joe Johnson thriller, *The Afghan*, which is a prequel to the series and normally sells at $2.99/£2.99 (paperback $9.99/£9.99).

The Afghan is set in 1988 when Johnson was still in the CIA. Most of the action takes place in Afghanistan, then occupied by the Soviet Union, and in Washington, DC. Some of the characters and story lines that emerge in the other books have their roots in this period. I think you will enjoy it!

The Afghan can be downloaded **FREE** from the following link:

https://bookhip.com/LFMAWM

If you only like reading paperbacks you can still sign up for the email list at that link. A paperback of *The Afghan* is for sale on Amazon.

You should also enjoy the other thrillers in the Joe Johnson series, if you haven't read them yet. You may find it is best to read them in order, as follows:

Prequel: *The Afghan*
1. *The Last Nazi*
2. *The Old Bridge*

3. *Bandit Country*
4. *Stalin's Final Sting*
5. *The Nazi's Son*

To find the books, just type "Andrew Turpin Joe Johnson thriller series" in the search box at the top of the Amazon page — you can't miss them!

IF YOU ENJOYED THIS BOOK PLEASE WRITE A REVIEW

As an independently published author, through my own imprint The Write Direction Publishing, I find that honest reviews of my books are the most powerful way for me to bring them to the attention of other potential readers.

As you'll appreciate, unlike the big international publishers, I can't take out full-page advertisements in the newspapers or place posters on the subway.

So I am committed to producing work of the best quality I can in order to attract a loyal group of readers who are prepared to recommend my work to others.

Therefore, if you enjoyed reading this novel, then I would very much appreciate it if you would spend five minutes and leave a review—which can be as short as you like—preferably on the page or website where you bought it.

You can find the book's page on the Amazon website by typing "Andrew Turpin The Old Bridge" in the search box. Once you have clicked on the page, scroll down to "Customer Reviews," then click on "Leave a Review."

Reviews are also a great encouragement to me to write more.

Many thanks!

THANKS AND ACKNOWLEDGMENTS

I would like to thank everyone who reads **The Old Bridge**—which is my second novel in the Joe Johnson series, following **The Last Nazi**. I hope you enjoy the book and that it proves entertaining and even informative.

Throughout the long process of research, writing, and editing, there have been several people who have helped along the way.

Once again, my brother Adrian read through several early drafts of the book and gave me various ideas for improvements while also giving me advice on the television studio scenes in the book—something he's well qualified to do as a broadcast engineer who now runs his own professional photography, lighting design and cinematography business, The Light Direction, based in Kendal, Cumbria. Adrian also helped with the graphics for my website and reader emails. But most of all, he kept me at the coalface by giving endless encouragement at times when I was stuck or feeling as though I was struggling to make headway.

Other people also read the book at early stages and gave me feedback that helped me to improve it. In particular, I would like to thank David Cole. My parents, Gerald and Jean Turpin, also read it and provided encouragement.

My two editors, Katrina Diaz Arnold, owner of Refine Editing, and Jon Ford, again did a great job in terms of improving the manuscript. I would like to thank both of them—the responsibility for any remaining mistakes lies solely with me.

But I also have a growing team of advance readers who go through my books at a later stage, just prior to publication, and have been able to give me a few useful pointers and have spotted the odd error. If you would like to join my Advance

Readers team, send me an email at andrew@andrew-turpin.com and let me know. Make sure to tell me a little about yourself — including what part of the world you live in and the type of books and authors you like.

Once again, I would also like to thank the team at Damonza for what I think is another great cover design.

I guess I should also thank our dog, Coco, because I tend to get many of my plot ideas and crystallize my thoughts while out on my daily one hour walk with him.

AUTHOR'S NOTE

I am aiming to set the Joe Johnson series in the "real world," against a broadly factual historical backdrop, although the key characters and the plots are obviously fictional. This is true of *The Old Bridge,* just as it was with *The Last Nazi.*

Today, Croatia, Bosnia and Herzegovina, and the other countries of the former Yugoslavia are popular and beautiful holiday destinations for many people. For a casual visitor, it is easy to forget that in the early 1990s, a series of brutal civil wars—Europe's worst since the Second World War—raged across that region as the six republics that formed Yugoslavia fell apart.

These wars, sectarian in nature, involved battles between the various ethnic groups that comprise the population there. Bosnia and Herzegovina and Croatia were the principal theaters for this conflict as the Bosnian Serbs, Muslims, and Croats turned on each other after several decades of relative peace following the formation of Yugoslavia post the Second World War.

During those decades, the type of marriage portrayed in *The Old Bridge* between Franjo Vuković, a Bosnian Croat, and Aisha Delić, a Bosnian Muslim, was relatively common.

However, once the conflict began, that all changed. And despite the peace agreements and the redrawing of borders, the fault lines between ethnic groups and the underlying political and social tensions remain. It has been a difficult peace.

As is often the case in wartime, and particularly in wars that are sectarian in nature, a large number of war crimes were committed by all sides—although principally by Serbs and Croats against Muslims—as attempts were made by the various ethnic groups to drive others out of territories that they wanted to claim for themselves.

In fact, the conflict in Bosnia led to the first crime of genocide seen in Europe since the Second World War, at the town of Srebrenica, in Bosnia and Herzegovina, where Bosnian Serb forces killed about 8,000 Muslim men and boys. Many other similar incidents have not been officially categorized as genocide—but were in all but name.

There were also many instances of crimes against humanity, rape, and ethnic cleansing. Hundreds of thousands of people were driven from their homes, and many ended up in the concentration camps run by the Serbs and the Croats, of which the Croat-controlled Heliodrom, mentioned in this book, was just one. Other notorious camps included the Serb-controlled Omarska, Keraterm, and Trnopolje sites, among many.

Estimates of the number of people killed during the conflicts across the region range from 130,000 to 140,000. There is no question that the majority of these were Bosniaks —Bosnian Muslims.

The United Nations established the International Criminal Tribunal for the former Yugoslavia (ICTY), based in The Hague, to prosecute the most serious crimes committed during the conflict. It indicted 161 people in total, and the final trial to be completed was that of the former Bosnian Serb commander Ratko Mladić, who was sentenced to life imprisonment in November 2017 after being found guilty of genocide, war crimes, and crimes against humanity. Some of the charges were related to the Srebrenica massacre.

The ICTY also gave its final judgment on November 29, 2017, in the case of an appeal by six men, including the Bosnian Croat army commander Slobodan Praljak, against their previous convictions in 2013 of crimes against humanity, murder, and many other charges while persecuting the

Muslim population of Bosnia. The charges included the destruction of the Old Bridge in Mostar. The Appeals Chamber upheld the 2013 convictions and confirmed the sentences, which in Praljak's case was twenty years of imprisonment. Praljak immediately drank a poison that he had smuggled into court and died shortly afterward. The ICTY documents relating to this case can be found here: http://www.icty.org/en/press/the-icty-renders-its-final-judgement-in-the-prli%C4%87-et-al-appeal-case

Praljak is mentioned in chapter thirty-nine of **The Old Bridge.** Another character mentioned in that chapter, Branko Perić, is fictional.

Finally, I should note that as Joe Johnson, the lead character in this series, is from the United States, and most scenes are from his point of view, it makes sense to use American English spellings and terminology in most cases, rather than my native British English. Any mistakes in this respect are mine alone—please do point them out to me.

BACKGROUND READING AND BIBLIOGRAPHY

There were a great many fascinating sources of information that I read through and watched as part of the lengthy research process prior to and during the writing of **The Old Bridge**.

I could not possibly list them all, but I thought it would be good to give you a flavor of the ones I found most useful here, so that if you would like to find out more about the issues that inspired my plot, you at least have a starting point.

The classic six-part BBC documentary, *The Death of Yugoslavia*, first broadcast in 1995, is still available on YouTube. It is probably the best starting point for those who would like to get a feel for the scale of, and background to, the conflict that tore the region apart. It includes dramatic footage of the destruction of the Stari Most—the Old Bridge—in Mostar, by tank fire in November 1993. You can find it at https://www.youtube.com/watch?v=DdS9M70SVOg

There is a BBC book, also called *The Death of Yugoslavia*, that was published to accompany the series, written by correspondents Laura Silber and Allan Little. It is well worth reading and is still available on Amazon.

The transcripts of the trials conducted at the International Criminal Tribunal for the former Yugoslavia (ICTY) in The Hague are fascinating to read and give a wealth of useful material.

A good example is the trial summary and six volumes of judgements from the combined trials of Jadranko Prlić, Bruno Stojić, Slobodan Praljak, Milivoj Petković, Valentin Ćorić, and Berislav Pušić. This trial dealt with the destruction of the Old Bridge in Mostar using tank shells. The documents can be found at http://www.icty.org/case/prlic/4 and Judgement Volume 2, Section V, gives the most detail on the destruction of the bridge. You will see how I have loosely built my story around the facts outlined in this case.

There is also a large amount of detail in Volume 2 of this judgement on the war crimes committed at the Heliodrom, the concentration camp near Mostar, by Croat HVO forces against mainly Muslim detainees. Again I have drawn on this detail quite heavily in *The Old Bridge*.

A book written by Jadranka Petrovic, *The Old Bridge of Mostar and Increasing Respect for Cultural Property in Armed Conflict,* also gave some fascinating background on the destruction of the Stari Most. It is an academic study that also makes good use of the ICTY transcripts among the many sources used by the author. See: https://www.amazon.co.uk/dp/9004210288/

Ed Vulliamy, a journalist with *The Guardian*, wrote an eloquent and hard-hitting book, *The War is Dead, Long Live the War,* about the conflict and the postwar attempts to seek justice for those who were victims of war crimes. This formed very helpful background reading. It can be found at https://www.amazon.co.uk/dp/B0080GV1ZE/

For a broader overview of the ethnic and religious conflict that has existed in the entire Balkan peninsula region for hundreds, even thousands, of years, I would recommend *Balkan Ghosts*, by Robert D. Kaplan, a journalist who writes for *The Atlantic* and other media outlets.

Regarding US policy toward Bosnia and support for the Bosnian Muslim government of Alija Izetbegović in their battles against the Serbs and Croats, there are very many publications offering deep background of various kinds.

One that focuses on the role of the CIA and other intelligence services is Cees Wiebes's book, *Intelligence and the War in Bosnia 1992-95*. This examines the detail behind the controversial US decisions to effectively allow Iran to supply weapons to Bosnia and the thinking behind it, and to permit mujahideen into Bosnia to fight alongside Bosnian forces. At the time, of course, these decisions were driven by the situation on the ground, in which the Muslims were being hit hard by Serb and Croatian forces. Wiebes's book can be found at https://www.amazon.com/Intelligence-War-Bosnia-1992-1995-Studies/dp/3825863476

There is an illuminating 1996 report by the US House of Representatives' Committee on International Relations, which examines the US role in arms transfers from Iran to Bosnia and Croatia and discusses the effective "green light" given by the Clinton administration to allow this to happen. See: https://archive.org/stream/ finalreportofsel00unit/finalreportofsel00unit_djvu.txt

A thorough *New York Times* analysis of Clinton's Bosnia policy, "The Clinton Record," can be found at: http://www. nytimes.com/1996/07/29/us/the-clinton-record-foreign-policy-bosnia-policy-shaped-by-us-military-role.html? pagewanted=all

There are various media reports about the relationship between Izetbegović and Osama bin Laden. See, for example, this summary: http://www.historycommons.org/context.jsp? item=western_support_for_islamic_militancy_2091

On Aisha's life in New York, I was inspired by a blog, Slavs of New York, and in particular a piece on Bosnians in Astoria, which led me to the Ćevabdžinica Sarajevo restaurant that I've depicted as her favorite hangout. The blog can be found at: http://nycslav.blogspot.co.uk/2006/02/bosnians-in-astoria.html

Like Aisha and Franjo, there were many couples in mixed marriages across the sectarian divide in Bosnia whose lives were torn apart by the conflict. One harrowing story that illustrates the issues very starkly is this one in the *Chicago Tribune*: http://articles.chicagotribune.com/1996-09-08/news/ 9609080294_1_banja-luka-bosnian-serb-serb-authorities

A large number of refugees from the war in the Balkans subsequently made their way to the US and other countries, who have all done their bit to accommodate the displaced and the persecuted, many of whom endured extreme ordeals during the conflict and then a tough period of adjustment in their new homeland. For those interested in reading some of their stories, a good starting point is this article in *The Independent* by one refugee: http://www.independent.co.uk/voices/im-a-refugee-who-escaped-bosnian-concentration-camps-if-you-think-the-resettlement-process-is-easy-a6749781.html

An excellent source of news and analysis across the Balkan region can be found at the *Balkan Insight* website. This news site keeps a close watch on ongoing trials for war crimes at the various courts across the former Yugoslavia. It can be found at: http://www.balkaninsight.com/en/page/all-balkans-home

Balkan Insight also recently published an excellent article about the ongoing political unrest across Bosnia and Herzegovina as a result of the artificial carve-up of boundaries, and the potential for further unrest. It can be read at http://www.balkaninsight.com/en/article/bosnia-marks-dayton-anniversary-amid-growing-crisis-11-21-2017.

An interesting article about how the divisions between ethnic factions in Bosnia have never gone away since the end of the war, and the potential for more conflict in the future, can be found in this analysis article in *Foreign Affairs*, see: https://www.foreignaffairs.com/articles/bosnia-herzegovina/2009-08-17/death-dayton

ABOUT THE AUTHOR AND CONTACT DETAILS

I have always had a love of writing and a passion for reading good thrillers. But despite having a long-standing dream of writing my own novels, it took me more than five decades to finally get around to completing the first.

The Old Bridge is the second in the **Joe Johnson** series of thrillers, which pulls together some of my other interests, particularly history, world news, and travel.

I studied history at Loughborough University and worked for many years as a business and financial journalist before becoming a corporate and financial communications adviser with several large energy companies, specializing in media relations.

Originally I came from Grantham, Lincolnshire, and I now live with my family in St. Albans, Hertfordshire, U.K.

You can connect with me via these routes:

E-mail: andrew@andrewturpin.com
Website: www.andrewturpin.com.
Facebook: @AndrewTurpinAuthor
Twitter: @AndrewTurpin
Instagram: @andrewturpin.author

Please also follow me on Bookbub and Amazon!

https://www.bookbub.com/authors/andrew-turpin
https://www.amazon.com/Andrew-Turpin/e/B074V87WWL/

Do get in touch with your comments and views on the books, or anything else for that matter. I enjoy hearing from readers and promise to reply.

Printed in Great Britain
by Amazon

36605134R00274